DISORDER

Novels by Johan Fundin

SCHIZOID
DISORDER

Rave Reviews for Johan Fundin's
DISORDER

"Psychological suspense and thriller readers are in for a treat with Johan Fundin's *Disorder* ... Outstanding in its many connections and genre-busting approach ... Packed with twists and turns ... Medical thriller tension ala Robin Cook."
—*Midwest Book Review*

"Fascinating ... *Disorder* starts with a bang and culminates in a mind-bending finale ... The world of this book is as twisted as the shadows that make up the central metaphor of the narrative ... Thriller lovers will be intrigued by the concept."
—*San Francisco Book Review*

"A fast-paced, suspenseful read that brings up questions of reality and perception. The author's idea to explore this through a medical lens is an interesting twist."
—*The US Review of Books*

"Very interesting and clever ... Creative and enjoyable yet unsettling at the same time ... A frightening cast of characters: dead, undead, and alive ... The ending is very satisfying."
—*Manhattan Book Review*

"A pleasure to read ... A brilliant techno-thriller, full of suspense, with rich and detailed characters ... With this book, Johan Fundin has established himself as a definite talent to watch in the thriller genre."
—*OnlineBookClub.org*, Official Review

PRAISE FOR JOHAN FUNDIN AND HIS NOVELS OF SUSPENSE

What readers are saying

"An excellent read—a real page turner throughout."

"Johan Fundin has a gift for creating atmosphere."

"Creepy and captivating."

"A fascinating way of playing with genre."

"Really exciting from beginning to end."

"What a shocker! It's really, really good! It has everything a suspense novel needs: mystery, murder, red herrings, characters, love."

"It's very suspenseful. There's finesse in the train of thought, and the use of language differs from that of other thrillers."

"Exciting, entertaining, vividly described, electrifying."

"Reminiscent of Dean Koontz."

"Enjoyed it immensely. Thrillers are at their best, for me, when there is something cosy and human and likeable at their heart. It makes you care much more about the characters."

"Johan Fundin has built a steadfast reputation for crafting gripping, thought-provoking fiction that twists the minds of its readers into a frenzy of suspense."

"What a thrilling story! Impressive!"

"Keeps you guessing all the way."

DISORDER

JOHAN FUNDIN

ASIONI PRESS

This book is a work of fiction. Any references to historical events,
real people or real places are used fictitiously. Other names, characters,
places and events are products of the author's imagination,
and any resemblance to actual events or places or persons,
living or dead, is entirely coincidental.

DISORDER

Copyright © 2019 by Johan Fundin

The right of Johan Fundin to be identified as the
author of this work has been asserted by him in accordance
with the Copyright, Designs and Patents Act 1988.

First published in Great Britain and the U.S.A. by Asioni Press

First Asioni Press trade paperback edition: May 2019

1 3 5 7 9 8 6 4 2

All rights reserved. No part of this publication may be reproduced,
stored in a retrieval system, or transmitted, in any form or by any means,
electronic, mechanical, photocopying, recording or otherwise,
without the prior written permission of the publisher.

Cover art by RLSather
Book design by Asioni Press

A CIP catalogue record for this title is available from the British Library

ISBN 978-1-9999817-0-9
e-ISBN 978-1-9999817-1-6
Subjects: BISAC: FICTION / Thrillers / Suspense. |
Thema: FH – Thriller / suspense fiction.

Printing information on the last page.
Published simultaneously in Great Britain and the U.S.A.

ASIONI PRESS
asionipress.com

DISORDER

• ONE •

"WHO'S THERE?" CAT sat bolt upright in bed. "Who's there?"

The man in the raincoat and hat didn't answer. He clung outside the half-open bedroom window, staring, grinning.

Cat pulled the quilt closer to her bare bust. "Get out of here right now, you perverted freak!"

Why didn't he say something? Why was he only watching? *Because he likes to watch, Catriona. And you're naked.*

The August heat was as aggressive as the dreams. Therefore, she had chosen to go to bed without wearing a nightgown. The alarm clock on the bedside table showed 5:36 a.m. She had fallen asleep with the bedside lamp on and a window open. A mistake.

Every paparazzo kept an eye on Cat Milton. Anyone who read the tabloids knew where she lived. The trespassing bastard wasn't here by coincidence. He would climb in, rape her, kill her and empty the luxury house of valuables.

The bedroom was upstairs. Had he climbed the facade? Via a balcony? Or across the roof via another side of the house? This side had no fire escape.

At twenty-three, she was too young to die, too busy to die, too beautiful to die. Her heart was slamming. The shriek rushed out between her lips. She screamed so loud that her throat and ears hurt. "Who are you? What do you want? What are you doing here? Is it about money and jewellery?"

The man grinned like a shark. His teeth flashed in the morning sun. "I'll show you what I want, Cat."

He climbed in through the window and moved towards the bed. The intruder reached for her long hair. Cat swung herself out of bed just in time and slipped away from his hands. Her knee collided with the bedside table. She screamed, floundered, fell. The gold and diamond ornate glass crystal vase overturned, crashed to the floor and exploded into a thousand pieces.

"Don't be afraid, Catriona. I could never hurt you. I just want to caress your lovely hair."

It must have been raining during the night. The man left wet footprints on the carpet. He wore leather gloves as black and shiny as his coat. His ugly grin turned invisible. His wide-brimmed hat hid his face. "Will you let me caress your beautiful tresses before we start our serious conversation?"

Again, his hands shot out at her.

Now she saw. The man had sixteen fingers. Eight fingers on each hand. He wore the most absurd example of customised gloves she had ever seen. She screamed again, backed towards the door, not bothering to try to cover her most intimate body parts. The situation was already pathetic enough.

"Will you let me touch your ravishing hair before we begin our important discussion?"

My hair? To begin with? What next?

She jerked the bedroom door open, jumped out, slammed the door shut, dashed through a corridor, saw from a distance how her bedroom door opened again, stumbled down the stairs to the ground floor, sprinted through the lounge, heard his approaching footsteps from the stairs to the ground floor, ran through the fitness room, sprinted past the kitchen, skidded into another corridor, heard footsteps from the fitness room, rushed into the bathroom, knocked the door shut behind her, fumbled with the lock, caught the clicking sound of the rotary-bolt door-lock and staggered backwards until she hit the basin. She swallowed her cry and gasped.

In spite of the heatwave, she shivered. Her glossy nipples were as hard as frozen wild strawberries. Where could she escape to without clothes? She would never sprint out of the house stark naked—not in central London. She stood stock-still in semi-darkness, listening. Only heard her racing heart. She bit her lower lip, wondering why the house was silent. The man must have lost her. There were many doors in the house. The madman didn't know she was hiding in the ground-floor bathroom. Somewhere in the building he stood motionless, listening for Cat as intensely as Cat was listening for him.

There was no slit under the bathroom door which allowed light to seep out into the hall. She flicked on the light switch. She studied the face in the bathroom cabinet mirror door. Scrutinised the sky-blue eyes. The outline and cool shade of the cheeks. The subtle splash of freckles across the bridge of the nose, like amber dots of watercolour. The hair ringlets whose lustre was reminiscent of a scarlet sunrise.

She tried to see what the top photographers, the top editors and the top designers saw. The girl in the mirror had illuminated the front covers of hundreds of fashion magazine issues, including a phenomenal number of issues of the most prestigious magazines in the world. The face in the mirror had given Cat Milton an average weekly wage of between 110,000 and 215,000 US dollars. The face in the mirror had given the girl several multimillion contracts—calculated in dollars—thanks to a handful of lucrative fashion and beauty deals. In the last twelve months, she had pulled in more than fifteen million dollars. The invader in black coat and hat had attacked one of the world's best paid supermodels. *Does he want to kill me and rape me and burgle the house and kidnap me? In any order? Rape a strangled girl? Steal the corpse and preserve it?*

She opened the bathroom cabinet and looked at the five bottles on the middle shelf. Venlafaxine: an antidepressant. Two bottles each of two wakefulness-promoting agents: Dexedrine, an amphetamine-based stimulant; and Liglitrem, a medicine whose wakefulness-promoting effect was similar to that of amphetamine-based substances but with a different chemistry and mechanism of action. In accordance with the medical prescription, she was finishing her intake of 10-milligram Dexedrine tablets and had started taking 5-milligram tablets, thereby reducing the Dexedrine dosage; at the same time, she was using Liglitrem. Overlapping recipes were not uncommon. *Somehow, I must have mixed up the doses yesterday. Or confused the bottles?*

A sound destroyed the silence. She froze. Listened. Footsteps. In the corridor. Or in the hall. Approaching steps. Brisk steps across the parquet floor. The treads stopped cold. The intruder had located her. How? Had she made a noise? Had the cabinet door squeaked?

Three knocks on the door.

Cat screamed.

• TWO •

"I HATE YOUR face." Janice trod in the same spot before the full-length mirror in the guest room. "Your face is disgusting." The monster stared back at her through the mirror glass.

She was helping Mum to prepare the room for Cat's arrival. Cat didn't know yet that she had to come home to Blackfield. Sis hadn't yet heard the terrible news.

Jan raised a fist at the girl in the mirror. "You're so horrible I want to vomit." The words came out as a mumble because of her misshapen mouth. Her lips were reminiscent of thick scars. Froth and leftovers clung to the corners of her mouth. Her head was asymmetrical. The left side of her skull had a chronic swelling, a pinkish-red malformation which resembled the pulpy flesh of a watermelon. The ears were of different sizes. The fleshy nose with forward-pointing nostrils looked like a pig's snout. The matted and rat-grey hair belonged to a troll. Her skin was inflamed and scarred by acne. Her humpback resembled a heap of stones.

Jan didn't like to be Cat's twin sis.

How could one twin sister be so annoyingly ugly when the other was so incredibly beautiful?

Her dislike of being Cat's sister wasn't about envy. It wasn't that Cat earned at least seventy thousand pounds a week while Jan got fifty pounds per week as a part-time pub waitress. It wasn't that Cat had had countless boyfriends since the age of fourteen while Jan had never been with a boy. It wasn't that Cat had seen the whole world thanks to her extreme beauty and glamorous profession while Jan had never travelled outside their hometown because of her monstrous disfigurement.

She didn't despise Cat. It was Cat's beauty she despised. Most of all, Jan hated herself. She hated herself for subjecting other people to her hideous looks.

"Janice! Janice! Help me to water the flowers!"

"Mum's calling," Jan said to the mirror monster. "I must go down to the ground floor and help her. When I come back, I want you gone. Do you get it?" She wiped a tear from her eye. "You know what, my sister is coming home and she'll sleep in this room. Let's see how you'll handle Cat. My sis is the most beautiful girl in the world. You'll have a very tough time coping, you stupid mirror."

It took an effort not to attack the mirror with her fists. "I doubt you can cope with my sis. Cat's beauty will burst you from edge to edge, if not shatter you into a thousand stupid pieces."

Exhausted, she turned away from the horror creature. She tolerated it less and less. Not just here, but anywhere. Anywhere in the home and in the city. Mirrors were evil. Mirrors plagued her with images of the freak.

"Come on, Dix. Mum wants us to help her."

A shadowy figure stirred. Dixie crawled out from under the bed. He miaowed and yawned.

"I agree with you, Dix. It's super-hot. During a heatwave like this, flowers are thirstier than usual. Therefore, we must help Mum to water the flowers. Are you thirsty too? I'm very thirsty myself. There's a six-pack of Fanta Orange in the fridge and I'm going to drink all six cans."

"Janice! Janice?! How many times do I have to shout at you?! Hurry up, you slacker!"

"I'm coming, Mum. I'm coming." Jan lumbered out of the guest room with Dix in tow. She patted the back pocket of her baggy jeans, ensuring the corkscrew was still there.

Since her T-shirt was as large as a tent and covered her fat butt, no one could see she carried the corkscrew. The pointed kitchen utensil was as dangerous as a stabbing weapon and could be used as such. Well, that was the whole idea.

• THREE •

"CAT? ARE YOU okay?"

The voice outside the bathroom door had that amusing Swedish accent. Cat moved closer to the door. Stopped. Listened. "Ebba? Is that you, Ebba?" She sobbed. "Is it really you?"

"No, it's The Little Mermaid ... Of course it's Ebba! Why don't you open the damn door?"

Cat sat at the kitchen table, curled up in a Versace bathrobe. She sipped green tea and nibbled at a cloudberry yoghurt. She had showered, washed her face with glycerine and rose water and begun to feel a little better. She had thrown her hair into a sloppy topknot. A few wisps of hair hung down over her ears.

Ebba stood at the stove, frying eggs and bread in olive oil. She was humming a pop song. Ebba Sjödal had the ability to renew herself from one day to the next like a chameleon to meet the fashion industry's ever-changing requirements. Any hair colour and any hairstyle worked for her. But today she appeared natural: black semi-curly hair; an interesting contrast against her green eyes and pale skin.

The pretty Swede had a personal sense of style and an immediate skill to match designer labels with classic items from popular high-street stores to create her own characteristic profile. This morning she looked stunning in a pitch-black knee-length dress from Valentino and sparkly red low-heeled shoes.

"Would you like a fried egg sandwich, Cat?"

"Thanks, but no thanks."

"As you wish, sourpuss."

Ebba could eat innumerable sandwiches without gaining weight. Cat took another sip of tea and gathered her thoughts. "How were your last few days?"

"Crikey, can't describe them." Ebba's eyes glittered like fireflies. "My new boyfriend is outright wonderful in bed. He's a tireless sex machine."

Cat sighed. Ebba changed boyfriends as often as she changed clothes or hairstyles. "I mean the photo shoot in the Bahamas."

"Aha." Ebba sat down at the table opposite Cat and grinned. "The photo shoot was outstanding. But I hate living out of a suitcase for more than four days in a row, I hate airport food, I hate hotel toilets and the dirty—"

"When did you get home last night?" Cat interrupted.

"Last night?" Ebba rolled her eyes. "Ask me about the small hours." She squirted ketchup onto her sandwiches. "Crikey, I ended up at some party in the West End and tried to cure the jetlag with a tremendous Bloody Mary, no, two; two large ones; but it didn't work very well. I only got an urgent need to piss and I nearly pissed myself. I got home at four and dropped straight into bed."

Ebba had an unrivalled ability to look beautiful the day after a hard night out.

"You didn't wake up when I screamed?"

"When?"

"At some time after half past five?"

"No, Cat. I heard nothing. Did you have one of your episodes? A panic attack? Something to do with your disease?"

It wasn't just another episode, Cat thought. "A man stepped into my bedroom."

Ebba giggled. "Sure."

"He climbed straight in through a window. A window I had forgotten to close and lock. I'm not kidding."

"A new admirer?"

"Stop it."

"Or an old admirer? Herbert Krass?"

Cat respected most photographers. Photography was an art form. Without the fashion industry's professional cameramen, she wouldn't have a career. She was smart enough to understand that. However, she didn't like the gossip photographers. Herbert Krass was part of the worst gang of tabloid reporters.

Krass had played a scurvy trick on Cat three years ago and she had never been able to forgive him. When she stepped out of a taxi in Leicester Square that night, the door frame caught one of her high-heeled shoes. She lost her balance, stumbled out of the taxi, almost fell. Perhaps it looked funny. Perhaps it *was* funny. And maybe she appeared to be drunk. Except she wasn't. She never touched alcohol. Because of her mysterious disease, she had chosen to be teetotal. Krass, who had already made up his mind about the joyful situation, took his chance. His camera shot up her short skirt. Later in the same week, a close-up picture of her knickers had been plastered on the front of Krass's gossip paper, accompanied by the headline: 'Look who's out on the town: Tipsy Catriona Milton shows off new sexy underwear'.

"Couldn't have been Krass," Cat said.

"Why not? It's obvious he's fond of you."

"The intruder had sixteen fingers."

Ebba giggled. "You can't be serious."

"Do I look like I'm joking?"

Ebba's sniggering dissolved. "Maybe not. But six fingers out of sixteen could simply have been false."

"For misdirection, you mean?"

"Yeah. Just a trick."

"Why?"

"How could *I* know? I didn't even see the freak."

What Cat saw in Ebba's eyes was disbelief.

"If there was an intruder here at all." Ebba munched on a ketchup-soaked sandwich and drank coffee from a beer glass.

"This time it was different. An overly vivid nightmare, even for me." The awful thing was it *could* have been Krass. The possibility existed. The probability, however small, it was Krass had a finite value greater than zero.

"Sure. This time it was different as hell."

"It was real, Ebba. It happened."

"Did he wear a mask?"

"No."

"So, you saw the guy's face?"

Cat thought about the grin, the disgusting grin which she had only glimpsed beneath the wide-brimmed hat. "Not really. Or not exactly, I mean."

"As I suspected. You don't know." Ebba paused, chewing her egg sandwich. "Listen. If some guy climbed in through my bedroom window, I would definitely remember his face. You would too, Cat. The conclusion: there was no guy here."

"How persuasive you can be."

"How would a fool reach your windows at all? Your bedroom has no adjoining balcony. Neither has mine, for that matter."

"He could have climbed the ornate sections of the facade. Used the fire escape, then the roof. Maybe a vigorous individual could jump from adjacent balconies to reach my windows."

"It's very hot. What if you were heat exhausted?"

"Unthinkable."

"You don't mean some idiot tried to rape you and rob you in your own bedroom?"

"Rapists and burglars exist, not least in London. And I can prove there was a guy in the house this morning. You want me to prove it?"

Ebba crossed her arms. "Okay. Prove it."

• • •

"I swear. The madman left a trail of wet footprints."

"No doubt. And now he's hiding in one of your wardrobes."

"In the sunlight, in this heatwave, the footsteps must have dried and vanished—"

"Your vase." Ebba grimaced, holding her head. "Your vase which was so nice. What a mess."

"A trace of the attack. I was in bed, stark naked under the covers. He rushed towards me. I escaped in the nick of time."

"Or you knocked over the vase in your sleep."

"No. The man exists. He was here. I'm certain."

Ebba gave Cat a hug. "You work too hard, my dear. Too hard for your own good. You'll beat Claudia Schiffer's magazine cover record before you even know it."

"I don't care about records." It was so typical of Ebba to count magazine cover appearances, as if it were a competition. "What I care about is to do a solid job, to handle my medical condition and to find out what happened here this morning."

"What does your boyfriend think about your ghost stories? Are you going to tell Roy about the sixteen-fingered man, uh?"

"Great idea." No, it wasn't.

Ebba looked at her wristwatch. "Damn, I'm in a hurry like a rabbit."

"You're going to the agency?"

"First the agency and then a fucking newspaper interview and then a representation assignment in Bond Street and then I'll do a quick trip to Harrods in my own time and then a speedy late lunch at the National Dining Rooms with Sophia and that wearisome marketing analyst Dooby from Analytics Limited with a capital A as in Arseholery and tonight I'll fly to Milan for two days of shoots."

"National Dining Rooms?" It wasn't like Ebba to go out in Trafalgar Square.

Ebba examined her painted nails and smiled. "I don't want to be seen at Dorrie or Nobu every week."

'Dorrie' was Ebba's own slang word for the cocktail bar at The Dorchester. Nobu, the restaurant chain co-owned by Robert De Niro, was a popular haunt among the celebrity elite. If Cat thought Nobu was okay, Ebba *loved* it.

"Say hello to Sophia from me, Ebba."

"Will do."

"Do not say hello to Dooby from me, Ebba."

"Dooby-Scooby-Dooby-Do." Ebba laughed. "Got it. What do your next few days look like?"

"Fully booked. Including a bikini photo shoot on the Riviera. No lunches with marketing analysts."

Ebba smiled again and put a cigarette between her red-painted lips. "See you next time, Cat."

• FOUR •

SHE DISCOVERED THE shoeprints in the flowerbed below her bedroom windows. Neither Attila the gardener nor Maggie the housemaid would leave footprints in the flowerbeds with such nonchalance. Besides, Maggie's feet were too small in this case. These shoeprints belonged to a big man.

A man in a black raincoat and a hat.

She gazed up at a certain window—and saw something which hadn't been there five minutes earlier when Cat and Ebba had looked out over the backyard from inside the room. Seen from the backyard, the words appeared mirrored, as if they had been written on the inside of the window glass. Reflected sunlight troubled her reading further. She went back into the house, went to her bedroom.

Unable to stifle her reaction, she screamed.

The text on the window glass:

I'LL GET YOU LATER, CAT

The person who had scrawled on the window—the man in the raincoat and hat, in other words—must still have been in the house while Cat showered. While the girls had had breakfast. While the girls had searched the bedroom. What if the man knew that Ebba had left the property? What if the intruder knew that Cat was alone right now? *I'm alone with a sixteen-fingered assailant.* She ordered herself to calm down. It didn't work.

From the laundry room she fetched a bucket with hot water and detergent. Even if the scrawling could pass for evidence she wanted to scrub it off before the gardener or the maid showed up. Neither Attila nor Maggie would ever ask questions about things which weren't their business, but Cat wasn't prepared to give them the slightest reason to suspect that murky events were taking place on the property.

She was still in her bathrobe when the phone rang.

She stepped into her room—her own shadow took a leap across the wallpaper, a detail which freaked her out—and snatched up the receiver. "Yes?"

"Cat?"

She shuddered. It felt like a cockroach scurried up her back. It was Janice, her sister, on the phone. "Jan, I have no time—"

"Listen—"

"No," Cat said. "You didn't catch me at a good time."

"Dad is dead."

"What are you babbling about? Where do you get your stupid ideas from? I called Dad the other day. Called him from Rio de Janeiro. Everything was fine with Dad. As fine as ever."

"The other day was the other day and means nothing anymore. I'm talking about the present. Do you understand, Cat? Natural cause of death, the doctors say. Heart attack. They found Dad on the floor of a laboratory. I wish ... Mum and I wish you were here."

Cat could hear Jan was crying. It came to her with dazzling clarity that her sis had delivered a terrible truth. Dad was dead.

Dead.

What a thing to hear over the phone. What a thing to tell someone over the phone.

She realised she wanted to hug Jan, here and now. But one hundred and seventy miles separated them. Just over two hours by train. An astronomical distance in the awful moment.

"I understand what you're saying," Cat said, "but I can't believe it." Tears began to sting her eyes. "Dad is a fit and healthy forty-three-year-old. He isn't a typical heart attack candidate." She couldn't bring herself to talk about Dad in the past tense.

"He worked very hard." Jan wailed. "You know that too, Cat. Perhaps Dad worked too hard for his own good."

"When did this happen?" Cat's voice faded.

"Five ... nights ... ago." Jan sobbed between her words.

"Five nights ago? And I'm told only now?"

"Getting hold of you isn't the easiest task. Egocentric people like you are elusive. But you *have* been informed. If you checked the messages on your answering machine better, you would know that I ... that Mum and I had sad news to tell."

Under the confusing veil of shock, Cat tried to arrange her thoughts. The answering machine's red message light was flashing non-stop, week in, week out. She had lived in luxury hotels and on board airliners for eleven days in the last two weeks, the period during which she had been working in Rio, Paris, Barcelona and Toronto. She simply must have missed that important message. Neither Jan nor Mum would try to track her through her modelling agency.

Regarding her mobile, there were very few people outside the fashion industry who knew her new number or new email address. Moreover, both Mum and Jan disliked Cat's world. Only Dad had shown interest in her career. Dad who now was dead. Dead and gone forever.

Cat wiped tears from her cheeks. "How's Mum?"

"Mum wonders if you're coming home for the funeral."

"I asked how Mum was."

"Are you coming home!"

"Don't shout in my ear. When is the funeral?"

"Tomorrow."

"So soon?"

"A hassle for you, isn't it? Poor you."

"Shut up."

"Don't talk to me like that, you vain bitch."

"Don't talk to me like that, you lazy cow."

"I'm not lazy! I'm slogging away at the tavern down the road and you know that!"

Cat sighed. "I'm coming home. I have a thousand things on my mind this week but I'm coming home for Dad's funeral. Tell Mum I'm coming home." The phone fell from her fist. Her knees were shaking.

She sank to the floor with her hands on her face. Her head was spinning. A lightless whirlwind overwhelmed her.

• FIVE •

OVER THE YEARS, Catriona had established an excellent professional reputation. She was always on time. She was easy to work with. She took care of herself. She was seen in the right places and socialised with the right people. She didn't stay out late at night. She never cancelled a shoot, a television commercial, an interview or any other commitment. She never tried to back out of a contract. Now, for the first time, she would breach her own rules and routines. A supermodel's schedule was planned months in advance. Industry people dependent on Cat Milton wouldn't be happy this morning.

She called Supreme, her mother agency with headquarters in Highbury. Supreme was an international group with one of the largest networks in the fashion world. She asked the receptionist if Anita was available at all.

The difference between model and supermodel was staggering. Anita Scriver was a star booker who handled only supermodels. Anita organised the supermodels' special projects, for example, book productions, videos, TV appearances and press interviews. Her girls were always in demand and received more requests than they had time for. A supermodel booker like Anita decided with whom a girl would and wouldn't work. It was essential supermodels worked only for the most prestigious magazines and the most important clients.

"Sorry to hear you've lost your dad, Cat," Anita said in an all-business voice.

Cat suppressed her tears. "The cancellations?"

"Problems, Cat. But I'll handle the problems."

Her confidence in Anita was limitless. The super booker would deal with the difficult client-oriented issues with undiminished professionalism. Then there were the people whom Cat wanted to contact herself: her publisher, her personal fitness coach, her stylist, her beautician, her nutritionist, her hairdresser, her aromatherapist, her dermatologist, her limousine driver. These people were more than professionals. They were her friends, like Anita was a friend. According to her agenda, she was supposed to need them all at least once in the next few days. She cancelled all the arrangements.

She considered calling Roy. Then she rejected the idea. The new football season had started and she thought he had a match today. Catriona Milton and Roy Beckman didn't see each other as often as they wanted, like many other celebrity couples with busy careers. However, they had told themselves that living stressful lives didn't have to have a negative impact on a romantic relationship. Their tough everyday schedules meant they valued the precious moments they were together.

She was happy for Roy's sake. According to the experts, Roy Beckman was the most talented midfield player in the Football League Championship. According to the papers, a major Premier League club would sign him as soon as possible. Chelsea, Arsenal or Manchester United. Last spring, Roy had made a hat trick in a cup tie against Liverpool. He was already of interest to the England national football team. Instead of calling her boyfriend, she sent him a text message:

> Good luck with the game, my handsome hero. Think of me and score. Will be away for a few days. Love you—Cat.

She refrained from mentioning a death in the family. Roy was preparing for a football game and she didn't want to disturb her sweetheart more than necessary.

Supermodels spent most of their time looking sensational. Whenever they got a chance to dress down, they did exactly that. Cat pulled on wrinkled jeans, running shoes, a lemon-yellow short-sleeved blouse. She hid her tear-filled red-rimmed eyes behind dark sunglasses and kept her hair in the not-so-neat bun. She looked ordinary now, she thought, maybe with the exception of the seven-hundred-dollar Chloé blouse. (In her line of work, around the globe, thinking in American dollars—by way the most traded currency in the world—made more sense to her than thinking in euros, Japanese yen or British pounds.) In her choice of handbag, there was no room for simplicity. The list prices of the forty-seven or forty-eight handbags she owned ranged from one thousand eight hundred dollars to eleven thousand six hundred dollars. At random, she grabbed a Kelly mini pochette in fuchsia-coloured alligator skin from Hermès, a cool nine-thousand-eight-hundred-dollar product.

She didn't care about the obscene combination of clothes and handbag. Someone would soon wake her up and tell her that her dad was alive. The bad news was a mistake which was due to nasty dreams. Everything was fine and under control.

She packed a Marcel Wanders luxury suitcase, or rather, heaved her stuff into it helter-skelter; a mix of everyday wear and designer clothes, all items in sombre shades: underwear, blouses, skirts, trousers, dresses. She made sure to throw in an all-black outfit to wear at the funeral and something appropriate for her feet. From her collection of two thousand pairs of shoes (there were reasons why the girls had a big house) she snatched up a pair of new black three-thousand-four-hundred-dollar Prada shoes.

The brightest garment (yet discreet) which ended up in the suitcase was a grey-purple Calvin Klein silk dress with a list price of four thousand seven hundred dollars. She owned many items for which she hadn't paid a penny or a cent. It was a perk of the job to own clothes of the designers who demanded her services.

She wrote three messages. Although she could have used SMS, or sent a Direct Message from Twitter as most people would have expected, the old-fashioned handwriting felt less direct, less definitive, less trackable by high-tech gadgets, as though she were a paranoiac.

She put Ebba's note in the wall-mounted box in the corridor outside the Swede's room. She left the notes to the gardener and the maid atop the chest of drawers in the main hall. In each of the messages she mentioned only she would be away for a few days. Not a word about her dad's death. Not a word about where she was going. Nobody needed to know right now.

In the house there were precious stones with a combined value of at least two point seven million dollars. Diamonds. Rubies. Sapphires. Emeralds. Kept in various safes. She felt like a girl in a hallucination when she programmed the burglar alarm, grabbed her baggage and left the property through the backyard fence.

Tabloid journalists often surveyed the front of the property. No paparazzo had yet been caught camping in the backyard, not even Krass. Nobody would know Catriona Milton had gone outside. Now she only had to flag down a taxi.

In the heat, in the downward-sloping street, the suitcase became a bigger problem than she had imagined. She lost her grip on it in the intersection between Blenheim Crescent and

Ladbroke Grove. It rolled downhill, straight towards the vehicle traffic. Why didn't the suitcase's automatic brake system work? She chased the suitcase and saw how it stopped at the junction with Lancaster Road, or rather how a man stopped it with his foot.

Her secret escape out of Notting Hill was demolished.

"Hey, Cat. This yours?" Herbert Krass grinned.

• SIX •

THE GOSSIP REPORTER'S golden hair looked like crusty crustose lichen. With a body shape like a wine barrel, he seemed to suffer in the heat. Krass must have been outside all day. His skin was as red as a boiled lobster. His shirt's armpit sweat stains were as large as pizza plates. His blue-and-white-striped tie with the Millwall football club logo hung loosened around his neck.

Cat stopped dead in her tracks, considered her words, kept a good face. "Thank you for catching my suitcase, Krass."

"And my reward? Can I hope for something wonderful?"

"Don't be silly. May I have my suitcase?"

"May I have a kiss?"

She sighed. "Please, Krass. May I have my suitcase back?"

"Okay." He gave the suitcase a push in her direction. It rolled on its wheels. "But I'm going to write about this. Stay tuned for next Saturday's edition, baby."

She took her suitcase. "Stay away from me, Krass."

"Call me Herbie. We know each other too well to use surnames, Cat." The camera bag dangled from his shoulder.

She watched his hands. They looked normal. Five fingers on each hand. But that didn't mean Krass was innocent. He wanted her to see his hands were normal. The rascal must have used eight-fingered gloves to hide six fake fingers. Despite the heatwave, Krass's grin was as icy as that of a snowman.

"You don't want to forget, Cat, do you?"

"You were mean to me." The memory flashed. The memory of the camera eye which had peered up her skirt.

"It was three damn years ago."

"Feels like yesterday."

"What do you want me to do?"

"Go to hell? How does that sound?"

His grin didn't melt.

"The new spokeswoman for one of the world's largest cosmetics companies isn't supposed to use that tone with her admirers, is she?"

"Why are you doing this to me?"

"Doing what? I know your type, Cat. You love publicity."

"There is good and bad publicity."

Krass laughed, sounding like a honking elephant. "There's no such thing as bad publicity. Furthermore, this is my job."

"There are serious newspapers."

"What if I adored you, Cat Milton? What if I was secretly in love with you? What if I thought you were the most beautiful and sexiest girl I've ever seen? What if I told you about my nightly fantasies? What if I thought, because of you, that Roy Beckman was the luckiest guy on the planet?" He took a step forward.

Cat winced. "Stay away from me."

His grin was so deep it seemed to split his face. "Have you had a tough morning?"

What did the snake know about her morning? "What do you know about my morning?" She moved backwards.

"What do you mean?" He took two steps forwards to offset her two steps backwards.

"Do you own a black raincoat and a black wide-brimmed hat?" She pulled back another two steps. Walking backwards with a heavy suitcase was anything but comfortable. The sky, devoid of clouds. The air, filled with pollution and traffic noise. The sun threw its fiery glow. London became a bobbing concrete island beneath her feet.

"What on earth are you talking about?" The gossip reporter advanced another couple of steps. His strides were longer than hers and he wasn't burdened by the weight of a suitcase. Soon he would be close enough to grab her if he wanted to.

"Never mind." It didn't matter they were on a street in central London in broad daylight with innumerable witnesses if something nasty happened. She had to get away from this guy.

"I'll get you later, Cat."

I'll get you later, Cat. The cold finger of terror poked her between the shoulder blades. "What did you say?"

"I said I'll get you later. The most beautiful girl in the world is obviously in a hurry somewhere. Herbie the nice guy is doing her a favour. He's leaving her alone."

That was when it happened. Like a gunslinger in a Wild West duel, Krass pulled—faster than his own shadow—the camera out of his shoulder bag. A hail of photo flashes hit her in the face. Krass guffawed. "I got you, baby. I got you."

She spun around, almost tripped and began to move southwards along Ladbroke Grove, now uphill, with convulsive grips on the suitcase and the handbag. She knew Krass wanted her to lose her temper, wanted her to make a scene. She refused to be lured into the paparazzo's trap.

"Where does the event take place, Cat?" Krass called. "The suitcase reveals a secret: you're on your way somewhere. And you didn't want anyone to know because you took the way through the hidden gap in your backyard fence. Where're you going?"

She heard his clicking camera again. At least ten times. She didn't look back over her shoulder. Ignorance was better. *So, Krass knows about the hidden gap in the backyard fence.*

As a model, she knew a few things about camera technology. Shooting in bright daylight could be a daunting challenge for an amateur photographer but Krass was a pro. Depending on the sun's position and strength, the camera's flash could be used in various ways to overcome this challenge.

She waved to a taxi, a classic black cab, and discovered it was vacant. The vehicle found a gap in the traffic and stopped. She yanked the cab's back door open, heaved the suitcase onto the floor, tossed the handbag onto the back seat, jumped in, slammed the door shut. "St. Pancras railway station, please. Drive as fast as you can."

• SEVEN •

EBBA DROVE HER purple Porsche towards new adventures, wondering if Cat had bought the lie about the two-day job in Milan. A life without impulsive action, fast cash, wild parties or speedy cars was no real life.

The Porsche flew past Victoria Station and Gordon Hospital, then skidded with screeching tyres onto Grosvenor Road. The temptation to stomp a little extra on the accelerator became too great to resist. Her pretty foot had a life of its own. The spontaneous movement accelerated the car to the border of her imagination. Difficult in the dense London traffic, she suspected, but nevertheless fun as hell. You had to rush like crazy to switch between different lanes here and there and to seize the rare gaps between snail-paced vehicles.

Her hometown of Kungsör out in the Swedish boondocks was too small for quick thrills and rollicking fun. Kungsör was reminiscent of a weather station in Antarctica. Thank God and the Devil's aunt for London. London was civilisation.

She would soon arrive at his residence. Only two blocks away now. Sunrays danced across the windscreen. She was there now, finally there. The luxury vehicle slipped into the car park outside a white stuccoed multi-storey building.

What if Cat found out that she, Ebba, didn't go to Milan? Maybe Cat would find out, or maybe not. It didn't matter. If Cat for some reason wanted to check the details of her best friend's work schedule, it would be easy for her to do so. If Cat learnt the truth, Ebba would fabricate a new lie to save the party. Life was one big party, which had to be saved at all costs. Her ruminations had begun to merge with Cat's troubles in disturbing ways. What was done was done and couldn't be undone. A few things had gone too far. She had passed the point of no return. She had to think forwards, not backwards.

Earlier today, she had found a note in the box on the wall in the corridor outside her bedroom. Cat had left a message which said she would be away for a few days but mentioned neither a reason nor a destination. Ebba didn't like the sketchy text. It wasn't like Cat to express herself in that way. Cat wouldn't write such a message if it was about a job somewhere. Jobs belonged to everyday life. The girls never left longhand messages to each other about everyday things. Something was wrong.

She snatched up her pink Fendi handbag, stepped out of the Porsche, activated the car alarm and spat out the cigarette butt.

Holy crap, how hot it was in the evening sun.

Soon it'll be even hotter, she thought, giggling. She strolled towards the main entrance. A smile played at the corners of her mouth. A euphoria bubbled in her stomach. Not only did she desire him. It was *fun* fucking Roy Beckman.

• EIGHT •

CAT HURRIED INTO St. Pancras railway station, purchased train tickets, boarded the earliest Intercity service to Blackfield.

She sank into a seat in the mobile-phone-free carriage. Sorrow, fatigue, anger, confusion. The mixture of emotions took their toll. She wanted to be alone, and found she was alone, here in carriage A.

She had told her sister she was coming home, but 'home' wasn't the right word. Five years ago, she had stopped thinking of Blackfield as 'home'. London, or the entire planet, was her home since she, at the age of eighteen, had reached superstar status. If you were one of the fashion industry's ten most sought-after models, there was no room for Blackfield in your life. She wasn't going home for her father's funeral. She was going away. Away to the place of her childhood—backwards in time and space. Here and now it reappeared, her memory of the moment nine years ago which had changed her life forever.

Just like Kate Moss, Catriona Milton was discovered by chance in an airport at the age of fourteen.

Victor and Rita Milton and their daughter Catriona return home to England and Blackfield after a holiday week in the Algarve. (Janice has, as usual, refused to travel anywhere. Sis has spent the week at Aunt Hilda's home in Colvin Street.) Cat must go to the toilet and insists she cannot wait until the family has passed through the security at Crow City Airport. She must *hurry*, she explains, or she's going to pee in her knickers. She tells Mum and Dad she needs only a minute to pee, or two minutes, or at most three. She dashes into the nearest ladies' room.

It's here, in this very ladies' room, where no one less than Anita Scriber, star booker at the modelling agency Supreme, spots the girl with the exciting appearance. As a fourteen-year-old, Cat is an ordinary schoolgirl. As an eighteen-year-old, she will be world-famous. Anita would build Cat's career and guide her to superstar status. Supermodels wouldn't be what they are without their super agents. Anita is more than a professional, more than a friend. If Ebba is like a sister, Anita is like a mother.

The train started to roll. Northwards. Towards Blackfield. Unbelievable, but true. She was sitting on a train bound for Blackfield. Too late to change her mind. Too late to get off. *Blackfield—the City of Crows. The city of dark secrets.* She was still alone in carriage A. The quiet carriage was the train's emptiest carriage. In this day and age, people would ideally be contactable around the clock.

She got a new insight: it was pleasant to have her mobile turned off.

No hair stylist or makeup artist had worked on her today. She felt ordinary. She was a simple girl. Her average look today had become a sort of disguise, she decided. Most people who were enchanted by the sight of Catriona Milton saw her in flashy magazines, commercials and televised fashion shows.

She closed her eyes and became drowsy. Everything had a price. She was convinced. The disease was the high price she had had to pay for her beauty, her success, her wealth. She had met Dr. Stockmayer for the first time six years ago ...

The robust man in the white coat sits in an armchair behind a metal desk. His hair is soot-black, his eyes steel-blue. Black hair and blue eyes are a striking combination. He asks her to sit down in one of the visitors' chairs. She obeys.

"I'm Roger Stockmayer. Neurologist, neuroscientist, and Director of Oberon Clinic."

A snowfall stabs at the view outside the windows, cutting grey-white stripes out of the sky. The daylight is as inhospitable as splinters of ice. She hates February.

"Victor Milton is familiar to me," Stockmayer says.

"Do you know my dad?"

"I'm aware of your father's work in the arena of molecular biology."

"What's wrong with me, Doctor? Why do I sleep so much?"

"Miss Milton, you're suffering from narcolepsy."

Cat doesn't know how she is supposed to react. Is she already dying? She's only seventeen. "Narco—what?"

"Narcolepsy. A relatively rare disease which affects the brain's ability to control sleep and wakefulness. The disease makes the REM sleep, or the dream sleep, occur very fast, sometimes in the waking state. A narcoleptic person may doze or fall asleep at any time without warning."

"Relatively rare disease, you say? How rare?"

"No precise figure exists. It has been estimated that less than 0.05 percent of the population has some form of narcolepsy."

"Why is this happening to me?"

"The disease is a mystery, even if successful research suggests we are on the right track to solve it. It has been discovered there seems to be a correlation between narcoleptic humans and certain genetic factors involving the HLA complex."

"The HLA complex?" She grimaces. "What's that?"

"An organisation of genes on chromosome 6. The HLA complex encodes antigen-presenting proteins on cell surfaces and coordinates the immune system. It is believed specific variations in the complex increases the risk of an autoimmune response against the brain's protein-producing neurons. There are roughly eighty to one hundred billion cells in the human brain. Only ten to twenty thousand brain cells secrete a couple of important substances called hypocretin-1 and -2, or orexin-A and -B. Your immune system destroys those cells."

"Am I going to die?" Ripples of panic grow into waves.

"We're all going to die. We're all beginning to die from the moment we're born. Life is a transport route to the grave."

"I'm referring to this disease you say I have!"

"Aha. Then the answer is no. Your disease isn't fatal."

"The nightmares are worse than anything else. They're real, roaring, powerful. Explosions of light ... riots of colours ... The creatures ... the creatures are coming ... they're chasing me ... Often it feels as if the nightmares ... are killing me."

"The extraordinary nightmares are a classic symptom."

"To me they're more than extraordinary. They're real."

He smiles, pretending to believe her. "They are hypnagogic and hypnopompic hallucinations—sensations you experience at the transitional states from wakefulness to sleep and from sleep to wakefulness, respectively—episodes you feel are extremely vivid nightmares. They should not be confused with ordinary nightmares."

"How long will it take to cure me?"

"There is no cure, Miss Milton."

"No … cure?"

"Not today. Maybe never. Even so, the condition is treatable. Medication keeps narcolepsy under control. The severity of the disease varies widely among patients."

Her eyes hurt. She tries not to cry. "Why me? Nobody else in my family has this condition."

"Though the disease may be genetic, the inheritance pattern is unknown. Most narcoleptics come from families where no other family member has the problem. Your future children will most likely be healthy."

"I feel sick, Doctor. The news makes me feel sick."

"Remember what I said. Your condition is treatable."

"Including the nightmares?"

"Yes." Stockmayer leans forward, as though he needs to take a closer look at her. "You are a model, aren't you? Or should I already say supermodel?"

A tear falls from the corner of her eye. It rolls down her cheek. "Is my career at risk because of this?"

He shakes his head. "It shouldn't happen. I'm not saying you'll never experience problems, but with the right actions you'll be able to live a good life."

"Actions? What kind of actions?"

"Drug therapy. Scheduled naps. Non-stop communication."

"Medicines?"

"Yes."

"How long?"

"For the rest of your life."

She falls silent. She makes an effort trying to understand the long-term consequences of the worst news she has ever received.

"Although it has been discovered a lack of hypocretin or orexin causes it, the situation isn't as simple as just restoring the process. The medicines address the symptoms, not the cause of the problem. A potential future cure would first and foremost require new scientific breakthroughs."

"How much medicine do I need?"

"The treatment in its entirety, including specification of drugs and dosages, is tailored to the individual. It'll take some time until we've found a programme which suits you. The time required to obtain maximum control of symptoms varies from case to case. As your healthcare provider, it's my job to help you deal with the practical and emotional effects of your condition."

(((*Miss?*)))

Cat hears a new voice.

((*Miss?*))

Stockmayer's voice disappears.

The new voice advances.

(*Your ticket, miss?*)

"Your ticket, miss?"

She opened her eyes, felt the rushing train. She remembered the departure, not her drowsiness. Her head was as heavy as lead. She turned her eyes in the direction of the voice. He stood in the aisle of the carriage, less than ten feet away. Herbert Krass.

She gasped. Tried to say something. Couldn't utter a word.

"Are you all right, miss?"

She rubbed at her eyes, squinted at the figure. It wasn't Krass. "I'm sorry, Conductor. I ... I must have dozed off."

The conductor smiled. "Tickets from St. Pancras, please."

"No worries." She ruffled through her handbag.

"Where are you going?"

"Blackfield."

"There are nicer places."

"I know."

"Do you have a valid travel ticket?"

"Here." She showed him the ticket.

Did he know who she was? Had he recognised her?

The conductor left carriage A.

She glanced at her watch. A Bvlgari for four thousand eight hundred and seventy dollars. Among the three dozen watches she owned, the mint-green Bvlgari was one of her favourites. It looked amazing on her porcelain-smooth wrist. The time was eleven past six p.m. By now, Ebba was probably on board her flight to wonderful Milan. Lucky her.

She went to the cafeteria carriage, bought a carton mug with filter coffee and returned to carriage A less than five minutes later. The horror which struck her was as clear as starlight, as cold and hard as an iceberg. She was no longer alone in carriage A, yet she felt lonelier than ever. The sixteen-fingered figure in a raincoat and a hat moved along the aisle towards her.

• NINE •

"**I GUESS YOU** saw the piece of writing on the bedroom window." The man blocked the aisle. "Had I completed my errand this morning, I would have had to kill your friend. But killing Miss Sjödal is not a prioritised option among primary solutions. Therefore, I postponed my commission, as Miss Sjödal showed up and disturbed my plans."

"Errand? Commission? Leave me alone."

"The mission must be completed, Cat."

His hands. Scaly, mustard-yellow. Eight-fingered. Hands like paws. Fingers reminiscent of claws. Claws like stilettos. The rest of the stalker's body was hidden beneath the raincoat and the hat. How had he managed to track her from Notting Hill to St. Pancras and to this particular train? *I'll get you later, Cat.*

"I need you, Cat." He moved closer to her. "I need you more than you can ever imagine. It's the truth."

Desperation snatched at the outskirts of her understanding. She wanted to see other people. Fellow passengers and members of staff. Since she had boarded the train, she hadn't seen or heard any other passengers.

"Talk to me, Cat."

She blinked. "Why do you need me?"

"Because you're special."

The man threw out his right paw. He was quick like a weasel. A claw penetrated the back of her blouse.

"I said I need you, Cat. It's important." His voice was as chilly as a midwinter breeze. She screamed, floundered. The man—the creature—was too strong. His claw kept the grip on her blouse, pulling her backwards.

How could such a big guy jump such a small girl? What a coward. She had the same body statistics as her professional role model, Kate Moss. She was short for her profession. She now mustered all the strength a five-foot-seven catwalk queen could possibly have. She struggled, wrested, twitched. The fabric of her blouse burst. Her momentum threw her off balance. She lost her footing, crashed to the floor. An electric swarm of stars circled her head. Her body ached. She moaned. "Please don't kill me."

"If you don't calm down, Cat, I'll have to apply a much less pleasant discussion technique. Be a good girl and stop fighting."

"You're threatening me while telling me to calm down?"

"I'm not threatening you. I want to be your friend."

"Your method of making friends is not convincing."

Despite her tight spot, she was glad she'd worn running shoes, not high-heels. She sprang to her feet, dashed to the far end of carriage A and struck with a fist the control panel which operated the door mechanism. "Come on, come on, come on."

The door slid open. She threw herself out. As the windowed door jerked back to its closed position, she saw the hat-clad figure sprinting towards her. His face remained invisible in the hat's shadow. He reached out a paw towards the control panel in carriage A. She spun around and away from the door and knocked on the carriage-B control panel. The electronics didn't work. The door to B refused to open.

The sun-baked countryside whizzed past the windows of the exit doors. Where was the nearest emergency brake? How far was it to the nearest station? She hammered again with her fist on the door control panel. Nothing happened. The door to B still refused to open. A swishing sound behind her. She whirled around. The door to carriage A glided open.

The world turned as black as a certain hat shadow. The power cut must have coincided with the train passing through a tunnel. A darkness as thick as tar enveloped her. There were several tunnels along this railway line. She didn't know in which one the train now happened to be. The compact blackness reinforced her feeling of loneliness. She was alone with a monster on board a motionless rail vehicle. Fellow passengers and all staff had already evacuated the train. Cat was forgotten.

It was him, she thought. He had cut the power. He had shut the train down in the middle of the tunnel to make it easier to get at her. He had done it so neither personnel nor passengers would notice when he killed her.

She winced. Something crawled on her back. As though a huge spider scampered from her lower back all the way up to her neck. Now it climbed up her hair. *No eight-legged creature but a hand with eight fingers.* The Bvlgari watch face had revealed her position. The mint-green glow couldn't be missed in the gloom. He was here. In the blackness. With her. Where exactly?

"Disobedient girls should never be alone in dark spaces," the pursuer said. "Naughty girls can get into trouble in darkness."

She screamed. Or tried to. A feeble cry fell from her lips.

• TEN •

THE TAVERN, THE Red Unicorn. Jan surveyed the premises, paying attention to orders of food and drinks both at the tables and at the bar. A mix of regular customers and new faces. Families, singletons, businessmen, businesswomen, students, academics, factory workers and the occasional lost tourist.

She didn't want to work today. Dad had died. But she had already taken four days off because of the family tragedy. The employment conditions weren't great. She couldn't afford to be off any longer. She needed her fifty pounds per seven-day period. The current week she had already lost out on forty pounds. A tenner remained to be saved.

At the bar stood a Smurf-sized guy with shaved head, flattened nose, and ears the size of jug handles. The metal in one of his nostrils wasn't a ring but a fish hook. Despite the heat, he wore a fur-lined leather jacket with text on the back which read: 'Do I look like a fucking people person?'. He was in the company of a tall anorexic blonde dressed in a small white piece of cloth which might have passed for a slingshot bikini.

Behind Jan, someone said, "Two cappuccinos. If they arrive at lightning speed. If not—forget it."

The snappy order had come from one of two costume-clad men with briefcases in their hands. They gave her no eye contact. She wasn't offended. She was used to people's lack of eye contact. Customers were afraid to lose their appetite if they had to look at her as she took their orders. She blamed no one. If you hated yourself, if you were disgusted by your own appearance, you couldn't criticise people for their lack of eye contact.

"Have a seat, gentlemen." She smiled as best she could with her misshapen mouth, gesturing towards a free table. "Two cappuccinos will arrive straight away."

Today the number of staff was just six. A busy day. Customers shouted their orders: "Tortellini with four cheeses in tomato sauce." ... "A bottle of the house white, the drier variety." ... "Three cheesecake special." ... "Four espressos, two double." ... "Three Red Unicorn luxury burgers but only two with mustard." ... "A half-pint of orange juice with ice and a pint of Blackfield Bitter Ale." ... "Five mackerel sandwiches, though two without onion, and extra mayonnaise on all of them." ...

Was the hot weather an omen? Was something terrible destined to happen soon? Jan thought of the corkscrew in the back pocket of her jeans. How would it feel to use it as a self-defence weapon? Just a hypothetical question. An uninteresting thought experiment. She already knew how she would use the corkscrew. She intended to use it on a particular person.

A man waved at her. He sat alone at a corner table at the far back of the room. He seemed familiar. Jan guessed she had met him before, not here at the Red Unicorn but somewhere else, and perhaps only once. Yes, she remembered.

"Good afternoon, Dr. Stockmayer."

"Good afternoon, Miss Milton."

Roger Stockmayer. Age fifty plus. Tousled hair. Three-day beard stubble. Tall forehead. He wore a beige summer jacket and a navy-blue shirt. He looked outlandishly cool in the heatwave.

"You remember me, Miss Milton."

"You are my sister's doctor."

"I want to take this opportunity to express my condolences."

"Thank you." Tears dotted her pig eyes. She had to blink. She managed to keep the tears away. Her sight became dry and clear again. *Can pigs cry? Maybe I'm the only pig who can cry.*

"Your father's obituary in the *Blackfield Telegraph* was beautiful. It did his career justice. Milton was a true force in the field of modern molecular medicine. He made a difference."

He gave her eye contact. He gave *her*, Janice Milton, eye contact. For some reason, he thought it was worth looking at her. *I don't disgust him. Why don't I disgust him?*

"I need to see my patient. Your twin sister, in other words. Your sister's contact details do not seem to be up to date and, because of her busy work schedule, it is anything but easy to get hold of her, if you see what I mean."

"Even when Catriona's contact details *are* updated from time to time, it's difficult to get hold of her. She says if there are umpteen million text messages and voicemails on her mobile, umpteen million phone messages on her landline answering machine and umpteen million fan mails received at her agency's fan club division, then it's easy to miss one or two. You couldn't guess how many followers my sis has on Twitter, Facebook and Instagram. You would be shocked if I told you."

Stockmayer smiled. "Earlier, I talked to your mother on the phone. She said her other daughter, your twin sister, comes home tonight, but your mother didn't know when."

Mum should know the time of Cat's arrival, Jan thought.

"Moreover," Stockmayer said, "your mother said that if I need to get in touch with your sister, it'd be better to talk to you about how I should go about it. How does that sound?"

"Mum was busy watching TV, wasn't she?"

"Do you have time to sit down a while?"

What does he want to talk to me about?

She cast an anxious eye on the wall clock. "I finish my shift in ten minutes."

"Excellent."

"Something else?"

"Indeed. A glass of rosé, please."

"I don't want to intrude on your family reunion, Miss Milton. Not under present circumstances." Pause. "A wonderful wine." Pause. "Could you take a message for your sister?"

"I suppose I could." Jan munched on a Danish pastry.

"Thank you. Please ask your sister to contact me. Tell her it's about a remarkable new drug."

"Aha." Jan's mouth was full of pastry. "Was that all?"

"That should be enough to arouse her interest. Tell her she can get in touch at any time during normal office hours. My contact details are the same as before."

She wanted to get up and away from the table. The awkward chat had to be over. "Have we finished?"

"May I ask you a personal question?"

She trembled. Her body stiffened. "Be my guest."

"Miss Milton, are you horrified by your appearance?"

She hadn't been prepared for such a question. She didn't know how to react. The background noise of the pub was sucked out of her ears. The world went out like a dead light bulb. She was alone with Stockmayer on a deserted planet.

"Yes. I'm horrified by my appearance."

"Have you ever considered plastic surgery?"

"No."

"Why not?"

She hesitated. "Two reasons."

"Which are?" Humility filled the lines in his face.

She pursed her lips. "Look at me."

"I am looking at you."

"I'm too malformed. Even the most optimistic surgeon wouldn't think there was any hope for me. Moreover, I have no money. The costs must be astronomical."

"Your sister has money. She's a multimillionairess."

"Catriona's wealth is uninteresting to me. I want to manage my own private economy. I wouldn't be able to accept Catriona's money if she offered to pay for the operations. Also, I'm a hopeless case. The discussion is meaningless." She gasped for air. "Why all these questions about me?"

"Professional curiosity. A good friend of mine happens to be one of the most respected plastic surgeons in Europe. Anyway, thank you for the chat. How much do I owe you for the wine?"

• ELEVEN •

CAT FELT A tug at her hair from behind. Curls of hair fell out of the topknot and cascaded over her back and shoulders. The stalker fingered the elastic strap of her bra. Another soundless scream dribbled from her mouth. For a second, she considered opening one of the side doors and jumping off the train and into the tunnel, out of one darkness and into another.

The light returned. The floor lurched. The train restarted and accelerated. The unwelcome touch, the cold fingers, fell away from her back. An unspent fraction of survival instinct prompted her to act. She punched the carriage B control panel. This time, the door coughed, then slid open. She threw herself into carriage B, collided with a service trolley. Chocolate bars, plastic spoons, sugar cubes and bags of peanuts and potato crisps scattered in the aisle. A thermos crashed to the floor with a bang, spilling steaming tea. A miniature bottle of sparkling raspberry juice hit the edge of a table and exploded like a clay pigeon. The unchilled juice sprayed like a deep-red rain.

Carriage B was jam-packed. Glaring adults, sobbing kids, passengers' pets. Barking dogs, hissing cats and croaking birds.

She spun around the overturned snack trolley, tripped on the thermos, skidded on sugar cubes and chocolate bars, regained her balance and kept running along the aisle. About thirty feet in front of her, the door to carriage C opened.

They sat talking in the train manager's compartment: Cat, the conductor and the train manager himself.

She looked at the conductor. "Don't you recognise me?"

"Of course I do," the conductor said. "You're the lovely lady in carriage A, the phone-free carriage. The lady who's on her way to hideous Blackfield."

"I've already learnt Blackfield isn't your favourite city."

"You look familiar to me," the train manager said. "I can't put my finger on it. Have you ever been on TV?"

"Never," she lied.

"Why are you wearing sunglasses?" the conductor asked.

"Is it a crime to wear sunglasses on board this train?"

"Of course not," the conductor said. "I'm just curious."

"Me too," the train manager said. "Curious."

"My eyes are sensitive," she said.

"Uh-huh," the conductor said.

"What's your name?" the train manager asked.

"Mary Smith," Cat heard herself say. She hoped they wouldn't ask her to show ID.

"Is it Miss or Mrs.?" the conductor asked.

"Miss," she said. "Why does it matter?"

"Well, Miss Smith," the train manager said. "Do you want us to believe a man dressed in a raincoat on the year's sunniest and hottest day tried to rape you?"

"Yes."

"Nobody on board the train fits the description, and that's no surprise."

"The attacker might have changed clothes," she said. "He would have had time."

"Just a speculation on your part," the train manager said.

"Listen, you two; I don't know what intentions he had but he was here. He attacked me." She refrained from mentioning eight-fingered hands.

"Of course he was here," the conductor said.

"If he was here," the train manager said, "where is he now?"

"The train is moving at high speed," the conductor said. "The last time we stopped at a station was before the power cut. No attacker could have jumped off the speeding train or got off the train at a station. So, where's the guy?"

"I don't know where he is," she said. "But I'm not lying."

"Of course you're not lying," the conductor said.

"The tear in my blouse? Isn't it clear I'm telling the truth?"

"The tear in your blouse may have occurred anytime," the train manager said. "You could have caused it yourself."

She couldn't believe her ears. "What did you say?"

"I think you've had a fight with your boyfriend. It happened on the platform at St. Pancras, didn't it?"

"Of course." The conductor snapped his fingers. "There we have the explanation. A quarrel with the boyfriend and things turned too passionate." He chuckled.

She got up from the chair, gritting her teeth and clenching her fists. "Let's go to carriage A. There may be evidence there which proves the attacker was on board."

"Of course there's evidence," the conductor said. "Let's go."

• • •

"Look." Cat pointed at the window.

"What?" the train manager said.

"Yes, what?" the conductor said.

"On the window," she said. "You can't see it?"

The train manager looked. "Oh, that? Sure, I can see it."

"Of course we can see it," the conductor said.

"A child probably did that," the train manager said. "A child who's missing a cat."

"Sounds reasonable," the conductor said.

"The window will be cleaned," the train manager said. "And very soon."

She couldn't care less about window cleaning. It was so beside the point.

"Is your baggage in order?" the conductor asked.

"Yeah." She wouldn't check the contents of her suitcase or her handbag now, not in the presence of these men.

"There's nothing for us to do here," the train manager said.

"At least nothing which has something to do with our job," the conductor said. He gave Cat a perverted look, grinning.

"Anything else, Miss Smith?" the train manager asked.

"No, thank you. I'm fine."

"You might have had a nightmare," the train manager said.

"Or else it's the heat," the conductor said.

"Would you like an aspirin?" the train manager asked.

"No," she said.

"Are you sure?"

"Yes."

"Of course she's sure," the conductor said.

She shuddered. "You'd finished here, hadn't you?"

The men shrugged and left the carriage.

She turned back towards the window.

The scribbling read:

I NEED YOU, CAT

• TWELVE •

LEO BAGINSKI JUGGLED an apple in the queue at the supermarket in Croydon, south London, listening to the radio news through his media player. Later, he would wonder how the day would have proceeded had he decided to buy his lunch apple elsewhere. He put the player with the accompanying earphone back into his suit-jacket pocket. The supermarket cacophony roared in his ears like tinnitus. The oven-hot air turned his shirt into a self-adhesive film. He could do with a glass of iced water. His tongue had the dry texture of a brick, yet he ignored every discomfort. An attire consisting of T-shirt, shorts and flip-flops was incompatible with a professional appearance and therefore unthinkable. He eased his tie knot a tad.

In front of him in the queue stood an old woman with a shopping cart in one hand and a baby stroller in the other. A woman with a grandchild or great-grandchild, he guessed. She appeared to be in her mid-seventies. Her shopping cart was filled to the brim. The baby was crying.

She glanced at his apple, wearing an apologetic expression. "Are you having your lunch break, young man?" Her features were overall round or circular: round rosehip-coloured cheeks, circular bright-blue eyes, round nose, circular ears, circular mouth, round belly. Her skin marked by age spots and wrinkles.

Baginski understood what she was driving at. "Yes, madam. I'm on my lunch break. But don't worry. I'm in no hurry."

"Are you certain, young man? You only have an apple there while I have a fully loaded shopping cart. I would be more than happy to let you go before us in the queue."

"Us?"

The old lady beamed. "Little Oliver and I."

He glanced at the baby in the stroller. "Ah, little Oliver. Does he cry because he is hungry?"

"No. The problem is the heat. He has got plenty to drink, and we can't do anything about the heat." She leaned over the stroller and tickled the baby under his chin. "Little Oliver looks forward to tonight's barbecue with the whole family."

"Barbecue sounds nice."

"The papers say it's the hottest August for forty-six years."

"I see."

"You're not on a diet, are you?"

"Uh?"

"A young man in the prime of life should have more than an apple for lunch."

"I had a proper breakfast, madam."

"And a cooked meal for supper every night?"

"Your assumption is correct, madam."

"You don't want to go before us in the queue?"

"I'm too well-mannered to accept your offer."

The woman laughed. "Where did you grow up, if I may ask?"

"In an Orthodox home in Slovakia. My father is a priest and my mother is a schoolteacher."

"That explains your courtesy, young man. The son of a priest and a schoolteacher."

He returned a dutiful smile.

The woman paid at the checkout. Meanwhile, he kept an eye on little Oliver. Then she returned her groceries to the shopping cart. She would use the cart to transport her purchases to her car in the multi-storey car park.

He paid for his apple.

"Thank you for watching Oliver," the lady said.

"No problem at all."

"Uh, how heavy the cart is."

"You also have the stroller. Let me help you with the cart."

"Wouldn't that be troublesome to you?"

"How could the son of a priest and a schoolteacher think it would be troublesome to help a fellow human being?"

The woman laughed. "Where are you headed?"

"Like you, I have my car in the nearby car park."

The lady took the stroller. Baginski gripped the shopping cart. They left the supermarket and walked towards the multi-storey car park.

"I hope you don't lose time because of us."

"No worries, madam. My employer's sales office is within a ten-minute drive of here."

"So, you're a salesman?"

"Yes. I've been on a mission in Croydon the whole day."

"What do you sell?"

"Industrial consulting."

"How exciting! Your employer?"

"Alphatrone Computing Limited."

"Been with them long?"

"About four years."

"Your title?"

"Industrial Consultant." *What an inquisitive lady.*

They reached the car park. One of the lifts opened. A dozen people stepped out. Eight people entered, including the old woman and Baginski, with stroller and shopping cart.

"What level?" Baginski asked.

"Third," the old lady said.

He pushed the lift control panel's 3-button.

"Where's your own car?" the lady asked.

"Sixth." He pushed the panel's 6-button.

Three of the other people in the lift also pushed buttons. One person got off at level 2. Baginski, the old woman and two other people got off at level 3.

Baginski and the woman started across level 3 towards the woman's car. "Now you have to push the button again to make the lift return to third and then up to sixth," she said.

"Shouldn't a young man in the prime of life survive that?"

"Yes." She beamed. "And then you get to enjoy your apple."

They approached a conspicuously empty parking area. There were many vacant parking spaces and only four people in sight.

Three of the four people departed towards the staircase or the lifts. One person got into his car and drove off.

"Which car is yours, madam?"

"The yellow Vauxhall there." She pointed.

They arrived at the Vauxhall. Baginski parked the cart.

"Thank you so much, young man."

"When was the last time you filled up your car with petrol?"

"This morning. Why do you ask?"

"Because I could use the information, madam." He let go of the apple, took the gun out of his jacket pocket and shot the woman in the head.

The apple seemed to hang motionless in the air. The next moment, the Glock pistol was back in his jacket pocket and the fruit was back in his hand. The apple had defied gravity.

The lady fell backwards onto the concrete floor, still with a smile on her round mouth. She seemed just as happy in death as she had been in life. High expectations on the barbecue with the grandchild or great-grandchild and the rest of the family still sparkled in her bright-blue eyes. The bullet hole in her forehead represented yet another circular shape among her overall circular features.

Baginski knew that when he had fired the silenced pistol bullet, the nearest surveillance camera had caught his back only, not the shooting. The film would show nothing but the back of a medium-sized man in a dark suit. He hadn't planned to eliminate the woman. She had just been in the right place at the right time. The London police had searched a stolen Volvo linked to the recent murder of a popular politician. The Volvo had been sighted in Croydon. This Vauxhall was inconspicuous enough to suit his next mission.

The woman's ungraceful body didn't fit into the space under a private car but it did fit beneath the chassis of a van at a nearby parking space. As he dragged the corpse, he wasn't bothered by the streak of blood on the floor. The corpse would be discovered sooner or later anyway. He opened the cadaver's handbag, grabbed the car keys, reunited the handbag with the body under the van. By nature, he wouldn't steal money from the corpse's handbag. His outstanding morals prevented him from doing so. An industry consultant didn't nick money from lifeless old ladies.

Scattered voices erupted from different directions. A dog barked somewhere. A young couple's loud quarrel. A tipsy woman's high-pitched laughter. A man shouting at his dog to shut up. Baginski took it all in but there were no people in the immediate vicinity of the scene of the murder. He surveyed the distance between the Vauxhall and the nearest stairway door. Two surveillance cameras were scanning the section through which he wanted to move. The make and model of the cameras told him the system wasn't bulletproof. He raised the semi-automatic pistol and squeezed off four shots. Two rounds per camera. The high-tech sound suppressor did its job. The gunfire wasn't louder than the dead, dull thump of a double bass.

With the smooth motion of a tiger, he slipped into the stairwell. Earlier, in the lift from the ground level, eight people (little Oliver excluded) had heard him say his car was parked on level 6. False information. He walked onto level 4, munching on his apple. He met people. Stressful individuals. Stress was a health hazard. Today, people died of stress. People should eat more apples. He opened the Volvo's boot, changed his grey suit jacket for a beige blazer, took off his tie and grabbed the briefcase. Back at level 3, he opened the Vauxhall's front door on the driver's side, put the briefcase inside, closed the door. He went over to the stroller. "I have news for you, Oliver." Baginski wore his flawless industrial-consultant smile. "Both good and bad news. Which do you want to hear first?"

The baby moved his arms in the air, up and down, up and down (waving?) but didn't answer. At what age did babies answer when spoken to? Oliver's eyes were wide. His toothless mouth opened, closed, opened. No words came out. No noise either. The baby neither laughed nor cried. Drool dripped from a wet corner of his mouth. Unconcerned, the baby was playing with a pram toy—five colourful teddy bears on elastic, clipped to the pram. Baginski decided not to waste any bullets on the baby. His good morals prevented him from doing so. He never spent more ammunition than necessary. Thrift was a virtue his father the priest and his mother the schoolteacher had taught him before he, as a ten-year-old boy, had killed them.

"The good news is you'll see the daylight of tomorrow. The bad news is tonight's barbecue is cancelled. Take care, Oliver." Baginski got into the Vauxhall, started the engine and drove off.

• THIRTEEN •

PARIS. LE CARROUSEL du Louvre, Rue de Rivoli. The latest shows of the ready-to-wear collections. The superstar Catriona Milton has been booked for shows presented by a number of the most prestigious fashion houses in the world.

It happens during the third show on the closing day of Paris Fashion Week. Cat waltzes down the runway in a black glittering dress and is struck by the feeling she is about to have a seizure.

Her head gets filled with Dr. Stockmayer's words ... EDS, Excessive Daytime Sleepiness, is a classic symptom. Another is cataplexy, a sudden and temporary loss of muscle coordination, from the slightest weakness to total body collapse. She is certain an EDS-cataplexy attack is about to strike her, on this very catwalk, before the eyes of everyone at the venue and millions of TV viewers.

False alarm. The medicines work. Later, in the backstage chaos, with a Styrofoam cup of orange juice in her hand, she tries to laugh off the horrible moment. Backstage staff and other models giggle when they hear what Cat says. Ebba giggles louder and wilder than anybody else. Everything is as it should be. Cat's harmony with herself is restored.

• • •

The girls prepare for yet another show. The backstage is hurried, turbulent. That's how it should be. A fast-paced environment maximises the suspense.

Everybody is doing last-minute corrections to outfits and makeup. Everyone is yapping at the same time. Ebba trumpets the latest industry gossip. A few girls laugh at a dirty joke. It is popular to let the audience wait. The longer the wait, the better the show. The fashion press with VIP status. The dealers. The fashion magazine managers. The right celebrities. The arena is filled to the brim with the high-class invited. The lensmen want to be close to the runway to obtain the best camera angles.

Every catwalk scene is coordinated with conscientious attention to detail to ensure each girl gets enough time to change clothes in between scenes. Once a model steps off the runway, she must carry out a hectic change of outfit and get her makeup and hair perfected. It is the job of the backstage dressers to get the models runway-ready. Clothes hang organised on a rail in sequence so both model and dresser know which outfit to pick at each change. The dressers are ready to quickly open and close zippers, undo buttons and button up, as well as help the models with accessories.

The show begins. This time, Cat is fourth in the order of girls. She appears in a superb silk dress, moving through bursts of camera flashes.

• FOURTEEN •

HOW COULD BLACKFIELD exist on the same planet as Paris? What an unfathomable contrast. She stood outside the front door of the suburban terraced house at the dead end of the world. Farnwood might be one of the finest neighbourhoods in the City of Crows but it wasn't exactly Notting Hill. It took an effort to place her finger on the doorbell.

The door creaked as it opened. Her sis was there. Jan was the size of a walrus.

"There you are," Jan said. "Better late than never, uh?"

"The front door is still squeaky," Cat said. "After all these years, it's still squeaky. Damn annoying."

The sisters burst out sobbing. They hugged.

"I'm sorry I called you a vain bitch."

"I'm sorry I called you a lazy cow."

"Your blouse is ruined, Cat. A tear in the back."

"Thank you for the information."

"What happened?"

"It got stuck in a door. I'll change it in a jiffy."

Dixie miaowed and stepped out from between Jan's legs.

"Hey, Dix." Cat scooped him up in her arms. "I've missed you, big boy." She kissed him on the nose.

Dixie miaowed again.

"Mum!" Jan called. "Mum, Mum! Cat is here!"

The sisters sat opposite each other at the table in the bustling kitchen. Mum stood at the cooker, handling multiple pots and pans. Gravy simmered, butter sizzled, mustard seeds popped. The kitchenware clattered, tinkled and rattled. The air smelled of pancakes, onions, peppers, mushrooms and chips.

Mum's body shape was intermediate between Cat's fabulous figure and Jan's elephantine appearance. Her hair was a mix of Cat's adorable tresses and Jan's unruly mop. Her eyes were a fusion of Cat's exquisite eyes of a star model and Jan's repulsive gaze of a Halloween skeleton.

Mum clattered amongst saucepans. "Why must your father die before you show any interest in coming home, Catriona?"

Cat sighed. "Good to see you too, Mum."

"Don't be rebellious. There's no room for rebellious girls in this house." Then, "How many pancakes would you like, girls?"

"Is there bacon in them?" Jan asked.

"Lots of bacon."

"Good." Jan clapped. "Four pancakes."

"If you say four, it means at least five, Janice," Mum said.

"One please," Cat said. "Without bacon."

Jan stared at Cat. "Only one?"

"Your sister is a so-called 'fine lady', Janice," Mum said. "They count calories."

Cat couldn't be bothered to comment on that. It was the wrong moment to have a fight with Mum.

"How was your trip?" Jan asked.

"Awful," Cat said.

"What happened?" Mum asked.

"Yes, what happened?" Jan asked. "Why was the trip awful?"

"You don't want to know."

"Life can't be too awful for a girl who is on seventy thousand pounds a week," Mum said.

"Or *at least* seventy thousand a week," Jan said.

Mum put the food on the table and sat down across from Cat. "How can a financially independent girl be so damn whiny?"

"I have paid a high price, Mum. You know that."

"Aha?"

"She has, Mum," Jan said. "Don't fight, you two. Please don't fight. Let's eat. I'm hungry."

"I have to take medication for the rest of my life," Cat said. "Nevertheless, I'm forced to put up with occasional nightmares and hallucinations of extreme terror."

"Dad is dead," Jan cried. "Stop fighting, stop fighting."

"Shut up, Janice." Mum slammed her fist on the table. Plates and cutlery rattled. A creepy silence gripped the kitchen. Mum sobbed and wiped at her eyes. Another silence. Then, "We need something in our glasses, girls." She came back with a bottle of white wine and a carafe of elderberry juice. "Wine or juice, girls?"

"What a question," Jan said. "Juice, of course."

"Yes." Cat tried to muster a smile. "Juice for me too. Who can resist the most delicious homemade elderberry juice?"

"Help yourselves to the pancakes, girls," Mum said.

They ate. They drank. There should be plenty to talk about, Cat thought. No one said much. An uncomfortable feeling. A funereal mood already. Cat finished her only pancake in the same time as Jan devoured her five. Mum had three. After the dinner, the twins helped Mum to clear the table.

"Janice, could you show your dear sister to her room?" The tone in Mum's voice made the question sound like an order. "There's a programme on TV and I can't miss it."

Mum hasn't seen me in a long time, Cat thought. *Yet she prioritises the TV. Why can't you hug me, Mum?*

"Come, Sis," Jan said. "Let's go upstairs."

"Mum hasn't changed," Cat said.
"You'd expected her to?" Jan said.
"It's about time she did."
"You're too good-looking."
"Is that what you think, you and Mum?"

The room was a perfect example of bad taste: a cheap bed with olive-green bedspread, a grey-painted wooden wardrobe, beige curtains, dark-blue-and-brown-striped wallpaper. The London elite would go nuts, Cat thought. Luckily no friends knew how she would spend the next few nights. Only the mirror looked decent. A full-length mirror with an ornate frame. "I don't recognise the room, Jan. It's changed. You've altered it."

"I hope you like it."
"I do," Cat lied.
"We call it the guest room."
"Since when?"
"Since the last time you disappeared after a brief visit and a fight with Mum."
"The room was ours—yours and mine—when we were kids. Our shared bedroom." Cat paused. "The mirror is new, isn't it?"
"Dad bought it a few months ago. He said it was an antique mirror in the baroque style. It's eerie, isn't it?"

"It's nice."

"Although it's nice, you can't exclude it's eerie."

"It isn't eerie."

"Do you see the contrast?"

"What are you talking about?"

Jan pointed at the mirror glass. "We're reflected at the same time, Sis. You and I. Beauty, ugliness. Side by side. The mirror isn't used to dealing with extreme contrast."

Cat watched the girls in the mirror. "Don't talk like that."

"The contrast between us could crack the mirror glass."

"I told you not to talk like that."

"I talk the way I want. You're my sister, not my mother."

Dixie sneaked into the room, stopped at the mirror, sniffed at it and miaowed.

"There, you see?" Cat said. "Dix has approved the mirror."

"I hope it can handle you, Cat."

"What do you mean?"

"I do hope the mirror can handle your beauty—without breaking."

"Don't be silly."

"I met your doctor today."

"Stockmayer?"

"Is there anyone else?"

"What did he want?"

"See you."

"I understood. Get to the point."

"He said it was important."

"He wouldn't seek me if it weren't important."

"He showed up at the tavern after talking to Mum on the phone. He said your contact details weren't up to date."

"What a great revelation."

"It's about some new medicine."

"Aha." Cat yawned. "Now I would like to have a shower and then go to bed. Could you please explain to Mum?"

"I could always try."

"Goodnight."

"Try to be on time for breakfast." Jan left the room. The floor moaned under her clumsy feet. She closed the door behind her. A pleasant stillness filled the room.

Cat was alone.

Or so she thought.

• FIFTEEN •

EBBA SNIFFED THE cocaine off the bedside table. All of it in one go.

"Take it easy with that stuff, Miss Sjödal," Roy whispered. "The tip of your pretty nose is all powder-white." He penetrated her from behind. He was hard, rough and deep inside.

"Oh, so nice ... Oh, so nice ..." Ebba glanced over her shoulder. "Lick the tip of my nose."

He obeyed. "You're so mischievous. Sexy and mischievous."

"Don't come too soon, handsome." She squeezed the pillow before her, giggling. "Dare not come too soon."

The bed springs whined. The mattress bobbed. The bed legs rattled.

"Harder, Roy ..." She tittered.

His teeth nibbled her hair at the back of her head. She trembled. He stroked her stiff nipples. She moaned. He grabbed her hips. She pushed herself firmer and wilder against his throbbing penis. Her already hammering heart was sent into overdrive. They climaxed together. Ebba shrieked. Roy panted in her ear. She gasped.

Her eyes swam about somewhere beyond the ceiling. A window was ajar. They were silent, holding each other, only just aware of the rumble from the Pimlico traffic four floors below. She rested her head on Roy's chest. His hand caressed her waist.

"You're a great girl in bed," Roy murmured.

She met his gaze. "As great as Cat?"
"Greater."

She kissed him. Roy Beckman. The handsomest football player anywhere. Athletic body. Eyes like amber. Dusk-dark hair. Roy was with her. Only Cat didn't yet know.

Today's fashion magazine headlines made Ebba sick: 'Cat Milton—The Girl of the Year', 'Cat Milton—The Outstanding Professional', 'Cat Milton—Beauty Incarnate', 'Cat Milton—The Hottest Catwalk Girl Right Now', 'Cat Milton—A Role Model of Role Models'. Cat was as perfect in her leisure time as she was on the job. Too perfect. If Ebba ordered a Tequila Slammer, Cat had a protein shake. If Ebba had a Vodka Russian, Cat ordered mineral water. If Ebba smoked a cigarette, Cat nibbled on a carrot. Ebba loved crisps and cheese puffs. Cat enjoyed natural nuts and dried fruit.

She grows up in a cramped and shabby rented flat in Runninge, a notorious district on the southern outskirts of the Swedish town of Kungsör. On Ebba's fourteenth birthday, the family is gathered at the cracked kitchen table. The overcooked potatoes and the gooey gravy disgust her.

An older bro, nineteen-year-old Micke, guffaws. "Little Sis no longer looks like an ugly duckling, guys. She's developing nice little titties as well."

The rest of her bros, four of them and all older than her, guffaw like idiots. Dad swings a fist in Micke's face. The nosebleed spatters the boy's T-shirt. Micke howls. Then Dad starts to laugh. Mum sits soundless like a doll. Mum has a tragic expression in her eyes.

On a day she skips school, her life changes and will never be the same again. Ebba wants to get away from Kungsör and the terrible district of Runninge. She gets on a train to Stockholm, absconds conductors and manages to make the entire trip to the capital without a ticket. She wanders around the posh NK department store on Hamngatan, with no money whatsoever, pretending to be interested in clothes she can only fantasise about buying. That is when it happens. A strange woman talks to her. A woman who turns out to be a reputable talent scout in the fashion industry, both in Sweden and abroad. Ebba says something, though she can't remember what. More words are exchanged. Why me? she wonders. How can a girl like me have an interesting look? The strange lady wonders if she may offer Ebba a cup of hot chocolate at the French cafe. Ebba hesitates but accepts. When you're broke, it would be stupid to turn down an offer of a free cup of hot chocolate.

They move towards NK's floor 3. She is convinced she dreams a peculiar dream. She is the ugly duckling, and therefore this must be a dream. Except it is no dream. Ebba is no longer the ugly duckling. When she returns home at night, she tells her family what is about to happen in her life. No one believes her. They laugh her to scorn.

Roy kissed her. "You're shorter than the tallest catwalk queens and taller than the shortest ones. You're neither tall nor short."

"First, Cat is short for her profession," Ebba said. "I'm two inches taller than Cat. Thus, I'm five feet nine. Overall, I have the same body statistics as Miranda Kerr."

He kissed her supple breasts. "There was a time when I thought all Swedish girls were blonde and blue-eyed. A certain Miss Sjödal revealed my ignorance. The combination of black curly hair and bright-green eyes is super-sexy."

She giggled. "I'm glad I don't disappoint you."

He paused. Then, "Cat is like a sister to you, isn't she?"

Ebba nodded. "She is."

"More than just a catwalk-sister? Strange. You two are so different. You are but shadows of each other, if that."

"We're sisters *and* mere shadows of one another." She pondered. "We're like twisted shadows. We're each other's twisted shadow."

"Oh."

"Cat and I have always been together, always looked after each other."

"How was it that you met and got to know one another?"

She sat up in bed and lit a cigarette. "We first met when we were fifteen, at a gala dinner in Brussels. After my move from Stockholm to London, we socialised more and more. As sixteen-year-olds we experienced Paris together and lived in the agency's apartment complex in the Bastille area along with twelve other models. Back then, we were a bit naive. Our first visit to the fashion capital of the world and we thought we would be raised to stardom as soon as we stepped off the plane.

"But the penny dropped quickly. We worked our butts off to survive in this very competitive work environment. Several of the girls cried themselves to sleep every night. We made like seventeen or eighteen castings per day and met with the same business people, again and again and again.

"And every night we hung out with these guys. We knew the guys we met in Paris were paid to invite models to nightclubs, but we didn't care about this status competition between the clubs. We girls had fun and the drinks were free. We were sixteen-year-olds and met men in their fifties—rock stars, sports managers, movie stars, artists, entrepreneurs, filmmakers, media moguls."

"If you and Cat are that close, I can understand if this new thing which you and I have together gives you a bad conscience."

"It's a tough world. Everything costs something. Romantic relationships shatter and new ones start. Money and competition make the globe spin."

"I thought you thought teetotallers were boring."

"Catriona is an exception. She is my best friend and my housemate. Sometimes I wish we were biological sisters." She stubbed out the cigarette and sank into bed again.

"Ebba?"

"Mmm?" She fidgeted, clung to him.

"How bad is it with that other stuff in your life?"

"Nothing I can't handle."

"That's no answer."
"Okay, I guess it's as bad as you can imagine."
"Then it's very bad indeed."
"My career is threatened. The secret operation will save it."
"How dangerous do you think it is?"
"They are powerful people. I'm only a tool to them."
"Is that how you see it? That you're a tool?"
"It facilitates the situation."
"You mean it relieves feelings of guilt?"

She didn't answer. She let Roy form his own opinion. "I've already played my part in the plan. I don't participate anymore, not in an active way."

"Is that what they've said?"
"Their silence speaks for itself."
"Who are they, Ebba?"
"I can't tell you. Not now."
"Why not?"
"I just can't."
"Okay." Pause. "Okay."
"Our careers and our love are a top priority."

"Our careers and our love, baby." He kissed her. "I'll play in the Premier League and the Champions League next season. And I'll play for England in the World Cup. I know I will. I have both the talent and the motivation."

"Promise you won't disappoint me. I demand that Roy Beckman becomes the top goal scorer in the Champions League and at the next World Cup."

"I love your Swedish accent, Ebba. It's sweet, sexy."
"Roy?"
"What is it, gorgeous?"
"You licked cocaine from the tip of my nose."
"I love to lick the tip of your pretty nose."
"Do you risk getting caught in a doping control now? How often are professional players tested?"
"No worries, gorgeous. I have luck on my side."

She giggled, kissed his lips and thought about another, intimate, spot on her body which Roy had also licked. She lay on her back now and it felt so good. "Come here, sweetheart." She spread her knees. "Come here again, you big bad boy." Her soft hand encircled his penis. "Any energy left in you?"

• SIXTEEN •

CAT CLOSED THE window in the guest room, lowered the Venetian blinds, drew the curtains, went over to the wardrobe, tossed the cool one-hundred-and-sixty-dollar L.K. Bennett washbag onto a shelf and felt a growing irritation. Despite the draped window, the room was too bright to allow good sleep. The wallpaper was still ugly. And she wasn't alone in the room.

A rustling sound hung in the air.

She wheeled around and her gaze fixed on the mirror. Even if she recognised what she saw in it—a full-figure reflection of a beautiful model in a bathrobe—she didn't like how the mirror glass trembled, rattled and clattered.

She didn't like that a mirror behaved at all.

'Dad bought it a few months ago. He said it was an antique mirror in the baroque style. It's eerie, isn't it?"

"No, no." She shook her head. "Mirrors don't behave."

The mirror stopped behaving. Order was restored. Not for long. From behind the mirror, it crept forward.

A beige creature. Cat cried out.

"Dix!" She cried out again, this time from relief. "How could you do this to me? How could you? My heart stopped."

Dixie said nothing, did not apologise.

She jerked the door open. "Step out, boy. Out! It's not nice to spy on a girl like that."

Dixie miaowed, yawned and slipped out of the room.

• SEVENTEEN •

THE DAY OF the funeral. Three tearful women had dressed for the occasion. Jan wore a black tent-size T-shirt, black jeans and black flat childish Mary Jane shoes. Even though Sis had showered, her unkempt hair was as greasy as bacon strips. Mum, the widowed Rita Milton, appeared in an unassuming crow-black dress from the discount store Primark. She had styled her hair with a cluster of curlers. Cat wore a night-black five-thousand-seven-hundred-dollar dress from Christian Dior, black tights and the black luxury shoes from Prada. Too tired and upset to do anything special with her hairdo, she kept her radiating tresses in the simple topknot. Dixie appeared in his natural colours: thin streaks of white in the ginger-coloured fur; shimmering green eyes; pink nose.

The funeral package included the undertaker's services, the priest's fees, the cost of flowers, newspaper ads, the cremation fee, the cost of grave space and grave services, plus a multicourse dinner for eighty people. A bill of about ten thousand pounds, almost five times the typical cost of a funeral. Cat wanted to split the bill with Mum. Mum rejected the proposal, insisting she would pay for everything herself. Cat improved on her original idea, offering to pay the total bill herself. Mum took it the wrong way, calling her daughter's generosity indecent.

The undertaker, Mr. Whale, had arranged funeral limousines. Three black Cadillacs, two of which were divided between relatives and friends. The third car was reserved for the closest colleagues of the deceased, including Karl-Heinz Zimmer and Sandra Kallikrinos, the BioFutura Systematik Deputy CEO and Deputy Director of Research, respectively.

It was high time. The people, and one cat, left Mum's house. The drive towards the church began.

The time in church both escaped and stood still, Cat thought, as though man-made clocks meant nothing in God's house. Something inscrutable was at stake, heaven only knew.

She shuddered. Some unknown presence had stepped out of the steep shadows.

The post-funeral reception took place in a venue for hire in Farnwood, the Milton family's suburb on the western outskirts of the city. How could you get an appetite worthy of the name? Cat wondered. How could you eat at all on a lousy day like this?

Given the vast amount of food and drink, the venue seemed to have been set up for a celebration. From a caterer, Mum had ordered a smorgasbord which included classic beef lasagne, vegetable pies, marinated salmon, garlic bread with mixed salad, quinoa with meatloaf, gourmet beef stew, fettuccine Alfredo with shrimps, chicken Kiev, roast potatoes, garden peas and gravy. The assortment of bottled drinks was reminiscent of that of a bar, from sparkling water and fruit juices to beer, wine, martini, whisky and cognac.

In Cat's immediate vicinity sat three of BioFutura Systematik's eight representatives this afternoon: Sandra Kallikrinos, the BFS Deputy Director of Research, Greek, in her fifties, bronze skin, rosewood-coloured hair. Fernando Asensi, Chairman of the BFS Scientific Committee, Spanish, bulky raven-black hair, a strained expression pasted on his lips. Arnold Butler, the BFS Administrative Manager, bald, sallow face, eyes like ping-pong balls. Cat excused herself and went to the ladies' room. On her way back through the gloomy corridor towards the vestibule, she almost collided with a man.

"Miss Milton," the man said.

"Mr. Zimmer," Cat said.

"My deepest condolences."

"Thank you."

Zimmer was tall, at least six feet three. Early or mid-forties. Hair like spun ivory. His eyes, as friendly as a dolphin's, radiated an ocean-blue gaze behind hexagonal glasses.

She continued through the corridor, heard Zimmer follow

her. His footsteps sounded rapid. Did he hurry to catch up with her? She avoided glancing over her shoulder. As she arrived at the vestibule, she stopped. The man was with her again.

"Did you have any interest in your father's work?"

She cleared her throat. "No, not particularly. Besides, Dad was reluctant, or at least hesitant, to talk about his job."

"Did you understand why he was secretive?"

"I don't need a background in science or technology to see that BFS is associated with top-secret research projects."

Zimmer's eyes became motionless, as if they had turned into enamel. "Your incredible beauty stuns me, Miss Milton."

How can someone who has wept as much as I have today be beautiful? Is it attractive to have red-rimmed eyes, strained facial features and tired body movements?

They returned to the dining room. Most people had finished eating. People mingled.

"Something to drink?" Zimmer said.

"Apple juice, please." Cat sat down at an abandoned table. The disposable tablecloth was torn and spattered with gravy and lasagne meat sauce.

Zimmer moved to the bar and came back with a cylinder-shaped glass of apple juice and a tumbler of cognac. He sat down opposite her.

"How long did you and Dad work together?"

"For nearly eight years. After twelve years at Pfizer in Germany and in the United States I was headhunted by BFS. At the same time, I moved to Britain."

"What will happen now?"

"With what?"

"With BioFutura Systematik."

Zimmer's smile was too wide for a post-funeral reception. "As Deputy CEO, I'm the boss until we find the greatest man or greatest woman to succeed your father. I could progress to the CEO post myself at the end of this mess, though it doesn't have to be me. We have a number of splendid internal candidates. As an alternative, your father's successor could be recruited from the outside. All BFS appointments are based on competence."

"What are you doing at BioFutura?"

"Advanced boundary-crossing research." Zimmer sipped his free cognac and seemed to like it. "BFS is an interdisciplinary facility which combines expertise from natural science, medicine, computer science, nanotechnology, and so on. Research across conventional boundaries is crucial in today's high-tech reality."

"Um, right."

"Many research areas are related one way or another, and as we see advancements on all fronts, the number of sub-disciplines is increasing all the time."

"Are you a molecular biologist? As Dad was?"

"No. I'm a biophysicist."

"Oh. Um." *Must he have hexagonal glasses?*

"Molecular biology is the study of functional and structural properties of biological systems with the goal of understanding the roles of different molecules in cells and the interaction between those molecules. The area stems from biochemistry, genetics and biophysics. Biophysics, in turn, is precisely what it sounds like."

"Um, right."

"A link between biology and physics. Biology explores life's complexity and variety, describes how organisms communicate, reproduce, experience habitats and acquire fuel. Physics looks for mathematical laws of nature and demonstrates predictions about the forces that drive different systems.

"Biophysicists study life at all levels, from atoms and molecules to cells, organisms and environments. The challenge of biophysics is to bridge the gap between life's complexity and the simple laws of physics."

"I wish life were simple rather than complicated."

"I understand what you mean, Miss Milton. And I agree."

"Are all BFS projects brought about in collaboration with industries?"

"Not all of them but many. We carry out contract work for private multinational corporations. We also conduct our own research programmes."

"Research no one outside BioFutura knows about?"

Zimmer hesitated. "Why all these questions about BFS?"

"I want to get to know Dad better. I thought I knew Dad well, but the more we talk, you and I, the more I feel like I didn't know him as well as I thought. Sorry if this sounds strange."

"You have more in common with your dad than you think."

What a strange comment. "What do you mean?"

"The daughter—a supermodel. The father—a mastermind of molecular medicine. Fashion and biotechnology. In both industries, the stakes are sky-high and the competition is fierce. We're talking about global multibillion-dollar industries. The pharmaceutical industry is even a trillion-dollar business. It's tough at the top. You know it, and I know it. The threat, from anywhere, can show up when you least expect it. You must look over your shoulder all the time. Do you understand?"

Yet a strange discourse. She had no idea what he was talking about. She nodded anyway, pretending to have a clue.

"Any more pressing questions about BFS, Miss Milton?"

"I don't think so."

"You don't think so? You mean you're not certain?"

"Thank you so much for your time."

"No problem at all, Miss Milton. The pleasure, I assure you, was all mine." Karl-Heinz Zimmer rose and disappeared in the direction of the mingling crowd.

Cat remained seated with her thoughts for company. She sensed the man had withheld something she deserved to know.

Cat stood before the full-length mirror in the guest room. She undressed, undid the hair bun, put on a motley nightgown from Féraud. She stepped out into the silent corridor and went to the bathroom. Less than fifteen minutes later she was back in the guest room. Her eyes landed on the full-length mirror and she couldn't repress her dread. The shock seized her with a crackling sensation, as if her mind was on fire. The floor swayed underfoot. She put her hands over her mouth to prevent the cry. She swallowed hard, tried to swallow both the scream and the mental pain. The text, in black ink, on the mirror glass:

NICE FUNERAL, CAT

• EIGHTEEN •

THE KARLA SCHOOL, Kungsör, Sweden, a Friday in a sixth-grade classroom. Twelve-year-old Ebba sighs. The schoolmaster is pissed off, not only because the fartful codger is worn out at the end of the week but because it's his only freaking mindset. Schoolmaster Stenlund is always pissed off.

"What's wrong with you, kids?! Do what I say, when I say, how I say, and you'll be okay!"

It's hot in the classroom and even warmer outside. Only three weeks to the summer holiday. Mr. Stenlund wears a lambswool cardigan. He has worn the same piss-yellow lambswool cardigan every day since the spring semester started. His soiled shirt collar shows a matching piss-yellow ring. When the codger gets mad, his cheeks swell like balloons. He looks like an overgrown hamster with a chinstrap beard, ready to breathe fire like a dragon. Ebba imagines liquorice-black smoke pouring out of his ears and his arse.

"Hey, Mr. Stenlund, this snoozefest is over now." Benke taps a finger on his stolen wristwatch. "Besides, I'm an atheist. I don't need religious studies."

The king of the class, Bengt 'Benke' Bengtsson, has worn thuggish leather jackets since first grade. Tattoos since second grade. Ear and nose rings since third grade. Neon-green haircut since fourth grade. Stilettos and brass knuckles since fifth grade.

Now, in sixth grade, Benke is not only the king of the class. He is also the emperor of the Karla School. The emperor has a busy schedule kicking down fourth- and fifth-graders in the school canteen and in the playground. Benke's buddies, six dumbwits at the far back of the room, laugh at the emperor's arguments. Boys mature later than girls, Ebba thinks. Everyone knows that. Immature boys are so tiresome. The lads in Benke's gang haven't developed in the least since kindergarten.

The schoolmaster glares like a doomsday prophet. He slams a fist onto his desk. In the shadow-drenched afternoon, the windows rattle like animated skeletons. "Your watch is wrong, Bengt. There are five minutes left in class."

"Another five minutes of this fuckshit?" Benke grimaces. "I'm bored out of my skull."

"I think the subject is interesting," Marja says. "You're disturbing the class, Benke."

Benke's head turns with reptilian quickness in Marja's direction. "I'll fix you for that, you bitch."

"Could you knock it off, Benke?" Ebba says.

Benke looks astounded. Then his eyes darken. "Funny how the bitches in class have become cocky of late. I'll fix Ebba too."

"You've fixed enough, Bengt," Mr. Stenlund says. "You have yet another detention to look forward to. Monday afternoon. And yet another therapy session with the school psychologist. The headmistress wants to have a word with you for the hundredth time. And the school will send another letter to your parents about your unacceptable language and behaviour!"

"You fucking howler monkey," Benke mutters.

"What did you say?" Mr. Stenlund asks.

"Nothing." Benke leaves the classroom, slamming the door.

The school bell rings. Kids holler and goof around. Chairs and benches rattle and bang. The awaited weekend is here. Benke's buddies throw themselves towards the door. When the tough boys have disappeared, the rest of the class spills out. Before the end of this beautiful day, horror and grief will strike.

The Karla School was inaugurated on September the eleventh, 1904. Ebba was an unplanned child, born on September the eleventh many years later. It feels a bit spooky to share a birthday with the old Karla. She wonders what it was like to be a pupil at Karla in the 1910s. How were the teachers back then? As easily irritated then as today? As strident then as today? As pissed off then as today?

The best friends Ebba and Marja cross the schoolyard. Ebba's black semi-curly hair is short and spiky. Marja's cloud-bright loops are well-combed and gathered in two braids. Ebba sports a wrinkled T-shirt. Marja wears a well-ironed blouse. Both girls wear jeans and running shoes. They stop, peer to the right, to the left. Four of Benke's closest friends pass the school workshop and then leave the schoolyard via the exit towards Skolgatan. Another two yobs trot past the school gym and skulk across the parking lot, in order to vandalise Mr. Stenlund's car—to puncture the tyres and to scratch the paint surface, according to Benke's orders—if the rumours are true. Benke himself will get to Headmistress Mrs. Helena Nyberg's house on Åsgatan and smash a few windows by throwing rocks at them, if the rumours are true. When the coast is clear, the two girls slip out of the schoolyard via the exit towards Karlavägen.

Ebba and Marja have accompanied each other on their way to and from school since they were first-graders. Both of them live in Runninge, the ramshackle area just east of the brook Runnabäcken, a twenty-five-minute walk from the Karla School. In Kungsör, it takes at most twenty-five minutes to walk anywhere, but more often just five or ten: Kungsudden ('King's Cape'); the King's Grillroom; the medieval Queen Kristina's riding track; the Kungsör Ridge—the forest where King Karl XI hunted bears. And so on. The Big Square is so big it takes no less than twenty seconds to cross it on foot. That must be why it's called the Big Square.

Scores of thugs and small-time crooks live in Runninge. Benke Bengtsson is not one of them. His asocial style is a mystery.

The boy comes from a wealthy family, lives in a luxury villa with a view of the lake, not far from King Karl's Church just north of downtown. No family member subjects him to beatings or taunts. On the contrary, his parents spoil their only child with an endless stream of presents. How can Benke under those circumstances have turned into such a monster? His upbringing is not consistent with that of the stereotypical goon.

"Are you hungry for a vanilla custard doughnut, Ebba?"

"I'm always hungry for a vanilla custard doughnut, Marja. And so are you." The vanilla custard doughnuts from Kungsör's Pastry Shop on Drottninggatan are a local sensation. "But I have no money."

"My treat. I got a tenner from Mum." Marja's cornflower-blue eyes glisten behind her red-framed glasses.

Ebba finds it difficult to accept being offered a free vanilla custard doughnut because she knows she can never afford to return the gesture. "Thanks, but I'll have a rye crispbread at home instead. Have to hurry home before Mum and Dad get crazy with rage."

"Your parents are pretty tough on you, huh?"

"Tougher than my bros."

"One has to be able to offer one's best friend a vanilla custard doughnut. Vanilla custard doughnuts have a special place at the heart of friendship."

Ebba musters up a smile. "Okay."

The girls stroll up Karlavägen, towards Drottninggatan and Kungsör's Pastry Shop. On a level with the Baptist Church and on the opposite side of the street, they pass the bronze statue of Thor Modéen, the productive comedy actor whose career pinnacled in the 1930s and '40s. The girls have seen most Thor Modéen movies, on TV or at the local cinema, aptly named The Thor Modéen Theatre.

Kungsör's Pastry Shop first opened in 1925 at an address further down on Drottninggatan and reopened twenty-two years later at number 19. The interior from the 1947 reopening is largely preserved to this day. In the cafeteria section, there is a decorated window created by the artist Ulla Skogh. The etched glass shows characters associated with the local royal history of Kungsör: King Gustav Vasa, Queen Kristina, and a bear-hunting King Karl XI.

"Ebba? Do you think Queen Kristina ate loads of vanilla custard doughnuts when she was staying in Kungsör?"

"I'm sure she did. Her horses too. But not at this pastry shop. It didn't exist back then."

"And kings, queens, princes and princesses don't have to pay for doughnuts at all. I guess the royal family had their own supply of doughnuts out at Kungsudden."

The girls giggle.

"Would you like to sit in the cafeteria, girls?" the female shop assistant asks.

"Not this time," the girls say at the same time. They want to eat their custard doughnuts outside, in the afternoon sun.

The girls sit on one of the benches by the fountain between the bus station and the town hall. As soon as they have finished their doughnuts, they continue their walk homewards. They cross the Big Square southwards, then ramble up Freigatan.

"Stop." Marja grasps Ebba's arm. "Wait."

"What's the matter?"

They stop in the middle of the intersection between Freigatan and Drottninggatan.

Marja's gaze scans the terrain. "Not a good idea to walk home this way today." Spots of sunlight sparkle in the lenses of her red-framed spectacles.

"You think we would risk meeting Benke, right?"

Since Benke was going to get to Headmistress Mrs. Helena Nyberg's house on Åsgatan and smash windows by throwing rocks at them, he will be eerily close to the southern part of Drottninggatan. Which way does Benke intend to take, to and from Åsgatan? Anytime, the emperor of the Karla School could show up at the intersection where the girls are hesitating.

"Let's walk via Torsgatan instead," Marja says. "Torsgatan and Kungsringen." The tone of her voice belongs to an indisputable decision.

Ebba shrugs. "Okay."

"We could then take the opportunity to pick flowers along Kungsörsleden. What do you think?"

"I'd love to pick flowers. It's been ages since last time."

They return along the short Freigatan, then turn left onto Torsgatan, pass the pharmacy and turn right onto the walkway along Kungsringen. Kungsör is the paradise of the mistletoe. Nowhere in Sweden are there as many mistletoes per unit area as here. There may be twenty thousand mistletoes in this small town. Only, in the trees which line Kungsringen there are hundreds if not thousands of mistletoes.

"Marja?"

"Yes?"

"Shall we count mistletoes?"

"How does anyone have the time to count all the mistletoes before the sun goes down?"

"Some clever inventor must invent a mistletoe counter machine. In Kungsör there are more mistletoes than people."

The girls titter. Soon they find themselves on the bush-lined trail known as Kungsörsleden. Since they left Freigatan they have met no more than seven cars, a maximum of five pedestrians and at least four cats. The girls happen to be all alone right now at this particular section of the trail. From here, it takes only a quarter of an hour to walk home. *It doesn't matter if I'm a bit late or not. Mum and Dad always find some reason to yell at me all the same*, Ebba thinks.

The girls walk off the trail towards the brook. Here, flowers grow in all sorts of colours. They know which flowers they're allowed to pick and which ones are protected. The air is still. No crickets play here in May. The shades of the afternoon sun sprinkle the fields. The brook murmurs like carbonated water.

"Now we've got them, guys, ha-ha. The four-eyes and the

duckling." Benke strides out from his hiding place. His stiletto throws reflected sunrays onto the surrounding greenery.

• NINETEEN •

CAT WENT BY bus to Oberon Clinic in the district of Selmore Village. She hid behind dark sunglasses and was in her casual attire consisting of jeans, a simple T-shirt and running shoes. Today she wore her hair in a ponytail with an elastic ribbon. The diamond-decorated smartphone beeped. A new text message:

> Hi Cutie. Thank you for good luck wishes. Thought of you during the game—and scored three goals. I'm on the move to Premier League and Champions League. Love you. Miss you. Roy

The match had taken place yesterday. Why didn't he get in touch until today? Despite the heatwave, Cat felt something icy in the pit of her stomach. Not significant enough to make her tremble. Not insignificant enough to make her dismiss it either. She had informed him she would be away. It struck her that Roy didn't ask where she was. Why didn't he ask?

She had taken her medication, like every morning. Still, she felt an onset of drowsiness, here on the bus. It could be the heat. She didn't fall asleep. She slipped into a daydream. She was seventeen again. She found herself in Dr. Stockmayer's office ...

"How effective are the treatments?" She looks into his eyes. "Will I live a worse life than most people?"

"You're too brusque when you assess your situation."

"Am I?"

"At the age of seventeen, you're already one of the fashion industry's most sought-after models. You're considered one of the most beautiful girls in the world. You have begun to earn tens of thousands of pounds a week. Contracts with prestigious cosmetics companies have turned you into a multimillionairess. It would be obscene to say you live a worse life than most people. Do you understand?"

She assumes she has said something stupid. She can't meet his gaze. "I'm trying to figure out how I feel."

"I have an idea about how you feel. I'm not saying I know how you feel, because I can't, no one can, and it would be wrong to talk that way, but I have an idea."

She looks up. "Have you?"

"This is my territory. Neuroscience includes all study of the nervous system. Psychology, the study of mental processes, is related to neuroscience. Neurology and psychiatry are medical disciplines which address the diseases of the nervous system. Neurology deals with structural, electrical and biochemical disturbances, while psychiatry focuses on emotional disorders, behavioural abnormalities and cognitive diseases. Neurology as well as psychiatry influence research in neuroscience."

He wears a salt-white coat, pitch-black shirt, plum-purple tie. His dark hair is uncombed, ruffled. His steel-blue eyes are brilliant. The tall forehead gives the man a peculiar as well as an intellectual trait.

Today there is something else about him too. Or something else about *her*. She experiences something she has never imagined before. She finds him attractive.

"You have to regain your optimism, Miss Milton. And it is my job to guide you."

She nods. The cold of February outside the windows has crept into the office and into her. She shivers.

"You're cold," he says. Then, "A cup of tea?"

Cat nods. "After all these strange years ... finally a diagnosis. It feels like the mystery of my awkward teen years is no longer a mystery. Teachers and other pupils thought I was just lazy, stupid, uninterested. Well, that's what they still think."

"The public's misunderstanding. The public's ignorance of sleep disorders leads to many awful misunderstandings." He goes out to an adjacent kitchen and comes back with two cups filled with steaming tea. "What I want you to do next …"

((((((*Miss?*))))))

Cat hears a new voice in the distance.

(((*Miss?*)))

Stockmayer's voice is vanishing. The new voice is growing.

((*Are you sleeping, miss?*))

(*Your bus stop, miss.*)

• TWENTY •

ABOVE THE WINDY horizon of Middlesbrough, the milk-white factory-emitted plumes of steam mingled with streaks of white nature-made clouds. The Generous Paradise Hotel looked all but generous from the outside.

The male receptionist grinned. "Are you here for the art critics convention, madam?"

"No. I'm here for the biomolecular science congress. My name is Sandra Kallikrinos. I represent BioFutura Systematik."

"Never heard of them." Then, "ID? A *valid* ID, that is."

The receptionist examined her ID card like a TV detective, looked at a computer screen and tapped on a keyboard. "Aha? Already paid and all meals included. But don't forget to pay extra for everything which costs extra, madam. Using the room phone costs extra. Using the room minibar costs extra. Using the gym costs extra. Using the car park costs extra. If you don't finish your breakfast by nine-thirty a.m. you have to pay extra. And there's a four percent surcharge with your card payment." He handed over a plastic key. "Welcome to The Generous Paradise Hotel. Enjoy your stay."

• • •

Sandra inspected the bathroom, then began to fill the bathtub. The water pressure was poor, both from the cold and the hot tap. The water sprinkled like rain in a drainpipe. Fortunately, she was in no hurry. She put the computer on the room's only desk, started a word processing program, began to write a first draft:

YOLEXUS ENT. CLINICAL TRIAL COVER-UP

NanoScoop is a global contract organisation with headquarters in Pasadena, California, USA. The contractor provides a range of services for companies in the pharmaceutical, biotech and medtech sectors. It offers comprehensive solutions through all phases of the development of a new drug, from design to commercialisation, including strategy development, clinical trials, biostatistical analysis and consultancy.

A NanoScoop-handled clinical study contracted out by the pharmaceutical company Yolexus Enterprise, concerning the YE drug Nargontanac, caused mental disorders in seven volunteers of different nationalities at the Parjanya Hospital in New Delhi. (Nargontanac, a substance which controls sleep disorders within the category of dyssomnias, including hypersomnia, sleep apnoea and narcolepsy.) According to official data, the study included thousands of patients. In fact, the patient volunteers were only seven. The scandal was not discovered. Scientific prestige and political morality were at stake. A fictional version of the events in New Delhi was delivered to the media.

NanoScoop became the subject of legal proceedings initiated by lawyers representing the drug-injured 'volunteers' after the Yolexus insurance policy failed to offer financial compensation. In addition, uncertainty surfaced regarding the existence of files which Yolexus according to standard practice should have sent to the

DHPRA (Drugs and Healthcare Products Regulatory Agency) before the clinical trial, detailing whether Nargontanac had been adequately tested on human blood in vitro. Questions arose over whether Yolexus had established a safe dose of Nargontanac. The DHPRA concluded neither NanoScoop nor Yolexus could be held responsible and 'the unfavourable incidents' had been caused by an unexpected biological effect of Nargontanac in humans.

The seven subjects at the Parjanya Hospital, New Delhi—gender, age, nationality, cause of death: 1) male, 56, American, car accident; 2) female, 49, Swedish, car accident; 3) male, 41, German, suicide; 4) male, 37, Greek, suicide; 5) female, 30, Indian, sport accident; 6) female, 25, British, slip-and-fall accident; 7) female, 21, Japanese, sport accident.

Sandra paused. She looked up from the computer screen. All seven patient volunteers had lived and worked in New Delhi. The Greek man's name: Alekos Teknetzidis. Sandra's brother had hanged himself in the string of the yo-yo which the night before he had bought for his six-year-old son. Alekos had wrapped the yo-yo string around his neck and then, in the kitchen, used the handle of the cooker's oven door as a hanger.

She tried to repress her thoughts, or at least restructure them. Even though Yolexus Enterprise was to blame for her brother's illness and subsequent suicide, it was crucial her article didn't appear like a text written for the satisfaction of personal revenge.

The world must learn about the cover-up. Sandra's action wasn't about her brother. Had Alekos not been one of the victims, she would have informed the world anyway.

She saved the document, closed the file, exited the word processor and launched the BIOZYM8 application, an all-bells-and-whistles specialist computer software for the processing of biochemical data.

The figure which appeared on the laptop screen showed a Lineweaver-Burk plot, a common type of graph in enzymology, the branch of biochemistry which studied enzyme activity. Enzymes were molecules which speeded up chemical reactions in biological systems without being consumed in the process. The reaction rate could be measured using a variety of laboratory-based gadgets.

Inhibition of enzyme activity was an important control mechanism in biological processes. Many drugs functioned as enzyme inhibitors. In one way or another, Nargontanac inhibited the enzymes cytochrome P450 2C9 (CYP2C9) and cytochrome P450 2C19 (CYP2C19). Cytochrome P450 was a supergroup consisting of thousands of enzymes.

Sandra's hand hovered over the keyboard. The most interesting part of the figure was the slopes of the three graph lines. Series 1 demonstrated the CYP2C9 enzyme kinetics in the absence of inhibitor (Nargontanac). The increase in slope of graph line in the presence of inhibitor indicated the strength of binding of the inhibitor to the enzyme in question. Series 2 and Series 3 showed a fabricated and a true version, respectively, of the CYP2C9 enzyme kinetics at a given concentration of inhibitor. The untrue Series 2 had appeared in several documents composed in connection with the legal procedures implicating NanoScoop and Yolexus.

Someone had cheated. Or rather a group of people from the inner circle of Yolexus Enterprise. Nargontanac demonstrated a much stronger inhibitory effect than had been reported. If that fact had been irrelevant to Sandra's case, there wouldn't have been any reason for Yolexus Enterprise to cheat in their report on the enzyme kinetics.

Biochemical systems were complex. Multiple reactions and interactions competed for space and equilibria. A particular change in a certain parameter could result in effects at some other level in the system. Through her research and her contacts, Sandra had come across the true Series 3. It was high time the DHPRA and the media were aware of the fraud at Yolexus. She closed the file and exited the app.

The bathtub was filled to four-fifths. Enough water. She added a scented bubble bath and turned off the taps. On a shelf by the sink, she placed her phone, with the alarm set to ring in half an hour. She undressed, climbed into the tub and pulled the shower curtain. She slid into the lovely bubble bath.

Sandra froze. She wasn't alone in the bathroom. Someone loomed just outside the shower curtain. A fuzzy character, as silent as a shadow.

The cleaning lady? Sandra hadn't hung the sign which read 'Please do not disturb' on the door handle towards the corridor, but if the room hadn't been ready she wouldn't have been able to check in, would she? "Hello?" she said.

The curtain was pulled aside. A costume-clad man with blond hair and very black sunglasses looked down at her. His face wore an ultra-neutral expression, the blandest look which Sandra had ever seen. The man grabbed her neck and pushed her down under the water. She tried to scream but couldn't. Pain and foamy bubble-bath water invaded her throat. She flapped her arms. The man squeezed her neck, harder and harder.

A broken wave of darkness drifted in behind her eyelids. More water rushed into her mouth. She coughed, spat, flailed her arms, kicked out with her legs, swallowed bubble-bath water, sputtered, coughed, struck out with her feet, swung her arms, clawed at the air, spat water, hit her head on the bottom of the bathtub and became dizzy, dizzy, dizzy …

Leo Baginski surveyed the bathroom. The dead woman in the tub appeared to have drowned. A perfect accident. Water had splashed onto the floor but it didn't matter. Water on the bathroom floor would be associated with the woman's own activities. If he wiped the floor, the woman's naked footprints would disappear. A persistent detective might get the idea the scene of the accident was a murder scene.

He regarded the corpse. The skin on both the neck and bust was undamaged. The skin was as nice now as before he'd started his necessary job. Since he wore gloves, he hadn't left any fingerprints on the lady's body or elsewhere in the hotel.

He stepped away from the bathtub, took off his disposable plastic shoe covers and latex gloves, dropped them into a polythene bag, transferred the bag to a briefcase, put on a pair of brand-new leather gloves and left the still fluorescent-lit bathroom. He moved to the computer on the desk. The machine was on, logged in and running on battery. The woman in the bathtub no longer had any use for the laptop but he wanted neither to destroy it nor to steal it. The slightest trace of a crime would arouse suspicions surrounding the drowning accident. He wouldn't steal money from the cadaver's handbag. Baginski's outstanding morals prevented him from doing so. An industry consultant didn't nick money from deceased ladies.

He moved a black-gloved hand across the laptop keyboard and performed a file search by entering a few keywords: Nargontanac, Yolexus, NanoScoop, Clinical study New Delhi.

Two files of interest. A word processing file and a BIOZYM8 spreadsheet file. The woman in the bathtub would never publish a finished article. He erased the files from the hard drive.

• TWENTY-ONE •

EBBA SCREAMS. MARJA screams.

"You're afraid now, bitches, aren't you?" Benke cackles. "You can show yourselves now, guys."

Benke's cronies reveal themselves. The country bumpkins had hidden behind other shrubbery nearby. Frizzy-haired Berra is tall and thin like a full-grown skeleton. His eyes are writhing in contortions, like two blue-green glow-worms. Sigge is a skinhead, short with a drooping posture like an orangutan. His lips are thick like cocktail sausages. The idiot grin with half-open jaw shows dense rows of brown teeth.

Berra and Sigge guffaw.

The girls shriek.

"Who should we fix first?" Berra asks.

"The four-eyes or the duckling?" Sigge asks.

"I want to begin with the four-eyes." Benke points at Marja with his stiletto. "The four-eyes was smart-mouthed as hell in the classroom today."

Marja drops her schoolbag. Fear contorts her face.

Ebba regains her voice. "Stop messing about, guys. Leave us alone." She looks at Benke. "Weren't you going to Headmistress Mrs. Nyberg's house to smash her windows, Benke?"

"Change of plans." The emperor of the Karla School swings his stiletto around and points it at Ebba.

"Two cocky bitches need to be fixed first," Berra says.

"Guess which two," Sigge says. His moronic grin is as wide as his apish skull.

"Wow, how brave you are," Ebba says. "Three guys against two girls." A moment later, a pain stings her cheek. Benke has hit her in the face.

"Shut your cakehole, you duckling," Benke says. "You're as blabbermouthed as Stenlund the fat-arsed howler monkey. Such behaviour gets punished. Next time, I'll use the brass knuckles." He kicks Ebba's schoolbag. The bag flies out of her hand.

"Stop it!" Marja shouts. "Stop it, stop it." She steps back. "Go away. Leave us alone. Immediately."

Benke frowns, as though the girls' request to be left alone is incomprehensible. "Grab the four-eyes, guys." To Ebba, he says, "Stand still here, duckling, until it's your turn."

Berra and Sigge attack Marja. The boys hold her down, pressing her arms to the ground.

"Get away from her!" Ebba screams. "Let her go. Stop it!" No one hears her. Her voice is drowned out by the guys' boisterous laughter and Marja's crying.

DISORDER

Benke creeps up onto Marja's writhing body. His face is rosehip-tinged from excitement. The stiletto flashes. Marja's spectacle lenses sparkle. The boy's free hand wanders about inside Marja's waistband, deeper and deeper. His eager tongue explores her neck.

Help us, Ebba thinks. *Help Marja. Can't any adult show up and help us?*

"Isn't it enough now?" Berra asks.

"What if someone turns up?" Sigge asks.

"She's shrieking like a fire alarm," Berra says.

"It's me who decides when it's enough," roars the king of the class. "Just hold her down, arseholes, and do it firmly. She's stirring and twisting like hell." The stiletto in the brass-knuckle fist approaches Marja's ear while Benke's other hand moves deeper down inside the girl's trousers.

The turquoise sky preserves an inscrutable silence. The stillness separates, isolates, the horrific day from reality. Sagging strings of blue-grey clouds drift eastwards along the horizon, like tired factory smoke.

"You're not going to cut her with the stiletto, Benke, are you?" Berra's glow-worm-like eyes turn back and forth in their dead-black sockets. "You're kidding, right?"

"We were only supposed to scare the girls a little," Sigge says. The grin is still as wide as the shaved ape skull but the volume of the silly guffaw has dropped a few decibels.

"I'm not kidding at all," roars the emperor of the Karla School. He raises his head, shoots his pals a look which is hot like lava. "First we fix the four-eyes, and then we'll fix the duckling. You do as I say. Keep holding Marja down until I'm finished with her and check that Ebba doesn't run away. Get it?"

The skeleton and the skinhead nod. Like puppets they lack a will of their own. Again, they press Marja's arms to the ground.

"Lucky for you that you get it, dickheads," the emperor hisses, "otherwise I would have had to rearrange your already ugly mugs." He focuses again on the girl beneath him. Marja's blonde tresses are stained with dirt and soil. One of her blue-black ribbons has come loose. The crumpled strip of fabric lies abandoned on the ground like a dead snail.

"Don't cry, pretty little four-eyes," Benke whispers. He kisses Marja on the mouth and pokes her in the ear in a playful manner with the stiletto. "Don't cry, pretty little four-eyes."

His hand moves again between Marja's legs. She tries to squeeze her knees together but can't. The king of the class is too strong. "The corners of her mouth taste sweet from sugar and vanilla," Benke cackles. "She must have munched a vanilla custard doughnut. I bet Ebba has also munched a vanilla custard doughnut."

The skeleton and the skinhead laugh.

"We should have jumped them earlier," the skeleton says.

"And nicked their doughnuts," the skinhead says, nodding.

Ebba's heart rattles. She must do something. What can she do, outnumbered and with inferior physical strength? Each of the guys is much stronger than she is. The narrow bush-lined trail is deserted as far as she can see in both directions. No adults are out walking here at present, neither within earshot nor within sight. The land consists of strips of shrubs, thickets, and the open and empty farmland. She is in one of the least crowded locations on Earth. To try to call for help is hopeless. The boys would jump her and shut her up in no time.

"What was that?" the skinhead asks.

"What?" the skeleton asks.

"What the hell is going on?" the emperor asks. "Shut up. I'm busy with the four-eyes."

"Someone's coming," the skinhead says.

"You're sure?" the skeleton asks.

"Shut up, Sigge," the emperor says.

"Don't you hear the sound?" the skinhead says.

"I only hear Marja's sobbing," the skeleton says.

"Shut up, Berra," the emperor says.

"Someone's coming," the skinhead says.

The emperor puffs. "Where? Where the fuck?" His hand which has wandered around inside Marja's trousers returns out into the sunlight.

"From the thicket." The skinhead points.

A rustling sound. The deer appears, blinking in surprise, decides not to mix with human affairs, hurries across the road, out in a field, and disappears.

"You gullible idiots," the emperor says. "It was just a deer."

"It could be an omen," the skeleton says.

"An omen," the skinhead says, nodding several times, as if the word 'omen' was part of his vocabulary.

"What the heck is an o-men?" the emperor asks.

"Hmm, I don't know," the skinhead says. "But it sounds scary. Berra said it first."

The emperor roars, "Berra, what's an o-men?" He pats the crying Marja's cheek.

"An omen," the skeleton says, "is a sign that something nasty is going to happen."

The skinhead guffaws. "Nastier than us?"

"Exactly," the skeleton says. "Nastier than us, believe it or not. Come on, guys, let's get out of here."

"We're not finished with the four-eyes and the duckling," the emperor says. "Nobody leaves anywhere."

"Haven't we frightened them enough?" the skinhead asks.

"This is just the beginning," the emperor says.

"Mr. Stenlund will have our arses," the skinhead says.

"Fuck the howler monkey," the emperor says. "And fuck the school shrink and fuck the bitchy headmistress. Fuck them all. I'm going to burn down that fucking school and piss on the smouldering ashes."

"I'm leaving now," the skeleton says. "Mum is making Jansson's temptation for dinner tonight. My favourite dish."

"I'm heading home too," the skinhead says. "I have a new cool computer game to try."

"You don't have a computer," the emperor says, scowling.

"I play horror and torture porn games on Dad's PC," the skinhead says, grinning.

The skinhead's dad, Sverker, lives a secret double life. Officially, Sverker is a Christian priest in the church of the district of Torpa. Unofficially, Sverker is the leader of the religious sect PSK—Proud Satanists of Kungsör.

The skeleton and the skinhead let go of Marja's arms and walk off, brisker and brisker. Then they run. They're out of sight. Gone, like the deer. Jansson's temptation and violent computer games are waiting.

The emperor looks up from Marja's terrified face. "Berra? Sigge? Cowards! Get back here! Cowards! Get back here!"

The broken tree branch (which Ebba doesn't remember having picked up) swishes through the afternoon light. The wider end of the branch collides with the back of Benke's head. The emperor howls and there's blood. Marja shrieks. Crimson drops dot her skin like surreal freckles.

Marja is screaming beneath Benke's collapsed body. "What's happening? What's happening?"

Ebba wakes up. The daydream is not a daydream. She sees blood. To begin with, the candy-cane-red dots on her best friend's cheeks. Then, the change. A horrifying transformation of the blood, from quiet dots to violent splatter. The jet sprays out of the side of Benke's bull neck. The rose-red body fluid pulsates through the sunlight like splashes from a garden hose.

Marja bellows. "Why is there so much blood? Ebba?" She flails her arms, tries to shove Benke's body, but she's stuck.

The tree branch falls from Ebba's hands. She stares. *Why is there so much blood?* "Marja, wait, I'll help you."

Marja thrashes and screeches like a wildcat. She tries to push the thug's body upwards while Ebba tries to roll him sideways. It takes ages. Afterwards they just sit on the ground, looking at each other, crying. Ebba doesn't remember for how long. Fear and the surrounding silence distort time.

• • •

"What happened, Ebba?" Marja's gaze shows a non-expression as transparent as a polar wind. She wipes her mouth on her blouse sleeve and spits on the ground.

Ebba tries to say something but can't.

"What did you do, Ebba?"

Ebba shakes her head.

"Benke isn't moving," Marja says. "He's totally still."

Ebba says nothing.

"The blood has stopped spraying," Marja says. Specks of red glitter on her eyeglasses.

Ebba says nothing.

"My clothes are bloody," Marja says. "Yours too."

Ebba says nothing.

"Is he dead?" Marja asks.

Ebba still says nothing. She's thinking.

"Why is there so much blood, Ebba?"

Ebba shakes her head. "Something isn't right."

"That's certain," Marja says. "You see the blood, don't you?"

"I think there's something strange here."

Silence.

"Thank you for saving me, anyway," Marja says.

"You're my best friend."

"Did you put Benke's stiletto in his throat?"

"No. How would that have happened? I just hit him on the head with a tree branch, and not very hard." She looks around, then points. "The one that's over there." She gets up on unsteady legs and picks it up. It is short and narrow, like a baseball bat but crooked. She spots the nail. The bloody nail sits in the heavier end of the tree branch. "No ... How awful."

"What is it, Ebba?"

"A nail."

"A nail?"

"There's a damn nail in the tree branch."

The girls sit close together, studying their discovery. Is it us? Ebba wonders. Is it my best friend Marja and I who sit here on this trail with a dead school kid? Less than an hour ago we were in the Big Square, eating vanilla custard doughnuts. How have we got into this terrible situation?

"The nail may have been used for a birdhouse," Marja says. "Or for a dartboard? Or the whole branch, with the nail in it, may have been used for a kids' hut which used to be somewhere around here, maybe behind those thickets? What do you think?"

"It doesn't matter what the nail may have been used for," Ebba says. "We have to think forward."

"How should we think? What should we think about?"

"Let's hide Benke somewhere, before we start to think about something."

"Hide Benke? What do you mean?"

"He's no longer alive. Therefore, we must hide him before we start to think."

"How do you know he's dead?"

"He's not breathing."

"Perhaps he just passed out."

"I don't think so, Marja."

"You don't think so? What do you mean? You're not a doctor. Only doctors know if a kid is dead."

"The blood has stopped jetting from the hole in his neck."

"So what?"

"Well, the body must now be empty of blood? Therefore, he's dead. You can't live without blood."

Marja bites down on her lower lip. "It seems like we have begun to think anyhow, before we've done something."

"If we ignore thinking that we're thinking while we're doing something, everything will be all right."

"Everything will be all right, uh?"

"Uh-huh."

"A schoolkid is dead, Ebba. How will everything be all right if we have to go to prison for this?"

"Children don't go to prison. Only adults go to prison. Evil adults. We're neither adults nor evil."

"Social services take care of children who have to be taken into care. If you kill someone, you must be taken into care."

"You haven't killed anyone. It was me. An accident."

"You're my best friend. If everything will be all right we'll help each other."

"No, Marja. I alone take responsibility for what happened."

"No."

"What do you mean, no?"

"Could you stop thinking for a moment and listen to what I'm saying?"

Ebba looks out over the field. A carefree crow flaps through the dying afternoon. Ebba wishes she were a crow. As a crow, she would fly away, away, away and never come home again.

"Okay," Ebba says. "I'm listening."

"Whatever we do and whatever we think of when we decide to think, we'll do it together. What's the point of being a best friend if a best friend can't stand up for her best friend?"

"Okay. I got it."

"Lucky for you that you get it."

"Do you have a plan?"

"Plan?"

"Ideally a good one."

"We need no plan. Only criminals have plans. We just go to the police and tell them everything."

"No."

"Yes."

"No, Marja. It isn't possible. We're only twelve. Adults say twelve-year-olds have their whole lives ahead of them. How could we live our lives if we told people about this unfortunate accident? By the way, didn't you say you wanted to be a lawyer? Can you be a lawyer when you grow up if you've been involved in this kind of bloody accident?"

"We must obey the laws. If we obey the laws we'll be fine."

"Laws are decided by adults. There's no adult who could understand what has happened here."

"Someone must understand."

"Can we be sure?"

Marja picks up the dirty cloth ribbon from the ground. She twists it and turns it, shakes it and ties it into place (even though it's soiled), where it should be, in her left pigtail. She's silent for a moment. Perhaps she's reflecting on how it would be to apply for a job as a lawyer if you've had a bloody experience like this. Then, "Do you have any good suggestions for what to do next?"

"I have an idea."

"A good one?"

How good or bad is an idea if you don't have any other ideas to compare it to? Ebba wonders. "You see the maintenance hole cover over there?"

The manhole cover is visible forty feet away. The cylinder-shaped utility hole connects with the town sewer.

"I dare not say what I think your idea is, Ebba. You say it."

"Let's hide Benke in the utility hole. For the time being."

"For the time being, uh? How long?"

"Until we get a better idea."

"And if we don't get a better idea?"

"Then the sewer will do forever."

Marja shakes her head. "How nasty. Imagine lying in a dark and wet sewer. There must be a lot of rats down there."

Benke won't complain in the least, Ebba thinks. "The lout is fricking heavy but if we help each other I think we'll be able to, hmm, to fix this." She gets up from the ground and looks around. A ball of anxiety is churning in the pit of her stomach. A wave of sour taste drifts up her throat. She swallows hard.

Marja looks up and meets Ebba's eyes. "Benke's mum and dad will be wondering where he is."

"A lot of people will be wondering where Benke is. For example, the schoolmaster."

"Mr. Stenlund would be pissed off if he knew what we were planning to do."

"That codger is always pissed off. No matter what we do."

"I wonder how heavy a manhole cover is."

"Well, soon we'll know."

The atheist Benke Bengtsson has his own way. He won't take any more classes in religious studies and he won't have to attend the end-of-school-year ceremony in King Karl's Church in three weeks. The girls help each other trying to push the maintenance hole cover ajar. Nothing happens.

"Why doesn't it work?" Marja says. "What's wrong?"

Ebba identifies the problem. "Seems like we have to lift and push—at the same time."

They fail to dislodge the metallic cover. It won't budge an inch. They could as well have tried to move a mountain. The girls are puffing, the sun is dazzling. After an incomprehensible effort, the utility cover does begin to move, albeit at a snail's pace, upwards and sideways.

"Ouch." Marja grimaces. "A heavy, heavy manhole cover."

"Of course it's heavy." Ebba gasps for air. "Kids like us aren't supposed to mess around with the damn thing."

"Benke was evil. And I hate him for that. But is it right to hate him now he's dead? Is it ever right to hate?"

Ebba says nothing. She doesn't know what to say. She squeezes her eyes shut, forcing back tears.

The girls bathe in the brook with their clothes on. Blood and dirt flow away in the swirling water. Only memories remain. Memories can't be washed away.

They walk home in their sodden clothes. They're late.

"Thanks again for saving me," Marja says.

"Best friends are always best friends," Ebba says.

"Wait, I want to give you something." Marja stops on the pavement. She's looking for something in her schoolbag, finds it and picks it out. "This." She holds out the little bear, a two-inch-tall figure in multicoloured glass mosaic. A lottery win at a travelling amusement park five years ago.

"Your glass bear? You want to give me your glass bear?"

"Yes, that's what I want."

Ebba shakes her head. "I can't accept it, Marja." The glass figure isn't worth more than fifteen kronor but to Marja the sentimental value is astronomical.

"I want you to accept the bear, Ebba. I want you to do that."

"Why? You love that bear. You've always loved it."

"And I will always love it." Marja wipes a tear from her eye. "But now it's time for the bear to move on. There'll be a new beginning for the bear, while you and I have a new beginning ahead of us."

"We have? A new beginning?"

Marja sobs. "A new beginning of a new future."

A new beginning of a new future. Ebba lit a cigarette, slid in behind the wheel of the Porsche and, as the car tore away, she stomped harder on the accelerator.

The Porsche jerked forwards through the London traffic like some aggressive metallic monster. It stopped dead, it tore away. Stopped dead, tore away. Over and over. From Vasco & Piero's Pavilion Restaurant in Soho (one of the best Italian restaurants in London, she thought; an opinion she shared with her friends among prominent politicians, movie stars and media people) via Regent Street northwards.

At Oxford Circus, she ignored a red traffic light, avoided a collision with a double-decker bus and hammered on the horn with a rapid fist. "Stay out of the way, dickhead." She giggled and blew smoke at the same time.

The sports car shot forwards and skidded on northwards through Portland Place.

She opened the glove box and smiled at the mosaic figure. "Are you all right, my little friend?"

The glass bear's eyes glimmered in the sunshine-draped summer day.

• TWENTY-TWO •

ROGER STOCKMAYER HADN'T changed much. He looked like he did in her freshest memories. The attractive steel-blue eyes. The tall forehead. The midnight-black hair, always tousled. The three-day beard stubble. He was a young fifty-two-year-old. Today he wore a light-blue short-sleeved shirt, black trousers, black shoes. No tie. No clinician's white coat. *Why isn't he in his chair behind the desk? Why doesn't he ask me to have a seat in a visitor's chair?*

"Welcome, Miss Milton." He walked straight out of his office, passing her just inside the doorway. "Follow me."

"Where are we going?"

"Let's take a walk."

Oberon Park in Selmore Village, a botanical garden, was privately owned by the Oberon Clinic and not open to the public. A maze of avenues, decorated with marble statues and bird ponds. Only Oberon staff, patients accompanied by Oberon staff, and Oberon professional contacts, had access to Oberon Park. The most beautiful park in Blackfield was a local secret. Catriona and Stockmayer walked along a double-sided avenue with Japanese cherry trees, a winter variant of the tree with several flowering times between autumn and spring.

"My most sincere condolences," Stockmayer said. "Your father was a significant character."

"Thank you, Doctor." She paused. "You wanted to see me."

"We value patient satisfaction. If a new promising drug is launched, I'm keen the patients who could benefit from it get the chance to try it. I'm sure your father would have agreed. After all, he paid good money to let one of the best private clinics in the country handle your case."

"What's the new medicine?"

"It's called Roxonodonol." He nodded to two colleagues who

were passing through the avenue in the opposite direction. "How long have you been using Liglitrem? Two years?"

"Ever since I was finishing the prescription of Provigil." Provigil (Modafinil), a well-known wake-promoting agent.

"Roxonodonol makes Liglitrem seem like mere aspirin."

Cat guessed it sounded impressive. On second thought, it sounded too good to be true. "If our discussion had been less serious, I would have asked you if you were joking."

"Roxonodonol is a super drug. It replaces all of the classical medicines which address some or all of the principal symptoms: EDS, cataplexy, hypnagogic and hypnopompic hallucinations, sleep paralysis and automatic behaviour."

What a sales talk, she thought. "Maybe I can even learn to spell the name of that medicine."

He smiled. "Roxonodonol has the short form Rox-1."

"Rox-1 doesn't sound too bad."

"How many side effects have you suffered from in the past?"

"Side effects of Dexedrine, Liglitrem or Venlafaxine?"

"Overall."

"Several." She bit down on her lip. "Back and forth."

"Nineteen side effects. Some mild, others unpleasant."

"Just one is one too many. And unless the nightmares kill me, the headaches will."

"Rox-1 makes all the side effects disappear."

"I'm impressed." She wasn't.

They passed through a square open area lined with linden trees, park benches and statues of lions and elephants. In a corner of the square stood an ornate building with marble columns and white brick facades: Oberon Park Restaurant.

"May I offer you a drink, Miss Milton?"

"Thanks but no thanks."

Was it disappointment she could read in his eyes?

"After only one month of prescribed intake of Rox-1, you won't even remember how it feels to hallucinate."

Cat was surprised. "Is Rox-1 that good?"

He nodded. "There aren't enough superlatives to describe its positive effects."

"Oh. Is it a cure?"

"No. Narcolepsy is still an incurable disease. Like the market's conventional medicines, Roxonodonol treats the symptoms but doesn't solve the underlying problem. We're still talking about a substance which a patient may need to take for the rest of their life. However, as I said, Rox-1 is better than the market's other relevant drugs combined."

"Has this Rox-1 just been launched?"

"The product is already included in drug therapies of about fifteen hundred narcoleptics around the world."

"Is it expensive?"

"The manufacturer's suggested retail price is competitive. But then, money isn't something which one of the world's most popular models needs to worry about."

She suppressed a smile. "Okay. I understand."

The man hesitated. "You're even more beautiful than I remembered. How that could be possible, I don't know."

She smiled dutifully.

He glanced at her. "Is there anything special you're wondering about right now? About Rox-1 or anything else?"

A persecutor. A sixteen-fingered lunatic dressed in black raincoat and black hat. "No. I have no special thoughts at all."

They walked along a three-row avenue of chestnuts and birches. Back to the clinic. "When is a good time for me to try this Rox-1?"

"Now. As soon as we get back to my office, I'll write a prescription and give you a list of pharmacies which currently stock the drug. You'll be able to collect it in town later today."

"And my current, yet unused, medicines?"

"Return all unused medicines to the clinic."

"Why didn't you tell my sister that when you saw her at the pub? I could have brought the medicines today."

"I decided on this procedure just now."

"And the medicines back home in London?"

"Please hand them in to the branch in Earls Court."

"I didn't know the clinic had a branch in London."

"It's new. Opened in June."

"I see."

"For convenience, it may be a good idea to have your case referred to the London branch. If you agree."

"Who's the manager of the London branch?"

"I am. But I delegate responsibility."

"Can I send my unused medicines by mail? That is, those I brought on my current trip to Blackfield."

"Mail gets lost. I would prefer you brought them here in person. Also, such a scenario would give me another opportunity to converse with the most beautiful patient I've ever had."

She forced a short laugh. "I'm flattered." *Am I?*

All of a sudden, her limelight life in Paris, New York, Milan and London belonged to another universe. Here and now she found herself in a clinic park, her eyes red-rimmed from crying, without makeup, with non-stylised hair, dressed in worn jeans and a wrinkled T-shirt. Yet she was told she was beautiful.

They moved through a courtyard with flowers and shrubs in all the colours of the rainbow and passed through an iron gate on the way up to the main building of the Oberon Clinic.

"Could I ask someone else to bring the medicines in case I were prevented from doing so?"

His smile lacked the slightest touch of genuineness. It balanced on the verge of a grimace. "Of course, Miss Milton. How long are you in town?"

"Just until the end of the week. My grief hurts and will hurt for a long time but I have to be back at work on Monday."

"Are you staying with your mother the whole week?"

"Yes. Why?"

"Oh, no particular reason, just making conversation."

His cryptic comment puzzled her.

He pulled out a desk drawer. "I'll give you my card."

"I already have your contact information, Doctor."

"You don't have my home phone number." He took a pen from his chest pocket and wrote the number on the back of the business card.

"Thank you." She let the card disappear into her handbag.

"That was all for today." He tore a sheet from a notepad and scribbled down the new prescription. He finished by putting his personal stamp on it. "Remember, you can call me whenever you want. Your well-being is my professional responsibility." He handed her the prescription.

"Feels good to know. Thanks."

Your well-being is my professional responsibility.

• TWENTY-THREE •

CAT FOUND THAT both doors to Mum's house, the front and the back door, were locked. She got in with the spare key which Mum had lent her. Sis was working at the tavern. Mum must be out. In the kitchen, Cat got her speculation confirmed. The handwritten note by the sink read: *Settling the funeral director's invoice. Then to Tesco. —Mum.*

She would only take a short nap, one of her regular daytime naps, to fight her EDS. She set her phone's alarm to ring in ten minutes and lay on the bed in the guest room, still in her jeans and T-shirt. No need to undress for as short a nap as ten minutes.

"Don't scream, Catriona. Please don't scream."

Her sleepiness was destroyed by a violent immediacy. She sat up in bed, staring out into the room. "Dad?"

The man shushed. "It's me, Catriona. It's me."

"Dad, you're dead. Your funeral was yesterday."

"Don't scream, Catriona. You haven't lost your mind." Victor Milton stepped out of the shadow beyond the wardrobe.

"Dad, you're dead. Dead. Dead."

"Yes, Catriona. I'm dead."

"You're ... you're ... cremated."

"I know I'm cremated. That's why I'm going to be brief."

He moved deeper into the room. Dad. Vic Milton, founder of BioFutura Systematik. She was awake. She wasn't dreaming. The man who had stepped out of the shadow was in his early forties. His hair was shoulder-length and gathered in a rubber band. Distinct cheekbones. Elegant nose. Clean-shaven.

"It can't be you, Dad. Can't be." She couldn't move.

"I'm sorry, Catriona. I didn't mean to scare you."

The paralysis broke. She scrambled for a pillow, pushed it behind her back. "Don't tell me it's you."

"I'm not resurrected. I'm still dead, but still here right now."

"Are you a ghost?"

"There are no such things as ghosts."

"What's going on here, Dad? What in heaven's sake is going on?" She discovered she was shaking. Her body ached. She wiped tears from her eyes. "Was the funeral fake?"

"Who would do such a thing? It would be crazy."

"Don't you dare come here and correct me. If something is crazy, it's this conversation."

"Sorry. I should have expressed myself better."

"Answer me. Was the funeral fabricated?"

"I was dead. I am dead. My lifeless body was in the coffin."

"The cremation? Was it fake?"

"No."

"The burial?"

"No. Not bogus. Ashes to ashes. By the way, the tombstone is genuine. Everything about the funeral was authentic. I'm dead, cremated, gone."

"Not quite gone," she cried.

"I'm not here without reason."

"I need proof that you're here, Dad. Proof that I'm not crazy. You have five seconds." She shivered despite the heatwave. "Four seconds." The words flew from her mouth between sobs.

"What would pass for proof?"

"Figure something out. My dad was smart. Three seconds."

"What an extraordinary time pressure."

"Two seconds."

"There are two things I want to do. First, I want to hug you. I want you to feel it's me, that I have a physique, that I'm not just a shadow figure in your mind."

"Okay. Let's hug." She crawled out of bed. Hesitated.

"Come here, Catriona."

"I'm afraid, Dad. Terribly afraid. Horribly afraid."

"I know you're afraid."

"I was there. At the funeral. And Mum ... And Sis ..."

He shushed. "Come here."

She closed her eyes and took a deep breath. Her mental preparation reminded her of the first time she had dived into the sea, off the coast of Scarborough. She had been a little child then. Now, several years later, she was once again starting to get into unchartered waters. The room became a deep-sea trench.

Careful footsteps. She found she was moving across the floor. She opened her eyes. They hugged.

She could feel him, his shape, and recognise the scent of his aftershave. It was him. Dad.

"I've mourned you, Dad. I'm still mourning. Just like Mum and Sis are mourning you. I refuse to go through the whole awful thing again. The funeral of one's dad is something one shouldn't have to experience more than once."

"You're right. There won't be more times. Vic Milton has been buried for the first and last time."

"You're dead. How can you be here?"

"You're asking the wrong person."

"Who should I ask?"

"I said I wanted to do two things, Catriona. The other thing is more permanent than a hug. I need a computer and a printer."

• TWENTY-FOUR •

I WON'T LET the painful heat ruin the party, Herbert Krass thought. The flat in Becontree, London, was warm and moist like his fat mother's armpit. When the latest clandestine transaction was over, he would buy a fresher and better flat. In fact, he would get a luxury home. He wondered what his colleagues would say if they knew how much his latest job paid. It was hard to be humble when you were the best journalist in town. Sad the papers would never see the photographs which would have resulted in sensational front-page news nationwide and would have given him front-page credits nationwide, but the compensation from elsewhere was irresistible. They, from elsewhere, were prepared to offer him four point five million pounds to give up his spectacular Ebba Sjödal pictures. Four point five million was comparable to a lottery jackpot. Also, by preventing the pictures from reaching the papers, he was doing Ebba a favour, wasn't he? A favour which he would use. He had to take advantage of her. After all, he was Herbie Krass. It was fun to have a hold over that rude Swedish girl.

As a scoop hunter, he harboured a limitless curiosity about everything which sold. He did wonder why they were prepared to offer him four point five million to hand over a series of pictures of a bad-mannered Ebba Sjödal. With twenty years in the gossip industry, he had developed an ability to assess whether it was healthy to ask questions in connection with black-market transactions or bribes. This time he wouldn't ask any questions. Herbie grinned at the thought of his own cleverness. His latest Ebba Sjödal pictures were wonderfully indecent. If the pix hit the papers, they would destroy her career.

He had covered the bedroom walls and the ceiling with fashion-magazine pictures of Cat and Ebba wearing nothing but bikinis. The bonus was that the wallpaper itself was now invisible, the wallpaper which Mother had chosen for him. Thus, the first thing he saw when he woke up every morning was pictures of Cat and Ebba in bikinis. A day couldn't start any better. Luckily, Mother was in a wheelchair. The fat cow seldom visited him. She still didn't realise these images were artworks. Photography was an art form. Herbert Krass was an artist, too.

Thoughts about Cat and Ebba in bikinis put him in a marvellous mood. And of course, he fantasised about nude images. Cat Milton stark naked? How much would such photographs be worth on the unofficial market?

A number of Cat and Ebba pictures were framed behind glass. In the kitchen hung three framed Cat photos and two Ebba. In the living room, five Cat and three Ebba. Exciting the girls shared a home. Fascinating they were best friends. Captivating they were both alike and different, like each other's twisted shadow. Cat—a timeless beauty queen. Ebba—adorable, though somewhat inferior to Cat. In his dreams, he was still having sex with both girls at one time, but more often than not Cat was arriving alone. Ebba's lifestyle was becoming Herbie's headache. He didn't like dream-sex with drug-snorting party-girls, no matter how gorgeous they were.

Although ninety-nine point nine percent of his dreams had the same theme and action, there was one favourite dream which belonged to the remaining tenth percent of non-erotic extravagances: a recurring dream about a wedding.

He, Herbert Krass, marries Catriona Milton. The scene is a chalk-white church. The colleagues from the paper are present, including the boss. Cat's family and fashion-industry friends are also there. "Herbie, you lucky devil," cries a journalist colleague, "you're marrying the most beautiful girl in the world."

After the reception, Herbie and Cat sneak away to spend their wedding night in a secret location. Later, they spend their honeymoon on an exotic island, without his mother's company. In the nightmare fantasy version, Mother accompanies the honeymooning couple as advisor, supervisor and organiser.

Herbie was back in the present and the stuffy two-room flat. He unbuttoned his shirt's top button, wiped his face with a paper towel which was already wet from sweat, took a swig from the beer can and grimaced. In the heat, it didn't take long for a drink to get lukewarm. The beer tasted worse and worse.

He wondered what Cat would say if he asked for her hand in marriage. She was dating the football star Roy Beckman but Herbie could propose to the beauty queen anyway, couldn't he? There was no law which said he couldn't.

What if his imagination came true? Imagine how proud Mother would be. Mother would sit there in her wheelchair, gaping and staring like an ape, forced to admit she was proud of her only son. But if Cat laughed at him, or if she told him to get lost, he could say his proposal to her was just a joke. No embarrassing situation would arise.

The doorbell rang.

The visitor's pinewood-blond hair was trimmed like a golf green. Lips as thin as rubber bands. The smile as sharp as a paper-cutting blade. Dark-grey suit, white gloves, black briefcase. The business card said: Leo Baginski—Industrial Consultant.

"Please come in, Mr. Baginski."

"Thank you, Mr. Krass."

"Let's sit down in the living room. This way."

"Thank you, Mr. Krass."

The photos were stacked on the coffee table. Herbie and the visitor sat down across from one another. Herbie took a chug of beer. "Would you like something to drink in this terrible heat?"

"No thanks, Mr. Krass. I'm fine. Is the collection complete?"

"Certainly." Herbie suppressed a belch.

The visitor flipped through the stack of pictures. "Attractive lady, this Miss Sjödal. But the circumstances in which she appears are far from attractive." He looked up. "How did you manage to take these?"

Herbie shrugged. "The best photographers find the right place at the right time."

The visitor smiled like a diplomat on live TV. "Which sometimes means the wrong place and the wrong time for the photographic object."

Herbie grinned. "Ebba Sjödal is living proof."

"Anyone else know about these photos?"

"You're kidding? As a journalist, I know how to keep my reporting material secret."

"Good." The visitor looked at another stack. "And these are all the negatives?"

"Sure."

"Videos and/or digital images?"

"Sixteen."

"Where?"

"In the digital camera." Herbie took another swig of beer, pointing at the Panasonic.

"Cloud storage?"

"Nope."

"Copies transferred to computers or flash drives?"

"Definitely not."

"Excellent, Mr. Krass." The visitor fired off his razor-sharp smile. "All the traces surrounding these pictures will disappear."

"Without doubt."

"The transaction, four point five million, is untraceable."

"No shit."

"My client would never risk his reputation through fraud, Mr. Krass. To my client, four point five million is a mere trifle."

"That's what I guessed." Herbie chuckled. "It's been a real pleasure doing business with you people."

"There's only one formality left, Mr. Krass."

"What's that?"

The visitor pressed a pistol barrel against Herbie's temple and squeezed the trigger. Herbie heard nothing. His head exploded in a cloud of darkness.

• TWENTY-FIVE •

"**YOUR WORKROOM HAS** been cleared out," Cat said. "Your stuff has been packed in boxes and will be picked up by BFS representatives. You want me to look through the boxes?"

"Is there a quicker solution?" Dad said. "We're in a hurry. We're running out of time."

"We?"

"Is Rita's computer available?"

"I think Mum took her computer to work."

"Is there no word processor at all in the house?"

"I have a tablet in my handbag. It has both word processing and spreadsheet programs installed. It can be connected to a wireless printer if you like."

"I used to have a spare laser printer, stored in a cupboard in the garage. Always loaded with paper. You think it's still there?"

"I don't know, Dad. I'm not equipment manager here."

"If the printer is available, we rig the kit."

"We? Again 'we'? Do you take for granted I've agreed on some sort of action plan?"

In the garage, they found the equipment Dad had said he wanted. Dad then wrote something and printed it. He put the printout in a light-yellow envelope, which he sealed, then wrote with a black ballpoint pen on the front: 'To my twin daughters Catriona & Janice Milton'.

"Keep this in a safe place until further notice," he said.

She weighed the envelope in her hands. It had texture, shape, weight, dimensions and colour. The envelope with content possessed all the qualities of a physical object. The document existed. Printed by the late Vic Milton. "Can Sis and I do what we want with it?"

"No. Once you've read the letter, you'll know what to do."

"Thank you for being so clear about it."

"You're welcome."

She rolled her eyes. "We look forward to the surprise."

"Trust me. Read the letter as soon as possible. And be careful. Use your common sense. Don't tell anyone I've written a document the day after my own funeral."

"I understand. Hope Sis understands, too."

"Could you and Janice do me a favour?"

"Wait a minute ... you're dead. Sis and I have cried a lot. And now you're back, asking us for a *favour*?"

"I want you to contact the medical examiner Ursula Ellis."

"Why? The cause of your death is known. Heart attack."

"I know Mrs. Ellis's statement."

"How do you know the medical examiner was Mrs. Ellis?"

"My dead body was cremated."

"I repeat: How do you know Mrs. Ellis was the practitioner who examined your dead body?"

"My ashes were interred. Cremation is a non-reversible process. Too late for another autopsy. However, I must know if it's possible I was murdered."

"*Murdered?*"

"I'm not stating it. I just wonder if it's possible I was murdered. That's why I want you and Janice to see Ursula Ellis."

"Why Sis and I?"

"You, Catriona, are the only person who has met me since my funeral. You can persuade your sister to help you with this."

"Exciting logic."

"My twin daughters are the only thinkable investigators."

"Investigators ... A mysterious word in this context."

"What do you think of the word 'questioner'? Or the word 'scrutineer'?"

"Awful. Does it matter what I think?"

"The only thing my daughters need to find out is how the medical examiner decided I died of a heart attack."

She was thinking.

"Do you have any enemies, Dad?"

"I wonder why I died at forty-three. I wasn't the typical heart attack candidate. My lifestyle was healthy. I wasn't overweight. I didn't smoke. I exercised every day. My diet was balanced and varied, rich in vitamins and minerals and the right types of fats."

"If you know you've died and if you're aware of the medical examiner's statement and if you suspect you may have been murdered, how come you don't suspect who murdered you?"

"You're already thinking like a detective, Catriona."

"I'm a fashion model. May I have my life back, please?"

• TWENTY-SIX •

EBBA STEPPED INTO Roy's kitchen and tossed the newspaper onto the table. "Look at this shit. Look."

Roy was eating breakfast in his underwear. He looked up at her. "What's up, darling?"

"A fucking newspaper article. I think I'm going nuts." She put her hands on her hips and pouted.

GOSSIP REPORTER COMMITTED SUICIDE

The notorious paparazzo Herbert Krass was found dead yesterday in his flat in Becontree, east London. Mr. Krass had shot himself. Journalist colleagues became suspicious when Mr. Krass never showed up for a press conference. Colleagues, as well as Mrs. Krass (the mother of the dead man), tried to phone him on several occasions. The police found Mr. Krass dead in a chair in his living room. The cause of death was a gunshot to the head. The weapon with the dead man's fingerprints lay on the floor next to the chair. According to technical expertise, Mr. Krass had pressed the pistol barrel to his temple when firing the weapon. The cartridge discharge residue analysis confirmed CDR residual particles were present on the dead man's hand.

Ebba sat down. "Scary shit, uh?" She stretched out a hand under the table, squeezed his thigh. "What if it was murder?"

"It says it was suicide, Ebba."

"Yeah, but what if someone blew Krass away and made it look like suicide?" Pause. "Professional killers must know how to make murder look like suicide."

Roy laughed. "And Ebba Sjödal the fashion model knows better than all the forensic specialists combined."

She grimaced. "Don't tease me. I'm serious."

"Do you have a reason to believe the guy was taken out by a contract killer?"

She shook her head. "I'm just wondering."

"Did he have a hold over you?"

She suffered a crisis. *Should I lie?* She lit a cigarette. "Maybe."

"What's it about?"

She shrugged. "I don't want to talk about it."

"I think you should."

"I don't think so."

"Think again, sweetie. You're suspecting murder. A bullet shattered the guy's skull, right? And you and I are together. I deserve to know." Roy kissed her cheek.

She sighed. "Krass had photos from an exclusive cocaine party in Los Angeles, pictures of me in intimate company with two powerful men from an international crime syndicate. These guys are wanted criminals and they're dangerous. They're being hunted by both Interpol and the CIA."

Roy held his forehead. "Ebba ... Ebba ..."

She sucked hard on the cigarette. "I didn't know jack shit about their backgrounds. I thought they were reputable and successful businessmen. Also, I was attracted to their looks. Also, I was high on snow. Another girl joined us in one of the many individual rooms."

"Who was the other girl?"

"The girl, or the young lady, is a well-known politician."

"Who?"

"You don't need to know."

"Right."

"It was an exciting, innocent sex party. Two guys and two girls at the same time. The champagne was flowing. The cocaine was flying around the room like dust. Do I need to add what this story, if leaked to the public, would do to my career?"

Roy shook his head. "What do the pictures show, Ebba?"

"One picture shows, with a gripping sharpness, one of the gangster bosses snorting cocaine off one of my breasts while the other boss is relieving me of my knickers."

"And this other woman? The politician? Is she in the same picture?"

"Oh yes."

"What's she doing?"

"You don't need to know, Roy, in view of the next general election."

"Well. Is this the most devastating image?"

She made a face. "It's the mildest image."

"What does the worst show?"

"You don't want to know."

"In view of the next general election?"

"You got it."

"How did this Herbert Krass manage to take these pictures?"

"He was a skilled photographer and had access to advanced camera systems. There was a gap between two curtains. Krass snapped the pictures from his parked car on the opposite side of the street. The magnification and detail of the pix are frightful."

"Why was he in LA to begin with?"

"His paper had sent him to report from an event which I attended myself. He must have learnt I was there.

"Later, at night, he must have shadowed me and my friend the politician."

"Could his death have anything to do with you?"

"Um, I don't think so." She couldn't look him in the eye. "A slimeball like Krass was probably involved in lots of shadowy deals. He may have killed himself, but not because of me."

"Could someone have blown him away because of you?"

She shook her head. "No."

"Where are the pictures now? Who is in control of them?"

• TWENTY-SEVEN •

"YOU'RE DEAD. HOW can you be here?"

"You're asking the wrong person."

"Who should I ask?"

Cat phoned from her mobile.

"Thank you for calling Oberon Clinic. Dr. Stockmayer speaking, how may I help you?"

"You haven't been honest with me."

"Miss Milton?" Pause. "What are you talking about?"

"We know there's something wrong with me, something wrong in my brain, except the malfunction is more serious than you've implied. You're hiding something. What and why?"

Silence. Then, "How about a walk in Oberon Park?"

"No more walks." She tried to keep her voice down but couldn't. "No more walks, neither now nor later."

"As you like. I am waiting for you at the clinic. My office."

She went to the clinic. This time she took a taxi. She was about to step into his office but she wasn't fast enough. He was just walking out the door, like the previous time.

"Come here, Miss Milton." He passed her and kept walking along the corridor.

Her anger flared up again. "I said I'm done with walks."

"I suggest no walk. We're going to visit Oberon Museum."

She huffed. "As if I were interested."

"Trust me. You're interested in your brain's condition. I'm also interested in your brain, among other things about you. I want to use the museum's environment to explain something."

The pyramid-shaped Oberon Museum was located opposite the clinic, on the other side of Epsilon Street. The clinic and the museum were connected via a glass-enclosed footbridge and escalator. The museum held exhibitions and screened film shows about the newest research and development in biochemistry, biomedicine and neuroscience.

"I haven't tried to keep you in the dark, Miss Milton. On the contrary, I'm trying to protect you. The reason I've kept certain details secret is they're new and not yet proven. I can and will explain today what I suspect you want to know, though the world isn't yet ready for the amazing truth."

Cat shot him a rock-hard look. "For the time being I'll be satisfied with a simple explanation, without frills. Understood?"

They passed a stairwell and arrived at a peculiar room with eighteen sides, eighteen angles. The shape of a polygon, he explained. The angles pointed either inwards or outwards. At six of the eighteen corners of the room stood a painted lion statue. Six different colours. One colour per lion.

"The structure of the venue is inspired by a type of important cyclic chemical compound called crown ether," Stockmayer said. "Crown ethers can be of different sizes. This particular room is modelled after the crown ether which has six oxygen atoms at the positions 1, 4, 7, 10, 13 and 16. These six positions are marked by the lion statues."

"The statues are beautiful."

"You're unbelievably beautiful yourself."

"Don't deviate from the subject. Explain what I want you to explain. And why are we here?"

"The mind and the body belong to the same universe."

Cat blinked. What was he talking about?

"The mental world is anchored in the physical world."

She huffed. "It sounds like science fiction."

"It isn't science fiction. Modern cognitive science has taught us how mental processes work. The basis of the mind is physical. Emotions, behaviours, thoughts and dreams are controlled by circuits in the brain which follow the laws of chemistry and physics. In addition, all electrons in the universe are identical and therefore indistinguishable. The electrons in your brain which contribute to the design of your desires, memories and fantasies are identical to the electrons in chocolate ice cream or in the circulatory system of blue whales or in the stars of the Andromeda Galaxy."

She was thinking. It felt like her head was spinning. On the catwalk you didn't have to worry about electrons. What on earth was an electron again? "Even if all these … hmm … electrons … are identical, I don't see how they can be inseparable. You must be able to keep track of which is which and which was where? Based on their positions? And measure how they move?"

He smiled. "Quantum mechanics states positions of electrons and other subatomic particles are unknown during periods between measurements. Instead, particle positions are described by so-called wave functions, which tell us the likelihood of finding a particle at each specific position. Over time, wave functions tend to overlap. Thus, it becomes impossible to say which particle positions at a specific measurement correspond to the particle positions in earlier or later measurements."

She sighed. "Why are we here? What do the lion statues have to do with anything?"

"What's the colour of the lion at position 10?"

Her eyes swept through the room. The lions were numbered 1, 4, 7, 10, 13 and 16.

Her eyes stopped at number 10. "Red."

"And I say green."

"You see a green lion at 10?"

"Yes."

She frowned. "The green lion is at position 13."

"At 13 there's a dark-yellow lion."

"Uh? And the red lion?"

"Nowhere."

"Nowhere? Who's right? You or me?"

"We're both right. Right in different ways."

"This is crazy."

"Not at all. Colour doesn't belong to the physical world's objects. Colour is constructed by the visual system of the brain. Colour sensations arise from reflected particles of light being detected by the eye. We have different colour vision, Miss Milton. Because our brains have different wiring. Your colour vision is normal while mine is abnormal. Modern research has also shown there's a certain colour dimension which is invisible to people with normal colour vision and visible only to people who have a particular form of abnormal colour vision. Moreover, many animals perceive the world in colour palettes which differ a lot to those of humans. And there's fish that can see colours which humans can only dream of experiencing."

Cat thought about her hair. "What's the colour of my hair?"

"To me, it's olive-green. To others it's scarlet. Or golden-yellow. Or any other colour. Or no colour at all. The observer's physiology determines the colour. All viewers are right, often in different ways, though most people see you as red-haired."

She tried to imagine herself with olive-green hair. It didn't work. *Cat Milton—the model with the long olive-green hair.*

"My so-called hallucinations are much stronger than mere hallucinations. People and weird creatures from my memories and imaginations have begun to stalk and chase me in my physical world. I mean they're here for *real*—not fantasised. Is that the trifle you chose to keep secret?"

"We're now approaching the fantastic aspect of your case. I suspect your disease has mutated into something unknown."

"Are you trying to scare me?"

"I'm trying to avoid it. As the experiment with the lion statues demonstrated, the image in the eye is not a copy of any objective reality. Both vision and emotional reaction are inner constructions of our brain. In your case, an unknown mutation has triggered a corrupted internal quantum biochemistry."

Corrupted internal quantum biochemistry? An impossible phrase to utter. Her tongue tripped on the alien words. Her sensation of instability made her lightheaded. Her foothold jolted. Six spinning lion statues became a spinning rainbow in the spinning room. "Which means in plain sane English?"

"Which means the balance between your inner and outer realities has shifted, Miss Milton. Your hallucinations have begun to assume physical properties."

• TWENTY-EIGHT •

THE FIERCE SUNLIGHT was shooting through the windows of Roy's kitchen. London was preparing for yet another day in the heat of the most preternatural summer in recorded history.

"Ebba?" Roy broke the pressing silence. "Did you put on that dress only to go out and buy the paper?"

"Mmm."

He grinned. "Why don't you take it off again?"

"Okay." She rose from the table and pulled off her dress.

Roy raised his eyebrows. "No knickers? No bra? Did you go out just like that? Wearing nothing but the dress?"

"I was only going to buy the fucking newspaper."

"You're so wild, Ebba. That's why you turn me on. Cat is nice and kind but too prudish. You are naughty as well as pretty. The pretty naughty Ebba Sjödal is my dream girl."

She giggled. "When are you going to tell her about us?"

"Why me?"

"You're her boyfriend. Or, um, ex-boyfriend."

"You're her best friend. Or is it ex-friend?"

Ebba didn't like Roy's question. She couldn't imagine Cat as an ex-friend. You could dump lovers but you couldn't dump best friends, could you? "We don't owe Cat anything. But we don't want her to find out through the tabloids."

"You have a point, Ebba."

"Imagine the following media headlines: 'Beckman and Sjödal are a couple' or 'Cat Milton and Roy Beckman's love story is over—Who dumped whom?'"

Roy nodded. "We have to keep it secret for a while."

"Until we decide who's going to tell her."

"We could tell her together."

"Maybe. If we don't mind being seen together."

"Can you save your friendship?"

"I want to save it."

He pushed out his chair. "Come here, gorgeous."

"You want me now? Just after breakfast?"

"Breakfast isn't complete without you."

She put her arms around his neck and kissed him. "We don't have the time, Roy. I have to be at work in an hour. What about your training session at the football club? Aren't you going?"

"We have time for a quickie."

Their lips met again. "You're mad, Roy."

"But you like me to be, right?"

She snickered. "Perhaps."

"Let's do it on the kitchen table, baby."

He grabbed Ebba's hips, lifted her and put her down on the edge of the table with an exaggerated thud. Plates rattled. The bread basket tumbled over. Round breakfast buns rolled off the table and kept turning over and over on the floor. Spilled breakfast cereals crunched under her naked rump.

"Oh, oh, wow." She laughed. "Did you and Cat do it on the kitchen table?"

"You're kidding? Cat is too decent."

"Come on then, tough guy." She pulled down his boxer shorts. Her eyes widened. "Before I fuck the shit out of you again I want to feel you in my mouth."

Roy grinned. "Cat never used such colourful language." He

paused. "She did like to blow me once in a while but only in a darkened bedroom."

She returned the grin, looking up into his eyes. "I'm not Cat. The kitchen table makes a refreshing change."

"Your lips are newly painted."

"No problem. I'll paint them again in a minute." She bent forward. "Stand still now."

"Your rudeness is priceless, miss."

• TWENTY-NINE •

"AWFUL NEWS. I just want to scream and cry."

"My disclosure doesn't alter anything I've said before, Miss Milton. Rox-1 restores the internal quantum biochemistry of the nervous system in patients who suffer from this amazing problem. It keeps the demons of the mind at bay. It prevents characters and situations from your inner reality crossing the boundary towards your outer reality."

She still wanted to scream but decided not to. "Are there other patients whose cases are the same as mine?"

"Every patient is different, even when they present with the same conditions or symptoms. There are similar mutations in other patients. Not many other patients, just a few."

"Where are those other patients?"

"Spread all over the world."

"Can I meet them? I want to meet them."

"You want. But do they want? I'm not authorised to disclose patient contact information to other patients. It's the principle of confidentiality. Research on the unknown mutation must be kept secret until further notice."

"More secrets," Cat thought aloud. "Would you be able to contact the other patients on my behalf? That way, I wouldn't need anyone's contact info."

"It would still be unprofessional. Now, have you started using the Rox-1 tablets which I prescribed?"

"Not yet."

"Have you collected them from the pharmacy?"

"Not yet."

"Please do it, Miss Milton."

• THIRTY •

THE FULL-LENGTH MIRROR in the guest room exploded. Shards of glass spurted through the air like a silver rainbow. Cat screamed. Flying splinters of mirror clattered against the floor and the ceiling and the opposite wall. The stalker in raincoat and hat stepped out of the mirror frame and into the room.

"Mum, what's that noise?" Jan shambled into the living room with a bowl of popcorn in her arms. "What's that noise?"

"Did you turn off the cooker?" Mum lay on the sofa in the living room. A bunch of curlers were back in her hair.

"Yes, Mum. I turned off the cooker."

"The fan?"

"Still on. Until the popcorn smell disappears. As you have decided. But what's that noise? Dix is worried."

"It's just the TV. An action movie just started."

"Is there something else on TV tonight, Mum?"

"Of course there's something else, but this channel shows three action movies in a row and I'm going to watch all three."

"I wondered if the clamour might be coming from somewhere in the house." She scooped popcorn into her mouth.

"That's a ridiculous idea, Janice."

"Perhaps from upstairs. Don't you th—"

"Be quiet, Janice. I'm seeing this film and you're becoming an annoyance."

"Come on, Dix. Let's go outside in the garden." I must have imagined the crash from upstairs, Jan thought. Sis had gone to bed. Since Sis hadn't come down from upstairs to complain about noise, there couldn't be any.

"You again?"

"Have you missed me, Cat?" The sixteen-fingered intruder moved towards her. He wore his signature raincoat.

"The disease has mutated into something unknown." ... *"The mind is a physical organ."* ... *"The brain acts like a biological computer."* ... *"The language of the mutation pattern is translated by hydrogen quantum superpositions in the brain."* ... *"You're unbelievably beautiful."* ... *"The boundary between your internal and external realities has shifted."* ... *"Your hallucinations belong to your physical reality."* ... *"Have you picked up your prescribed medicine from the pharmacy?"*

Cat yelled at him. "You could have injured me or even killed me, you madman."

"Calm down, Cat." He took off his hat. "I calculated the moment to get into the room. I knew you would be at a safe distance from the spray of mirror splinters. I knew you were standing at the window to pull the curtains, though you haven't pulled them yet." The reptile's face and head were as yellow and scaly as the eight-fingered paws. His eyes were glowing like a sunset. He had a broad snout and powerful jaw muscles. And teeth like those of a crocodile.

"I've learnt something lately," Cat said.

"I bet you have." In the moonlit room, the stalker's teeth flashed like polished silver.

Cat pulled the curtains. "Like my dad, you're dead. You're a product of my sick dreams. But if you wanted to kill me you would have done it already. You've had plenty of opportunities. In London, on the train, or here in Blackfield." She looked into his eyes, thinking she noted a human presence in the reptilian look. "Who are you? What do you want? Why do you need me?"

"My name is Umberto Antonetti. Or it was my name. In my human life. My family, from Verona, Italy, emigrated before I was born. I grew up in Birkenhead, Merseyside. I had both Italian and British citizenship. I was Professor of Biochemistry at Liverpool University—later Professor Emeritus—and involved in projects at BioFutura Systematik. I died from old age eleven weeks ago. I was ninety-two."

"My dad returned as my dad. You have obviously come back as something other than human."

"In my precious spare time, I've been investigating my current appearance. The study was made possible via Umberto Antonetti's own international contact network."

"Ridiculous."

"Shut your pretty mouth and listen, Cat. I discovered this body belongs to a prehistoric animal which lived in the time of the first dinosaurs, the Triassic period, about two hundred and twenty million years ago. This lizard is as dead as Professor Antonetti. The reason why Victor Milton came back as Victor Milton is you know him as Victor Milton, your own father. However, you've never met Umberto Antonetti. Consequently, you have no memories of Antonetti's appearance or character. Understanding how we perceive and react to the world is rooted in our understanding of neurobiology. Your disease-infected mind created this monster before your eyes. I'm real because of your own perception of reality."

The floor swayed under her feet. The light cast by the ceiling lamp began to drain away from her vision. "I'm so tired. I think I'm about to faint."

Roxonodonol (the letter 'o' appears five times in that freaking name) will scare away the sixteen-fingered stalker. No more walks in the park with Dr. Stockmayer. Janice? Mum? Where are you? Help me. I need your help.

Rita cranked up the volume on the TV. The loud action film became a shield from the grief which tried to steal the spark of her life. It was the night after Vic's funeral. She took the liberty of doing what she wanted and not doing what she didn't want. Her life as a widow had started early and it frightened her to death. She was only forty-two.

How did you plan the rest of your life?

Jan panted in the heat and put Dixie down onto the backyard lawn. "Dix, you know Cat goes to bed early, don't you?"

Dixie miaowed.

"Sis has scheduled sleep because of her disease, and Mum is watching TV. Therefore, we're going to be alone tonight."

Dixie miaowed.

"We don't need them, Dix. We're better off on our own. We can do without a grumpy mum and a bitchy sister tonight."

Dixie miaowed. Then he ran across the lawn, chasing his toys, a selection of plastic rats which were scattered among the apple trees.

"I can't even imagine running like you, Dix. I'm too heavy." She sat on a sunlounger with the popcorn bowl in her arms. "I'm staying here for a while." She shovelled popcorn into her grotesque mouth, chewed, gorged. Melted butter dripped from her lower lip.

What if she quit as waitress at the Red Unicorn and opened her own tavern? How would that come about? To start your own business with twelve pounds and fifty-three pence in your bank account? Ho-ho-ho. In any event, her dream of opening her own tavern was alive. Dreams were free of charge.

She stretched out on the sunlounger and gobbled more popcorn. The darkened sky arrived. The street lamps came on. Dixie's restless shadows were rushing back and forth across the backyard. Jan's gaze wandered onto the house wall, continued upwards, to the guest room window. The curtains were drawn but the light was on. Sis was probably reading in bed. Glamour magazines. How surprising. Sis was too fixated on glamour.

• • •

"Don't pass out, Cat. I'm not yet done with you." The lizard Umberto Antonetti grabbed her arm. "Don't dare to faint. You won't get away that easily."

Cat came to. "I'm wide awake. Ouch. Let go of me, you psychopath." She pulled herself away from his paw.

"It's high time we changed the topic of our conversation," the creature said. "Now, let's talk about biomedical research."

"I'm a model. I know nothing about biomedical research. You're terrorising the wrong person. Do you understand?"

"It's enough to focus on the implications of my mission."

"What mission?"

"For security reasons, I don't want to categorise it. It's about resolving a conflict between a variety of industrial interests."

"What does that have to do with me?"

The reptile put his hat back on. "Did your father mention a certain Karl-Heinz Zimmer?"

"No."

"If you're lying I'll kill you, Cat." Antonetti smiled like an alligator. "I repeat, for the first and last time: Did your father mention a certain Karl-Heinz Zimmer?"

"What if he did? Would it matter?"

"It sounds like your father did mention Zimmer."

"It sounds like Zimmer is one of the key players in your so-called industrial conflict, Professor Antonetti."

"You're too cheeky for your own good, Cat. I could crush you like a fly."

"Will you kill me if I try to contact BioFutura Systematik's Deputy CEO?" She strived to keep her voice steady but her words trembled like maple leaves in an autumn storm.

"Zimmer mustn't be disturbed. The man is busy working out the near future of BioFutura Systematik. In addition, he's occupied with renewing patent applications at the world's three largest patent organisations: EPO in Europe, USPTO in the United States, and JPO in Japan. Next week he'll visit the EPO headquarters in Munich."

"For a product of my mind—if that's what you are—you seem mysteriously versed in the world of science."

The lizard grimaced. "I've had enough of your impudence, Cat. You have to cooperate for your own good. Your life is in danger, and not just *your* life. Your obstinate appearance also endangers the lives of your mother and sister."

"I don't like the tone in your voice, Professor."

The dinosaur in raincoat and hat pressed itself close to her. "Give me the letter."

"What letter?"

"Don't tell me you don't know what I'm talking about." He grabbed her arm. "The letter from your father. Give it to me."

Cat said nothing. Her thoughts were in overdrive. How on earth could Antonetti know about Dad's letter to her and Sis?

The prehistoric lizard's grip on her arm hardened. "Have you read the letter?"

She hadn't yet shown the letter to Sis. It was still in her jeans pocket. The jeans hung in the wardrobe. The wardrobe stood at the perimeter of her field of vision. She wore a bathrobe. She was about to go to bed. "How do you know about my dad's letter?"

"Give it to me."

"No."

The scaly monster shook her. "You do yourself a favour by handing the letter over to me. It's not healthy for you to have it in your possession."

"Ouch. You're hurting me. Let go of me."

"The letter, Cat."

"Never."

He threw her across the room. She yelled. She landed among splinters of mirror a few feet from the door. Pain pulsed through her. She writhed in pain, gasped, sobbed. The beast moved towards her. Glass shards crackled under his shoes. "Where's the letter, Cat? It would be a shame to ruin your attractive face."

She craned her neck, looked upwards, reached for the door handle. "Janice? Mum? Dix? Where are you? Help me. Help!"

He swung his arm towards her head. The arm and the hand with eight claws swept through the air like a lethal club.

She ducked. His claws brushed a strand of her hair.

He seized her foot and pulled at it. "How stubborn Dr. Milton's daughter can be."

She sobbed. "Let go of me, you disgusting freak."

"The conversation isn't finished." The reptile began to drag her back across the floor. "You need to practise your rhetoric. Where's the letter?"

She hissed, floundered, paddled with her arms and sought something to hold on to but there was nothing within reach. She was sliding backwards through the room over a bed of crushed mirror glass. She clawed at the floor. Five nails broke, three on her left hand, two on her right. Her fingertips began to bleed. He was dragging her towards the mirror frame. One of the legs of the bed showed up in the corner of her eye. She stretched out a hand, groped for the bed leg, caught only air.

"Imagine if I pulled you through the mirror frame, Cat. Imagine if I forced you to discover the universe beyond the back of the mirror frame."

Her heart jolted. "No. No, I don't want to. Let go of me."

The dinosaur flashed a hideous smile. His blood-red eyes twinkled beneath the brim of his hat. "To kill you right away would be counterproductive. Instead, I'm going to tie you to the mirror frame before I search for the letter. I won't leave the house without the letter."

With an effort she didn't believe possible, she twisted her foot away from the grip of the horror lizard's paw. She spun on the floor, got hold of something cold and shiny, a long splinter of mirror, sat up with a jerk and rammed the splinter into Antonetti's throat. "*I got you there, you yellow-scaly freak!*"

The creature howled. A terrible scream with both human and animal qualities. Bright-red blood sprayed all over the floor. The thing shrieked. Blood splattered on the walls and the curtains and the ceiling lampshade.

• • •

"I'm going back inside, Dix." On the sunlounger, Jan yawned, noting the light was still on in the guest room. "The night is quiet and nothing exciting is happening. Even the insects have gone to bed. Nothing buzzes in the garden anymore. Dix?"

Dixie threw a glance at Jan and miaowed.

"Stay outside if you want, Dix. Be kind to our neighbours' cat, Gabriella, if she happens to pass through your territory. Act like a gentleman, or, hmm, like a gentle cat."

Dixie's eyes narrowed.

"*Janice.*" Mum's voice.

Jan shuffled into the living room. "What's up, Mum?"

"Did you hear something?" Mum's eyes were on the TV.

Why can't you look at me when you're talking to me, Mum? Jan listened. "I hear loud action-movie sounds from the TV."

"I mean from upstairs."

That's what I thought earlier, but you didn't want to listen. "Upstairs is quiet. Cat must have fallen asleep with the light on."

Mum snorted. "Catriona shouldn't think it's okay to waste electricity in this house."

"I'm going to bed, Mum. Dix is still outside. Goodnight."

Mum didn't respond.

Go to bed, Catriona.
  I've already gone to bed.
  No, you haven't.
  I'm on my back and I can see the ceiling, so I must be in bed.
  You're on the floor, Catriona. You're still on the floor. You had a fight with Professor Antonetti. Do you remember?
  Mmm. Yes, I remember.
  Go to bed.
  Now?
  Now.
  What about Janice and Mum?

What do you mean?
I have to tell Sis and Mum what has happened.
Now you're too tired. Talk to your sister tomorrow.
Just my sister? What about my mum?
Don't tell your mother. She wouldn't believe you anyway.

• THIRTY-ONE •

DREAM FRAGMENTS DANCE, swirl, rustle.

New York Fashion Week. Cat and Ebba are there and ready. It will be a great week, Cat thinks, though something is wrong. A terrible heat absorbs her. The room in the luxury hotel on Upper West Side, Manhattan, shouldn't be hot. Not during New York Fashion Week. It's the middle of winter.

Not at all, miss, Stockmayer says. *You're in Blackfield. The City of Crows. City of Crows ... City of Crows ... Crows ...*

Her eyelids fluttered. She blinked. Sunlight was pressing against the curtains. She wasn't in New York. She was in Blackfield. The City of Crows. Mum's house (also Dad's house, until recently). The guest room. In the middle of August. The extreme heatwave. It was already morning and sizzling hot. Her back ached. The surface under her back was as hard as stone, as if the mattress had transformed into a block of granite during the night. The mattress? Her hands fumbled outwards from the sides of her body. Mirror shards. No mattress. She had spent the night on the floor. *The letter.*

Cat became wide awake. She sat up and gazed around the room. The full-length mirror was destroyed. Only the frame remained. Splatters of blood and splinters of mirror everywhere. She had killed someone, or something, in self-defence. The corpse? Where? Professor Antonetti's corpse—the cadaver of the prehistoric creature—was gone.

She inspected her body. The quality fabric of the bathrobe had protected her from cuts. She couldn't discern a single scratch on her body. Only her fingers were aching. She recalled the fight, how he had been dragging her backwards across the room. She examined her fingertips and the broken nails. The wounds were superficial. The blood had coagulated.

She rose, tripped between and around shards of glass, moved to the wardrobe, opened it and put her hand in the front pocket of the jeans. The letter was still there. How lucky.

"Give me the letter ... It's not healthy for you to have it in your possession."

Three quick knocks on the door. "Catriona?"

What luck that the door could be locked from the inside. "Give me half an hour, Mum. Okay?"

"What kind of talk is that? Have you become a spoilt diva or a petulant princess? There's no room for prima donnas here."

"Please, Mum. Don't fight."

"Did you plan to sleep away the whole morning?"

"What time is it?"

"Ten. Breakfast stopped serving at nine."

"Like a lousy hotel service," Cat mumbled.

"What did you say?"

"Nothing."

"The next meal in this house will be dinner."

"That's fine, Mum. I'm not hungry yet."

"And don't waste electricity. You left the light on all night."

"Where's Jan?"

"Where do you think she is? At work, of course. Unlike a model, she can't afford to sleep away the whole day."

If Mum was trying to pick another fight with her, let her try. Cat couldn't be bothered to respond to Mum's distorted idea about the everyday life of a supermodel. Instead, she said, "I'll go down to the tavern and order some breakfast from Sis."

"Do that. And take your time at the tavern. You don't need to hurry back here."

It's your own daughter you're talking to, Mum. Imagine if we could get along. Imagine if we could.

She found a dustpan, a broom, a mop bucket and all-purpose cloths in the downstairs broom cupboard. Mum didn't check up on her again. She was in the living room all this time, busy watching TV.

The cleaning took less than half an hour. Not a trace of blood splatter. The wet spots after the wash would soon dry. She couldn't restore the mirror by magic. She would be happy to pay for a new mirror, even if the damage hadn't been her fault. It was easier to accept the blame for the ruined mirror than to tell Mum the truth about what had happened.

She dumped the bag with mirror splinters in one of the garbage bins in the driveway. Then she walked down to the pub.

Cat browsed the menu. "A veggie sandwich but without butter and without mayonnaise, please."

Jan made a face. "What a pathetic order."

"Shut up, Jan. And give me water."

"If you ask kindly, Cat." Jan gave her sis the finger.

"I want bottled mineral water. Your finest brand."

"You get the water we have or none at all."

"Non-carbonated, please."

"A slice of lemon with the water?"

"No."

"Ice cubes?"

"No. Ice cubes are made of tap water and I hate tap water."

"When we were kids we used to drink orange juice with ice cubes. Do you remember the summer afternoons when we drank juice and played with our cute Disney dolls in the backyard? That was fun. I bet you haven't kept your Disney dolls."

"Times change, Jan, and we change with the times."

Jan plucked a notepad and a pen from a pocket of her tent-size waitress uniform. "Chips to go with the sandwich?"

"You're kidding? I don't eat junk food."

Jan didn't give her sis the finger this time. The manager was looking in her direction. She wrote down Cat's order and shuffled to the kitchen.

"We need to talk, Jan."

Janice put Cat's sandwich and drink on the table. "Do you want to talk here?"

Cat looked around. The pub wasn't too busy at the moment. "Here's fine."

"What do you want to talk about, Cat? What *is* there to talk about? We don't have much in common, you know."

"Could you sit down awhile?"

Jan threw an eye at the wall clock. "I'm on my morning break now. I can sit for a few minutes." She sat down at the table, opposite Cat. "What do you want to talk about?"

Cat told her sis everything. The exploding mirror. The creature in black raincoat and black hat. Professor Umberto Antonetti. The letter. The threats. The fight. Her cries for help. How she in self-defence had killed the prehistoric lizard and modern-day man Antonetti. How she had lost consciousness on the floor among mirror shards and blood splatter. Her confrontation with Mum. Her cleaning of the guest room.

Jan stared. "Why does it sound like the wackiest story I've ever heard?"

"It's the truth."

"You look like you always do. Clean and super-gorgeous. Not a single scratch on your beautiful legs or arms or on your adorable face. You smell very nice too."

"I've had a shower. I've changed clothes. And I was lucky. The thick bathrobe protected me from cuts and scratches."

Jan wrinkled her forehead. "You have cut your nails and repainted them. Why?"

"As you can see, I broke a few nails during the fight." Cat held up her hands. "I needed a manicure."

"Uh, have you talked to your brain doctor about this?"

"About the manicure?"

Jan sighed. "No, Cat. About the prehistoric dandelion-yellow horror lizard."

"Ah. Stockmayer has explained how my reality differs from the reality of healthy people. By the way, reality isn't an absolute concept. There are several different types of realities and there's a number of theories about what reality really is."

"What reality *really* is? Pun intended, Sis?"

"Knock it off."

"You've killed a person? This Professor Antonetti?"

"In self-defence, as I said. Besides, he was already dead. You can't kill somebody who's already dead. The prehistoric reptile originated from my evil dreams or hallucinations. The balance between my internal and external realities is damaged. The creature crossed the boundary between my inner world and my outer world. This phenomenon has to do with electrons but don't ask me how."

"How weird."

"I'm not mad. My narcolepsy has mutated into some unknown disease. The imbalance between my dream world and external happenings results from a set of undesired interactions between elementary particles at inter-cellular level. The issue is studied by a scientific discipline called quantum biochemistry."

I don't recognise my own language.
I sound like Dr. Stockmayer.

The crease between Jan's eyes deepened. "Are you for real, Cat? Does my posh sister belong to my outer world, or is she a product of my worst imaginations?"

"It's supposed to be possible to fix my condition."

"Was that the reason Stockmayer wanted to see you?"

"Right. It's about a new drug. It's called Rox-1."

"I see. Rox-1. That explains everything, Cat. All of a sudden, the whole conversation makes sense."

"I hate your sarcasm."

"Have you started using this Rox-1?"

"I just got it from the pharmacy."

"What happens next?"

"I'll show you something." Cat picked the envelope from her skirt pocket. "Look." She took out the letter, unfolded it and put it on the table.

"What is it?"

"A letter to us from Dad."

Jan frowned again. Her ugly lips expressed an even uglier non-smile. "The date says August the sixteenth."

"That's correct. The day after the funeral, in other words."

August 16th

Catriona, Janice,

If you read this letter, it means I'm dead. It also means I wrote the letter after my death. The significance of the following is still a secret. No one must see this letter but my twin daughters, and Karl-Heinz Zimmer, the Deputy CEO of BioFutura Systematik. Although some of the facts mentioned below are known to modern science, the letter in its entirety must be handled with the utmost confidentiality.

Hand over the letter to Zimmer. The codes far below are associated with top-secret data files. These codes complement Zimmer's own codes. You don't need to explain anything to Zimmer. All you have to do is give him the letter in its entirety. It's important my daughters don't retain any part of the letter as a memory. It would be extremely dangerous.

You're probably wondering why I don't send an email instead. After all, it's the twenty-first century, right? Now, emailing Zimmer is unthinkable, regardless of network protocol or server system. I have reason to suspect corporate criminals have hacked into all my computers. To send the letter via normal postal service isn't an option either, for all kinds of reasons. Therefore, I'm asking my daughters to be my couriers. There's no one else I trust like you.

The secret at BioFutura is a revolutionary discovery. A breakthrough in a field called gene therapy paved the way for this remarkable insight. In short, gene therapy is a treatment technique to correct damaged genes which cause diseases. There are several ways of doing this. The most common approach is to replace the pathogenic gene with a normal gene. A vector (carrier molecule) delivers the therapeutic gene to the right site in the patient's target cells. At present, the most common vector is a virus which has been manipulated to carry human DNA.

Gene therapy has for years been associated with several problems. Until now. BioFutura Systematik has managed to solve all of the gene therapy problems. The key to the secret is a special group of nanoparticles which act as vectors. Even if nanoscience methods as gene therapy solutions is a popular research area, no programme anywhere matches the BFS concept. BioFutura's nanotechnological operation is a solid cure for several hitherto infectious and fatal diseases, including cancer. BFS's unique strategy has zero complications, zero side effects, 100% success. Do you understand, girls? A cure for cancer alone would be worth trillions of dollars. Now I say goodbye. It's high time for you to contact Zimmer. And Janice? Be kind to your sister. She needs your cooperation and support.

/ Dad.

4K6OD(3x-91w)   93HFOS(8y+zc-2.154)
4M646HAPEN(5.2hj-0.77u)   4
2ISK(3.8375rb+0.1198vf)   FHE3453J(4m-

49238.2ug)(x^2-k^2)   423J(93.6238wrts-0.1a)
4NF98D(e^3+f^4.55111) 4D9D(a1+j6) FW(X^81cv-
H) 428(J^7.29yd+M) JJWR9F85JF9(i-12o+Z) 4U6
49FU(8E67gd-j^gs+w1-w9)   494   GHFU630
DLPEJD469 GJ5 9 2 f

• THIRTY-TWO •

ELMER GRITT WALKED out of the factory in Wintergreen, Blackfield. The blazing sunshine fell upon the car park like a carpet of heat. The cloudless sky was burning. The air seemed to be trembling. At once, the aggressive heat penetrated his summer jacket and shirt. He continued to the subterranean garage, where a new company car was ready for him. A strawberry-red BMW. Elmer liked the colour. Liked it a lot.

His phone rang. He took the call. "Hi, gorgeous."

"It's our wedding anniversary, Elmer. How long will you be working?"

"I've only one job left to do today, Veronica."

"Is your last job a long way from home? Don't tell me you'll be in Manchester or London."

Elmer chuckled. "Not at all. Central Blackfield. Afterwards I'll buy presents for you."

"I love you, Elmer."

"I love you too, Veronica. I can say it an infinite number of times and I never get tired of saying it."

"I know, Elmer. Hurry home."

"I promise I'll hurry. Tonight we're celebrating our wedding anniversary." Elmer returned the phone to his jacket pocket. He placed the spare equipment in the boot of the BMW: a Steyr AUG assault rifle, an Uzi submachine gun, an Instalaza anti-tank rifle, a Delkorel Multi-Mode rocket launcher and an Mk 47 automatic grenade launcher. On the front-passenger car mat he put a Zastava M76 sniper rifle, two SIG Sauer semi-automatic pistols and a Milkor MGL-140 six-shot revolver-type grenade launcher. He got behind the wheel of the BMW and drove out of the factory site towards the city.

"Dead people don't write letters," Jan said. "Admit you wrote this yourself."

Cat ignored Jan's words. "Dad doesn't mention Antonetti. The professor told me he had been involved in projects at BFS."

"Dad doesn't mention him because Dad didn't write this."

"The professor was a traitor. That explains it. The pieces of the puzzle fall into place."

"You're sick, Sis."

"I know I'm sick but it doesn't mean I must be wrong. Dad wrote that you should be kind to me. I need your support."

"You might have written this yourself because you want me to be kind to you."

"I don't want you to be bitter. We're different, you and me. It isn't my fault. No one else's fault either. Can we move on?"

"We're so different, Sis."

"We could try to prove to ourselves that we can work together, even though we are so different. Do you want to try?"

"For your sake?"

"Or for Dad's, if you can't do it for mine."

"My break is over. Have to get back to work."

"Answer me before you leave this table, Jan. Are you going to help me with this?"

Jan sighed. "What do you suggest we do?"

"We follow Dad's instructions, of course."

"The letter means nothing."

"Do you still think it's a fake?"

"There's no proof of anything."

"The date? August the sixteenth?"

"What does it mean? The letter might have been predated or post-dated anytime. Also, the year is missing from the date."

Cat sighed. "The reference to Zimmer?"

"If it were important we approach Zimmer, there would have been some contact information here. The absence of Zimmer's contact information weakens the credibility further."

"The secret codes at the bottom?"

"Just gibberish." Jan flapped her hands.

"Jan, you're hopeless."

"I'm trying to look at the letter with objective eyes. If it was from Dad, why didn't he mention Mum?"

"The less Mum knows, the safer she'll be. Dad realised that."

"Right."

"I'm tired of arguing with you. Will you accompany me to Zimmer's place to hand over the letter?"

Jan thought for a moment, maybe just for show. "Okay. Just because you happen to be my sis."

"Thanks."

Jan grimaced. "You will owe me a favour."

"Another thing. Before we search for Zimmer, I'm going to visit the medico-legal centre."

"Why?"

"Dad wanted me to seek something out. To have a word with the medical examiner, Ursula Ellis, who examined Dad's corpse. Do you want to tag along?"

Jan laughed without humour. "No."

"Dad wanted you and me to visit Ellis together."

"That too, huh?" Jan shook her head. "I've already agreed to accompany you to Zimmer's place. That's enough. If you want to go to the BMLC, you have to go alone. There's *no way* I'm going there."

Cat pulled a sour face. "How about the following? I'll visit BMLC alone. In the meantime, you'll find out Zimmer's contact information."

"Doesn't sound too bad."

"So, you agree?"

"Only just."

"Excellent. I knew you could be cooperative."

Jan glowered.

Cat grinned. "May I have your mobile number? In case of an emergency?" When you had to ask your own sis for her mobile number, Cat thought, it showed how little contact you'd had in recent years.

"I have no mobile phone and no plans to get one."

"I'll give you mine," Cat said. "My new mobile number." She wrote down the number on a napkin.

"Don't forget to pay for your sandwich and your mineral water before you disappear." Jan returned to waiting tables. Breakfast became lunchtime and new diners were entering the busy tavern.

The doorbell blared. Rita Milton put down the watering can and went out into the hall.

The male visitor was bald. Grey-brown eyes. Blunt nose. Apple-shaped cheeks. Broad shoulders. Dark-red spectacle frames. Beige summer jacket.

"Good day, madam. My name is Elmer Gritt."

"Uh-huh?"

"What a nice cat."

Rita scooped up Dixie in her arms. "How can I help you?"

"I'm looking for Miss Catriona Milton."

"For what reason?"

"Reason?"

"Why are you looking for my daughter?" Rita noted a red BMW parked next to the pavement in front of the house. A sports car.

"I'm an advertising sales agent with a reputable global cosmetics company. Catriona Milton has a contract with us."

"If that's the case, you should know my daughter Catriona lives in London."

The man flashed a smile. His teeth were white like lily-of-the-valley flowers.

"The model agency Supreme says Miss Milton is in Blackfield in connection with a funeral."

"Can't this wait till she returns to London?"

"I'm afraid it can't wait, madam."

"What was your name again?"

"Gritt. Elmer Gritt." He showed an ID card with a name, a photograph, a company logo and an employment number. The cosmetics company name was Galaxy999. "I would like to inform Miss Milton of some urgent detail changes."

"I've never heard of Galaxy999. Which retailers stock your products?"

"Exclusive shops all over the world, madam."

"And you just happened to be nearby, here and now?"

The visitor smiled again. "Galaxy999 has a sales office in Blackfield. And yes, I happened to be nearby."

Rita realised the man understood she was testing him. Enough now. She wanted to continue to water her thirsty flowers. She shrugged. "Catriona is at the Red Unicorn."

"The pub on Farnwood Street?"

Rita nodded.

"Thank you for the information, madam."

Elmer swung the BMW on to Farnwood Street. The sparse traffic gave him two hundred and fifty feet of unobstructed vision.

He spotted the young woman. The unpretentious attire, the casual hairstyle with a simple topknot and the dark sunglasses formed a disguise which only fooled amateurs. The girl in his field of vision was Catriona Milton, one of the world's most famous supermodels. Miss C. Milton had just left the tavern and was now walking in the oncoming direction, along the opposite pavement. Her body language signalled determination. She was in a hurry. Where? A pharmacy? Unlikely. According to provided information, she had already collected Roxonodonol.

Elmer increased the pressure on the accelerator. The BMW rocketed forwards. He pulled the gun from his jacket's inner pocket, considered shooting the girl from across the street, considered shooting her through an open window.

• THIRTY-THREE •

EBBA WONDERED IF the bartender had pissed in the coffee. She hissed, grimaced. How the fuck could this crap hole compete in London's competitive cafe scene? From now on she would stick to the cafes she knew. She spat in the coffee cup and pushed a cigarette between her teeth. At least she could smoke here in the outdoor seating area.

Her phone screamed. She snatched it up. "Hello? Who's bothering me in the middle of my fucking coffee break, huh?"

"Nice to hear you're on top form, Miss Sjödal."

She coughed out tobacco smoke and gasped for air. The sensation of terror made her cheeks quiver. "So, it's you, sir." *Oh my freaking God. Jarrow. Dirk Jarrow of all men. The CEO of Yolexus Enterprise. Why is he calling now? I've already played out my role.*

A picture of Dirk Jarrow forced itself into her mind. His skin had the same shade as marble. Ice-blue lips. Hair reminiscent of withered weeds. The man was so thin he didn't throw a shadow. The spindly figure was treacherous like a spider. He was both cunning and strong, much stronger and agiler than his appearance suggested. His suit appeared two sizes too small. Pink socks were visible below the hem of his suit trousers. His rugged head, which protruded from the mould-green tie loop, looked like a cadaver skull in a noose.

She was struck by nausea, and not because of the bad coffee.

"Are you alone, Miss Sjödal?" Jarrow asked.

She hesitated. The word choice must be correct. "We can speak undisturbed, sir. For the moment, at least. Some friends left the table just a few minutes ago. I'm alone right now."

"Where are you?"

The cigarette had fallen from her mouth to the stone floor. She shook out a new one from the packet and fumbled with the match. "At the outdoor seating of a cafe in Covent Garden. I'm having a break between two modelling jobs."

"And enjoying the weather, I presume." His laugh echoed in the phone. "Soon you'll be in a luxury hotel in Paddington."

"Why, Mr. Jarrow?"

"Don't mention my name on the phone."

"Oh, sorry, sir."

"If you take pride in your appearance, do not mention my name on the phone. Something tragic might happen to your looks. Do you understand what I'm saying?"

"I understand. I'm so sorry."

"Something might also happen to Roy Beckman's health. Top clubs in the Premier League are not interested in investing in wheelchair-bound players."

"Forgive me. Please forgive me for having mentioned your name by accident on the phone." She wiped away a tear which was rolling down her cheek. "It'll never happen again."

"Excellent, Miss Sjödal. How nice that we understand one another. Mutual understanding is indispensable in business. Imagine if a bomb exploded in a certain house in Notting Hill. That would be a shame, wouldn't it?"

She sucked on the new cigarette, sobbing. There were a lot of people at the outdoor area of the cafe, though nobody looked in her direction. Everyone minded their own business. How lucky. No one noticed anything strange.

"You don't have to worry about that reporter any longer, Miss Sjödal. Your problem has been eliminated."

Her heart made a somersault. "I read the papers, sir. Herbert Krass is dead. He took his own life."

"As I just said, Miss Sjödal. Your problem has been removed from the equation."

What I was theorising about was not my imagination after

all, she thought. Oh my God. Krass was a murder victim. I was right from the beginning. "Did you arrange that, sir?" At once she regretted her question. She held her breath, hoping that Jarrow wouldn't explode.

"Yolexus Enterprise has several problem-solvers, including one Leo Baginski."

She puffed on the cigarette. "Who's that?"

"Someone who makes your worst nightmares look like infantile nonsense. You don't want Baginski to pay you a visit."

"Hmm, this Baginski, where is he now?"

"Wherever he needs to be." Dry laughter again.

"I understand. Thank you for the, hmm, information." Her voice fluttered. "Why are you telling me this?"

"To emphasise how serious we are about our agreement. To show how important it is for you to remain alert and focused."

"Okay, sir. Okay."

"Mr. Krass became a problem for you. And problems are there to be solved. Don't you agree, Miss Sjödal?"

"Sure. I agree."

"Good. Do you see Yolexus has done you a favour?"

"Hmm, yes, I think so. I definitely think so."

"You think so. A good start, Miss Sjödal. You have the right way of thinking. Because you think Yolexus Enterprise has done you a favour, the company has decided you should be grateful."

"I am grateful." The cigarette jiggled between her teeth. "I'm very grateful. Thank you very much."

"You're welcome, Miss Sjödal. Yolexus Enterprise estimated you wouldn't miss Mr. Krass."

"I ... I ..."

"Yes, Miss Sjödal? What are you trying to say?"

"I thought ... I was convinced you didn't need me anymore; that I had completed my contract; that we had terminated contact with each other."

"It's correct you've played out your role but we need you for a little while longer."

"Why?" Her heart scurried.

"Let's just say the pleasant Miss Sjödal is a guarantee whose expiry date has been postponed. Don't you agree guarantees are essential in connection with serious business transactions?"

"Um, yes."

"Miss Sjödal is a Yolexus guarantee. It would be irrational to finish your contract before the dust after the Victor Milton affair has settled. Do you see our point?"

"Hmm. I see your point."

"Fantastic that you see our point, Miss Sjödal. You're not just very attractive. You're also very clever."

"What do you want me to do?"

"You heard me say you'll be in Paddington soon?"

"Yes."

"The meeting is with me. The details of our meeting will be announced shortly. Stay contactable."

"Understood, sir."

"And Miss Sjödal?"

"Yes?"

"Don't hesitate to inform us if you happen to be troubled by other difficult reporters or other types of uncomfortable people. Your problems become our problems, and we don't want any problems whatsoever."

"I won't hesitate to inform you."

"Marvellous. Your communication skills are nothing short of admirable."

Ebba got into her Porsche and, as the car tore away, she lit a new cigarette. The supercar flew past the Theatre Royal and then skidded out on to Aldwych. She opened the glove box and waved to the bear, the two-inch figure in multicoloured glass mosaic.

What had Jarrow meant when he'd said 'the Victor Milton affair'? He'd meant just the revolutionary discovery at BioFutura Systematik, hadn't he? Cat's dad's death had been a natural death, hadn't it?

• THIRTY-FOUR •

CAT HEARD A whizzing sound. Screeching tyres. She turned her gaze across the street. A car accelerated in the oncoming direction. A red BMW. In the same instant, a tram, a classic orange-coloured Blackfield tram, approached from the opposite direction and blocked her view of the speeding BMW. The tram stopped and its doors opened. She noted the tram stop name—Line 3B: Farnwood Street A—and decided to board. Earlier, she had planned to take a taxi to BMLC, but now she wanted to get out of the sunshine as fast as possible. The tram would do.

Blackfield, like Rome or Sheffield, was a city of hills and valleys. The city rose from two hundred and thirty feet above sea level in the far east to one thousand two hundred feet above sea level in the far west. The tramline 3B, via Crow City College, Yarmouth Square and Roderick Avenue to Birchpark Top in Creake, ran constantly uphill.

The woman in the BMLC reception stared. "How can I help?" She sounded too grumpy for a service-oriented job.

"I would like to meet Mrs. Ursula Ellis," Cat said.

The woman sighed. "Have you booked an appointment or telephoned recently?"

"No, but I thought—"

"Where do you think you are? At a walk-in hair salon?"

"I know where I am. The medico-legal centre."

"The medical examiner is very busy."

"I'm sure she is."

"Unexpected deaths should be reported to the coroner."

"I'm not here to report a death."

The woman grunted. "Then why are you here?"

"I would like to talk to Dr. Ellis about an earlier autopsy, the one of my deceased father."

"The medical examiner doesn't usually open any sort of correspondence surrounding a closed case."

"Usually not? You mean there are exceptions?"

The woman scowled. "You don't seem to meet the criteria."

"Wait a second. Correspondence is written communication. I don't need anything in writing. I just want to talk to someone about this. Does Mrs. Ellis have any deputies?"

The receptionist's sigh was so forceful that droplets of saliva flew from her mouth. "The deputies are also terribly busy."

"Pathologists?"

"Busy."

"Can I wait here until somebody finds the time to see me?"

The woman puffed. "Your father? Did he have a name?"

"Milton. Victor Milton."

"And you've forgotten to introduce yourself."

"Catriona Milton."

"The same name and the same scarlet hair as that famous model?" The woman frowned. "What a strange coincidence."

The medical examiner looked like a corpse herself. Bluish skin, sunken cheeks, glazed eyes.

Ursula Ellis sat behind her desk, eating chicken salad from a plastic box with a plastic fork. The summer heat in the office was murderous. The stench of half-spoilt chicken salad hung in the air like a pollution cloud.

Cat almost gagged. "Thank you for welcoming me during your lunch break, Dr. Ellis." Thoughts pestered her, thoughts about dead bodies in the basement's cold room.

"I have a few minutes left before the next job." Ellis smacked her lips. Her teeth were green with pesto. Mayonnaise flowed from the corner of her chewing mouth. "What do you want? Your father died a natural death. The details are specified in the forensic report. Copies of the report have been sent to relatives."

"I'm aware of the statement. Heart attack."

"Your problem?"

"Could the cause of death have been something else?"

"Do you imply the postmortem was unprofessional?"

"No, no. Not at all. I've only had nightmares that my father's death wasn't natural."

"I see."

"A heart attack can be caused by different things, right?"

Ellis didn't answer. She licked chicken fat from her fingers.

"Did you perform the postmortem on my dad?"

"Maybe, maybe not. I don't memorise the names of the dead like some perverse pastime. The BMLC houses a team of forensic pathologists. We handle one thousand unexpected deaths per year, of which seventy-five percent require an autopsy. The BMLC performs annually around four hundred and fifty investigations surrounding deaths."

"All the data is in the computers, isn't it? Could we have a look at my father's file?"

"As I said, copies of the report have been sent to relatives."

Forget about the copies, Cat thought. "Could you possibly summarise the details of my dad's file, here and now?"

"Nothing would change."

"Please?"

Ellis swallowed the last piece of chicken and burped. "Very well, then. If you insist." She pressed a few buttons on the computer keyboard and leant back in her chair.

"Are you satisfied now, miss? The details of the file agree with the completed report. As expected. And as I said before."

Cat bit down on her lip, thinking. She didn't think the medical examiner needed to know that Milton had conversed with his daughter the day after his own funeral. "Mrs. Ellis?"

"Yes?" The medical examiner removed food from her spattered front teeth with the nail on her pinky finger. Her body language revealed her lunch break had ended. New cadavers were waiting to be dissected.

"What is an air embolism?"

"Why do you ask?"

Why do I ask? Where did that question come from? From Dad? "Could you please answer the question?"

"An air embolism is a blockage in a blood vessel caused by an air bubble. Why?" Ursula Ellis licked the pinky finger she had used to pick the remains of smelly chicken meat from her teeth.

"My dad said ..." *Did he?* "I mean, I dreamt my dad had an air embolism. Could you please explain this condition?"

"What are you insinuating?"

"Nothing. I'm curious about my dreams. I want to know."

"You want to know if an air embolism may have caused your father's death." Ellis turned off the computer and leant forward. "In connection with medical procedures such as surgery or drug administration, air may enter the bloodstream. Most of those embolisms are harmless. A serious embolism may be more or less dangerous. In the worst case, it can lead to death. A person with an air embolism shows symptoms such as cramps, pale skin, chest pain or heart problems."

"It sounds like an air embolism can cause a heart attack. Am I right?"

Ellis sighed. "If we follow your stubborn line of reasoning."

"Can you be honest with me?"

"I've been honest with you from the beginning."

"If my dad died of an air embolism, would your pathologists have discovered it in connection with the autopsy?"

Ellis sighed, checking her watch. "Autopsies have enormous significance for medicine. However, an autopsy can't always reveal the cause of death. The answer to your question is probably no. We can detect a heart attack but not always what caused it. Not in one hundred percent of cases."

"So, my dad *may* have died of an air embolism."

Ellis made a great show of looking occupied with the settings of her wristwatch. "Nothing indicates your father was at risk of getting such a complication. If a person has engaged in activities associated with the risk of an air embolism, a physician might prescribe immediate treatment. Tests can be carried out to confirm the diagnosis."

"But in the case of my dad, the possibility exists all the same, doesn't it? No matter how small, the possibility is still there?"

"Why are you pushing this question so hard?"

"I have to."

"Because of your nightmare?"

Cat nodded.

"How will you use what I've communicated today?"

"I'll keep it to myself."

"Have we finished?"

"Another question. A very final one."

A painful grin distorted Ursula Ellis's face. "Okay, young lady. A very final one."

"If we imagine the following. Imagine if someone injected air into a person's bloodstream. Injected air with a syringe."

"What are you driving at?"

"Could the outcome be fatal?"

"Provided that—"

"And in connection with a possible autopsy, you wouldn't find any mysterious, poisonous substance in the corpse," Cat interrupted.

"But a pathologist would detect the spot on the skin where the cannula went in. In the statement, the file, no cannula mark is mentioned."

"Is the scenario I describe *possible*?"

"It would be murder."

• THIRTY-FIVE •

WHEN JAN HAD finished her shift at the Red Unicorn, she didn't go home. Instead, she shambled down Drury Road, past Pinewater High School in the direction of Endsleigh Wood at the southern boundary of Farnwood. She looked around in the woods, searching for a lonely place close to the water. And found one. Not a person in sight or within earshot. The shiny brook wriggled through the terrain like a sky-blue worm. She moved towards the brook and stopped at the edge of the bank. The mirror image in the water surface made her pull back in disgust. It was like looking down at a lost sea monster. An underwater creature which had emerged from the depth of the brook. She mobilised the energy she needed and took the corkscrew from her trouser pocket. The lethal tool in stainless steel had been in her pocket too long.

What was the quickest way to end the monster's existence? She squeezed the corkscrew with both hands, raised it, pointed it to her neck, closed her eyes and waited.

Waited for what? What are you waiting for, you ugly freak? Do what you have to do. It's about time you freed the neighbourhood from this mutant.

Are you a coward, Janice?
No. I'm not a coward. At least not in the way you think.
So, what are you waiting for?

She opened her eyes and let her gaze sail on the surface of the brook. "Dad and Sis count on me," she thought aloud. "Dad and Sis count on me." The glimmer of the corkscrew blended with the sun's rays. She returned towards home. She dumped the corkscrew at a roadside recycling station.

"Janice? Catriona? Girls?" Mum's voice from the kitchen.

"It's just me, Mum." Jan stopped in the hall.

"Janice? Come here."

Jan shambled to the kitchen doorway.

Mum sat at the table, sipping wine, reading today's issue of the *Blackfield Telegraph*. She looked up. "Where is your sister?"

"Cat had things to do in town."

"Aha. *Things*. How informative." Mum paused, taking another sip from the glass. "The rest of my life begins today,

Janice. I want to deal with the future. To mark this new start, I will clean the whole house."

"Do you want any help with the cleaning, Mum? I'd be happy to help you."

"No. I want to do it myself. You and your sister would only be in my way. How long will Catriona stay in Blackfield this time around?"

"She says she must be back at work on Monday. I guess she'll stay here till Sunday night."

"That long? Not a fabulous idea to clean the guest room until Catriona is gone."

"I'm going to my room now, Mum. If I may."

Mum said nothing. She had returned to reading the paper.

Jan cracked open the door to the guest room and peeked inside. The quiet room was bathing in sunlight. She shuffled inside and closed the door. Cat's story began to play in Jan's head. She had a rigor, a brief one, already gone. What am I afraid of? Afraid of what could be hiding here? Afraid Sis has lost her mind?

The room was in order. With one exception. The full-length mirror was destroyed. The exquisite frame was intact but the back panel was thrashed. A few pieces of glass still hung around the edges of the frame. Not a trace of glass splinters or blood splatter or some other drama. If Cat's story was true, she had managed to clean up the room very well. Jan looked under the bed. Cat's suitcase was there. Nothing else.

She moved to the wardrobe, grabbed its door handle, hesitated. The rigor wasn't all gone after all. The chill had returned, weaker this time but unignorable, running along her malformed spine. She searched her memory, looking for the exact chronology of Cat's story. Sis had said she and the intruder had been fighting. Sis had killed him in self-defence, but if that was true, where was the body? The more she thought of Cat's story, the surer she became. Cat hadn't mentioned anything about any corpse. Sis had stabbed the intruder with a shard of glass, assumed she had killed him, then fainted. Umberto Antonetti? Could the man still be alive? Could the professor still be in the house? This simplified idea neglected all theories about prehistoric horror lizards.

Jan opened the wardrobe door.

Cat left the BMLC and hurried through the square Birchpark Top towards the tram stop.

"Wait, Catriona. Wait."

She stopped, turned around and started.

The approaching man was in his early forties. His hair was shoulder-length and gathered in a rubber band. Distinct cheekbones. Elegant nose. Clean-shaven.

"What's up, Dad?"

He caught up with her. "What did Mrs. Ellis say?"

"You got your suspicions confirmed, Dad. It seems there's a theoretical possibility you were murdered. If it's true, you're a victim of some conspiracy. That's all I can say." She wondered if Dad was disappointed she hadn't more to say.

Dad looked at her. When he spoke again, he almost whispered. "Could someone have shadowed you to the BMLC?"

"How could I know? I'm a supermodel, not a super-agent or a super-spy. Do you know the difference?"

Dad, unfazed by his daughter's anger, said, "Have you and Janice sought out Karl-Heinz Zimmer?"

"We haven't had the time yet. I prioritised the BMLC, okay? Now Sis and I will try to see the distinguished Mr. Zimmer and hand over the letter. Can we then return to our own lives?"

"I want you to do something else too."

"Again?"

"Not for my sake. For your own."

"What are you talking about?"

"There's a hair salon on the corner of Roderick Avenue." Dad pointed. "Visit it. I want you to get your hair dyed."

"Something wrong with my natural scarlet hair?"

"Nothing wrong. The natural colour of your hair stands out in a wonderful way. The fashion industry loves your scarlet hair, and I do too. But a detective on a top-secret mission wants a discreet look. Therefore, I recommend a temporary change of your hair colour, as a safety measure, for your own good."

"So far I've managed to hide behind dark glasses."

"You've been lucky. Someone may have begun to shadow you. It doesn't hurt to be extra careful. Do you mind getting your hair dyed a common colour?"

She puffed. "What do you suggest?"

"Could you imagine being a blonde?"

She shrugged. "Okay."

Dad walked away and disappeared in the crowd of people.

She crossed the square, completed her errand and left the hair salon *black-haired*. Now I almost resemble Ebba, she thought, grinning. Blonde or black-haired didn't matter to Cat. She just wanted to defy Dad.

The wardrobe door squeaked. Jan was convinced someone or something would jump out. It didn't happen. There was nothing there except Cat's clothes and accessories. A mix of everyday items and luxury fashion pieces. Suspended from a hanger, the designer dress which Sis had worn to Dad's funeral appeared like a crow-black ghost.

She returned downstairs. "Mum?"

"What's up, Janice? Must you disturb me again and again?"

"May I take the cordless landline phone to my room?"

"Who are you going to call?"

"The pub."

"Must you call from your room? Do you have secrets?"

"No secrets, Mum. I just want to be able to sit and make notes at my desk at the same time. If I may."

"You may. If you hurry up. And if you pay for the call."

"I always pay for my calls, Mum, at the end of each month."

"Good. Now, leave me alone. I'm watching TV."

Jan returned upstairs. She sat down on her bed with the phone in her lap and dialled.

"Thank you for calling BioFutura Systematik, how may I help you today?"

"Good afternoon, sir. I'd like to talk to Dr. Zimmer, please."

"I'll see if Dr. Zimmer is available to take your call. Could you please hold for a minute?"

"Okay."

"Thank you. I'll be right back."

"Okay."

"Dr. Zimmer is not in his office."

"How can you know so quickly? I was on hold for, like, two or three seconds. I heard two beeps in the receiver and then you were back on."

"When I say Dr. Zimmer is not in his office, it means he's not in his office. Do I make myself clear?"

"When will he be in?"

"How would I know? Who do you think I am? Zimmer's secretary?"

Stay calm, Janice. "Could he be out of town?"

"Who wants to know and why?"

"It's important I speak to no one but Zimmer. I could call at a better time, sir."

"If there is a better time. Or a less bad one."

She wondered why the man was so unfriendly. Didn't she have the right to be anonymous? Perhaps he disliked her voice. Her malformed mouth affected her voice and her spoken words. Strangers often found her voice repulsive, as disgusting as anything else associated with her person.

Jan said, "Can I leave a message?"

"If you don't mind waiting until next Christmas for a reply. Dr. Zimmer receives about three hundred and fifty letters, emails and voicemails per week."

"But this is very important."

"That's what everyone says when they call."

"Zimmer isn't in the local telephone directory."

"A correct observation."

"Could one of Zimmer's colleagues know where he is?"

"If Dr. Zimmer wanted to be found, he would have left a message about where he was. No such message exists. How long will you stay on the phone? My coffee break is coming up."

This moron is driving me mad. "Would you be able to provide me with Zimmer's home number and, or, home address?"

"BFS never discloses employees' private contact details, especially not to callers who can't be bothered to introduce themselves. You should know I can track this call. Do I make myself clear?"

The caller is the daughter of the BFS founder Victor Milton, you rude idiot. She hung up.

Jan got a daring idea. If Mum knew, she would go nuts.

The cardboard boxes containing Dad's miscellaneous items might hold a clue about Zimmer's private contact information. The filled and sealed boxes were still in Dad's office. Mum had said BFS representatives would arrive any day to fetch them.

She sneaked into the office, if it was possible to sneak when you weighed as much as a hippo. When she moved across floorboards, she couldn't avoid making noise. She closed the door behind her. The room contained an empty desk, three empty bookcases, a floor lamp and, in the middle of the floor, five cardboard boxes.

The boxes were labelled: Laboratory equipment, Books, Magazines, Binders, and Miscellaneous, respectively. She opened the Miscellaneous box. It contained all kinds of documents, invoices and notepads. Nothing of interest. She was close to giving up when she spotted the envelope. It was wedged upside-down in a corner at the bottom of the box. The sender's handwritten name: Karl-Heinz Zimmer.

The envelope wasn't sealed, had no stamp, and the sender's address was missing. She shook out the letter. It was an invitation to a dinner.

Jan skimmed the text. A few weeks ago, Zimmer had invited a handful of BioFutura colleagues to dinner at his new home. The invitation was written in the first-person singular and didn't mention wife or family. She guessed the man was single. The letter ended with information about a new home address and a new home phone number.

Cat sat on a bench in the shade of a tree in the square Birchpark Top. She picked up her phone and called. Emotions came back with full force. Her feelings about how much she loved Roy. How much she missed him and wanted him. How much she longed for his touch and his breath on her neck. Two weeks had passed since the last time they had slept together. She had decided to wait until she saw him again before delivering the surprise, though now she felt she couldn't wait. She would call Roy now and tell him about the trip she had won at a lottery in connection with an advertising job in Central Europe. A weekend trip for two. To Berlin. One of her favourite cities. *Any* weekend. Perfect. Cat and Roy would be holidaying in Berlin whenever they both had time. Roy would be thrilled when he heard about her surprise trip.

So, she called.

It took a while before he answered. "Cat?"

He didn't sound overwhelmed with joy. He came across as a bit troubled. Or was it just her imagination? "I miss you, Roy. I would have called earlier but a lot has happened."

"No problem, Cat. I've been busy too."

She thought she heard a giggle in the background. A brief, high-pitched laugh, now gone. A girl? Or was it just her imagination again? "How's the football going, Roy?"

"I can reveal the England manager has contacted me. He says I'm in the forthcoming World Cup squad."

"Congratulations, Roy. I'm very happy."

"Where are you, gorgeous?"

"I had to go up to Blackfield."

She heard it again. A snicker in the background. Then, a

whisper. She was certain now. Roy wasn't alone. He had a girl in his flat. *A girl.*

She heard Roy whispering back, "Cat can hear your giggle." His words sounded distant, as if he had put the phone down and whispered in some other direction across the room.

The room. Which room? The bedroom or the living room? Roy had two landline phones in his Pimlico flat.

A thousand years passed. Then, "Cat?" Roy's voice on the phone again. "Cat, you still there?"

She felt sick. "What happened?" Her voice fluttered. Her anger grew. Roy was cheating on her. Who the devil was the girl?

"I'm sorry," Roy continued. "I had to chase away a wasp. Anyway, it's gone now. It flew out a window."

A suppressed giggle in the background again. Without doubt a girl in Roy's bedroom. Who?

"Aha," Cat said, for want of something better to say. "A wasp. Luckily the wasp didn't sting you."

The sound of her heart rumbled in her ears. Her head was aching. Her throat was dry like the sand in an hourglass.

Water, she thought.

I must drink water before I faint.

"Why did you call, Cat? What did you want?"

"I ... I wanted ... Never mind; it can wait until I get back to London. You see, it's a surprise. It wouldn't be a surprise if I told you over the phone, would it?"

Roy laughed. "A surprise?"

"Mmm." She squeezed her eyes shut, pushing her tears back.

"Sounds great. I love surprises."

"I know." She stifled a sob.

"You all right?"

"Yeah, I'm all right."

"I look forward to the surprise."

She turned off the phone, lowered her head and held her face with both hands.

• • •

Jan sneaked out of Dad's workroom, not without creating noise. A walrus couldn't be clumsier, she thought. The floorboards groaned beneath her feet.

"Janice?" Mum's voice from the living room.

Jan froze. "Yes, Mum?"

"What are you doing?"

"Nothing special."

"What do you mean?" Mum showed up in the doorway towards the hall. "You've been in your dead father's workroom. You know I've forbidden you to sneak around in the workroom but you did it anyway. What did you do in there?" A fire flared in Mum's eyes.

"I apologise, Mum. I was just looking for Dix. I can't find him. I've been looking everywhere, except in the attic and the garage. I was worried he had slunk into the workroom and then maybe got stuck there behind a closed door."

"Dix is in the kitchen for the moment."

"Okay, Mum. Thanks. He must have been playing hide and seek. Dix loves hide and seek games. I'm going to give him a new bowl of water. It's terribly hot."

Mum stood silent for a while, frowning and glowering at the same time. "Well, Janice, I guess I can accept your explanation, at least until further notice." Her face didn't brighten. "Now, go to the kitchen. Give Dix a new bowl of water. It's terribly hot."

Later, Jan lumbered into her room, planted her bum on the bed again and dialled Zimmer's home phone number.

After four ringtones, an answering machine kicked in: *"Good morning, good day and good night. Enjoy your time zone wherever you are. This is Karl-Heinz Zimmer speaking, though you might already have guessed that. Please leave a message, provided you have something important to say. Goodbye."*

Jan ended the call. Indeed, it was an important matter, but she didn't want to mention a single word on the answering machine.

How long would Sis be gone?

Roy, unfaithful. With whom? Who was that girl? As if Cat didn't already have enough trouble. The pile of problems grew like a malignant tumour. *I'll get you for this, Roy.*

A southbound tram arrived at Birchpark Top. She boarded it. All the seats were occupied. She squeezed into the aisle among standing passengers. The doors closed. The crowded vehicle restarted. Her subconscious warning bells should have begun ringing. They didn't.

• THIRTY-SIX •

JARROW LICKED THE blood from the scalpel blade. Fox's blood was refreshing, even more so than red wine. Now he would preserve the fox skin. The fox meat would become another meatloaf. The freezer in the kitchen was still only half full with meatloaves from fox, squirrel, badger, otter, hedgehog, snake, rat and his wife Lisa-Marie.

He made no dishes from dog or cat. After all, in London, dogs and cats were established companion animals. No sane person would consider eating their companion animals.

He stood in the basement under the house in Greenwich, wiping the sweat from his forehead with his shirtsleeve. It wasn't so much the heatwave which triggered his perspiration as the excitement associated with his work on the fox skin. The basement itself was as cool as an ice queen's groin.

One interest had led to another, from drug development and invaluable laboratory animals to taxidermy, companion animals and meatloaves. He was a visionary. A man without vision would never be the CEO of a successful company.

You didn't have to come from a pharmaceutical background to become the CEO of a pharmaceutical corporation. Jarrow had studied law, economics, biology and solid-state physics. He had discovered his interest in animals as a young technical assistant. Soon, a range of pets in his home became a complement to the laboratory animals. In later years, taxidermy became a hobby. The corridor on the first floor of his house was filled with stuffed creatures. Sparrows, starlings, pheasants, crows, hawks, owls, parrots, cats, dogs, squirrels, foxes, deer, fishes, lynxes, snakes, one bear and his wife.

The mounted Lisa-Marie stood naked at the bottom end of the corridor. Curly, amber hair. Eyes like blue crystal. Red-painted fingernails. Nice breasts with light-pink areolae. Shaved pubic area. A seductive pose. Lisa-Marie as a stuffed figure was as attractive as she had been as a living woman. Her vagina and anus were as pleasing now as before. Why she had married an ugly man like himself was a mystery, he thought, though it proved physical appearance wasn't essential to a successful marriage.

It would be a waste to throw away the meat of the animals or his wife. Although Mother's meatloaf recipe was based on beef, it was fine to replace the beef with, for example, fox or dolphin or Lisa-Marie. Mother didn't need to know everything about her son's inventiveness. The meat of his wife had been enough for five meatloaves. The exact number of meatloaves was irrelevant. Smaller loaves would result in a larger number; bigger loaves would result in a smaller number.

That Jarrow consumed his wife's intestines, flesh and brain was neither shocking nor startling. Cannibalism wasn't fiction. Cannibals had existed for hundreds of thousands of years in many parts of the world. Regarding eating habits, Dirk Jarrow was thus a kind of gastronomic traditionalist.

Bruno sat in the middle of the kitchen table like a living decoration. The turtle seemed to be sleeping and eating at the same time. His head was in part retracted inside his shell, his eyes closed, his jaws working on a parsnip.

"I know the heat makes you drowsy, buddy," Jarrow said and tapped the turtle on the back.

Bruno didn't comment.

"You'll get your squirrel meatloaf," Jarrow said. "I love squirrel too but my meatloaf of choice for today is fox."

Bruno didn't comment.

"What do you want to drink with your meatloaf, Bruno?" He moved the turtle. "Pear-flavoured soft drink?"

Bruno opened his eyes but said nothing.

Jarrow nodded. "I see, buddy. Pear-flavoured as usual."

To reach the bag of Brussels sprouts, he first had to move the dead man's arm. The corpse had been in the chest freezer for fourteen days, ever since he had stolen it from a crematorium. An insignificant theft, if you could call it theft at all. No one would miss a supposedly cremated cadaver.

He put the Brussels sprouts in a saucepan with toilet water. He never used water from the kitchen for cooking. The kitchen sink tap was Bruno's shower, and the sink itself was Bruno's swimming pool. Jarrow waved to the turtle, who was swimming around in the water-filled sink. When Bruno had finished bathing, Jarrow wiped him dry with a dishcloth.

The oven-baked meatloaves were ready. He opened the oven and took them out. Both loaves were piping hot. "Dinner's ready. Are you as hungry as I am?"

Bruno nodded. He wasn't a talkative buddy, but a nod was always an answer.

Lisa-Marie said nothing. She already sat at the kitchen table, silent and naked and sexy. The tip of her electric tongue poked at the corner of her mouth. Her porcelain teeth sparkled like snow crystals. The ringlets of her hair glimmered like spun gemstones. Her bright-blue custom-made eyes in acrylic twinkled like vase filler beads. The artificial joints in her legs, arms, fingers, neck and lower jaw gave his wife an enchanting appearance unrivalled by any blow-up sex doll in his collection. Jarrow grinned. He understood why his wife was dead silent. She was longing for their upcoming bedroom activities.

• THIRTY-SEVEN •

ELMER GRITT STUDIED the young lady from the front of the first car of the three-car tram. She must have had her hair dyed. The girl's natural hair was brilliant scarlet. Too brilliant scarlet for a natural hair colour. Perhaps the result of a mutation. Now her hair was crow-black. For what purpose? Her pose, her figure, her anatomy, revealed the truth. The young woman was none other than Cat Milton. The famous model. Victor Milton's beautiful daughter. Stockmayer's patient. The girl who had been prescribed Roxonodonol.

The tram accelerated. The aisle of the first car was crowded but unproblematic. He pulled the gun out of his jacket pocket, aimed, and squeezed the trigger.

Cat noticed one of her shoelace knots had come undone. She crouched to tie the shoelace and heard, in the same instant, a dull thud from one of the tram car's side windows above her head, as though a sparrow had collided with the window. She then dismissed the bird theory. Something lay on the floor by her feet. Something which hadn't been there earlier. Something that had smashed against the *inside* of the window glass. The object looked like a miniature badminton shuttlecock. With a pointed top. An arrow-like projectile?

She rose from her crouched position. She trembled. Her heart thundered. Had no other passengers noticed the projectile?

A man at the far end of the car stared in her direction—stared at *her*. A bald man. Round cheeks. Broad shoulders. Glasses. Beige jacket.

Elmer fired the pistol again. The tram lurched. The projectile rattled against an upright steel post in the aisle and landed in the lap of an elderly woman. Passengers started to shout.

• • •

Baginski threw himself out of his seat with a semi-automatic pistol in each hand and fired a dozen rounds. The deafening noise from the discharging guns exploded in the confined space of the tram car. Elmer Gritt staggered backwards. Blood sprayed from his chest and neck. Passengers screamed. Children cried. Gritt expressed more surprise than pain. He shifted his attention from the girl to Baginski, put the tranquillizer gun back into his jacket pocket, produced an Uzi and squeezed off three bursts. Shrieking passengers in the aisle went down in the crossfire.

She couldn't believe her eyes or ears. She was caught in some zero time, denied time for reflection, robbed of her rationality. Was it the bald man who had fired the arrow-like projectile? Who was the man who had jumped out of his seat with booming guns in his hands? Cat had had a quick glance at this second man before she had tried to dive for cover. Pinewood-blond hair. Pale face. Tall, with an athletic build. Black suit, white gloves.

Two men. A duel. Gunfire with real, lethal guns. Innocent passengers dead or injured.

In a soundless gap between flying bullets, Cat heard one of the men shout, "Stay away from the girl, Gritt. She's mine."

The name of one of the men is Gritt? Who's he? And who's the girl the voice referred to? Are they fighting about me?

It can't have happened for real. It must be a nightmare movie, as dark as midnight, as alien as resurrected dinosaurs in hats and raincoats. The action sequence before her eyes appeared to be playing in slow-motion. The bald duellist had already been hit by a shower of bullets but he refused to go down.

Baginski ducked. The window glass blew apart above his head. The tram kept rushing downhill. In front of him, yelling and dying passengers were falling. The hard rain from Gritt's bullet-spitting Uzi submachine gun tore away the padding in the seats, thrashed the ceiling lights and blew out another four or five windows. The tram car's upright steel posts clanked and jangled in the spray of lethal metal. Bullets punched straight through the carriage wall behind Baginski. With the speed of a panther, he reloaded both Glocks.

The tram drove too fast down Roderick Avenue. He heard the blaring sounds from car horns outside, both to the left and to the right of the track. He wondered how the driver was doing. Was the driver dead? That would explain the uncontrolled speed. The conductor, a middle-aged woman, was dead. She lay on the floor of the first-car aisle. Three bullet holes in her forehead. Her uniform stained with gore and brains. Face distorted in horror. Her lifeless accusing eyes fixed in Baginski's direction. Why such a reproaching stare? He did have a valid travel ticket. He wasn't a fare-dodging passenger. His good morals prevented him from being one. The conductor's blaming gaze was therefore lacking substance. He disliked unfairness. He fired two shots into the dead woman's face—one bullet through each eye. Her accusing stare vanished. Justice had been served.

A loud bang shook the speeding tram. A collision with a car? Cat was flung sideways. She hit her head on one of the upright metal posts, tripped on someone's leg and fell to the floor. The world was spinning. Her eyelids turned heavy. A gloom embraced her. She floated away into the rolling darkness.

• THIRTY-EIGHT •

EIGHT MONTHS EARLIER. The Criterion, the historic restaurant at Piccadilly Circus. The night she first met him.

Cat is out on the town with two childhood friends. All three girls left Blackfield for London many years ago. All three found success. The brunette Rosanna is a top economist at one of the world's largest banks. She has her office in Canary Wharf, one of the most important financial districts on the planet. The blonde Marjorie is a prosperous and ever-sought-after stage actress in the West End. She has also starred in a number of Hollywood films. The three women live stressful lives and seldom find the time to see each other. This night out together is their first in three years.

The Criterion is one of the most enchanting and memorable restaurants in London, and the world, in Cat's opinion. The dining room and bar in neo-Byzantine design. The impressive gold ceiling. The wonderful marble columns. The massive windows. The fascinating mirror walls. The majestic decorations. The pearl-white tablecloths. The pleasant lighting.

The Criterion is crowded with celebrities and the rich. Film stars, sports personalities, tycoons, artists, politicians, entrepreneurs, writers. Even so-called 'common' people find their way here, tourists and Londoners. Cat, Rosanna and Marjorie are three happy singletons. Tonight, they aren't looking for boys. Rosanna drinks red wine. Marjorie has champagne. Cat enjoys mineral water. They look at the menu.

Further down the long room there's a bunch of boys. Fifteen professional football players. All of them are dressed in a dark suit, white shirt and colourful tie. Cat doesn't know a thing about football but she knows these boys are professional football players. As a supermodel, it's impossible not to recognise your contemporary celebrities. The right people should appear at the right parties at the right venues. No wonder the right people find the right love at the right moment.

She is in the Criterion's Long Bar to ask for vegetarian snacks to go with her mineral water.

Someone says, "Hi."

Cat turns her head and looks at him.

They don't have to introduce themselves. She can feel he knows who she is. She knows who *he* is.

"You have the most beautiful eyes in the world," he says.

Cat laughs—a mechanical laughter, just for show. She utters a dutiful "Thank you."

Despite his unoriginal pick-up line, a pleasant tingling arises in her stomach. This isn't the first time she's had compliments on her appearance, though tonight the words came from *him*. Roy Beckman isn't just the country's most talented new star in football. He's also very attractive.

"May I ask you something?" Roy says.

"How could I stop you?"

"Is it true what the papers say about your hair?"

She giggles. "What?"

"The brilliant scarlet is your natural hair colour. Is it true?"

"Same shade as the red maple in November. That's what my dad says. Maybe I was born with a genetic error? What do you think?"

"I think you're wonderful. You're the most beautiful girl I've ever seen."

"And how many times have you used that line?"

"Not creative enough?"

"Not creative at all. It's awful."

"Sorry."

"Don't be sorry. And don't try to be too clever. I don't want to hear lines which sound as if you've practised them a thousand times. Got it?"

He laughs. "You are ... what shall I say ... a very special girl."

They talk for a few minutes in the crowded bar. Roy is much taller than Cat. She has to bend her neck to meet his gaze.

Two days later, they will read about themselves in the gossip magazines: a fictional romantic story accompanied by innocent photos from the Criterion's Long Bar. Although the story is made up, the gossip press has predicted what will happen. Three days after the article's publication, he calls her and asks her out. It's the beginning of what will be known in the media as the Milton-Beckman saga.

• THIRTY-NINE •

THE TRAM SHOOK, lurched, groaned. People shouted and kids wept. Some passengers seemed apathetic, while others pounded on windows and doors. A fascinating mix of moods, Baginski thought. Human nature was captivating. At the calculated moment, he threw himself backwards in the aisle, aimed the reloaded Glocks upwards, staring into Gritt's face. In Baginski's field of vision, Gritt now appeared upside down. The bleeding giant searched for the girl. At the moment, he ignored Baginski. The girl had become more important than the fight.

Baginski discharged multiple semi-automatic shots from both handguns. The tram car was again drowned in ear-splitting noise. The bullets hit Gritt in the abdomen, the chest, the head. More blood and splinters of skull bone sprayed. The tram wobbled. Bullets smacked through the ceiling and shattered windows. Gritt raised his eyebrows. Again, he'd been reminded of Baginski's presence. The bald man swung the Uzi around and aimed at his opponent. The predominant expression on Elmer Gritt's blood-smeared face shifted from surprise to irritation.

Baginski noticed the lorry a fraction of a second before the collision. Somehow, he managed to hold onto something—a floor-mounted litterbin. The terrible crash hurled the tram off its track. The Uzi flew out of Gritt's fist. Gritt lost his foothold and was heaved backwards. Passengers, alive and dead, spun around inside the tram car like rags in a tumble dryer.

The tram turned in a semi-circle and ploughed forward on the tarmac, slamming into street lights and cars. Electric sparks flew. Metal and plastic twisted and snapped. Glass broke and clattered.

Baginski scrambled to his feet. Through a shattered window he saw the derailing tram had come to rest at the northern end of Yarmouth Bridge. The overhead wire had fallen and an electrical enclosure further up the street was on fire. He considered killing all the passengers who still could be killed. Survivors were potential witnesses. Now he heard the sirens from approaching emergency vehicles and decided to spare survivors. He had no time to stay here.

Gritt was already on his way out of the wrecked tram car. Baginski shot him in the back with several rounds. More blood splattered. Gritt just shrugged, pried the demolished doors apart with his hands and stepped outside. The doors snapped shut again with an electric spark and a popping sound. Gritt turned around and stared back through the cracked glass of the door. Baginski raised his pistols and fired a total of six shots straight through the glass. Gritt caught the flying bullets with his opened mouth and swallowed them. One bullet split two front teeth on its way down his throat. He grinned and then left.

Baginski tried to open the doors. The locking mechanism, an integrated slamlock type, had been smashed up pretty bad. He gave the doors a couple of shoulder tackles. Nothing happened. He pointed one of the guns at the lock and pumped off three shots. The lock exploded. He pushed the doors apart, scrambled outside and took up the hunt for Gritt.

Yarmouth Bridge was a one-hundred-and-fifteen-foot-tall cantilever bridge. It stretched over both train railway lines and a multilane road traffic thoroughfare. Adjacent to the northern end of the bridge lay Yarmouth Square. Beyond the southern end stood the concrete silhouette of Crow City District College. The burning-hot air was devoid of wind. The sun, a celestial ball of fire, loomed over the cityscape like a merciless monstrosity. No clouds. No birds. Not even crows. The glowing white-hot sky was reminiscent of a salt flat.

He spotted him. Gritt was running across the bridge in a southerly direction. The giant was a hundred feet away. Baginski fired both Glocks multiple times. Two rounds brushed the bridge steel railing and deflected. Four bullets slammed into Gritt's body—his shoulders, his back, his legs. More blood splattered.

Gritt staggered but refused to fall. He recovered his balance and continued towards the southern side of the bridge.

Fear thumped through her like an electric shock. However, Cat was determined not to faint. She realised the tram—or what was left of it—had crashed somewhere. Wailing, whimpering, injured and dead passengers lay scattered everywhere.

She could hear sirens. Her mental fight against the heatwave continued for an eternity. She managed to scramble to her feet. Her body was aching. Her legs were as steady as cooked spaghetti.

She peered through a cracked window and was struck by a vertiginous view of road and train traffic a hundred feet below. She pulled back from the window, her hand searching the aching bump on her head. The bump began to assume the size of a golf ball, or so she imagined.

She grimaced, wanted to weep, *refused* to weep. Instead, she clenched her teeth. *We have crashed on Yarmouth Bridge. Where's my mobile phone?*

Less than three minutes had passed since the crash, Baginski thought. Authorities hadn't yet closed Yarmouth Bridge. Traffic was still moving from south to north. The derailed tram was blocking the opposite lane. The sirens from emergency vehicles sounded stronger and stronger.

Gritt stopped, wheeled around, aimed the Uzi at his pursuer and discharged the weapon. Terrified drivers in the northbound lane tried to swerve.

Baginski threw himself and returned fire. He felt he floated on air. Bullets from his thundering Glocks cut through the dazzling daylight. He landed on the bonnet of a Ford, bounced against the windscreen, dropped onto the bridge road surface, got to his feet and kept shooting.

A few stray bullets rattled the overhanging structure of the cantilever bridge. The Ford was hit from behind by a Volvo, which was struck by a Datsun, which was rammed by an Audi. Vehicles honked everywhere. Baginski rounded the Ford and continued to fire, shot after shot after shot. Multiple rounds slashed into Gritt's body. The sun kept spraying its relentless fire. Blood spattered onto the bridge surface. Bullets rattled the bridge's railings. Pistols banged. Spent cartridges clattered. Reflections of sunlight danced across glass and metal. Gritt smiled a blood-dripping smile, dropped the Uzi, climbed one of the structural steel trusses and jumped off the bridge.

Baginski peered over the railing. Throughout the vertical one-hundred-and-fifteen-foot jump, Gritt kept his dynamic pose of a running man, not bothered by the sudden absence of a surface under his feet. The big man landed on the roof of an accelerating passenger train and continued to sprint along the roof in the train's direction of acceleration.

The bald figure stopped and looked up at Baginski. Gritt seemed unmoved. He didn't even appear to be concerned about his blood loss. Soon, the train with Elmer Gritt on its roof disappeared beyond the concrete horizon of the urban landscape.

Baginski wasn't surprised. He knew what was going on. Later he would be more effective in his dealing with Gritt. At the moment, to slow Gritt down, to make him lose time, was more important than to stop him. In that respect, Baginski had succeeded. Gritt hadn't got to the girl. Baginski, having the girl within easy reach, had the advantage. Any time, the police would be here. He returned to the crashed tram to finish his mission.

Elmer scooped up the mobile from his blood-filled jacket pocket. A gunshot had scratched the display. He called his home number. The phone seemed to be working.

"Veronica?"

"Elmer? Where are you? It's our wedding anniversary."

"I know it's our wedding anniversary, Veronica. I love you. I love you with all of my heart. I had some problems at work. Hence the delay. Everything is fine."

"What problems at work?"

"Nothing serious. I just had one of those days when not everything is straightforward."

"Hurry home."

"I'm on my way, Veronica."

Baginski checked the pistol magazines as he entered the wrecked tram. Seven bullets left. More than enough to finish the job. He only needed a single bullet to kill Catriona Milton. A well-placed gunshot in the girl's pretty head.

• FORTY •

"GET OUT OF the way, you damn plodder." Ebba stamped on the accelerator pedal. The Porsche whizzed past the slowcoach.

The lorry driver waved. Ebba gave him the finger. The driver frowned. She laughed. Her car speeded up. The lorry became a flea-sized spot in the rear-view mirror.

The flight to Barcelona would depart in less than two hours. Important work and big money were at stake. Then the luxury dinner and all-night party.

At last she saw the motorway exit. Terrible traffic. Awful exit ramp. The Porsche veered with screeching tyres. In the middle of the curve Ebba pushed a cigarette into the corner of her mouth. Traffic jam. The car stopped dead. The car tore away. Traffic jam. The car stopped dead. The car tore away. Traffic jam. And so on. The phone screamed in her skirt pocket. "Damn." She wanted the answering function to kick in but the call might be from Cat or the Supreme office or the event organisers in the Catalan capital, so she took the call. "Hello?" She blew cigarette smoke above the dashboard.

"Nice to hear your voice again, Miss Sjödal."

Holy crap. Dirk Jarrow. This time around, I won't mention his name on the damn phone.

She coughed smoke. "Sir ... what a surprise."

"A positive surprise, I hope." Pause. "Where are you?"

She honked the horn at another timewaster. "On my way in to Heathrow. And I'm stressed."

"You drive yourself?"

"Yeah."

"I thought top models preferred to ride in limousines."

"I love to drive. I love fast and fancy cars."

"Fast and fancy cars for a fast and fancy girl." Jarrow chuckled. "Flight destination?"

"Barcelona." She checked her snazzy lipstick in the rear-view mirror.

"Bikini photography at an exotic beach?" His hard chuckle rattled Ebba's ear.

"Um, that's right." She steered the Porsche in the direction of Terminal 5.

"Your return flight?"

"Late evening, the day after tomorrow."

"The pictures would have been extraordinary, no doubt."

Would have been? "What do you mean, sir?"

"I mean you won't travel to Barcelona today."

"What?" Behind the wheel, she twitched. She had modelling contracts to fulfil. She had the responsibility to live up to her many commitments. Industry people counted on her services. She must be in Barcelona this afternoon.

"I dislike having to repeat myself, miss. What did I say?"

A blazing shiver jolted her. "That I ... cancel ... I have to cancel my flight ... I won't travel to Barcelona today."

"Spot on. Your perceptiveness is outstanding, Miss Sjödal. We've reached another agreement. Brilliant."

"What do you want?"

"How's your best friend?"

"What do you mean?"

"Your best friend was your responsibility, Miss Sjödal. We don't know why your best friend has begun to dig into the circumstances surrounding her father's death. Could you provide a satisfactory explanation for your friend's actions?"

They won't hurt Cat, will they? No, they won't. Jarrow is only trying to scare me. He has succeeded in scaring me. This performance has been taken too far. I just wanted to hurt Cat in a figurative manner. I wanted Roy, I still want Roy, and Roy wants me. Roy doesn't want Cat. I just wanted to hurt Cat on the battlefield of love. Cat is my best friend. Best friends must be able to compete against each other, mustn't they? I had no idea how Yolexus Enterprise would use the information I provided. I don't want to be involved anymore. I don't want any further contact with Jarrow and his corrupt corporation.

"Are you listening, Miss Sjödal?"

The Porsche jerked into a parking space. "I'm listening, sir."

"And?"

"I don't know why Cat is acting in the way you described."

"Are you certain?"

"Yes."

"Untruths have negative health effects."

"I'm not lying."

"I would advise you to think again, Miss Sjödal. And now, a different matter altogether. I want to see you in the bar at the Golden Plaza Hotel in Paddington."

The memory returned. The memory of Jarrow's mention of a new meeting. "When?"

"At three p.m. the day after tomorrow. Thus, you have plenty of time to cancel your programme in Catalonia."

"How should I explain this to my employers?"

"You're an expert at lying and deceiving. You're a natural talent. You'll be able to come up with something smart to say."

"What's the meeting about?" Ebba remained in the driver's seat of the Porsche, smoking the cigarette, looking through the windscreen. Heathrow was wrapped in thirty-six-degree heat. How grim. She could do with a cold drink. A boozy ice cream cocktail would be nice.

"An update to your contract with us, Miss Sjödal."

She puffed on the cig. "I understand."

"Good. I'm a man of my word. If I were unreliable, I wouldn't be the CEO of a successful corporation. When I say this whole deal will be completed very soon, I mean it."

"Right."

"This is the last time the organisation will use your exclusive services. I promise."

"I see."

"Magnificent. And Miss Sjödal?"

"Yes?"

"You'll arrive at the Golden Plaza Hotel alone and you won't tell anyone about the meeting."

"I understand."

"How formidable. Mutual understanding is essential. A lack of understanding comes with negative consequences. Negative consequences, in turn, are both tragic and painful."

"I wouldn't even think of telling anyone, sir."

"A healthy attitude, Miss Sjödal. By the way, Roy Beckman happens to be your best friend's boyfriend. You're fucking your best friend's boyfriend and it doesn't seem to bother you in the least. Your skill to dupe is priceless."

They must be tapping the phones. The house in Notting Hill was probably bugged. Roy's apartment in Pimlico too. How else could Jarrow know so much about her privacy? Not even the gossip press knew she was sleeping with Roy Beckman. *Oh my freaking God. As if my life wasn't messy enough already.*

She puffed faster and faster on the cigarette. "I must finish the conversation now, sir. If that's okay."

"It's altogether okay, Miss Sjödal. You have a lot of things to do now, haven't you?"

"Well, I shall see you soon, sir. At the bar. The Golden Plaza Hotel, Paddington."

Jarrow's laughter was as friendly as the howl of a werewolf. "There's nothing I look forward to with greater joy."

Ebba ended the call, swore multiple times, got out of the car and spat out the cigarette butt.

She moved to the British Airways information desk in Terminal 5. She had a flight to cancel and she did it. Luckily, Barcelona would be waiting for her until the new deal with Yolexus was completed. Supreme didn't need to know what she was planning to do, she decided. She would later 'explain' to Supreme and Anita Scriver.

Jarrow was right. She was a great liar. Sometimes she was so good she fooled herself. This time she would fabricate a credible story which would explain why she didn't show up in Catalonia.

She wondered what Cat was doing. Jarrow had said Cat had started to look into the facts surrounding her dad's death. What on earth did that mean? Had Cat's dad been murdered? A murder staged by Jarrow's organisation? Cat's dad assassinated by a so-called problem-solver? What was his name again? Bagin something? No. Baginski. Who the heck was he? The problem-solver who had taken Krass out of the equation?

"Someone who makes your worst nightmares look like infantile nonsense. You don't want Baginski to pay you a visit."

She turned onto the motorway, returning to central London. She lit a cig and opened the glove box. The glass bear in multicoloured mosaic peered out at her. The memory of Marja. The symbol of old friendship and rotten secrets. An unwelcome voice in her head said: *If Cat's dad was murdered, it's partly your fault, isn't it?*

"No," she thought aloud. She was a victim of blackmail. In addition, she didn't know the details of Yolexus Enterprise's shadowy affairs. She wasn't aware of the extent of the conspiracy. She didn't know Cat's dad's life had been in danger.

Jarrow was a crackpot. Insane. And Krass? The creepy reporter was better dead than alive anyway. Regarding Krass, Jarrow had been right, after all. What if Krass had been double-dealing in several affairs? Imagine if the gossip journalist's plan had been to sell the nasty photographs, sell them to Jarrow, and pretend to her he still had the photos in his possession, to maintain his hold over her. Could that theory be possible?

Krass had been a sleazebag but no fool. What if the untiring paparazzo had found out about Yolexus's interest in BioFutura's research? Ebba found no reason to reject her speculation. Krass had been a specialist in finding out stuff about celebrities. He had shown a perverted interest in Cat and seemed to know everything about her. Therefore, he must have known about Victor Milton. How much did Cat know about what was going on? Should I warn her? Warn her about Jarrow? Do I dare to warn her about Jarrow? I'm sleeping with Roy, but Cat is my best friend after all. Cat is still my best friend. Isn't she?

• FORTY-ONE •

CAT CROSSED YARMOUTH Square, half-stumbling, half-running. A double-decker bus was about to depart from the stop at the corner of Hill Street and Denton Crescent. She boarded it on impulse. It turned out to be a number 93 with the destination of Wintergreen, via the city centre. The bus number didn't matter. She would have got on any bus. She just wanted to get away from here. Away from here to anywhere, as fast as possible.

Passengers ogled her. The driver glared at her. She didn't blame them for staring. She knew she looked like she felt—unkempt. Was she bleeding from somewhere? She touched the bump on her forehead, then looked at her hand. No blood. The last time she had looked in a mirror was on her visit to the hair salon. She took a seat on the upper deck, as far back as possible, as distant from other passengers as possible. What could she do? What on earth was going on? Who was the big man who refused to die despite dozens of pistol shots in his body? Who was the suit-cladded gunfighter?

Stay away from the girl, Gritt. She's mine.

She didn't dare, and couldn't, go home. If she did, she would endanger Mum and Jan's lives. Perhaps Mum and Sis were already in great danger. What the heck could she do?

Her hands trembled. She fumbled in her handbag, shook out her phone and called.

"Oberon Clinic." An unknown woman's voice.

"I called Dr. Stockmayer's direct number."

"Dr. Stockmayer isn't available at the moment. Your call was forwarded to reception. Are you a patient?"

"Hmm. Yes."

"Do you want to leave a message?"

"No, thank you. Goodbye."

She dug out the card with the home phone number scribbled on the reverse. She took a deep breath, called the number and wondered why she had needed to take a deep breath. *Your wellbeing is my professional responsibility.*

He took the call. "Hello? This is Roger Stockmayer."

"It's me—Miss Milton. Sorry to bother you at home."

"An irrational thought, Miss Milton. If I thought you were bothersome, I wouldn't have provided you with my home phone number. I gave you my number so you could call me anytime. How are you doing? I've been thinking about you."

"Er, you've been thinking about me?"

"I mean I was wondering how you were finding the drug. Any problems?"

"No problems at all. At least not with Rox-1."

"What's up?"

"I ... I don't know ... I dare not be alone right now and I don't know who to talk to."

"You sound sad."

"I *am* sad. Distraught."

"What's happened?"

She cleared her throat and restrained a sob. "The horrible event will be reported on tonight's TV news and in tomorrow's papers. As we speak, it's all over the Internet."

"Where are you?"

"I'm on a bus on the way to the city centre." The images from the gunfight rushed back to her. She swallowed a cry.

"Does it pass via Central Station?"

"I think so. Bus 93. Yes, it passes via Central."

"Get off at Central. I'll pick you up."

Stockmayer's cool snow-white Mercedes-Benz swept through the heatwave like an out-of-place ice floe. Cat imagined the vehicle constituted an extension of the man's snow-white office. The front passenger seat was as treacherously comfortable as a visitor's seat at the clinic.

He glanced at her. "You have a bump on your forehead and your eyes show anxiety. You may have been on board a crashing tram or bus. The famous model wanted to avoid attention. That's why she disappeared from the scene of the accident. Is it something along those lines which will be reported on tonight's television news and in tomorrow's papers?"

"Are you always that fast with your theories?"

"You've dyed your hair. Why?"

"It's a long story."

"As part of establishing an apparent image of yourself."

"What's that supposed to mean?"

"The crow-black hair camouflages the real Catriona Milton. You have so far tried to hide your identity behind the darkness of sunglasses and beneath unglamorous clothes. Then you wanted to do something extra."

"Are you always that fast with your theories?"

"Black hair suits you."

"No."

"Your natural scarlet hair suits you too."

"You mean olive-green?"

The corners of Stockmayer's mouth tipped up.

She didn't return his smile. "On Monday, I'll be back at work. I cannot turn up with black hair."

They were quiet for a while. She understood he had realised she didn't want to talk about the black dye. He didn't need to know the details of permanent, semi-permanent or temporary dye types. He didn't need to know the black was temporary. If she wanted, she could wash her hair and regain the natural scarlet as soon as tonight. And she would. After just a few washes, the black would be gone.

The Mercedes rolled up Colvin Street and then turned onto Westminster Road.

She looked at him. "Where are we going?"

"To my place."

Something tingled in her stomach. "I thought we were going down to the clinic."

"I haven't finished today's work in my library just yet."

"I don't want to be an inconvenience."

"You'll never be one. Without patients, I wouldn't have a career." His smile was a bit too wide. "You're an interesting case, and in more than one respect."

She said nothing. She didn't know how to respond to the comment. She wondered how Sis was doing. Had Jan found Zimmer's contact details? Cat checked her mobile for new voicemails. Nothing from Sis. Phone battery down to almost zero. Dammit. She put the phone back into her handbag and looked up. "Where do you live, Dr. Stockmayer?"

"In the Springlake district."

"Nice. Have you lived there long?"

"Just long enough to fall in love with the area."

"I see." Pause. "I was just curious."

"Curiosity is a healthy characteristic, Miss Milton. Without curiosity, humanity would remain stagnant and primitive. We have curious people to thank for our modern, advanced society. Could you imagine an indifferent Bill Gates or Nikola Tesla?"

She looked at him but said nothing.

The Mercedes swooshed northwards via sunlight-spattered city pictures of concrete, granite, steel and glass. At Crowfield

Way, the car passed the modern skyscraper Rainbow Tower. She cast a glance at the tall building.

"The day after tomorrow I'll give a talk at Rainbow Tower," Stockmayer said.

"About what?" She peered towards the building's top at the edge of the sky.

"Dyssomnias. A category of sleep disorders characterised by disturbances in the volume, quality and timing of sleep."

"Sounds interesting," she said, not because she meant it but because it appeared to be an appropriate thing to say. "Is it something I ought to attend?"

"No. You already know everything you need to know. Also, narcolepsy is just one of many dyssomnias recognised by modern science. Your particular illness occupies less than five minutes of my sixty-minute talk."

But I'm special, she thought. You said so yourself earlier, my dear Dr. Stockmayer. It seems like my disease has mutated into something unknown. The amazing effect must be kept secret until further notice. Is the subject too sensitive to have me at your upcoming event at Rainbow Tower?

"Miss Milton?"

"Yes?"

"Do you remember our discussion about the lion statues?"

"Whizzing electrons and molecules in our nervous systems. And something about something called photons. Just don't ask me whether I grasp how these particles function."

He glanced at her. "I didn't mention, by any chance, neural cell surface glycoproteins or atomic force microscopy analysis of central nervous system cell morphology, did I?"

"Uh?"

"Never mind. Does the bump on your head have anything to do with the effects associated with the imbalance between your internal and external realities?"

"No. Not at all. What happened today was experienced by a lot of people."

He nodded. "The TV news tonight will confirm your story."

The car crossed the River Claxton via Springlake Bridge in a northeasterly direction. On the horizon, Paradise Park came into view. She was furious at Roy. She missed Ebba. How far was it from here to Stockmayer's house? How much did she dare tell her doctor about today's ordeal? How long could she stay at his place tonight? How fast could she get in touch with Sis? Had Ebba returned from Milan? What would Ebba say when Cat told her about Roy's infidelity?

An inexhaustible stream of questions invaded her mind.

• FORTY-TWO •

BAGINSKI STOLE A navy-blue Vauxhall Astra from a car park on Hill Street. Bad luck the girl had got away. Priorities had changed. It would take time to retrieve the girl, while the tracking transmitter, which the High Court judge and triple spy from NanoScoop Technology Group, Esmeralda Northcutt, Baginski's sporadic mistress, had kindly placed in the red BMW, unveiled Gritt's movements. Gritt was once again the primary target and the girl the secondary target. Gritt belonged to the same organisation as the late Umberto Antonetti and was at least as immoral as Antonetti. Baginski would focus on Gritt now and fix the girl later.

The computer in his suit jacket pocket wasn't larger than an e-book reader. The GPS program said Gritt was driving his BMW through the city centre. Baginski drove the Vauxhall Astra along Chapman Avenue, Kingfisher Street, Carriage Lane, High Street and past Blackfield's Cathedral. He was closing in on Gritt. The BMW was less than two miles away. How did Gritt's newest plans look? Was he hot on the trail of the girl again so soon? Or was his current action, driving through the city centre eastwards, a deception?

His hunt for Gritt continued towards the hilly district of Goston. The distance between the BMW and the Vauxhall wasn't greater than eight hundred yards and kept shrinking. Gritt turned onto Goston Road. When Baginski steered the Vauxhall onto the same road, he saw the BMW with the naked eye. Gritt stopped in front of the main entrance to Goston Cemetery. The graveyard where Milton's ashes had been buried.

• FORTY-THREE •

(((((((((((**MISS MILTON?**)))))))))))
She dreamt someone called her name.
(((*Miss Milton?*)))
The voice. Closer and closer. The familiar voice.
His hand on her breast.
No, not at all. It was a car seat belt which touched her breast.
Miss Milton?
Yes? I can hear you. But I can't see you. Where are you?
"Miss Milton?"
Her eyelids opened. Cat looked around. She found herself in a car. Indeed, her seat belt was brushing against her left breast. The memories surfaced. The tram crash. The bus journey into the city. Stockmayer's Mercedes-Benz.
"I'm sorry. I must have fallen asleep."
"You did fall asleep. Nothing to apologise for."
"Why did you let me sleep? Why didn't you wake me?"
She looked through the windscreen. How fast an afternoon could pass. Already twilight? The Mercedes wasn't moving. She didn't recognise the urban landscape outside the car windows. She had no idea where she was. Somewhere in Springlake, she guessed. He had said he lived in Springlake.
He leaned towards her, very close, almost too close. "Every opportunity to take a daily nap is good for you. Reduces EDS."

"How long did I sleep?" The scent of his aftershave floated up her nose. She couldn't deny she enjoyed the scent of it.

"No more than five minutes."

"My guess was five hours."

"You look refreshed. Do you feel better now?"

Your well-being is my professional responsibility.

"Yes. Are we … there? At your place?"

"Yes."

"What will Mrs. Stockmayer say?"

"There is no Mrs. Stockmayer—any longer."

"Why is it dark outside? Is it night already?"

"Illusions conspire." His handsome eyes glimmered. "It isn't evening yet. It's late afternoon. The car windows are somewhat tinted to shield the sharpest sunlight. The car is, at present, in the shade of an oak. The sun just passed behind a strip of cloud. And you're still wearing your dark sunglasses."

Roger Stockmayer lived in a Victorian house at the top of a steep street with a view of Paradise Park. The artificial lake in the middle of the park shone like a mirror. The motley flora, the multifaceted buildings and the rich birdlife of the lake radiated harmony, like in an artist's oil-on-canvas masterpiece.

Cat stood by the panorama window in the living room. "I can understand why you don't have a garden of your own. You don't need one."

"You think I have a nice view?"

"It's phenomenal. I guess you have one of the best views in the City of Crows." She turned away from the massive window. "Before I can even start talking about today's events I need to wash my face with cool water."

He nodded. "I'll show you the bathroom."

The bathroom shone, just like the Oberon office and the Mercedes. Bathroom walls and floor in sparkling white marble. Bathtub, shower cubicle and toilet in dazzling lemon-yellow.

Her doctor looked at her, holding his chin between thumb

and forefinger, like a man deep in thought. "Would you like to use the shower?"

"Thank you for asking, but I'm okay with the washbasin."

"Are you sure?"

"Yeah, I'm sure."

He handed her a bath towel. "Just give me a shout when you've finished. I will treat that bump on your head and that bruise on your upper arm."

"Thank you."

"I'll wait in the living room while you wash your face." He turned away and left, leaving her alone.

She didn't just wash her face. She also washed her hair. To remove all of the black dye with a single wash wasn't possible, though she did manage to rinse away most of it. Her natural scarlet hair reappeared. Thus, she ignored Dad's (*my dead dad's*) advice once again. She didn't want to be blonde, she didn't want to be black-haired, she didn't want any hair dye at all. The bump on her head was still aching, not much now, just a bit. However, the letter to Zimmer was burning in her pocket, hotter than ever. Regarding the letter, she would obey Dad.

She sat in the bathroom armchair and he sat on the lid of the toilet. He lifted her arm. "How did you get the bruise?"

"Antonetti bruised my arm. Professor Umberto Antonetti."

"Who's he?"

"The man who has been stalking me and chasing me ever since the morning I travelled up to Blackfield."

"Do you mean the man who got into your outer reality through your hypnagogic and hypnopompic hallucinations?"

Cat nodded. "The same guy who entered through a mirror in Mum's house."

"Remember, it's about *your* reality. Yours and nobody else's. *Your* truth, nobody else's truth."

"But today's tram crash isn't just about *my* truth. The crash belongs to the real world, the official reality."

"I said earlier I guessed you'd been on board a crashing tram or bus. I was right."

"Aren't you always right about everything?"

He chuckled. Then he wrapped a thin towel around her head, placed an ice pack against her forehead and put another, folded, towel on top of the ice pack.

"Could I have a concussion?"

"I don't think so. None of the symptoms are there. The bump on your forehead isn't a bad bump; it just looks a bit awkward on such a pretty girl."

"Er, I'll be back at work on Monday and the bump must be gone by then."

"I think it will. If not gone altogether by Monday, it can be concealed."

"Okay. If you say so."

"Hold here. Hold the bag against your forehead."

She let his hand guide her fingers to the folded towel on top of the ice pack. "How long?"

"Fifteen minutes." He wrapped another thin towel around her bruised upper arm and placed another ice pack on top of it. "Let's kill fifteen minutes. Tell me about today's events."

They remained seated. In her doctor's bathroom of all places. He seemed to consider every word she spoke. He appeared to study her facial expression, her lips, her eyes. She perceived his presence in a different way than ever before. A denser presence. There wasn't much she could hide or lie about. The media reports would say what had happened anyway. The media reports would confirm her own truth.

Now, talking to her doctor, she omitted only two details: that she had visited the BMLC earlier today, and that the two duellists on board the tram had been fighting about her. She saw no reason to burden Stockmayer with problems of such calibre.

• FORTY-FOUR •

GOSTON CEMETERY. IN front of the main entrance. A deserted strip of road. Dead silence. Triple rows of trees along Goston Road screened Baginski's Vauxhall and Gritt's BMW from the residential buildings along the opposite side.

The cars snailed. Gritt slowed down even further. Baginski braked even more. The BMW halted. The Vauxhall stopped. The distance between the vehicles was less than fifty-five yards. They were caught in a predicament. Baginski knew it, and Gritt knew Baginski knew. A no-extrication-type problem. They had reach the point of no return.

Baginski eased out of his suit jacket. The blood streaked his shirtsleeve, dropping onto the seat and dotting the car mat. The 9mm P round from Gritt's Uzi had ripped his upper arm. He had to do something about it now. Yolexus Enterprise would later arrange professional healthcare. He noted the exit wound. The bullet had passed straight through his arm. He removed his tie, wrapped it over the wounds and pulled tight. It was hard to estimate the extent of the damage caused by a gunshot wound but he thought no major blood vessels had been destroyed. He should have used an antiseptic but had to do without. The bleeding had subsided, at least for the moment. He ignored the pain and put on his jacket again, switched on the car radio and tuned in to the local station, Radio Blackfield.

The news broadcast was dominated by updates about a derailed and crashed tram, dead and injured passengers and a gunfight on Yarmouth Bridge. Victims' descriptions of offender characteristics were fuzzy. The villains' features described by civilian drivers on the bridge were vague as well. Authorities speculated whether there was a correlation between the events on Yarmouth Bridge and the theft of a Vauxhall Astra from a car park at nearby Hill Street.

He wasn't dissatisfied. The authorities knew nothing. Not a single alarming word was uttered about Yolexus Enterprise, Delkorel BioElectronix, BioFutura Systematik or NanoScoop Technology Group. Not a single inconvenient word about a Dirk Jarrow, an Umberto Antonetti, a Victor Milton or an Esmeralda Northcutt. The staggering secret surrounding Nargontanac was invaluable. Was it even possible to relate it to any symbolic multitrillion-dollar value? He didn't think so. The woman in the bathtub in the hotel room in Middlesbrough had drowned just in time.

Sandra Kallikrinos hadn't been aware of the secret, only the circumstances surrounding patient subjects in clinical trials in New Delhi, but that knowledge alone, with a BioFutura employee, had been unfortunate. Jarrow wouldn't be impressed by the publication of a Yolexus–NanoScoop scandal.

He turned off the radio. The deadlock remained, the BMW standing immobile in front of the Vauxhall. Goston Cemetery used to close around sunset. He checked the time on the dashboard clock. About an hour till twilight, though Goston seemed already closed, at least the main entrance. That was when he spotted the sign on the cemetery's ironwork:

CONSTRUCTION WORK IN PROGRESS:
WESTERN GOSTON CEMETERY.
MAIN ENTRANCE CLOSED 1–31 AUG.
NORTHERN ENTRANCE VIA PORTOBELLO LANE
REDUCED OPENING HOURS.

He lowered a window, listened. Nothing. The construction workers must have finished for today. No traffic for the moment on Goston Road. No buzzing insects. Calm ruled both sides of the iron cemetery gates.

Shrieking tyres made his gaze whip forward through the windscreen. The BMW had accelerated with explosive force, the road dust whirling behind it like grey smoke. Elmer Gritt aimed at the closed gates of the cemetery's main entrance. The BMW smashed through the gates with thunderous noise. Baginski raised the Vauxhall's window, put the reloaded Glocks on the passenger seat and stamped on the accelerator. The time had come. The time for the game's final phase. With no return.

He downloaded a detailed map of the area to the pocket computer while the Vauxhall rolled forward on a low gear. Goston Cemetery had the shape of an irregular pentagon. It sloped from west to east. A grid-structure of paved roads for both pedestrians and vehicles covered the entire pentagon. From the western main entrance, there was a downhill start in every direction. The BMW was already out of sight and out of earshot. A trick? Was Gritt waiting, with the BMW's engine turned off, in one of the downhill passages? No other vehicles or pedestrians could be seen or heard. The cemetery was deserted, closed for the night. The northern entrance also seemed to be closed. The area was empty of visitors.

He tried to analyse the situation from Gritt's perspective. He understood why Gritt had come here. The primary reason was the temporarily reduced opening hours had turned the cemetery into an appropriate battlefield. A showdown in an empty cemetery was discreet, whereas a fight in a populous environment, such as a street in the city centre, would attract unwanted attention. The battle aboard the tram had been unfortunate, however inevitable. The girl's movement pattern had triggered the confrontation aboard the tram. The fact that Victor Milton's grave was in Goston Cemetery constituted a mysterious secondary reason for why Gritt would come here. It couldn't be a coincidence that Milton's grave was here.

Baginski stopped dead. He was at an intersection. Splinters of glass lay on the paved road to the far right. Not many shards. Only three. They sparkled like ice in the sunshine. Splinters from a broken headlight? A trace from the BMW? If one of the BMW's headlights had been crushed as the car had rammed the entrance gates and the shards of glass hadn't fallen to the ground until the vehicle had passed here? He estimated the chance was greater than zero.

He steered the Vauxhall onto the road to the right and continued down the gentle slope. To the far right, beyond a vast number of rows of gravestones, he glimpsed the southern cemetery wall with its overhead barbed-wire fence. The view to the left was striking, a landscape of thousands of tombstones and contrasting green sloping lawns as far as he could see, a land of the dead which dissolved in a blurry horizon to the north.

He continued in the easterly direction and reached another intersection. The sinking westbound sun threw light into the car's rear-view mirrors. The reflected sunshine didn't disturb him. Something else bothered him. A reflection of light which shouldn't be there. An artificial backscattering.

He ducked instinctively.

Both front windows exploded.

• FORTY-FIVE •

THEY LEFT THE bathroom and returned to the living room.

"An amazing story," Stockmayer said.

"Frightening is the correct word."

"You must contact the police."

"No. I don't want to."

"Why not?"

"I'm scared. I don't want anything to do with it. I want to be anonymous. Invisible."

"I haven't forgotten you're famous. I understand you're afraid and have a supermodel image to preserve. On the other hand, you witnessed the events. Therefore, you're needed."

"I'm not needed. There are other witnesses."

"What did the two offenders look like?"

"One was bald, broad-shouldered, had a blunt nose, round

cheeks, wine-red spectacles. He was firing with some kind of machine pistol or rifle. The other guy was athletic, had blond hair, spooky face. He had a gun in each hand and wore a suit and gloves like an assassin from some gangster movie."

"What do you mean by 'spooky face'?"

She thought for a while. "The suit-clad man's face was pale like an eggshell and lacked a connection to empathy."

"Your descriptions of the men are remarkably good. How come? Did you get the opportunity to study them before the shooting started? Did you and the men have eye contact?"

"You're asking a lot of questions."

"Was it clear what the conflict was about?"

"No."

"Did someone say something?"

"I don't know. I didn't hear anything."

"Are you certain?"

She hesitated. "Yes." A lie which couldn't be checked out.

"Sit down on the sofa and rest for a while. I'm going to prepare our dinner now."

Cat raised her eyebrows. "Dinner?"

"Don't you eat dinner every day?"

"I do but—"

"Excellent."

His living room was twice the size of Mum's kitchen and living room combined. Black leather armchairs, black wooden chairs, black gate-leg dining table, black leather sofa, black bookshelves, dark-red wallpaper. What a contrast to his office down at the clinic.

The dining table was already set for two. He must have planned to invite her to dinner before they even arrived here. He must have started planning as soon as she'd ended her phone call aboard bus 93. Had he already prepared the food as well?

She called out in the direction of the kitchen, "Is there anything I can help you with?"

He showed up, somewhat changed. He had put on a nice tie

and must have drawn a comb through his hair. "Thank you, but it isn't necessary. Dinner will be ready in a minute."

Let me guess, my dear Dr. Stockmayer. You had already planned to invite me for dinner, and now you're only heating the already cooked food in a microwave oven? Cat smiled. "Okay."

Janice sat on the floor in her room, resting her humped back against the two foot-end bed legs. On the floor, she was invisible from across the street. As long as she sat on the floor nobody could see the ugly Janice Milton from across the street. She did the neighbourhood a favour by being invisible.

Daytime, like now, there was no alternative to sitting on the floor. Daytime, the days she didn't work at the pub, she couldn't darken the room by closing blinds and curtains, since she needed the sunlight, including the blood-red sunset. The window in her room faced westwards. The sunlight helped her fight the many shadows in her mind. Earlier today she had broken that rule of thumb. When she had called Dad's company, she had sat on her bed. An inexcusable negligence. When you sat on the bed you were visible at certain angles from across the street unless the blinds and the curtains were closed. Imagine if someone had seen her. What if someone had spotted the disgusting monster from somewhere across the street?

In her room clung all kinds of dolls and soft toys. On the bed. On the floor. In the bookcase. In the rocking chair. On the small table in the corner. In the wardrobe. On threads hanging from the ceiling. Puppets. Cut-out paper dolls. Animal soft toys. Hard plastic dolls. Porcelain dolls. Voodoo dolls. The room was more than just a space to be, more than just a place for her forced existence. The room was above all a refuge. A hideaway, which allowed her to isolate her ugliness from society. A place where she could fight the demons, tackle the depression, escape into herself and flee into her most intense daydreams.

The cordless phone rang. Jan sat on the floor with the phone in her lap. She answered. "Hello?"

"It's me."

"Cat? How long will you be gone? Where are you? How was it at the BMLC?"

"I'm not sure how it was at the BMLC. In any case, I don't think you can say with certainty that Dad didn't die under mysterious circumstances."

"Where are you now?"

"At Stockmayer's place."

"You mean you're at his clinic?"

"I mean what I said."

"At his home? In his house? Why?"

"I've had an eventful day. Can't talk about it on the phone. I'll tell you later. I've discussed my day with Stockmayer and he has invited me for dinner. Please tell Mum I won't have dinner at home tonight."

"Dinner with Stockmayer? At his place? Are you kidding?"

"Don't mess with me. Could you inform Mum?"

"How? What should I say?"

"Tell her the truth. We're twenty-three, Sis. We're not kids any longer and we can take care of ourselves. We're free to do whatever we want. We don't need Mum's permission. Got it?"

"Mum will get enraged, Cat."

"Mum gets enraged whatever I do."

Jan sighed. "At least I've found information on Karl-Heinz Zimmer. He lives on Montrose Place in Rockthorpe."

"Brilliant."

"I also found a home phone number. I rang. An answering machine started. Zimmer is neither at home nor at BFS."

"He's probably working somewhere else today. We'll go to Montrose Place with Dad's letter a bit later. Later tonight."

"Uninvited?"

"Dad said the matter was urgent."

"Uh-huh."

"After dinner I'll take a taxi to Farnwood. Could we meet outside the Red Unicorn? Shall we say ten p.m.?"

"If I can leave the house without Mum getting suspicious."

"I said we're twenty-three. What if you could stop worrying about what Mum might say about anything? You're old enough to leave the house without Mum's consent. Do you understand?"

"But what should I tell Mum if she asks where I'm going?"

"Tell her you're going to work an extra shift at the pub."

"What if Mum calls the pub to check it out?"

"She would get upset, I guess. But we'll survive."

Candles threw swaying shadows onto the walls of Stockmayer's living room. At the partly opened windows, dark-red curtains stirred like sails in a breeze. His eyes held hers from across the table. A claustrophobic silence filled the room. Time must have halted. The drawn-out soundlessness pinched her like a psychological test. The chair under her bum felt like one of his clinic's visitors' chairs. Why didn't he say something?

"What are you thinking about?" he said.

"All the strange things which have happened. And all the mysterious things which are still happening."

"Mysteries like being here with me tonight?"

"What is reality? How do you define reality?"

"Shall we eat while we talk?"

"Dinner smells wonderful. What is it?"

"Lecsó."

"A Hungarian vegetable stew."

"That's right."

"You guessed I'm still vegetarian."

"And you're still teetotal. There is both pineapple juice and bottled water as an alternative to the wine."

"I can see you're prepared. You guessed right in both cases."

"I hope you'll enjoy the stew."

"I'm sure I will."

"Pineapple juice or mineral water?"

• FORTY-SIX •

THE DEAFENING BANG which tore through the Vauxhall sounded like a discharged rocket launcher. The ducking Baginski had had time to plug his ears with his forefingers. The sparkling tail of a comet whipped through the car, accompanied by a whirlwind of smoke and splinters of glass. The ceiling was demolished but nothing in the car caught fire. The projectile had flown straight through the Vauxhall and detonated on impact with the ground further away in the cemetery.

He used his hand to put pressure on the accelerator pedal. The vehicle rolled through the intersection. He reached for the steering wheel, grabbed it and turned it to the left. He peered through the shattered window. The Vauxhall swung onto a lawn, collided with a headstone and stopped. The car engine whined. The wheels spun on the watered grass. He straightened up, snatched one of the reloaded Glock pistols from the passenger seat, aimed at the BMW through the wrecked window and fired, again and again, almost emptying the fifteen-round mag. The bullets smashed into the BMW's passenger side, blasted two windows and hit Gritt in the head.

Gritt let go of the rocket launcher and turned his gaze towards the Vauxhall. The shots which had slammed into his head didn't seem to bother him at all. The distance between the two cars wasn't greater than twenty yards. Their eyes met. Gazes filtered through two pairs of sunglasses.

Baginski fired again, the last three rounds in the mag. Gritt's right spectacle lens exploded. The bullet must have destroyed his eye and torn through his head. Blood sprayed down Gritt's cheek. The grin on his lips was disturbing. The BMW rolled forward, made a left turn through the intersection and crossed the lawn behind the Vauxhall. Baginski reversed, flooring the accelerator. His car slipped on the grass before the wheels caught. The rear end of the Vauxhall walloped into the BMW's passenger side. The noise of tortured metal cut through the stillness of the cemetery. The dented BMW careened and coughed but didn't stop. Gritt steered down the hill.

Baginski pushed the gear lever, made a tight turn to the right and accelerated. He picked up the other reloaded Glock, pointed the gun through the destroyed side window and fired five shots. Two bullets punctured one of the BMW's rear tyres. Three bullets tore through the rear window. The BMW skidded and swayed and lost speed but kept going. Baginski increased his speed. The Vauxhall closed the gap. The two cars flung forward and downhill, side by side.

Baginski tried to force the BMW off the road. Gritt tried to ram the Vauxhall. The cars pounded into each other, bounced against each other, back and forth.

Metal ripped, screamed, cracked and crushed. Bright sparks whirled like golden snowflakes in a storm.

He controlled the steering wheel with his left hand while firing the Glock with his right. He kept pumping bullets straight into the BMW.

Gritt didn't care to return fire. He focused on driving. Baginski reloaded the first Glock while steering the Vauxhall and shooting at the BMW. A flying rain of bullets hit Gritt. Blood splattered on the dashboard and the windscreen. Baginski let go of the steering wheel altogether, snapped up the other pistol and aimed both weapons at the BMW's bonnet, left front tyre and Gritt's neck and left temple. The guns thundered. The BMW coughed, rattled and whined. Blood flowed from Gritt's gunshot-wounded head.

The burial chapel grew in size in the corner of Baginski's eye. He turned his head forward, grabbed the wheel and swerved to the left. The rushing Vauxhall thrashed the wooden staircase of the chapel, spun around and recovered its forward motion. He braked but not quickly enough. The car ploughed across a surface of loose gravel. He floored the brake pedal. The Vauxhall came to rest in a cloud of dust. He looked for the BMW. He couldn't see it anywhere.

Tranquillity settled over the cemetery. A fragile silence. Baginski had no illusions. He opened the glove box, took out two new and loaded handguns and left the Vauxhall. He sneaked around the chapel, prepared to open fire.

No BMW, neither in sight nor within earshot. No Elmer Gritt. Where had he gone? And so fast?

He had only just rounded the chapel when the Vauxhall exploded in a roaring sea of fire. Baginski threw himself on the ground, shielding his head with his forearms. Pieces of the car wreck sprayed across the gravel field and rattled against the exterior of the chapel. Soot-black smoke, smouldering rubber, molten plastic and burning petrol washed through the dying daylight. He guessed what had happened and peered towards a knoll north of the chapel. What he saw should have been impossible to see. The weapon resting on Gritt's shoulder was an Mk 47 Striker AGL, a high-tech grenade launcher typically fired from a tripod-mounted position on the ground, though it could also be adapted to land vehicles, watercraft or helicopter-weapon mounting systems. Nobody fired the Mk 47 from their shoulder, except Gritt had just done so.

Gritt dropped the Mk 47 and walked away. He wasn't in a hurry. Soon, he disappeared below the horizon of the knoll. Baginski got to his feet, recovered his two pistols and put one of them in the inner pocket of his suit jacket. He moved, rounding the knoll, crossing between gravestones.

• FORTY-SEVEN •

"**WHAT IS REALITY?**" Cat sipped her pineapple juice. She had to quench her thirst. "How is reality defined?"

"A good question," he said. "Many people have a definitive

idea of what reality is. But problems arise when we try to define reality." He sipped his wine. "How would you define it yourself?"

She thought. Then, "Reality is what our senses can register. What we can see, hear, smell, touch or taste. Only those things. Everything else is unreal."

"That definition has shortcomings. It ignores many real things or phenomena we cannot perceive with our senses, for example, quarks, monetary value, or the number 7."

"Quarks?" She frowned. "What are they?"

"Building blocks of protons and neutrons."

She thought again, chewing vegetable stew, pretending she knew what protons and neutrons were. This time she put down her fork. "Now I know how to define reality." She looked at him, smiling. "We must eliminate the subjective perspective. The reality condition must be free of personal disorientations. Then we can say real things are what the vast majority of people perceive as real."

"That definition is also unsatisfying. Different forms of mass psychoses demonstrate delusions can affect entire communities. And from our discussion at Oberon Museum, you came to know mind and body belong to the same universe. Hallucinations result from the physico-chemical activity of the nervous system. Therefore, hallucinations are not unreal. They exist. They are as real as dreams and fantasies and other products of the brain's electrochemical work."

"I give up." She huffed. "I don't want to try to define reality anymore. What if *you* did it?"

"Okay. I think reality is a continuum. A multidimensional spectrum."

"Oh? That sounds, hmm, exciting."

I love his tie.

"Reality can't be reduced to a single definition. I judge it can only be explained at a higher analytical level. To grasp it, we have to consider the whole—the reality spectrum or the reality continuum.

"Moreover, I think everything is real. There's no unreality, only different variants of reality. Different reality frequencies in different directions within the reality spectrum."

"How are we supposed to work it out, then?" She sipped her juice, grateful it wasn't her problem to work out.

"We need to revolutionise our way of thinking about reality. Today, several strained theories exist. Inferior reductionists supply theories which neglect the human point of view or reduce reality to nothing but a mathematical concept, as if human subjectivity and awareness, as well as all macroscopic objects in the world, were incompatible with reality."

"Uh-huh. What are reductionists?"

He passed her the bread basket. "There's good and bad reductionism. Bad reductionism tries to explain a phenomenon completely in terms of the smallest or simplest elements of the phenomenon. In contrast, good reductionism, also known as hierarchical reductionism, never replaces one area of knowledge with another, but combines different areas of knowledge."

That's pretty cool, she almost said. Instead, she said, "How intriguing."

"As I guess you can see, good reductionism is related to multidisciplinary attacks on problems. It isn't surprising interdisciplinary research is much more successful than isolated research. I'm convinced hierarchical reductionism is the key to understanding our reality. But must we define reality? Is a definition required? I don't think so."

She smiled. "I don't think so either." *Do I mean that? Or does it just feel good to agree with the handsome Dr. Stockmayer?*

"The laws of quantum mechanics permeate the universe," he said. "Do you know how many atoms there are in the universe?"

"Me? No."

"There are an estimated ten to the power of eighty atoms in the observable universe."

"What kind of number is that?"

"A one followed by eighty zeros."

"Sounds like a large number."

"It's an extremely large number."

"Oh."

"Everything in the universe forms a gigantic quantum superposition. You included. You and me. Everything, everyone."

"Oh."

"To some extent, you are physically correlated with each and every point in the universe."

"I see. Since when?"

"Since the Big Bang. Since the beginning of time."

They had coffee on the porch. The glow from the candles in the living room leaked out and interacted with the twilight. The air was still but stirred as well. Strange, albeit true. A dog barked in the distance. The view of Paradise Park was even more beautiful than before. Stockmayer served himself a brandy to go with his coffee. Cat got a wonderful non-alcoholic liqueur, not overly sweet, just right. She now told her *complete* story, from the beginning. From the intrusion of her bedroom in London to the gunfight on Yarmouth Bridge in the City of Crows. She filled in new details. Things she had omitted during her previous conversations with him. Stockmayer understood her feelings in a way which Roy never would or could. She had to dump Roy. It's better to dump than be dumped, as Ebba used to say. She would call Ebba and tell her about Roy's infidelity. She needed psychological support from her best friend. Perhaps Ebba had an idea who Roy's new girl might be.

They sat on the sofa in his living room, watching the TV news. Shootings aboard a tram and on a bridge dominated the broadcast. News like this never remained local, she thought. This event would become nationwide and international news. Authorities had ruled out a terrorist attack. Two guys were shooting at each other while innocent passengers only happened to be in their way. The number killed was less than she had at first feared. Five. Three passengers and the conductor and the driver. Five dead was bad enough but it could have ended much worse. Eight wounded passengers underwent surgical operations at Crow City Hospital.

The TV screen glimmered in the dark. They were quiet. Words were superfluous. Her hand sought Stockmayer's hand. He held her. Her lips sought his mouth. He kissed her.

• FORTY-EIGHT •

HE FOUND GRITT before a headstone beneath the northern side of the knoll. The man in blood-spattered and gunshot-ripped clothes stood still and silent. He seemed to focus on the grave and not care that Baginski was approaching from behind.

Baginski raised the pistol again, aimed at the back of Gritt's head, moved closer, stopped, sighed, lowered the gun. He wiped dirt and soot from his forehead with the sleeve of his suit jacket.

"Leo Baginski," Gritt said, still standing with his back to his opponent. "We have a problem."

"I know what you are, Gritt."

"What I am."

"You're a robot. A cyborg."

"Robot. Cyborg."

"You belong to a series of humanoids manufactured by Delkorel BioElectronix. Your model is DEBE-902A."

"Belong. Manufactured. Model."

"I saw the prototype of your model at iREX."

Elmer Gritt hesitated. "iREX?"

"The International Robot Exhibition in Tokyo."

Gritt said nothing. He remained immobile, standing with his back to his opponent.

"You're a double agent for Delkorel Bio-E," Baginski said. "Mr. Jarrow demanded I find you and expose you. And I did find you. In connection with the Yolexus–NanoScoop affair, you leaked secrets to Delkorel about the drug Nargontanac. But now it's over, Gritt. It all ends here."

"How would it end? How would you stop me?"

"Jarrow expects me to find a way to stop you."

"You can't stop me."

Baginski thought. Gritt could be bluffing. There could be some way of stopping a DEBE robot.

"Why did you come here, Gritt? Here to Milton's grave?"

"Your left arm is bleeding, Baginski."

"From our encounter on the bridge." The pain from the wound reminded him of his human mortality. "Speaking of blood ... What red body fluid is pulsing through your body? Biological or synthetic blood? The model DEBE-901A at the Tokyo exhibition had biological blood in its system."

"My heart is pumping synthetic blood."

Baginski wasn't surprised. He had heard about the medical-research breakthrough surrounding artificial blood. Synthetic blood didn't belong to the realm of science fiction anymore. Ultramodern stem cell therapy had generated a method of manufacturing red blood cells. More or less successful attempts to produce artificial blood had been carried out for decades in different parts of the world, but British scientists were the first to use stem cells and with successful results. However, he hadn't known Delkorel was in possession of the technology.

"The traces of your blood in the tram car and on the bridge," Baginski said. "Can forensic experts track your blood to DEBE or somewhere else? To any DNA database for human embryonic stem cells?"

"No. By the way, my blood is inseparable from biological blood. Authorities, criminal investigators, will assume the blood they find is common blood."

"How and when was the inseparability between natural and artificial blood achieved?" As far as Baginski knew, this was still impossible. Meticulous blood tests should reveal differences.

Gritt didn't answer. Instead, he said, "I'm going to steal the girl. You can't stop me."

"Stay away from the girl. She's mine."

"Delkorel BioElectronix will own the girl's genetic code."

"No. Her DNA sequence belongs to the Yolexus archive."

"Why does Jarrow want to delete the girl?"

"She is a risk factor. An inconvenience. She is better dead than alive. Yolexus already owns the complete truth about the girl's distorted reality, in every detail. We don't need her anymore. That's why Jarrow wants to see her silenced for good."

Gritt waited until now to turn around to face and study his opponent. "Unless I get to her first." The cybernetic organism raised a smile. "I'm completing Professor Antonetti's work."

"Tell me."

"I started at the point where Antonetti stopped. The work must be completed."

"We knew BioFutura Systematik's external partner worked for Delkorel Bio-E. When Antonetti passed away, we anticipated detecting new Delkorel activities. How does Delkorel want to use the top-secret gene therapy programme which Antonetti tried to steal?"

"Why would I answer such a question?"

"You don't have to answer and I can't force an answer from a DEBE cyborg. I'm only interested. Therefore, I'm asking the question. It doesn't matter if you answer or not. Victor Milton's discovery will in any case be demolished."

A frown emerged on Gritt's gunshot-damaged face. Blood flowed from the artificial eye threshed by a bullet. "Mr. Jarrow's plan? Is Dame Esmeralda Northcutt involved?"

Baginski dodged the robot's question. "Milton's epoch-making discovery stands in the way of Yolexus Enterprise. Therefore, Yolexus will eliminate the BFS secret, not steal it. Yolexus will alter the conditions of human existence. Milton's work threatens long-term Yolexus plans. Invaluable strategies."

"Intriguing."

"Intriguing enough to give me something in return?"

Gritt laughed. A laugh which sounded like clattering nails in a toolbox. "Okay, Baginski. I'll answer your previous question. Delkorel Bio-E wants to utilise and refine Milton's pioneering gene therapy method. Why? For the repair and maintenance of advanced cybernetic DEBE products. For example, the organic parts and functions of my body need to be maintained, just like it's important to humans to stay fit in order to remain happy. I care about my health. I want to feel good. I want to stay happy."

It didn't cost Gritt or DEBE anything to reveal why the corporation wanted to steal Milton's discovery. If you didn't know how DEBE's newest cybernetics programme was designed, the information was unusable.

Delkorel Bio-E's latest humanoid series was impressive. Gritt had been an engineer at Yolexus Enterprise for two years without anyone suspecting anything. Gritt also had a human wife, Veronica, who didn't suspect she was married to a man–machine hybrid.

"Our marriage is perfect," Gritt said, as if he had read Baginski's thoughts. "I love Veronica, Veronica loves me. It's our wedding anniversary today. I'm going to buy gifts for her today. Our sex life is refreshing. We're planning to get children."

"How would that work? To get children?"

"Organic nanomachines in one of my circuits are building reproductive cells. Atom for atom. Molecule for molecule. DNA segment for DNA segment. Chromosome for chromosome."

Baginski shook his head. "Do you mean your reproductive cells are similar to those of the male human?"

"I want to say identical. They have twenty-three synthetic chromosomes, including the human sex chromosome Y or X. Delkorel Bio-E's artificial reproduction technology is a further development of existing state-of-the-art biotechnology. DNA can be computer-generated, then chemically manufactured in a lab and finally transferred to recipient cells."

"How do a DEBE robot's reproductive cells work?"

"Just like natural haploid gamete cells. They are synthetic macromolecules with biological functions. A synthetic sperm from me will merge with a human egg cell from Veronica when she and I have sex. This organic mathematics will result in our child. Our child will be named either John or Marie."

"You're a damn robot. A machine. You have no perception of sex or love or family."

"Modern robotics have resulted in emotional machines. I have a signal-transporting system. My synthesised neurons and synapses respond to stimuli. Veronica knows how emotional I can be when we have sex."

"Your circuitry imitates human emotions. That doesn't mean you're genuinely emotional."

"I'm more genuine than humans. Humans are corrupt, evil, impure, selfish, dishonest, treacherous, greedy. Humans are barbaric beasts who cause wars and environmental destruction."

Baginski shook his head. "Let me see if I've got this right. Veronica will give birth to a synthetic organism, or rather a human–android hybrid? A creature with fifty percent natural DNA and fifty percent synthetic DNA? Are you serious?"

"I'm serious. Unlike humans, I never resort to bad jokes."

Was it possible? Delkorel BioElectronix was manufacturing reproductive humanoids? Why? What was the point?

Reproductive cybernetic organisms would threaten human domination on Earth.

"Our beloved offspring," Elmer Gritt said. "A boy or a girl. Veronica becomes the child's biological mother. I become the child's cybernetic father."

"You have a big shortcoming, Elmer Gritt."

"What's that?"

"You lack human decency." Baginski raised the gun and fired three shots. The rounds ploughed through the robot's scalp. Blood, tissue and skin fragments flew. The shots echoed.

Gritt faltered but kept his foothold. He recovered his balance and showed his teeth. The blood-stained dental crowns looked even redder in the light from the sunset. "That almost hurt, Baginski."

"Can you experience pain?"

"Not like humans. In a different way. My nervous system detects various kinds of touch, such as pain. However, the sensation is not painful like it is in humans. When I have sex with Veronica, my nerve endings are stimulated in a different fashion. Another type of sensation. Enjoyment? As powerful as pain. Perhaps pleasure and pain are two sides of the same coin. What do you think?"

"I don't have time to think about that."

"Are you carrying exactly two Glock 9mm semi-automatic pistols? No other weapons?"

"No Glocks anymore. Two Rigal 10mm Auto high-velocity, with more powerful loadings than known to authorities. I'm also carrying extra magazines. I shifted guns in the car."

The Rigal was a French pistol inspired by the Austrian Glock. High-strength plastic-based design, trigger-oriented safety mechanism, lightweight, heavy-duty, reliable. The most significant difference between Rigal and Glock was that Rigal could be fired both in semi-automatic and fully automatic mode, whereas virtually all Glock models were semi-automatic. The founder and chief executive of the Montpellier-headquartered weapons manufacturer Rigal-Solutions, Jean-Baptiste Rigal, had, like Gaston Glock, a solid knowledge of polymer science. On the board of directors at Rigal-Solutions served a certain Dirk Jarrow.

"Well," Elmer Gritt said. "For the moment, I'm armed with two SIG Sauer handguns. In my jacket pockets. One pistol in each of my jacket's outer pockets. Extra mags in my trouser pockets. We're facing a fair ending of the game."

"Hardly fair. My opponent is a cyborg."

"We can approximate. The game is as fair as it can be."

"Thank you very much."

"You're welcome."

"You have an entire arsenal of weapons in the BMW."

The robot didn't comment.

"Where is the BMW?"

The robot didn't answer.

"What are you after, Gritt?"

"Nothing. I have no secret agenda. I practise my humanity. I'm more humane than humans. I enjoyed my two years at Yolexus Enterprise. I want to give you a fair match. Unlike Leo Baginski, I'm not a cold-blooded killer."

Baginski didn't know how to interpret Gritt's machine-like reasoning. "One of us won't leave the cemetery tonight. And earlier you said it wasn't possible to stop a DEBE-902A cyborg."

"Veronica is longing for me. I'm longing for her. It's our wedding anniversary. Before I return home, I'll buy presents for my wife. Tonight, Veronica and I will have more sex."

"To see your wife again, you first have to get past me."

"You have a positive attitude. You think you have a chance."

"How could you allow Veronica to see you in your current state? Gunfire has destroyed your exterior."

"Before I return home, I'll visit a Delkorel Bio-E plant. The lab runs around the clock, all year round. Cybernetics specialists will give me a new exterior while checking my wiring and my interior. Takes thirty minutes to make me new again."

"Can Delkorel repair one of their wrecked robots in just half an hour? Too bad we don't have time to talk about that. Too bad Veronica didn't hear what you just said."

Gritt once again turned his back on his opponent. "I'm going to count to five. Meanwhile, you can do whatever you want. When I have counted to five, I'll pull my SIG Sauers out of my pockets, turn around and start shooting."

Baginski needed a new plan.

He needed new plan, like, now.

Gritt began to count. "One ... two ..."

• FORTY-NINE •

SHE DREAMS AN evil dream about Goston Cemetery and Dad and Mum and Sis and a sixteen-fingered gravedigger. The bad dream is a continuum. It starts frightening and ends in terror.

The twin sisters are at the MAC coffee shop in the city centre, eating the locally produced ice cream, Crow's Paradise, an award-winning liquorice-and-melon ice cream. Ice cream is the last thing on Cat's mind. Cat wants to talk. Jan wants ice cream. They have reached some sort of sisterly compromise. Cat is grateful for the anonymity she has managed to preserve so far. To be invisible was less complicated than she had thought. Grey blouse, blue jeans, black Reebok shoes, dark sunglasses, no makeup, non-stylised hair in a mediocre knot. She isn't conspicuous. Nobody in the crowded cafe seems to suspect that one of the world's hottest models is right here right now. Customers are occupied with themselves.

Cat has a small ice cream waffle cone and is more than satisfied. Jan has three extra-large ice cream waffle cones, two cheesecakes, two jam doughnuts, sixteen gingerbread cookies, a Crazy Candy Factory Rainbow Swirl lollipop and three large glasses of Coca-Cola. Cat offers to pay the bill. Jan disagrees. Instead, it'll be as usual. The rich superstar pays for herself and the poor waitress pays for herself. It's a question of principle, according to Jan. The difference between the two sisters' weekly salaries is at least seventy thousand pounds, but it is irrelevant here. Each sister pays for herself.

Cat says, "Sitting here reminds me of the summers when we were kids and the countless ice creams we ate back then."

"When you didn't count calories," Jan says.

Cat ignores Jan's acid comment. Instead, she says, "I'm going to visit Dad's grave and I want you to come along. There's something I have to check."

"What the dickens do you want to check?" Jan is gaping like a walrus. "Why would anyone want to check anything?" Jan's voice, in Cat's dream, is clear and cold like iced water.

"I'm only going to check if the grave is intact."

"You're crazy, Cat. Pretty but crazy. Too pretty but also too crazy."

"Will you come along to the cemetery?"

Jan puffs. "Forget it."

"Please, Jan. I can't do this alone."

Jan appears to think. Then, "I'll come along. But only because you're my sis. You'll be indebted to me for this."

"Must we waste time and energy on arguing?"

"Who else would I argue with, Cat? There's no one but you."

"Silly you."

"Silly you."

They stroll down Crowhill Gate in the direction of Central Station. The station complex is crowded but the twin sisters attract no special attention. Cat's extraordinary beauty and Jan's provocative ugliness cancel each other out. As a pair of sisters, they're as neutral as air to the crowd.

"The tram is arriving." Jan points.

The tram driver waves. The man is a skeleton in uniform. An obscene smile pulls at the jaws of the bone-white skull. The sisters board the tram and find two free seats opposite one another. The conductor, a woman, appears. Her eyes have been thrashed by gunshots. She stands in a growing pool of blood. The sisters buy tickets. In the next moment, they're in the cemetery. The sun is blazing. Jan's malformed face sizzles in the heat, like plum tomatoes in a frying pan. Her clumsy shadow is a midnight-blue bug.

"Mum will worry," Jan says.

"Forget about Mum," Cat says.

"But it's time for dinner."

"Not yet."

"I'm already hungry."

"How can you be hungry? You've just had three extra-large ice cream waffle cones, two cheesecakes, two jam doughnuts, sixteen gingerbread cookies, a Crazy Candy Factory Rainbow Swirl lollipop and three large glasses of Coca-Cola."

"I have room for more food."

"Stop moaning now and hurry up."

Cat keeps hiding behind her sunglasses. However, she's missing a sun hat and longs for one. Strong sunlight is a model's enemy. Sharp sunrays damage the skin. Next week she will be back at work and she cannot show up sunburnt.

The flaming sunshine falls upon the kingdom of the dead. She hears complaints from below the ground, the cries and whispers of the dead. The cadavers suffer in the heat and struggle to get out of their coffins. Hands and arms and heads protrude from the underworld. The dead are crawling out of their graves. Outside the crematorium stands a gravedigger, wearing a black evening tailcoat and smoking a cigar. He has a dandelion-yellow reptile head and sixteen scaly fingers. "Your arse is awesome, Cat," the gravedigger says, grinning. She ignores him.

The sisters find Dad's grave. The stone is a black granite stone with an engraved and gilded rose. The memorial features the name Victor Milton, his title (Executive Chairman), date of birth, date of death and an epitaph. The square area of ground in front of the headstone is decorated with red and pink roses. The flowers look thirsty in the heat. A discreet grave. Nothing flamboyant about it. No sign of ... *of what? What are you looking for? Signs which prove Dad has left his grave?*

Thousands of tombstones throw shadows. Now she sees them coming. They're here to take her. The creatures. Four-legged monsters with ash-grey fur step out from their lightless hideouts, a curtain of dread sweeping upon her. Ten-footed demons with mint-green skin climb down from the treetops. Eight-horned abominations creep up from underground and wander through the grass. Petrified, Cat screams and tries to escape. Her feet don't respond. She freezes like a statue.

The burial chapel explodes. Splinters of window glass fly through the dream like crushed gemstones. Roof tiles are hurled everywhere like plastic bricks from a kid's Lego construction set. Roof beams, panels and rows of pews turn into clouds of burning sticks. Walls and ceilings cough and twist and catch fire and burst in the pressure wave. The balcony is smashed to woodchips and thrown across the cemetery like a grotesque Jack Straws pick-up game. The chancel and the altar flare up like a stage from hell. A tar-black coffin crackles in the licking flames. A sound emerges from within the coffin. Someone scratches on the inside of the lid. A corpse? The scraping noise gets louder. A cadaver hammers on the lid with its fists.

The corpse smashes the lid, creeps out of the coffin and gets to its feet. It is a she. The lifeless girl is in her early twenties. Her hair is waist-length and scarlet and as brilliant as the exploding fire all around her. In contrast, her breasts are cool and pale like hills of vanilla. She doesn't look dead. She must be dead. A living dead. The girl is Cat. She sobs, whimpers, shrieks. Her scream lifts her out of the dream, out and around and away.

Stockmayer pulled her towards him under the quilt, embraced her, kissed her. "What's the matter, Catriona?" He brushed hair away from her face, then looked into her eyes. "You screamed, Catriona. Did you have a bad dream?"

She nodded. "A nightmare, Roger. A horrible nightmare."

"Do you want to talk?"

"No. It's over. The bad dream is over. It's over now and forever." She straddled him. Her moist lips touched his chest, his neck, his mouth. Roger's stubble tickled her cheek. Her fingers groped under the quilt, found what they searched. His penis stiffened in her hand. She guided him, brought him where she wanted him. He slipped into her in a tender manner, just like before. She moved on top of him, bobbing. His hands shifted from her waist to her buttocks. The night floated like a new moon, dark but with a crescent of hope.

• FIFTY •

"**... FOUR ... FIVE." ELMER** Gritt drew his two SIG Sauer semi-automatic pistols, spun around and opened fire in Baginski's direction. In the stillness of the cemetery, the robot's guns thundered like cannons. Echoes of the shots bounced about like ghost whispers.

Elmer's cybernetic ears detected infrasound, ultrasound and all sound in between. He, or it, had better hearing than a cat.

A running Baginski heard Gritt reach 'five' in his counting. He threw himself. His suit jacket fluttered. Two or three rounds from the humanoid's cracking guns had passed through his jacket. It took forever to reach the ground, it seemed, as though he were running through water in a bottomless swimming pool.

A burning bullet singed an earlobe. Three flowerpots containing funeral flowers on a grave before him were blown apart like clay pigeons on a shooting range. He landed behind an ornamented tombstone.

The rain of bullets clattered and banged against headstones and metallic grave vases and plaques. He decided not to return fire right now. He chose to save ammunition for a while. His chances of defeating the robot could be greater than zero. Gritt might have bluffed. He made a mental summary of what he had learnt about the DEBE 900-series at iREX. You were never told everything at exhibitions or conferences. Corporations at the frontier of research always withheld information, to protect trade secrets or in-progress patent deals. Could he, however, deduce something? Any specific weakness of the humanoid, which he could attack?

Gritt could think much faster than humans. Even though the robot's brain operated with the speed of a supercomputer, Baginski was determined to expose the machine's weakness. The human brain, with its hundred billion neurons and hundred trillion synapses, was still the most advanced organ on Earth.

The whizzing rain of bullets declined and then stopped altogether. Again, silence. A trick? Baginski looked around. No cyborg in sight. He peered from behind the gravestone. No robot in his field of vision. He listened. Nothing. He got to his feet and began to move through the landscape of headstones, bushes, lawns and trees. He found it parked behind a hedge which ran along a series of tall tombstones. The BMW.

No humanoid in sight. He went over to the damaged car. He pushed the button on the boot handle. Locked. A gun solved the problem. The lock mechanism shattered. The bang echoed through the land of the dead. He lifted the squeaking lid.

He found an arsenal of firearms, ammunition boxes and two signature toolboxes which carried the yellow-hawk logo of Delkorel BioElectronix. One toolbox was filled with a variety of electronic equipment. The other one contained a multipack of Pemonirin (PMN7091), a plastic explosive developed by Delkorel Bio-E. PMN7091 was reminiscent of C-4 and Semtex but had a larger detonation velocity. He pocketed a package of PMN7091, searched the second toolbox and found what he was looking for. Electronic detonators, a remote control, an electric screwdriver, drill bits, silicone-tipped locking tongs. The screwdriver was a Ronix53D precision power tool, a non-commercial Delkorel gadget. He checked the screwdriver's organic light-emitting transistor (OLET) battery charge indicator and made sure the programmable functions worked.

He left the BMW, avoiding backtracking. He ran around the knoll, this time in the opposite direction. The burial chapel appeared again. He stopped dead in his tracks. The chapel doors were ajar. Only minutes earlier, the doors had been closed.

The chapel proved to be more than just a chapel. It resembled a small church. Fading daylight shone in through stained-glass windows. There was a chancel, an altar, a pulpit, a confessional, a pipe organ, rows of pews, a balcony, and hundreds of wax candles, most of which were unlit. He walked deeper into the church. Creakless shoes across a creakless concrete floor. The dead silence kept its grip. He stopped at the edge of the chancel and put down the equipment from the BMW. On the altar sat a black lacquer coffin. The quivering light from a few candles was reflected in the bloody handprint on the coffin lid.

Baginski raised a gun and pulled the trigger. The holy silence disintegrated. Five quick shots smacked into the coffin.

He lifted the lid. The corpse in the wooden box, an embalmed woman, sported four fresh bullet holes from the neck down. The fifth bullet had thrashed the head. Chunks of skull and brains dribbled down the pillow. Also, she was leaking embalming fluid. This wasn't a cadaver awaiting a funeral. The lifeless woman had already been buried, and not long ago. Someone had dug up the body somewhere in the cemetery, brought it here and placed it in the brand-new coffin.

Did Elmer Gritt do it? Why?

The confessional next to a long wall was an ornate structure in dark stained wood and red opaque glass. It featured violet curtains. On one of the curtains, a wide bulge emerged. The protruding part of the fabric grew.

He registered the movement from the corner of his eye, wheeled around and discharged his handgun into the confessional. Semi-auto fire, shot after shot after shot. Splinters of wood and glass whirled. The banging noise rebounded. From behind the bullet-riddled curtain, the figure appeared. It started to fall out of the wrecked confessional. Baginski continued to shoot. The figure, a statue of Virgin Mary, exploded into innumerable shards of ceramic. Someone had placed it on a leaning pallet, just behind the curtain.

A rattling pain in his arm made Baginski drop the pistol. Blood flew from the bullet hole just below his elbow. The shot had cracked from above and behind him. He gritted his teeth, raised his eyes and pulled the other Rigal out of his trouser pocket. The robot on the balcony aimed at him again.

Baginski fired five fast shots at the cyborg, snapped up the first gun from the floor and threw himself out of the chancel. He scrambled for shelter behind a pew in the nave.

The robot continued to fire. The rain of gunshots screamed and thundered. The bullets shrieked, jangled and banged in their contact with wood, concrete, marble, metal and glass.

Gritt had a superior position on the balcony. He kept his offensive, pumping bullets straight down into the nave. Something, however, had happened to the robot. It didn't aim as well as before. It staggered too, as if its programmed Ronix-902A batteries were damaged or were draining.

Splinters of furnishings swirled in the main body of the single-nave church.

Baginski leapt from his exposed position among the pews to the better cover of a marble column.

The chapel or church turned quiet again. A surprising calm spread through the building.

Now or never. He stepped out from his hiding spot behind the column, directed his pistols towards the balcony, aimed at the centre of the cyborg's body and emptied both magazines. Two full 19-round Rigal mags in semi-auto fire. Thirty-eight index-finger pulls—left-right combination. The end mark of temporary noiselessness.

The slam-bang sound rebounded. Elmer Gritt crashed through the railing of the balcony, dropped his two SIG Sauers, double-somersaulted through his fall and crash-landed on his back on a bullet-riddled pew in the nave. The pew collapsed upon impact. The building trembled. Dust swirled. Squeaking and creaking and snapping sounds were everywhere.

The robot coughed, floundered, whined. Artificial blood sprayed from a corner of its mouth. The irises of the cybernetic eyes were gyrating like spinning tops. From inside its ribcage, something rumbled like a distant thunderstorm.

Baginski went over to the flailing and kicking and croaking machine. A long and sharp splinter of wood from the destroyed pew had penetrated Gritt in his side, an inch below his left armpit. A sensitive area. He linked this observation to what he had perceived about the DEBE-900 machines at iREX. The 902A model had the same bio-port as the prototype 901A. The bio-port, a type of cybernetic power connector, looked like and had the same texture as a biological birthmark. He fetched the Ronix53D precision power tool, the electronic detonators, the remote control and the PMN7091.

Gritt coughed, croaked, spat. Red liquid the shade of ruby arsenic spilled between his teeth. The obscene smile was intact. "Good evening, Baginski."

"We're there now, Gritt. At the end."

The irises of the robot's eyes continued to spin, clockwise. "What end? The inevitable end? The end of an old beginning or the beginning of a new end?"

"The final end for one of us. From now on, there's room for only one of us. One of us leaves. The other one stays."

"I have to get home, Baginski."

"Why?"

"It's our wedding anniversary today. Veronica's and mine. I'll buy gifts and flowers for Veronica. Tonight, Veronica and I will have more sex. Must have sex to make the child. Vaginal sex is the basis for reproduction. Organic mathematics."

"Veronica will have to find a new husband."

"A new husband?" The humanoid looked confused. "Why?"

"She will soon be a widow. She will be free to find a new husband."

"But ... what about me?"

"It's time for your funeral, Elmer Gritt. There is no better place than a cemetery."

"Good evening, Baginski. I'm going to count to five—"

Baginski pushed the electric precision tool into the robot's right ear, set the rotational direction to counter-clockwise and pressed the start button. The auto-target-seeking Ronix driver found the right screw head in no time. He had to undo three screws, using three different types of drill bits. Then he removed the auricle. The humanoid's ear canal, twice as wide as that of a human adult, was a cobalt-blue cylinder made of the material Obrikalan-200, a metal-polymer alloy, a commercial Delkorel innovation. The cylinder featured two superpositioned screw caps and required two adjustments of the precision driver. An insider at Delkorel, unknown even to Jarrow and Esmeralda, had taught him how to use the Ronix tool.

He put the two screw caps aside, broke a rubber-like seal and lifted out the shock absorber. Now he was able to reach the central processing units. He mounted one of the silicone-tipped locking tongs onto the precision tool and pulled out the five disc-shaped CPUs. Then he filled the cavity with PMN7091 and inserted a detonator into the plastic explosive.

Done. Time to get out of here.

He activated the remote control and left the chapel. The forthcoming explosion would be heard a long way away.

First of all, he needed medical attention for his wounds. Not at a recognised hospital though. He would visit a WCP centre, one of Yolexus Enterprise's healthcare centres.

The humanoid and the chapel would be demolished in three minutes, he decided. At the southeastern edge of the cemetery, he climbed the wall and cut its barbed wire.

The gloom of the night wrapped the cityscape. He moved along a street which was free of residential buildings. Factories, warehouses and department stores lined the street in both directions. He checked his watch.

Forty-four seconds to detonation.

He stole a dark-green Honda, drove northwards and turned onto Portobello Lane. He heard the explosion. The thundering bang which would awaken everything and everyone. He kept his calm and drove out of the district. First, medical care, then report to Jarrow. And then he would find Catriona Milton again. Find the girl and silence her for good.

• FIFTY-ONE •

THE NEXT MORNING, they sat in the kitchen. Cat had showered and applied perfume to her hair and skin. In her handbag there was at all times a mini cosmetics bag with the most important toiletries. She leaned back on the kitchen sofa, her legs crossed. There was still moisture in her free-flowing back-combed hair. She was almost dressed. *Almost*. She was only in her blouse and underwear. Roger sat in a chair on the opposite side of the table. Ready for the clinic, he wore a short-sleeved shirt, a silk tie and creased trousers. She had tea. He had coffee. They both had toast with Hartley's Olde English marmalade.

"We have to talk, Catriona."

"I know, Roger."

"Last night …" He turned silent.

"We knew it would happen, didn't we? Sooner or later?"

He hesitated. Then, "Maybe."

"We gave in to our feelings."

"I'm your doctor. Your neurologist and expert advisor."

"Doctors aren't emotionless robots, are they?"

"No, but—"

"Doctors have feelings like everybody else, haven't they?"

"Yes, but—"

"Do you regret what happened?"

He turned silent again. Then he sighed. "I want to regret what happened but I can't. I spent the night with the most beautiful woman in the world."

"Did you like what happened?"

"I loved what happened, Catriona. What happened was the most wonderful thing that has happened to me in a long time."

She got off the sofa, went around the table and jumped onto his lap. Her fingers stroked his hair. She pulled his head towards her and kissed him. "I also loved what happened, Roger."

He caressed her bare knees. "What's going on between us?"

"You're about to fall in love with me, Doctor."

"I'm already in love with you."

"I've been longing to be with you." *How long? Since I came to know about Roy's infidelity? Had Roy's cheating triggered what happened last night?* She was surprised by her own forwardness. But it was nice to sit on her doctor's lap. His new erection pressed against her bum. "Remove my knickers."

Again, she was stunned by her own naughtiness. Did she force the situation as a kind of revenge action against Roy? Or as an attempt to postpone her phone call to Sis? She had missed yesterday evening's agreed meeting with Sis.

Roger glanced at her floral knickers and seemed to consider her words. "I wouldn't mind, Catriona."

"I know. The hard pressure against my bum reveals you wouldn't mind."

He looked embarrassed. "Could we talk for a while instead?"

"Okay." She remained on his lap.

"Five years have passed since I was last in an intimate relationship. You're the first woman since Henrietta."

"Henrietta?"

"My dead wife. Our love was endless. Henrietta was a concert musician. An outstanding violinist. She played several times in the internationally recognised Vienna New Year's Concert. While on a touring programme in the German Alps, she was involved in a fatal bus accident. There were several casualties. Henrietta received emergency treatment at a nearby hospital but died of her injuries. It was a long time before I started being interested in other women. My job became my therapy. I focused on work and ignored everything else."

She stroked his hair. "Heartbreaking, Roger." She paused. "I've been wondering how your private life looks, or looked, before. I haven't seen a single photo in your house."

"In all my life I've never photographed or filmed anyone or anything." He shifted on his chair but kept his gentle hold of her.

"People think they own something if they have a picture, a photo, of something. It's an apparent impression, created by the mass media culture. People see the world through the media and are therefore in danger of believing it's only through the media that reality exists. But the truth is just the opposite. A photograph of Henrietta would mean nothing to me, nothing more than a blank sheet of paper."

"How did Henrietta look? May I ask? I'm curious. I bet she was very beautiful."

"You may ask." He gave her a strained smile. "Henrietta had sky-blue eyes, bright eyelashes. Waist-length, straight, vanilla-blonde hair. She used makeup but never for a party-style appearance; only to emphasise her natural looks. She was a strong-willed woman. I observe the same willpower in you. I'm not saying you two are alike. I don't see you as a replacement for my deceased wife. That would be a deceptive view. I love you for the unique person you are."

"I think I know what you're talking about, Roger. Even though I can't agree with everything you say about photos, I grasp your perspective. I've begun to understand you, more and more, especially since your talk before about what reality is or can be."

"The beauty queen Catriona Milton, the real Catriona Milton, cannot be captured in a photograph. Real beauty isn't copiable as if it were an electronic file."

She smiled. "Photography and film are key concepts in a model's life."

"I know. I understand. And I respect it. Commercialism has countless shapes. Our different ideas don't have to compete. I'm in love with you. You're the most exciting woman in my life since Henrietta. Your status today as superstar and global celebrity is irrelevant to me." He paused. "We've known each other since you were seventeen. For long periods we haven't seen one another, though I've always kept an eye on you and your disease at a distance, in the spirit of a healthcare professional."

"I'm twenty-three now. I'm in charge of my life."

"The age gap?"

"You're a young, handsome fifty-two-year-old. There are countless relationships with similar or even larger age gaps, not least among celebrities."

He looked a little worried. "Shall we finish our breakfast? I have to drive down to the clinic. Can I give you a lift into town?"

She kissed him. "I'll be ready in a minute. Just need to get dressed." She slid off his lap. "And Roger?"

"Yes?"

"Thank you for telling me about Henrietta."

Roger drove his comfortable Mercedes-Benz towards the city. Cat was cosied up in the passenger seat, her hand resting on his thigh.

"Catriona? I suggest we keep our ... intimate relationship ... secret, as long as I am your neurologist. What do you say?"

"I was about to suggest the same thing."

"Officially, we have a strict and straight physician–patient relationship."

She smiled. "Officially."

He steered the Mercedes down Crowfield Way. "Where do you want me to drive you?"

"The Red Unicorn pub in Farnwood. If that's all right."

"That's fine. Are you going to see your sister?"

"Yes." To phone home was too risky. If she did, perhaps Mum would take the call. It was safer to seek Jan out at the pub.

"You're so incredibly different, you and your twin sister. You're mere shadows of one another."

She reflected on Roger's words. "We're twin sisters *and* mere shadows of one another." She pondered. "We're like twisted shadows. We're each other's twisted shadow."

"I see."

She looked out the passenger window, her thoughts darting to her London home. "My best friend and I are also like each other's twisted shadow. Ebba and I are more than best friends.

We're like twin sisters. We keep an eye on each other. Yet we're terribly different. Like night and day. Like shade and sunshine. Sure, we argue sometimes. I think it may be healthy to disagree once in a while. Disagreement is a fuel for discussion, and discussions open new perspectives." She looked at him. "What do you think?"

"Without disagreement, neither science nor technology would develop. If no one dared question established ideas, our understanding of the world would be a lot bleaker. New thinkers, such as Copernicus or Galileo, often encountered extreme and hostile opposition but they stuck to their guns, fortunately."

"I don't know who you're talking about. I can't name any scientists. But I don't need to know who Galleyo or Cooperniss are, or were. It's enough for me if you agree with me."

He smiled, reached out a hand and stroked her neck.

The Mercedes rolled past Rainbow Tower. The traffic got denser.

"Roger?"

"Yes?"

"Right now, my private life is more turbulent than usual. It has nothing to do with you or us. Sooner or later, there'll be new juicy articles in the newspapers. Would you be able to ignore all the gossip that's written about me in the papers?"

"Yes. I'm not interested in gossip. I'll do anything you ask me to do. That is, anything outside the physician–patient relationship."

"Thank you, Roger. By the way, don't believe everything that's written about me."

"I don't." He leaned towards the passenger seat, searched for her lips and kissed her.

The Mercedes turned into Farnwood Road. Roger opened the glove box and took out a blue envelope. "Here." He handed it to her. "Something for your sister."

She looked at the envelope in her hands. The text on the front read: To Miss Janice Milton. "What is it?"

"Information on how to contact a superb plastic surgeon in Vienna. A man I know very well. Jakob Ratzinger is one of the most prominent plastic surgeons in Europe. An amazing master. Dr. Ratzinger does wonders."

"Do you think he can do something for Janice?"

"Your sister is a difficult case, but my friend Jakob isn't afraid of tough challenges. It's worth a try."

"I appreciate your kind thought." She slipped the envelope into her handbag. "Janice is grotesquely malformed. What could be achieved through surgery?"

"She'll never work as a model, but surgical operations, if they succeed, would give her a more human appearance."

A less monster-like appearance, Cat thought, and was at once ashamed of herself. "Your superb contact is probably expensive. Janice has no money."

"She has a wealthy twin sister."

"I wouldn't hesitate to help my sister with money. I've tried many times in many contexts, with the same negative result. I'll try again though."

The Mercedes swung into the Red Unicorn's car park and stopped. "I'll call you," he said. "Or you'll call me. Anytime. You are, after all, my patient."

"Roger?"

"Yes?"

"Is my hair truly olive-green to your eyes?"

He delivered his attractive smile. "My reality."

She wrapped her arms around his neck. "I love you anyway."

His fingertips touched her face, exploring the contour of her cheekbone. "There's objective and subjective reality, sweetheart. The order of the four seasons is objective reality, just like the blowing wind, the burning fire or the flying bird. In contrast, subjective reality is free of predictability."

• FIFTY-TWO •

"GOOD MORNING, CAT." The waitress waved. "Rumour has it that Cat Milton is visiting her hometown, yes, yes." She cupped a hand over her mouth and giggled. Then she lifted an index finger to her lips, indicating silence. "Don't worry, Cat. At the Red Unicorn we're discreet. Our regular customers know discretion is an important part of our image, yes, yes. Non-regulars who seem too forward are informed of our policy. Celebrities always attract curious glances and they have to expect that, but we guarantee they're left alone."

Cat glanced at the girl's nametag. "Thank you, Gina."

"No problem."

"Is my sister here?"

"Yes, yes." Gina started to fill a glass display cabinet with cakes and pastries. "Janice is busy cleaning the toilets. When she's done, she'll have her morning break, I think, yes, yes, that's what the manager said."

"I'll just wait here, then."

"Can I get you anything?"

"An espresso, please."

"Yes, yes, good choice. Have a seat, Cat. I'll bring it over."

"Where have you *been*, Cat?" Thunder flashed in Janice's pig eyes. She held an extra-large Coca-Cola between her hands. "Our meeting last night at ten o'clock? Your own suggestion. You missed it."

"Please, Jan, lower your voice. I'll explain. Could you sit down?"

Jan sat down, against all expectations. The sis she hated to love. The sis she loved to hate. Fury still occupied Janice's malformed features. Her ugliness was provoking. She slurped her Coca-Cola like a rhino.

Cat took off her sunglasses. "I'm sorry, Jan. I apologise for missing last night. I had an important conversation with Rog ... with Dr. Stockmayer during dinner. We talked about my new medicine. A splendid drug, I must admit. No side effects. After dinner, I was resting on a sofa while he finished work in his library. I fell asleep. When I woke up, it was midnight. He let me spend the night at his place."

Jan stared. "You spent the night with Stockmayer?"

"I spent the night at his place, not *with* him. Big difference. I slept on the sofa in the living room. He slept in his bedroom, of course. Alone. By the way, he's been a widower for five years." With an effort, Cat met her sister's eyes.

"Do you think Mum is upset, Cat? Do you think Mum is upset because you've been gone all night?"

"Mum is always upset about something."

"What do you think Mum would say if she knew you were staying at Stockmayer's place all night, huh?"

"I'm twenty-three. Where I spend my nights is none of Mum's business."

It's none of Mum's business whom I'm sleeping with either. "But let's make things hassle-free for us, dear sister. If Mum asks where I've been, we'll say I spent the night at Louise Drum's place." Louise was a childhood friend with whom Cat, more than Jan, still had occasional contact.

Jan's wrinkled forehead turned even wrinklier. It developed the texture of corrugated fibreboard. "Imagine if Mum checks if you stayed at Louise's place. Mum might call Louise. Mum might also call Mr. and Mrs. Drum. And I might run the risk of getting caught out by your lie."

"Relax. Mum wouldn't think it was worth the trouble to check it out, either with Louise or with her parents."

"You've dyed your hair. Raven-black, right? And you've already started to wash away the dye. Most of the black is gone but not quite all gone. Why did you dye your famous hair?"

"Long story. Forget it. For now."

Jan huffed and changed the topic. "Haven't you seen or heard the news, Cat?" She waved her arms. "There's been a wild gunfight aboard a tram on Roderick Avenue and five people died and then the tram crashed on Yarmouth Bridge and the shootings continued and then the burial chapel in Goston Cemetery exploded—it fricking *exploded*—and in Goston the police found spent rounds from pistols and the smouldering remains of a stolen car."

"Well, I saw the TV news at Stockmayer's place. However, what you just said about Goston is news to me."

"It was a giant explosion." Jan waved her thick arms. "It thundered, banged and smoked. They're talking about some very strong explosive."

"I see. Has a connection been established between the events on Roderick, Yarmouth and in Goston?"

"No doubt, the experts say. However, they haven't revealed everything. Something was found in the smouldering ruins of the chapel. Something they're reluctant to talk about."

"And what's that?"

Jan shrugged. "Some info has leaked. Some info about some kind of advanced machine, electronics, or AI equipment. AI, I was told, means Artificial Intelligence."

"Oh. How exciting." Cat was thinking. Outside in the urban landscape, dangerous men were chasing her. She needed Jan's help. At the same time, she was exposing Sis to danger. "What time do you finish work today?"

"Five o'clock."

"We're going to Montrose Place tonight with Dad's letter. Five o'clock. I'll make it this time."

"Shouldn't we try to call Zimmer in advance?"

"No. We'll go there in secret. If we leave here shortly after five, we'll arrive in Rockthorpe a quarter to six or just before six, depending on rush hour traffic."

"Hmm. In secret. You do look secretive."

"If I do, there's a reason. I know things no one else knows."

"What?"

Cat lowered her voice. "That the violence in town and in the cemetery has to do with BioFutura Systematik and Dad's groundbreaking discovery and the letter to Zimmer."

"How could you know?"

"The events at Roderick and Yarmouth. I was there, Sis. I was aboard that tram. I saw everything. The crash on Yarmouth gave me a bump on my forehead."

Jan gaped. Remnants of onion-flavoured crisps smeared her teeth. "You were there, Cat? You were there when it happened?"

Cat looked around. Nobody glanced in their direction.

"The bump on your head is almost invisible now." Jan paused. "According to news reports, there were two men shooting at each other. The innocent victims, dead or wounded, just had the bad luck of being in the line of fire. What could all of this mess have to do with Dad's company?"

Cat told Jan everything there was to tell, or rather everything she could recall. That she had just left the BMLC building and that the two men aboard the tram had been fighting about her.

After a silent moment, Jan said, "Do you think Mum—"

"I know," Cat interrupted. "I know Mum would get upset if she heard my story. Don't say anything to Mum."

Jan seemed to be thinking. Then, "Your responsibility. And yours only."

"By the way, Sis, I've got something for you. Something which should put you in a better mood."

Jan glowered. "What?"

"It's from Stockmayer." Cat opened her handbag, took out the blue envelope and put it on the table in front of her sister. "To Miss Janice Milton, as you can see."

Jan scowled like a goat. "What is it?"

"Open it. Read it."

"Say something first. Say what it is."

"Info on how to get in touch with a formidable plastic surgeon. Stockmayer's friend and personal recommendation.

One of the most prominent plastic surgeons of today. Active in Vienna. There's hope for you, Jan, if you dare to listen."

Jan shook her head. "This is a total waste of time. When Stockmayer visited the Red Unicorn the other day and asked questions about you and the time of your arrival in Blackfield, he took the opportunity to mention his contacts in the field of plastic surgery. He already knows I'm not interested."

"There are specialists who do not see this as a waste of time. Stockmayer says his friend is a man who isn't afraid of difficult cases."

"I have no money. No money for expensive operations. Not even money for a flight to Vienna. I've never travelled anywhere. I do not plan to travel anywhere. I won't go anywhere outside the City of Crows. I don't want to."

"I'm prepared to pay for all your expenses. Your operations, no matter how many, no matter how expensive. Your return plane tickets to Vienna, no matter how many. Your hotel nights in Vienna, no matter how many. All your meals in Vienna, no matter how many. I'll pay for everything."

Jan shook her head. "Return the envelope to Stockmayer. I don't want it."

"No. I'm going to leave it here."

"When I clean the table, the envelope will end up in a rubbish bin."

"No. You should take care of it. You're going to read it."

"No. I decide for myself what to do and what not to do. You're not my boss."

"I'm going to leave the envelope here on the table anyway."

"Was there anything else, or are you done?"

"The espresso was delicious. Now, in this heat, I'm thirsty and want something cold to drink. Could you give me a bottle of still mineral water—your finest brand, please—and a tall glass without ice cubes? And give me the bill?"

Jan glared. "If you say what you're going to do until five o'clock. And you get the water we have or *none at all*."

• FIFTY-THREE •

ROGER STOCKMAYER SAT behind his desk at the Oberon Clinic. He had cancelled all his appointments of the morning and informed the reception staff he didn't want to be disturbed. On his desk sat a Styrofoam cup filled with steaming coffee. This morning, the Styrofoam cup functioned as an hourglass. When the coffee stopped steaming, he would pick up the phone and make the inevitable call. Planning the call in advance would be a waste of time. The development of the forthcoming dialogue wasn't predictable. He shouldn't forget to maintain the divide between his private life and his professional life. Last night had been dreamlike. It still felt like a beautiful fantasy. He had had his patient in bed. And not just any patient. No one less than Catriona Milton. One of the world's most desirable girls. It sounded almost too ...

Almost too good to be true? Except now it had happened. Admit you like the situation. Accept you're longing for a new woman. Henrietta isn't around anymore. Catriona is around. You're in love with her. She says she's in love with you.

The coffee stopped steaming. He lifted the phone and tapped the number on the keypad.

"Good morning, Roger." Dirk Jarrow's voice was almost cheerful, as if it belonged to another man.

"Good morning, Dirk. We have things to talk about. Did I catch you at a good time?"

"I always have time for you, Roger."

"Miss Milton, the one in question, contacted me straight after yesterday's events. I realised a Yolexus-designed solution had failed. What happened?"

"A problem. Delkorel Bio-E had sent an opponent."

"Who?"

"A difficult-to-stop humanoid from the DEBE 900-series."

Stockmayer reflected. Delkorel could have sent an AI robot as Professor Antonetti's substitute. Catriona had mentioned an Antonetti. He believed her. The girl had no reason to lie. "Do we have a triangular drama?"

"This triangle has four sides, Roger: Yolexus Enterprise, Delkorel BioElectronix, BioFutura Systematik and NanoScoop Technology Group."

"Go on."

"The robot is eliminated. We've lost the young lady but we know where to find her. She's staying at her mother and sister's place. We can hit the house anytime."

"To just enter the house and gun her down would be a bad idea, Dirk."

"Only if we decide the mother and the sister will live."

"I think we'll leave the rest of the Milton family alone."

"You're calling from an Oberon phone. Is she, by any chance, at the clinic as we speak?"

"I haven't seen her since yesterday. She's only one patient among a considerable number of patients at Oberon. I'm always very busy here. By the way, I have a new idea."

"I'm listening."

"Let's keep Miss Milton alive for the time being. I no longer think she needs to be eliminated right away. Her mysterious and concurrently intriguing physiology is still important to modern science. And, therefore, invaluable to us."

Jarrow chuckled. "Are you fucking her, Roger?"

Stockmayer sipped his coffee. "She's my patient, Dirk. I don't sleep with my patients. It would be unethical."

"We have her genetic profile, including the mutation pattern. We don't need the girl anymore. She's a loose end. Loose ends make me nervous. Let's bury her."

"We have the short-term mutation pattern, Dirk. Not the long-term one. It's beneficial to keep her alive until later."

"The plucky lady has begun to ferret around in the circumstances surrounding her father's death."

"I know. My contact at the BMLC informed me. I realised she'd visited the medico-legal centre only minutes before the attack on board the tram."

"She's a risk factor, Roger. Let's waste her."

"I agree she's a risk factor. But she's one we can handle. If we weigh all the facts, it's clear we have everything to win on keeping her in the equation for the time being."

"Is it clear? Or is it just your own wishful thinking?"

"Relax, Dirk. You worry too much."

"Catriona Milton is your responsibility."

"Trust me. I can handle the girl. I've gained her confidence. I answer her questions with honesty. Everything I've told her about the disease is true. At the same time, I lie by omission."

"Hasn't she suspected you've omitted information?"

"Yes. And I tell her the subject is sensitive and associated with secrecy. I've tricked Miss Milton into believing my partial discretion is in her best interests. I've tricked her into believing she knows everything she needs to know. I've tricked her into believing Rox-1 is already a launched drug."

Catriona thought she had collected Rox-1 at a righteous pharmacy. With Stockmayer's signature on the prescription, the order had reached the 'right' division. Private pharmacies gave Yolexus Enterprise additional leeway.

"What does she know, Roger? How much does she know?"

"She knows her dreams and hallucinations materialise in her external reality. I've explained to her what happens in her brain on a biochemical, quantum biological and neuroscientific level. However, I let her believe the phenomenon is limited to the imbalance between her own inner and outer realities."

"Do you mean she doesn't yet know it isn't just her own reality which is affected? You mean she still believes nobody but herself can experience the conversions of her dreams and hallucinations into physical forms?"

"That's right." He took another sip of the coffee. The taste of the coffee, he had to admit, was getting worse and worse.

"How long can that approach hold up, Roger? What would happen if you were confronted on that point? What would happen if she had her quasi-elastic observations in the presence of other people? What would happen if, for example, the mother or the sister saw the dead and returning husband and father?"

"Many questions at once, Dirk. For the first, I have reason to believe the returning characters want to keep as low a profile as possible. Milton doesn't want to upset his family. And Antonetti, in his capacity as a Delkorel Bio-E representative, wants to be as discreet as we are about this thing."

"Why haven't you mentioned Antonetti?"

"Well, I am mentioning him. Antonetti caught Miss Milton via her hypnagogic and hypnopompic hallucinations. However, she's strong. She defeated him. Antonetti is history."

"He became history when he died the first time around and now he returned, you say, and died again. History has a nasty habit of repeating itself."

Stockmayer thought of a quote by Karl Marx which seemed apt, but he didn't say it. Instead, he waited for Dirk to continue.

"Are there any more returning characters out there?" Dirk asked. "Beings you should have mentioned?"

Stockmayer glanced at the wall clock. "Antonetti and Milton are the only ones I'm aware of. I'm confident my patient would have mentioned other beings if they existed."

"Could she suspect she's a Nargontanac victim?"

"She's a supermodel, not a super chemist. My patient has stopped using Liglitrem and commenced using Roxonodonol. She has no reason to guess Liglitrem and Nargontanac are alternative names for the same substance."

"All the patient subjects from the New Delhi clinical trials are dead. Why is your patient still alive?"

"Because she's a strong woman. Stronger than any other known victim of Nargontanac. Although this unknown disease scares her, she isn't afraid to fight it. She doesn't avoid dealing with her problems in life. She attacks her problems."

"She must wonder whether there are other people who suffer from the same mutation?"

"Yes. She is concerned. Earlier, she even thought about trying to contact other patients."

"Go on."

"Through a rhetorical approach, I got her to give up that idea. She doesn't know she's one of only eight individuals on the planet who has had Nargontanac in their body. She knows nothing about NanoScoop or the clinical study in New Delhi. And, of course, she has no idea she's the only Nargontanac victim still alive."

"We can't afford a single mistake."

"I'm in total control of my patient."

"I'll consider your expert opinion."

"Do that, Dirk. Meanwhile, Baginski can step aside."

"Say something which puts a radiant smile on my face, Roger. Say Roxonodonol will be a global success."

"The brain regulator Roxonodonol will be a global success. The question is, in what way? With its amazing complexity, its awesome computational capacity and its boundless ability to imagine both actual and hypothetical worlds, the human brain is truly wider than the universe."

"I can live with that. Is there anything else to say for now?"

Stockmayer glanced at the letter on his desk.

The letter he had stolen from Catriona's handbag.

"Nothing more for the moment, Dirk."

"Keep me posted."

"As always."

Stockmayer put the letter in his desk drawer.

He remained in his swivel chair, gathering his thoughts.

Thoughts about work, about Catriona, about their night together.

The drug Nargontanac had a staggering, and at the same time scary, side effect. Neither dreams nor hallucinations stayed with the individual. The surroundings were affected too. The patient's fears, nightmares and fantasies coalesced in the objective reality which everyone shared. The later Catriona was told, the better.

The truth was related to an abnormal quantum biology of the patient's nervous system. You couldn't ignore or destroy the truth. Scientific spirit and intellectual curiosity required the discovery be preserved and refined, no matter how obscene the discovery might be. The job of the scientist was to question, to experiment, to theorise, to find, to conclude, to explain. Not to ignore or dismiss or condemn unpleasant ideas for the sake of the unpleasantness itself. Serious science was apolitical. It was irrelevant whether the Nargontanac effect was offensive or not. The finding was too intriguing to be thrown away.

Roxonodonol (Rox-1) was the prototype of a new drug for the treatment of neurological diseases such as narcolepsy, hypersomnia or sleep bruxism. The substance also controlled the changes of the individual's external daily life caused by Nargontanac.

A planned, refined Roxonodonol product (Roxonodonol-2, or Rox-2) would generate and direct the incredible side effect of Nargontanac. Roxonodonol-2 would replace both Nargontanac and the combination prototype Rox-Nargontanac.

Catriona now had Rox-1 in her body. She had it in her brain. He wanted her. He had to study her. He must love her. He loved to study her. He loved to love her. He must have her. Love was uncompromising. Desire was undistortable.

She's the best thing that's happened to me since Henrietta. And she says she's in love with me. We can love each other and still handle our jobs, can't we? Is she waiting for me to call tonight? Or does she want to call me?

Dinner with her again tonight? In town or at my place? Discretion has been agreed. Could we have a discreet dinner in town? Yes, we could. We have a physician–patient relationship. It wouldn't be a disaster if we were seen together in town.

Soon she will discover the letter is gone. An expected development. An exciting progression which I can handle.

Yolexus wants to destroy BioFutura's discovery. BioFutura's smart gene therapy concept threatens the Roxonodonol revolution. Milton's letter to Zimmer proves the side effect of Nargontanac exists. Milton wrote the letter after his own funeral. Catriona doesn't need to know how everything is connected. She doesn't need to know Yolexus Enterprise was behind the murder of her father. The letter may come in handy. I'll keep it. Through the letter, I could get a hold over Jarrow. Jarrow is a crazy gangster. A megalomaniacal psychopath.

A drug which realised dreams and imaginations in some controlled form would have unfathomable consequences. It wouldn't be possible to estimate the value of the substance in terms of trillions of dollars. The chemical would be invaluable, not least to the world's military forces. Its proprietor—Yolexus Enterprise, in other words—would own the planet.

• FIFTY-FOUR •

AMONG THE POSH perfume jars and hairspray cans stood a bottle of gin. Ebba twisted off the cap, splashed a generous dose into her grapefruit juice and stirred the mix with a forefinger. She sipped the drink, licked her finger, smacked her lips and puffed on her cigarette. After a booze-filled night out, she was on her way back into the game. She reached for the pretty little box. An old sweet gift box she had kept because it was so beautiful. A pentagonal box with a sparkling cover in red, orange and silver. She removed the lid. Dipped her saliva-wet index finger in the cocaine powder. Licked her finger. Dipped her finger again. Moved her finger to her nose. What lipstick should I wear tonight? Which perfume? What dress? Which shoes? The phone on the dressing table rang. The cigarette shifted from one hand to the other. "Yeah?"

"Hi, Ebba."

"Oh, hi Cat."

"I just wanted to hear how you're doing, Ebba. Is everything okay back home? The house and everything?"

"Good to hear from you, Cat. I'm fine and everything here's under control. We're lucky to have the best housekeeper and the best gardener in London." She sucked on her cigarette. "We've been worried about you."

"My dad died. I went to Blackfield for the funeral."

"That's what I learnt. It's so fucking *awful*. I want to hug you and comfort you, Cat. You said nothing about it in the note you left in my message box. Heard about it from Anita."

"Oh."

"There was always going to be a grapevine. Discretion about the girls' private lives isn't Anita's strongest skill."

"Yeah."

"When are you coming home?"

"I'll be back at work Monday morning."

"Everybody at the agency is longing for you, sweetie."

"Thanks. How was Milan?"

Ebba giggled. "Perfect, wonderful, awesome."

"You seem to be on top form, Ebba. Going out tonight?"

"You're kidding? Tonight's event is as big as fuck, Cat. You would also be going out tonight if you were here. It's the Kensington banquet. I just stepped out of the shower and got myself a yummy drink and I'm sitting at my dressing table thinking about what outfit to wear and the heatwave is freaky and it's like it's too hot to wear anything at all but you can't show up at a banquet stark naked, can you?" She tittered, adjusted her knickers and puffed on the cigarette. Damn knickers. What the fuck was up with knickers getting stuck in the crack of my bum on a sticky summer day, huh?

"I had forgotten it was tonight," Cat said. "The Kensington banquet."

"You've had other things on your mind. More important stuff, to be honest."

"Well, what do you think about the upcoming event, then?"

"The night will be what you make it. Smashing rumours have reached my ears."

"Tell me."

"Among tonight's guests there's a certain film producer." She snickered, stirred her drink and licked her finger.

"Aha. The Hollywood producer you mentioned a while ago? This Englishman who's interested in offering a certain Ebba Sjödal a contract? The horror movie producer?"

"Well, yeah, or the thriller and action movie producer."

"Who? Paul W.S. Anderson?"

"A secret, Cat. I won't say anything more for now." She grinned at herself in the dressing table's mirror. Her hangover was gone. "So far, in terms of acting, I've still only done that shampoo TV commercial ad. This influential producer just happened to see my little commercial and was impressed."

"Congratulations, Ebba. I'm sure you'll be a success in Hollywood."

She giggled and sipped her drink. "Don't you think it's a bit odd that a TV commercial can trigger a Hollywood giant's interest in a model?"

"Alfred Hitchcock discovered Tippi Hedren that way."

"Oh, oh, oh."

"What movie role, or roles, will you play?"

"Don't know yet. Things have yet to be decided. Lots of secrecy surrounds the movie project. The secrecy is part of the hype-generating strategy."

"With your sneaky appearance, Ebba, you'll be perfect for the role as the female villain."

"I'd rather play the nice and pretty girl."

"Just kidding."

Ebba laughed. "I know you're just kidding."

"You're the naturally nice and pretty girl."

They laughed, despite the circumstances. Ebba couldn't help but notice Cat's laugh was a bit forced. Her best friend's dad was dead. Dead. Murdered. Murdered by Jarrow's organisation. *Stop laughing, Ebba.*

"Ebba?"

"Mmm."

"Roy is cheating on me."

"Uh? Huh?"

"Roy is with another girl."

"Are you sure?"

"Yes."

Ebba dipped the cigarette filter end into the sweet gift box and put it back between her lips. "How ... How can you be sure?"

"Doesn't matter how I know. The essential thing is that I know."

"Damn. Roy Beckman. What a fucking pig."

"Who do you think the girl is?"

"Oh, I don't know, Cat."

"Have you heard anything on the grapevine? Anything at all? The slightest rumour?"

"I have no idea who the girl is."

"Have the tabloids started to speculate?"

"Do you know anyone in London who's always on top of what's written in the tabloids?"

"Ebba Sjödal."

"That's right. If the gossip papers had started to speculate, I would know."

"Okay. But if you find out who the girl is, I want you to tell me straight away."

"Of course. You're my best friend." Ebba checked her fingernails. "Now I have to hurry, Cat. I'm sitting in my underwear, sipping a delicious drink. I have to pick the right outfit and the right shoes and the right earrings and the right lipstick and the right nail polish and the right perfume and decide how I want to shape my hair and I have to buy more cigs."

"You'll be gorgeous tonight, Ebba. As always."

"Thanks."

"If you were in my place, what would you do?"
"What do you mean?"
"It's better to dump a guy than be dumped by the guy, right?"
"Oh, hmm, yes."
"I have to dump Roy before he dumps me?"

What was the safest thing to say? Ebba wondered. She shouldn't sound too eager to agree. A golden opportunity to put her acting skills to the test ahead of her Hollywood career.

"You do whatever you want to do. But perhaps you want to talk to Roy before doing anything at all. Hot guys like Roy Beckman don't grow on trees. It might be possible to save your relationship."

"The relationship can't be saved. It's over."

"You seem eager to break up with him, Cat. Have you met someone else yourself?"

"I'm going to dump Roy. That bastard won't have the pleasure of dumping me before I can dump him."

"Okay. Okay."

"Have fun tonight."

"Thanks. I'll be awesome tonight."

"I'm sure. And keep your ear to the ground."

"As always. Gossip is the most exciting thing there is. Gossip is the only real quality news."

Cat laughed a little. "See you on Monday."

"Monday, sweetie."

Two thoughts competed in Ebba's head: party on Cromwell Road in Kensington tonight, and the meeting at the Golden Plaza Hotel in Paddington tomorrow—with Dirk Jarrow.

• FIFTY-FIVE •

JARROW SAT IN a leather armchair reading a cosmology textbook. Lisa-Marie lay naked on the sofa, on her belly, ankles crossed. She was social, considerate, reasonable, compassionate, captivating and free from mood swings. As a stuffed sex toy, Lisa-Marie was the perfect wife. An unproblematic woman who neither nagged nor talked back.

He looked up from the book. "Listen, Lisa-Marie."

Her acrylic eyes twinkled in the light from the ceiling lamp.

"It says here that in the distant future, our galaxy, the Milky Way, will collide with the Andromeda Galaxy. Sounds bad, doesn't it?"

His wife didn't answer but the gleam in her eyes remained. Also, she had a smile on her mouth. Lisa-Marie's body language was more significant than a thousand words. He had captured her attention.

"On a different note," he continued, "before the sun explodes, mankind, if still around then, must evacuate to another world to have a chance to survive. Would you like to accompany me on such a gigantic journey?"

She didn't answer with words. Again, words were superfluous.

"I would bring you along on an interplanetary spaceflight, Lisa-Marie."

The tip of her motorised rubber tongue probed a corner of her mouth.

"I would build my empire with Roxonodonol in a parallel world. Create my empire with you. You're eternal, chronically young, constantly attractive. You *are* eternity. Roxonodonol is bigger than the biggest fantasies." He closed the book, undressed, went over to the sofa, turned his wife on her back, placed a pillow under her head and lay down on top of her.

What was Stockmayer up to? The neuroscientist seemed to be running parallel thoughts elsewhere. Even though he demonstrated a loyal commitment, something else hovered below the surface at the same time. What? A secret agenda? Jarrow lifted the phone and placed a national call to Blackfield.

"Thank you for calling Westerman Crescent Private Clinic, how may I help you?" The female voice carried a Yorkshire accent—Sheffield or Blackfield. Felicia Ricker sounded spirited indeed. In another life, she could have been a hyper-ambitious restaurant hostess.

WCP was a healthcare centre which belonged to the Yolexus Group. There was a total of five WCP branches scattered across Great Britain. Jarrow cleared his throat. "Good evening, Felicia. Mr. Jarrow here."

"Oh, good evening, Mr. Jarrow. What can I do for you, sir?"

"One Baginski is supposed to have admitted himself to WCP Blackfield. Correct?"

"Yes, sir. Gunshot wounds to both arms. Bullets fired with automatic weapons." Her voice was as lively and happy as ever, as though she was talking about a nice weather forecast.

Felicia knew what discretion meant at Yolexus Enterprise. If she didn't know, she wouldn't be a WCP receptionist.

"Felicia, connect my call to Mr. Baginski's room."

"Mr. Baginski has already left WCP, sir."

"When?"

"Earlier today, sir."

"That was quick."

"Very quick indeed."

"Who discharged him?"

"Mr. Baginski discharged himself, sir."

"I see. Did he leave a message?"

"No, sir. However, just before he disappeared, I heard him talking to himself. He said, 'The mission proceeds as planned.'"

• FIFTY-SIX •

SHE PHONED THE Oberon Clinic. His direct number. "Hi, Roger. It's me."

"Catriona … I'm longing for you."

"I'm longing for you too, Roger. But I have a problem."

"Tell me."

"I'm missing a letter. A letter in a light-yellow envelope."

"What kind of letter?"

"From Dad. A letter he wrote the day after his own funeral. On the front of the envelope it says, 'To my twin daughters Catriona & Janice Milton'. I kept it either in my skirt pocket or in my handbag yesterday. I'm both troubled and annoyed by this mess. Let me know if you should come across the letter by any chance."

"Unfortunately, I haven't seen it. Could you have lost it among the turmoil aboard the tram? Or during your run to the bus stop?"

"I guess it isn't impossible. But if I dropped it in town, someone should have found it and contacted my sister. Janice Milton is listed in the local directory."

"Such an optimistic theory assumes the letter is found by a benevolent person, and that it hasn't been destroyed by the traffic on Roderick or Yarmouth, or disappeared in a gutter. Blackfield is no idyll. Everything which falls to the ground in this town is regarded as junk."

"Yeah. You're right."

"There's an alternative explanation you must consider."

"What do you mean?"

"That the letter never existed."

"Now I don't understand what you mean."

"You do understand, Catriona. If you recall what I've said about your illness."

She was thinking. "Dad came back. You know that. I've told you, you believed me, and you explained the science. The equilibrium between my outer and my inner realities has been shifted in a sick way."

"That's correct. Your father returned to *your* outer reality. Your father wrote a letter to you and your sister through *your* reality. Your pathological perception of reality doesn't affect other people. It is limited to your own distorted subjectivity."

"My sister has seen the letter. How do you explain that?"

"Only from your perspective. Your mind, the circuitry of your brain, fabricated the scenario."

"My sister says she has seen it."

"Your imagination says your sister says she has seen it."

"Two members of staff aboard the Intercity train from London said they could see the message which Antonetti had scribbled on the train window."

"You imagined the train staff said they could see it. In fact, there was no message to see. No prehistoric lizards either."

"The figure in the black raincoat and hat, the sixteen-fingered Professor Antonetti, broke into my bedroom in London. You know that. I've told you and you said you believed me. The professor appeared as a yellow dinosaur. He was present and he chased me through the house."

"It's true and I still believe you. However, the scenario is still limited to your own person. The trespasser's physical presence resulted from abnormal quantum interactions between particles within your subjective universe."

"This is all crazy."

"There are crazy incidents everywhere. The perfect world is a utopia. Please answer the following question: How many people have seen Antonetti or your father in the last few days?"

"Hmm. Nobody. Nobody but me."

"Your experiences of a returning father and the creature in the raincoat are nothing but electrochemical byproducts of your damaged central nervous system."

She sighed. "How long will my crazy life continue like this? When will all the freaky stuff end?"

"You will be fine soon. I guarantee you will be restored."

She was thinking. With or without the letter she would get to Karl-Heinz Zimmer's place. With or without the letter she would convince Sis to accompany her to Rockthorpe tonight.

Visiting Zimmer could be more important than the letter itself. Dad must have known and taken into account that problems could arise. There must be a way out of this mess. *A way out ... a way out ... a way out ...* "I don't feel very well right now."

"I understand that. But I want you to feel well. I want you to feel well because I'm in love with you. I'm in love with you and I want to take care of you. May I take care of you?"

"I require you take care of me."

"I will. I promise."

"And I can take care of you."

"I know you can, Catriona. I've experienced it."

"How do you want to spend the night? You want company?"

"I want company."

"Me too."

"What will your mother say?"

"I'm a big girl. I can handle Mum."

"Shall we start with dinner? At seven?"

"I have things to do with my sister. I don't know what time we'll be done. Would dinner past ten o'clock be too late?"

"Not at all. I'll be working in my library, preparing my talk for the event at Rainbow Tower tomorrow."

"Yes, of course. I don't want to disturb your preparations."

"You won't. On the contrary, you're my fresh inspiration."

"What time tomorrow do you have to get to the Rainbow?"

"Not until the afternoon."

"So, we'll have a nice morning together, then."

"Without a doubt."

"Dinner tonight where? Your place?"

"I was about to suggest a nice little restaurant in Springlake, just three blocks from my house. The place is open well past midnight, serves superb dishes and is respectful of privacy. The owner is a good friend of mine. He knows what I want. He'll make sure we have a pleasant and discreet meal."

"Sounds exciting."

"You're an exciting woman. You suit exciting places."

She didn't comment. She waited.
"I'll pick you up," he said.
"It'll be more discreet if I take a taxi."
"Are you sure?"
"Yes. No problem."
"Okay. I'll see you at my place and then we'll walk to the restaurant. Send me a text message when you're ready. No hurry. Until I see you again, I'll be busy with work."
"I'll tell Mum I've been invited for dinner."
"Invited for dinner by your doctor?"
"To be honest, I'm old enough to dine with my doctor. It isn't my mother's business. By the way, my love life isn't my mother's business either. Even so, in order to make my stay in Mum's house as frictionless as possible, I think I'll lie about one thing or another."
"Do we have a serious romance?"
"I think so. We have to find out. In a perfect world we would already know, but someone said the perfect world is a utopia."
"I love you, Catriona."
"I love you, Roger."
"See you tonight."
"Tonight. Soon."

• FIFTY-SEVEN •

BAGINSKI SAT IN his stolen Honda, studying the Miltons' house from across the street. The Honda was one of about twenty cars parked along this side of the avenue. It attracted no special attention in the neighbourhood.

At the WCP a brilliant surgeon and a pretty nurse had treated and bandaged his injuries. While there, he had bathed and switched to new and clean clothes. He wore a dark-green blazer, dark-blue shirt, grey chinos and dark-blue Asics shoes.

He checked the local news on the 21st-century pocket computer. Neither Yolexus Enterprise nor BioFutura Systematik was mentioned in connection with the events of the last few days. Investigators had found the remains of a cyborg destroyed by an explosion in the ruins of a funeral chapel in Goston Cemetery. Not a word about Delkorel BioElectronix or NanoScoop. Did it mean the robot hadn't yet been identified as a Delkorel Bio-E product? Or had the authorities chosen to conceal they'd found a link to Delkorel Bio-E? As he'd expected, not a word about Pemonirin (PMN7091) either.

Commercial plastic explosives contained well-known high-explosive chemical substances such as RDX, for example, in C-4, or a mixture of RDX and PETN, for example, in Semtex. Materials scientists in Germany had developed a nanosensor which could detect a single PETN molecule among ten billion air molecules. A phenomenal invention. However, Delkorel Bio-E's non-commercial Pemonirin contained neither PETN nor RDX. The high-explosive chemical in PMN7091 had the unofficial name Triglaronal (TRGL).

None of the ingredients in PMN7091 could be derived, neither before nor after detonation. Today, no equipment or technology existed that could determine which explosive had destroyed a church in Goston.

He checked the time. Miss Milton, the model, had entered the house seven minutes ago. The spectacular beauty who happened to be Dr. Stockmayer's patient. Perhaps she was alone in the house. Perhaps not. He didn't want to shoot the girl dead in the street. His excellent morals stopped him. He condemned unprovoked street violence. The events aboard the tram and on Yarmouth Bridge didn't count as unprovoked street violence. The provoker was Delkorel Bio-E.

He would finish the girl indoors. The house was more discreet than the street. He opened the glove box and took out WCP receptionist Felicia Ricker's military weapon, a brand-new Beretta M9 semi-automatic double-action/single-action. He put the pistol and the silencer into his blazer pockets, got out of the Honda and walked up to the house.

He judged he was still undiscovered. None of the three women appeared in any of the windows which faced the street. He pushed down on the door handle. The house was unlocked. He heard the lock spindle rotate and the bolt clack back.

He swung the door open. The hinges squeaked—too loud. The brief noise must have been heard throughout the ground floor. A cat miaowed somewhere. Time wasn't reversible. The squeaking second belonged to history. He completed his movement, slipped into the house and closed the door. Again, the hinges squeaked.

He surveyed the hall, mounted the Beretta silencer and rested his index finger on the trigger. The door to the living room was ajar. Sound from a TV streamed into the hall. He was about to take a step towards the living room when he discovered he wasn't alone in the hall any longer.

The cat stared. A fat orange-and-white-striped cat with glimmering green almond-shaped eyes. Baginski stared back. The cat miaowed. Baginski said nothing. A staring contest with a cat was unwinnable. He turned his eyes away, accepting defeat. He wouldn't fire any shots at the cat. He was too well-mannered to do such a thing. To put a bullet in a cat indicated a lack of self-control. The cat yawned, miaowed, swung around and disappeared towards the kitchen.

Baginski moved to the door to the living room. The TV viewer had either missed the cat's miaowing because of the noisy TV or simply ignored the cat's familiar miaowing. The TV viewer wouldn't be disturbed.

He peered inside. Rita Milton, widow and mother, sat immobile like a wax doll on the sofa, with her eyes glued to the TV screen. If she pulled her gaze from the TV and looked his way, he would shoot her dead in zero time. She was watching an action film. He disliked entertainment violence. It had a destructive effect on people's discipline.

The beautiful daughter had to be in another room. If Catriona Milton were downstairs she would have reacted, like the cat, when the front door squeaked. Thus, the model must be on the first floor.

He didn't care where the other daughter, the ugly and malformed one, was. It didn't matter. If Janice Milton stayed away, she would live. If she stood in his way, she would die.

He walked up the stairs.

A framed wedding photograph stood on a chest of drawers in the first room. Only one side of the double bed was made. On the bedside table lay an electricity bill and a leaflet from an insurance company. At the desk was a condolence card. Rita Milton's bedroom.

The second room looked like it had been decorated by a depressed child. Voodoo dolls and bizarre puppets hung on strings and wires from the ceiling. Pink carpet. The bed with reinforced steel bottom seemed to be dimensioned for an elephant. The neon-green bedspread featured pink pigs of various sizes. Janice Milton's room.

The third room held a faint scent of some wonderful perfume. On the bedside table stood a mini-bottle of Chanel No 5. On the bed lay an August issue of British *Vogue*. On the floor next to the bed sat an exclusive handbag from Hermès and shiny black shoes from Prada. Underwear from the luxury brand La Perla had been tossed onto the backrest of a chair. Without a doubt, Catriona Milton's room, that is, the guest room. In a corner stood a destroyed full-length mirror. No splinters on the floor. The room had been cleaned. The thrashed mirror—both the glass and the wooden rear panel—puzzled him, then he pushed it out of his mind. The mirror wasn't his problem.

No girl in the room. Thirteen minutes ago, he had seen the model enter the house. The upstairs bathroom remained to be checked.

"Janice? Catriona?" Mrs. Milton's voice from the staircase.

The door between the guest room and the corridor was open.

"Are you home, girls? Sounds like you're home."
Footsteps. Mrs. Milton was on her way upstairs.

• FIFTY-EIGHT •

HE DRAGGED LISA-MARIE into the bathroom and tilted her voluptuous body against the washbasin. She never gained weight. His diligent wife kept her ideal weight of nine stone.

Jarrow had honed his craft. Lisa-Marie's metallic body frame weighed the same as her previous skeleton. Her tanned skin and resilient polymer fillings reflected the original Lisa-Marie's shapely curves.

He opened the door of the mirrored cabinet, took out toothpaste and toothbrush, then pried open her mouth.

As he brushed his wife's teeth, his free hand found her rump. Caressing her stuffed buttocks was like fondling an authentic woman's rear end.

"The toothbrush is done, sweetie. Time to rinse your mouth." He filled a glass to the brim with water, leaned his wife backwards and poured all the water into her mouth in one go. She had a hard time spitting. He had to bend her neck forward and slant her over the basin. The frothy mixture of toothpaste and water which flowed out of her mouth looked like melting pear ice cream. He licked her lips, then wiped her mouth with a terry towel. "Do you need to pee, baby?"

She didn't answer. Hence, she didn't need to pee. He looked into the toilet and found the turtle was still splashing around. The upper floor's toilet water wasn't used for cooking. "What luck you don't need to pee, baby. Bruno hasn't finished bathing yet."

He grabbed his wife under her arms, dragged her across the bathroom floor and leaned her against the shower cubicle. He embraced her and she embraced him. They were a happy couple. Happy couples liked to hug. Old love never dies.

"Time to have a shower, Lisa-Marie."

Her teeth and acrylic eyes glittered.

"Before we enter the shower, we have to fix a detail." He spread her legs, put two fingers into her elastic plastic vagina. His forefinger and middle finger squeezed the tampon and pulled it out. *Pop!* Sounded like a cork popped from a champagne bottle. The tampon smelled of lubricating oil. The electric vibrator was leaking oil. He must repair the electric motor as soon as possible, that is, before the next sexual intercourse.

"You're going to be nice and fragrant in all your three most significant holes, sweetie."

His wife didn't protest. She realised the importance of good intimate hygiene. She also understood he didn't count her urethra among her three most significant holes.

Lisa-Marie's anus consisted of two flexible O-rings in synthetic rubber. The custom O-rings had limited lifetimes, similar to tap washers. Lisa-Marie's well-maintained anus wasn't dripping. She underwent regular O-ring replacements every seven months. Her rectum was a special latex tube which offered adjustable friction during experimental anal sex. Through his knowledge of rheology, the science of deformation and flow properties of materials, Jarrow had recreated in meticulous detail the natural and original characteristics of Lisa-Marie's lovely anus and her just as lovely rectum.

Earth was a sick planet. The sicker the planet, the greater the profit for the pharmaceutical industry. Over the past twelve-month period, the world's population had bought drugs for more than five hundred billion dollars. Yolexus Enterprise (YE) was far from one of the largest pharmaceutical companies. YE was a stealthy organisation which thrived in the shadow of industry giants such as Pfizer, Johnson & Johnson, Novartis, Roche, Merck & Co. and Sanofi. Jarrow saw himself as a dark horse. He had the trust of the board. YE could only expand. The trust he had wasn't related to Roxonodonol. Not the entire board of directors was aware of the substance. Moreover, no member of the board knew the CEO had retained his wife's body since her passing twenty-four years ago.

He entertained no illusions. No one held a CEO post forever. A reputation could be short-lived and ruined overnight by social media. The average shelf life of CEOs had shrunk to three years. The board demanded rapid and positive results. At the same time, the board was worried a smart boss like Jarrow would accept a lucrative offer from a competitor. He enjoyed the choices in life. For the time being, he would direct and supervise the interests of Yolexus. The board recently identified three strategic priorities: to continue cultivating a varied and global business, varied without sacrificing expertise; to deliver more quality product variants; and to simplify the business model.

His self-confidence grew. He expected YE would meet the long-term goals of reducing risks and creating sustainable growth for the shareholders. His own long-term goal was to achieve sustainable growth for himself. The finesse was to give an impression of caring about shareholders. The Roxonodonol project was more important than YE. If he broke with YE or was forced to leave, he would develop the Rox project elsewhere. He would persuade Stockmayer to accompany him, provided it was still possible to rely on Stockmayer. He wanted to count on the top neuroscientist. Nobody knew Rox-1 or Rox-2 better than Stockmayer.

In intellectual circles, word had it that Stockmayer was a contender for a Nobel Prize. He was supposed to be a nominee mentioned in communications regarding either the chemistry or the medicine prize. If the fifty-two-year-old received the right phone call from Stockholm, it would boost the marketing and advertising profile of both Oberon and YE. More channels to new research grants could be opened. More secret and illegal projects could be launched in the wake of Rox-1 and Rox-2. And where to go from there? Together, Jarrow and Stockmayer would change the world. They were already busy changing it.

• FIFTY-NINE •

AT THE RED Unicorn pub, Janice cleared tables and set tables. Not without reason, she left for last the table where Cat had been sitting. The blue envelope was there. The envelope with the letter. The letter to Janice from Stockmayer. A fantasy letter about plastic surgery in Vienna. She was a monster, she thought. A freak. Therefore, the letter must be a crass imagination. She would throw the indecent letter in a litter bin. Did she want to throw it away unopened? Or first open it and then throw it away? Or first tear it to pieces and then throw it away? Or first burn it and then throw away the ashes? Or …

One table left to clear and set. But not just any table. The table with the blue envelope. The envelope with her name on the front. The envelope from Cat's physician. Did she dare open it? Did she dare peek at the letter? Not read it in its entirety, only look at the introduction? Did she dare?

Jan glanced around. Nobody was looking in her direction. No one noticed her existence. She was as popular as a weed. Her ugliness strengthened her seclusion. She was Cat's diametrical opposite. Sis was an attraction, an irresistible magnet.

Jan touched the envelope. Her index finger brushed the four words on the front: To Miss Janice Milton. In the lively tavern, she was both isolated and not isolated. She could open the envelope and peek at the letter, and nobody at the tavern would care. She was the disgusting waitress who was able to open the envelope in lightless solitude anywhere. People's indifference represented the safe barrier. In two minutes she must be at work behind the bar, pulling pints. She opened the flap of the envelope and plucked out the letter. A folded sheet of paper with text on both sides. She unfolded it. The text was concise. She dared read. She forgot she dared read.

Dear Miss Milton,

As a follow-up to our conversation the other day, please find below information about one of the most brilliant plastic surgeons working today. Jakob Ratzinger is a good friend of mine. Dr. Ratzinger's clinic is located on Südtiroler Platz in Vienna's 4th district (see overleaf for details). I'm not unaware of your financial situation but I want to urge you to listen to your sister.

If you decide to contact Dr. Ratzinger, don't be shy. I've already mentioned you and your case to my friend, and you should know the man is very easy to talk to. He is a pleasant and empathetic person. Whatever you decide about your future, I wish you all the best.

Greetings,
R. Stockmayer
Director—Oberon Clinic,
Blackfield (Selmore Village)
& London (Earls Court)

• SIXTY •

"DIX MIAOWED." HER voice, closer. "Are you home, girls?"

Still in the model's room, Baginski moved to the open door, slipped it shut and backed into the room.

"Do some housework, girls. Help me water the flowers."

Mrs. Milton's footsteps had reached the upper corridor. Even though he lacked empathy for Mrs. Milton, he would avoid dropping her, if it could be avoided. As a good-natured man, he didn't kill people without a qualified reason. Also, Jarrow had demanded a discreet operation on all fronts.

"Janice?" Pause. "Catriona?"

He pointed the gun at the door and waited. The cat miaowed somewhere in the depths of the house.

Footsteps moved along the corridor, stopped. Mrs. Milton knocked on the door to Janice's room. "Janice?" After a silent moment, she pushed the door open. Again, silence. Then the sharp sound of a door pulled closed by an annoyed mother.

Footsteps again. Closer and closer. The steps stopped outside the door to the guest room. "Catriona?"

His trigger finger stirred. If the woman opened the door, he would shoot her in the head.

Mrs. Milton knocked three times. "Catriona?"

Baginski stood as immobile as a mannequin.

"Catriona? Have you gone to bed? Now?"

Silence.

"Have you taken a nap to fight your EDS?"

Silence.

"Are you sleeping?"

Silence.

"Have you already fallen asleep?"

Silence.

"You're a spoilt diva, Catriona. You think appearance is the only thing which matters. You think you can come and go as you please and do whatever you want and get whatever you want if you're just gorgeous to look at."

Silence.

"You didn't even think it was worth the effort to tell your mother you were going to sleep at a friend's place last night."

Silence.

"Isn't your mother's guest room good enough? If you don't like it here, I suggest you check in at a hotel in town."

Silence.

"Janice says you slept at Louise Drum's place last night. Is it true? Or did you spend the night with some new boy?"

Silence.

"According to the papers, you're going out with that hotshot footballer Roy Beckman. Is that still right? What kind of a boy is he anyway? Is he well-behaved?"

Silence.

"Catriona? I've seen you in a new set of indecent posters. Adverts for some raunchy lingerie. You're posing in those posters wearing nothing but raunchy lingerie."

Silence.

"Catriona? How do you think it feels to a mother to see her daughter posing on posters wearing nothing but lingerie? Two of those shameful posters are on display down Central Station. Those posters are probably on display everywhere. Millions of people have seen my daughter wearing nothing but saucy lingerie. How could you do this to me? How could you?"

Silence.

"Imagine if the neighbours have seen the posters. What if my neighbours are gossiping, whispering and cracking jokes about those rude posters? My neighbours are also your sister's neighbours. Your obscene posters risk making life a misery for both your mother and your sister."

Silence.

Baginski noted how the door handle turned, stopped, stayed there, half-turned and then returned to its original position.

"Catriona? It isn't worth my time to argue with you right now. I have things to do and I don't want to be disturbed. I'll have a word with you later. When you're awake."

Footsteps again. Leaving steps. Audible only by a small margin. In the direction to the left. Towards the bathroom? The footsteps either vanished or stopped. "Catriona? Hello? Light is coming out through the gap under the bathroom door. Are you in the bathroom or have you forgotten to switch off the light?" Pause. "In this home, we're thrifty with the use of electricity. Remember that." Pause. "And don't waste hot water."

Silence. Then moving footsteps again. Back to the stairway, back to the ground floor. The cat miaowed again somewhere in the distance.

He swung the door open, stepped out of the model's bedroom, shut the door and checked the corridor. Not a cat in sight. As he approached the bathroom, he reflected on Mrs. Milton's last monologue. Most bathroom doors had locks, privacy locks rather than high-security locks. If this bathroom door had a lock, it had to be unlocked. Alternatively, the door had no lock. Would a daughter in a chilly mother–daughter relationship ignore to lock the bathroom door?

He was at the bathroom door now. Indeed, a sliver of light was visible beneath the door. The rectangular lock was a cheap, common model in polished chrome. Its vacant/engaged indicator showed vacant, the only indication which fitted Mrs. Milton's loud monologue. He pressed his ear against the door and listened. Running water. In a bathtub? The model was filling the bathtub. Perhaps she was already naked. Maybe she was about to step into the tub. What a nice coincidence. He had already murdered a woman in a bathtub. Only three days ago in Middlesbrough. Now another bathing lady was about to be added to his impressive track record.

He opened the door and almost started shooting.

The tub was empty. Hot water was flowing from a tap. The cabinet mirror was steaming up.

No Catriona Milton.

The bathroom was empty.

• SIXTY-ONE •

"ABOUT TIME," JAN muttered.

"I'm not late," Cat said.

"You look stressed, Sis."

"I feel paranoid."

"What do you mean?"

"Because of everything which has happened and is still

happening, I decided to leave Mum's house via the porch and the back garden."

"Did you suspect someone was watching the front of the house? Someone shadowing you?"

"I didn't suspect anything concrete. I just experienced a creepy paranoia. Never mind."

The sisters looked around. They were not alone in the Red Unicorn car park. Guests were coming and going. Cars were arriving and leaving. A normal atmosphere on a normal evening. No misplaced detail.

"Cat?"

"Mmm?"

"I've read Stockmayer's letter."

"Good."

"He suggests I contact this plastic surgeon Jakob Ratzinger in Vienna."

"Good advice. I agree with Stockmayer."

"The important thing is what *I* think. Do you understand?"

"We could contact Ratzinger together. I'd be happy to help you with everything. When I have the time. I mean, when I can make time for it."

"I've never travelled anywhere. I've never dared."

"I know."

"Have you been to Vienna?"

"Many times. Where is Ratzinger's clinic?"

"At a place called Südtiroler Platz."

"I've passed through Südtiroler Platz several times on my way to wonderful shopping streets. I love shopping in Vienna."

Jan scowled. "As if I were interested in shopping."

"Do you dare travel to Vienna and see Ratzinger?"

Jan didn't answer.

"Just promise me you'll consider it. I'll pay for everything."

Jan didn't answer.

"Speaking of letters ... Dad's letter to us has disappeared. The important letter we're supposed to deliver to Zimmer."

Jan raised her eyebrows. "You mean you've lost it?"

"It's gone. I don't know how but it's gone."

"Great, Cat. What are we going to do now?"

"We go to Rockthorpe tonight anyway."

"Without the letter?"

"Without the letter. Montrose Place? Which number?"

"Twenty-one."

"Come on, let's go. I'll pay for a taxi."

"Wait."

"We don't have time to wait."

"What are we going to say to Zimmer? We have no letter."

"What we are going to say, we decide when we arrive."

"Do you mean we're going to improvise?"

"Right."

"Do we dare?"

"We dare. Dad and Zimmer were close colleagues."

"The letter never existed, Cat. Right?"

"It existed. Don't whine now. We're in a hurry."

"Then, you wrote the letter yourself. As I guessed earlier."

"The letter was from Dad." It was true, Cat thought. *Roger mentioned alternative explanations for the missing letter. I may have lost it somewhere in town or fantasised about its existence. Sis doesn't deny she has seen and read it, though Roger suggested some details in a conversation with Sis may have resulted from the unhealthy distortion of my outer reality. Even now? No, I don't think so. If I didn't write the letter myself based on some hallucinated but correct knowledge of relevant sciences (how that could have been possible is beyond me), there's only one acceptable explanation: I lost the letter in town.*

The taxi turned into Montrose Place and stopped outside number 21. The time was half past six. Three hours until sunset. Fluffy clouds in the northern sky looked like dollops of whipped cream. The roundabout was abandoned. The August air was quiet, almost eerie. Holiday times.

"He may not be home," Jan said.

"That's what we're going to find out," Cat said.

"He may still be at BioFutura. Or at work elsewhere."

"You could have called and asked."

"I called yesterday."

"You could have called again today."

"Zimmer could be on holiday."

"Look at the windows. Lights are on everywhere."

"He may have forgotten to turn off the lights."

"You can forget to turn off a light or two, Jan. But not all the lights. The whole house is lit up."

"The lights could be on switch-timers."

"The point is, we don't know."

"Do we need to walk up to the house?"

"Yes."

"What if someone is lurking in the bushes, Cat. I'm afraid."

"Nobody is here but us. We can't see or hear anyone else."

"If someone is lurking in the bushes, we're not supposed to see or hear anything mysterious. That's the point of lurking."

"I'm so tired of your whining."

"You don't think I'm tired of you?"

"Dad said you should help me. You've agreed to help."

"That agreement no longer applies. Your trick with the so-called letter from Dad changes everything. A letter you probably wrote yourself."

"Shut up, Jan. We're walking up to the house."

The facade of Zimmer's house was a combination of red brick on the ground floor and white PVC on the first floor. Large and high windows on both floors. Blue-black roofing in synthetic rubber. The sisters reached the front door. Cat put an index finger on the doorbell's push button.

"Wait a minute, Cat."

"Wait? What now?"

"What if he's busy?"

"We're about to find out, aren't we?"

"He may have a visitor."

"Well, *we're* visitors."

"We're not invited."

Cat saw terror in Jan's eyes—and she realised something new. "You've never been to someone else's home, have you?"

Jan squeezed her lips tight, shaking her head.

"Visiting someone's home is a new experience to you. Your sad life takes place in Mum's house and at that unhip pub only."

Jan closed her eyes. Her hands trembled.

"Relax, Jan. I take full responsibility for this visit. You have nothing to worry about. Okay?"

Jan nodded, but her eyes were still shut.

"I think Zimmer likes to talk to me," Cat continued. "He gave me that impression when we chatted at the wake."

Jan opened her eyes. "There isn't a single guy anywhere who doesn't give the impression of liking to talk to you, Cat." She sighed. "Have you rung the doorbell? You were in such a hurry."

"I'll ring the bell now." Cat pushed the ring button.

They waited. Waited what felt like a long time, Cat thought. She glanced down at her diamond-encrusted Bvlgari watch. A mere minute had passed. She pressed the ring button again and was struck by a horrifying thought. What if Zimmer was one of them? This visit was a trap. Zimmer was one of them. Dad didn't know Zimmer was involved.

"You look strange, Cat. Did you just get sick?"

"I'm fine."

"You look mysterious."

"What if he's one of them?" Cat whispered.

"Them? Who?"

"The conspirators. Imagine if he's one of them."

"Zimmer?"

Cat nodded.

"The letter was to him," Jan said.

"Yeah, but what if Zimmer belongs to the same side of this affair as Antonetti did, and Dad didn't know. Antonetti didn't act on his own initiative. The professor worked on behalf of some shadowy corporation."

"You scare me when you talk like this. Come on, let's get home to Mum. I'm getting hungry. We could help Mum with the cooking."

"I'll try the door handle."

"Are you insane?"

"If the door is unlocked, I'll enter the house."

"Drop it, Cat. Don't you dare touch the door handle. Let's get out of here. Let's get home to Mum and Dix."

Cat grinned. "If the door is unlocked, we'll both go inside."

"No, no, no."

Cat grabbed the door handle and pushed it downwards. A metallic sound—*click!*—from the lock mechanism. She pulled and the door slid open.

"Look," Cat said. "Unlocked. And no burglar alarm."

"We're not allowed to be here, Cat."

"We'd better check out the circumstances surrounding the unlocked house. Zimmer will thank us for our consideration. Trust me. The BFS Deputy CEO likes to talk to me."

Jan moaned. "What if Mum knew what we were doing?"

They entered the house, Jan two yards behind her sister.

"Dr. Zimmer?" Cat moved through the lit hall. "Hello? Dr. Zimmer? Hello?" She paused. "This is Catriona Milton. I'm here with my twin sister Janice."

No response.

Jan caught up with her sister. "That's enough. Let's get out of here. Before something bad happens."

"It isn't enough. Not by a long shot. Mum can do without us a while longer."

"What are you going to do?"

"What do you think? I'm going to search the house."

"No, no. Are you nuts?"

"Something isn't right. We happen to be here and we have to investigate the situation. What if something has happened to

Zimmer? Imagine if he has slipped on a bar of soap or a banana skin and hit his head on the floor and fainted."

"Or lying in wait for us so he can torture and kill us, if your own conspiracy theory is correct."

"We're on a secret mission, remember? We owe it to Dad to see this through."

Jan snorted like a rhino. "Your responsibility, Cat. I owe nothing to nobody."

They moved deeper into the house.

"How quiet it is," Jan whispered.

"We don't have to whisper," Cat said. "Whispering people have something to hide." She called again, "Hello? Dr. Zimmer? Hello? The Milton sisters are here."

They arrived at the kitchen. Empty. They continued to the laundry room. Empty. The living room. Empty. Then to the next lit room, and the next, and the next. No Dr. Zimmer.

"Lots of family photos," Jan said. "When I found his contact details, I guessed he was unmarried. I guessed wrong. So, Zimmer has a wife and three children. Where is the family?"

"It's holiday times," Cat said. "If he's a workaholic, the wife and the children might have gone on holiday without him. Or they might have gone on holiday ahead of him. Mrs. Zimmer and the children might already be in another city or even another country, waiting for him."

"This is getting scarier and scarier," Jan said.

"Let's go upstairs." Cat went to the staircase.

"Are you serious? I don't want to go upstairs."

"You don't have to. Feel free to check the garage."

"No, no. I'm not going anywhere on my own."

"Come along upstairs, then."

Janice panted but she did move. The girls walked up the stairs and stopped at the top, listening.

The first-floor corridor held several shadows, including those thrown by two backlit sisters. Closed doors on both sides, though one door, at the far end on the right-hand side, was ajar. Yellow light fell out into the hallway. Cat shouted, "Dr. Zimmer? The Milton sisters are here. Hello?"

No answer.

"Let's get out of here," Jan said. "*Now*. I don't like this place and I'm *hungry*."

"No," Cat said. "We'll peek into these rooms. Let's start with the room whose door is open." She moved. "Come on."

Jan made a face but followed her sister.

They stopped where the strip of yellow light cut through the shadowed floor of the corridor.

"Hello? Dr. Zimmer? The Milton sisters here. Our dad sent us to see you." Cat crossed the threshold to the room. She froze to ice and screamed.

"What is it? Why are you screaming?" Jan caught up with her sister. Jan's piercing shriek drowned out Cat's brief yell.

The room featured bookcases along all walls. A wardrobe. A chandelier cast the yellow light. A desk lamp threw a cooler light. Zimmer sat in a chair behind the desk. His remaining eye stared at the sisters. The scientist was as clean-shaven now as he had been at the wake and he wore the same hexagonal glasses as before. However, the left lens was now shattered. A scalpel, not just its blade but almost the whole of its handle too, had been pushed into the man's brain through the lens and through his eye. The plastic eyeglass frame arms had been positioned not behind his ears but straight across his ears. Another two scalpels, rammed through the eyeglass frame arms and buried deep into the ears, secured the glasses to the cadaver's head.

"How awful," Jan croaked. "Who can have done such a thing?"

Blood stained Zimmer's shirt and trousers and the floor beneath the chair. On the desk, in front of the corpse, a blood-spattered notebook was open at a page which started:

August Notes #46—Last phone call from Sandra:

A clinical study commissioned by Yolexus Enterprise. A drug called Nargontanac. Patient subjects developed mental disorders. A legal proceeding followed but no convictions. Both NanoScoop and Yolexus were freed from liability.

Work-related scribble which meant nothing to Cat. She tried to collect herself, with more or less success. "How can you drive knives through solid eyeglass frame arms? How much force is behind such an act? With or without a hammer or any other tool? Do you see any tools anywhere?"

"What does it matter?" Jan started crying. "Let's get out of here right now. I don't want to be here anymore."

"I don't want to be here anymore either."

"Three knives." Jan whimpered. "Not one knife but three. As if the killer had a point to make."

What would happen now? Cat wondered. No letter. No Zimmer alive. Had she let Dad down? Had she believed she could play detective and be some sort of spy-like messenger? Would Dad return from his grave again? Would Dad pop out from the dark and shout at her because she'd failed?

"We just agreed," Jan said, sobbing. "Neither you nor I want to be in this horrible house anymore. Why are we still here? I'm afraid and hungry and tired and have a stomach ache. I want to get home to Dix and Mum. We're leaving. Do you understand?"

"We can't leave just like that."

"What do you mean?"

"Shouldn't we call the police?"

"You can call if you want. Don't involve me. Use your mobile, but not now. First, we disappear from here."

"I have a better idea."

"You have no idea how eager I am to hear about your idea."

"We call the police anonymously from Zimmer's phone."

"As you wish, even though I think your idea is inferior to mine. Don't leave any fingerprints on the handset."

"Thank you for the advice, genius."

"Won't the taxi driver remember us?"

"Maybe. We have to live with it. Either way, it's better to call from Zimmer's phone than from my or Mum's phone."

"We could let someone else find the corpse and call the police. His family, as well as BFS, are going to miss him soon."

"We've run out of time discussing what to do, Jan. You agreed to go ahead with the plan based on my idea."

"Do you have any more money with you?"

"Of course. As always. Without money I'd feel naked."

"Then, you could call the taxi company and get another car for us. Call from your mobile as soon as we get out of the house."

Footsteps emerged somewhere in the corridor.

"Help, help," Jan whispered. "Someone is coming."

"Imagine if it's the murderer," Cat whispered. "What if the killer is still in the house? We have to hide. Quickly."

"He must have heard us. The murderer is back to kill us. What are we going to do, Cat? There's only one door out of the room and there's no place to hide. We're trapped."

Approaching footsteps even closer.

"There." Cat pointed.

"The wardrobe? Are you kidding? How can you think there's space for both of us in the wardrobe? I'm big like a hippo."

"We must try," Cat whispered. She darted to the wardrobe. "In case you haven't noticed, we have no choice. Hurry up."

The wardrobe turned out to be the walk-in kind. Throughout the narrow space ran two rows of clothes racks, one for menswear and the other for womenswear. Nice suits. Beautiful dresses. Multiple shelves with men's and women's shoes. A dressing table and a mirror. Mr. and Mrs. Zimmer's shared walk-in wardrobe, Cat thought.

There was another door at the far end. A closed door. A possible escape route, if they wanted to leave that way, unless the killer also knew the wardrobe had two doors and was lying in wait for them at the other end.

Cat listened. Heard nothing.

They hadn't touched any light switches. They had left the door to the office open a crack. That way, the wardrobe wasn't all dark, just dim.

"I have to sneeze," Jan whispered.

"Don't," Cat whispered. "Pinch your nose."

Jan pinched her pig's snout with her forefinger and thumb. She flapped her free arm like a one-winged bird. She went up and down, up and down, on the balls of her feet. Her sickly skin looked even sicklier. She managed to prevent the sneeze.

The footsteps returned. The sisters peeped out through the crack in the door. A moving shape was glimpsed, then the man appeared in plain sight. Cat dared not breathe. She had no trouble recognising the costume-clad gunman from the tram.

The eggshell-pale face. The pinewood-blond hair. Lips as thin as bootlaces. A nose like a hawk's beak. The offensive smile.

Why had he returned to the office? Had he heard us walking around the house, calling Zimmer's name? Had he been in the house back then? If yes, why hadn't he attacked us then?

Cat's heart was slamming. She guessed Sis was scared to death as well. Sis didn't know who the man was or what he had done but his disturbing appearance should be enough to scare the wits out of anybody. Could he sense us? Could he smell my beautiful perfume? Or the stench from Jan's sweaty armpits?

The hawk-nosed killer stopped next to the corpse in the desk chair. His gloved hands pulled the three scalpels out of the dead man's head. Cat covered her ears with the palms of her hands and squeezed her eyes shut. Her vision was easier to block than her hearing. She couldn't imagine a more horrible sound than the wet and sticky sound as the killer jerked the knives out of the cadaver's head.

The murderer produced a plastic bag from a suit-jacket pocket, dumped the scalpels in it, tied it up and returned the bag to his pocket. He stood still for a while with his eyes rested on the periodicals, ring binders and books which lay scattered on the oak desktop. Then he left the library–office. The footsteps returned to the corridor and vanished.

Jan's sneeze sounded like an explosion in the confined space of the wardrobe. She gasped, whimpered, snorted and clutched

Cat's arm. Cat shot Sis a furious look and then peeked at her Bvlgari watch. Not until twenty minutes later—if they were still alive by then—would they dare step out of the wardrobe.

They ran along a dark alleyway until they reached the popular shopping and restaurant street Montrose Avenue. They blended into the crowd, catching their breaths, then waved to a taxi.

• SIXTY-TWO •

"YOU THINK YOU'RE on time, girls? Where the heck have you two been?" Mum wore pink plastic curlers in her hair and a lemon-sour expression on red-painted lips. She held a glass of white wine. Her outfit, bathrobe plus apron plus high-heeled shoes, gave a tragicomic impression. It seemed as though Mum had changed her mind about what to wear halfway through a decision to join the neighbours' party or leave for the bingo hall.

"We're adults, Mum," Cat said. "We've had things to do."

"Don't be lippy, Catriona."

"Please don't fight, you two," Jan said. "When are we going to eat? I'm starving."

"Dinner's been ready since six," Mum said. "I've already had my dinner. Got it?"

Jan's eyes fluttered. "What about me, or us?"

Mum laughed. "You know how the microwave works. You put leftovers inside, close the door, then press the start button. Microwaves were designed for lazy girls."

"At least there are leftovers?" Jan asked.

"Of course there are. With a permanent resident who has an appetite like a walrus, I have to cook in excess."

"I can't help having an appetite like a walrus."

"You're stinking of sweat, Janice. You must have a shower before your dinner."

"I'll also have a shower," Cat said.

Mum scowled. "You don't have to shower, Catriona. You smell wonderful, as always. We have to be thrifty with the use of hot water and electricity."

"I'm going out again tonight," Cat said. "I won't have dinner at home."

Janice raised her eyebrows. "You won't have dinner at home tonight either?"

Mum's eyes flashed. "What are you up to, Catriona?"

"I'll tell you, Mum. I promise. First, I want to shower and change my clothes. I won't use more hot water than necessary." Cat turned to Jan. "Please use the shower before me. But can we talk for a while first?"

The sisters sat opposite each other on the bed in Jan's room.

"How can you still be hungry after the horror show at Montrose Place?" Cat asked. "How can you still have an appetite? Don't you feel unwell after the sight of a corpse with three knives thrusted into its skull?"

"I do feel under the weather," Jan said, "but I'm hungry anyway. My belly screams for food. It's important to eat, Cat. Otherwise, you die."

"Right."

"And you? You said you'll eat somewhere else tonight. How's your own appetite?"

"I have zero appetite. But I have to pretend I have one. For the sake of politeness."

"Whom are you going to dine with tonight?"

"Stockmayer has invited me to a restaurant in Springlake."

Jan gaped. "Stockmayer?"

"It's not what you think. We'll talk about the new drug."

Jan's eyes narrowed. "Wouldn't it be more professional to discuss drugs at the clinic?"

Cat hurried to change the topic of conversation. "Mum seems to be struggling with grief."

"Yeah. Me too."

"When will she return to work?"

"Monday. Just like you."

"The day after tomorrow—how time flies."

"We haven't yet called the police."

"I've changed my mind. We won't call the police. I don't want to involve any authorities at all. I want to pursue this on my own. Dad trusts both you and I can keep industrial secrets. Authorities would make our already difficult lives even more difficult. I've had enough trouble here. On Monday, I'll be back in London, and I have to be on top form then."

"How can you change your mind without asking what I think? Doesn't my opinion count?"

"Have *you* changed your mind? You think we should call the police now?"

Jan shook her head. "Like you, I've had enough trouble."

"You *haven't* changed your mind?"

"First I changed my mind, then I changed my mind again."

"We *won't* call the police, then? Agreed?"

"Right."

"As amateur private investigators we can ignore dogma and bureaucracy. As amateur detectives we do as we please and it isn't necessary we know what we're doing. We take the liberty to be flexible, and we ignore what other people think about it."

"We could make an anonymous call to the authorities."

"Later. If we want. If we change our minds—again."

Jan grinned and guffawed. The load of crisps in her mouth had turned gooey, smearing her Pepsi-brown teeth. "Restaurant dinner with the doctor. Oh, how romantic."

"Knock it off. It's not what you think, I said."

"Do you want some crisps?"

"You're kidding? I'm a model."

Jan licked greasy crumbs from her fingers. She put away the bag of crisps and crawled off the bed. "Now I'm going to have a shower. Mum says I'm stinking of sweat. Am I?"

"Try to hurry up. And be thrifty with the use of hot water."
"Oh, shut up, Cat."

• SIXTY-THREE •

STOCKMAYER WAS IN his library, reading a periodical. He longed for the dinner and the succeeding night of love. Another adventurous night with the beauty. Catriona transformed him, rejuvenated him. Her presence had brought him back his long-lost joy of life. Her personality filled him with lust.

You're a young, handsome fifty-two-year-old, Roger.

The wall clock was showing the time nineteen-seven when his mobile phone rang. He put away the magazine and took the call. "This is Stockmayer. How may I help?"

"Good evening, Dr. Stockmayer."

Baginski's voice was neutral, free from fluctuations which could reveal emotions. However, Stockmayer knew the man was far from free of concern or worries.

"Hi, Leo."

"We have to talk, Dr. Stockmayer."

"I understand. Tonight?"

"Tonight."

"What are we going to talk about?"

"Yolexus business. More than that, I can't say on the phone."

'Yolexus business' could mean anything.

"Where are you, Leo?"

"Paradise Park. The part of the park which is right opposite your house. Is there somewhere we can meet undisturbed?"

It didn't surprise Stockmayer that Baginski was already in the neighbourhood. "You're welcome in my home, Leo. We could have a drink while we're talking."

"Thank you for the invitation, Dr. Stockmayer, but no thank you. I'm in a hurry and I need the fresh air."

"This time on a Saturday night, the park's northeastern department is empty of visitors."

"No visitors at all?"

"We can handle the situation. In the middle section of an avenue in the northeastern section of the park there are five statues of exotic birds. Do you know the statues?"

"I can find them, Dr. Stockmayer."

"I'll meet you at the bird statues in about fifteen minutes."

"I'll be waiting for you, Dr. Stockmayer."

Even though the unpleasant heatwave was over, the new, nicer temperature had already been suppressed by the intrusion of autumn. At least for now. The evening seemed removed. Dark and cool and unpredictable, like a Halloween night.

Stockmayer put on a dark-beige summer coat and left the house. The street lay deserted, silent. Dim cloud shapes towered in the western sky. One compact thundercloud blocked the evening sun like an eclipse.

He shuddered, pushed his hands into the coat pockets, crossed the street, walked northwards along the pavement and a dense hedgerow and entered the park via one of the still open gates. He continued straight ahead, then to the left, then to the right. Then he spotted the bird statues.

Peacock. Ostrich. Flamingo. Condor. Macaw. All five statues were eight-foot-tall marble sculptures organised in a straight line. A sixth figure appeared to the right side of the macaw. The immobile Baginski was reminiscent of a statue himself.

"Are you freezing, Dr. Stockmayer?"

"Bad weather is underway."

"Tonight?"

"On a number of fronts."

"I haven't had time to listen to any weather forecasts."

"You have to dress well, Leo, and move along the right paths, in order to dodge the bad weather."

"I can understand that, Dr. Stockmayer. I have a folding umbrella in my inner blazer pocket. Just in case."

"The woman in the car park in Croydon. A mistake, Leo."

"I needed a new car."

"You should have stolen a car without eliminating anyone. The Metropolitan Police has linked the Croydon murder to the car switch and the political assassination."

"The heat of the moment requires flexibility."

"And tonight? Did you drive here? In a stolen car?"

"Don't worry, Dr. Stockmayer. My stolen car is legally parked among other cars along the north side of the park."

"Not the dark-green Honda, I hope."

"Not the Honda. Another car."

Stockmayer paused. "What do you want to talk about, Leo?"

"About an unfortunate mistake, Dr. Stockmayer. Yours."

"Jarrow's idea?"

"Your intimate relationship with Miss Milton jeopardises the Rox project."

"Does Jarrow think I have an intimate relationship with Miss Milton?"

"Your mistake, Dr. Stockmayer, was to fall in love with your beautiful patient."

"The Yolexus boss is wrong about me and Miss Milton."

"Jarrow can't trust you, Dr. Stockmayer."

"He has no choice. No one knows Roxonodonol better than I. Jarrow needs me. And he knows he needs me."

"I can't trust you either, Dr. Stockmayer." Baginski pulled a pistol from his blazer pocket.

• SIXTY-FOUR •

THE SIGHT OF the corpse had destroyed her appetite. Falling in love didn't boost the appetite either. However, even if she wasn't hungry, she would eat something at the restaurant. In Roger's company she could. Time to get ready for the night.

Cat opened her L.K. Bennett washbag. First, base makeup. A light-coloured cream foundation, followed by powder. Then she turned to her eyes. Her sky-blue eyes, which over the years had made countless guys lose their composure. She put the ivory-matt eyeshadow over the eye areas, from eyebrows to eyelashes. Then she took a miniature brush to apply a grey eye shadow on and just above the eyelids. She was professionally careful with the edges and corners of her eyes. Then she used a soft black eye pencil to emphasise the outer corners of her eyes and the inner edges. For the eyelashes she chose a sumptuous black mascara. To define her eyebrows, she used a brown eyeliner.

Then, her cheeks. Evening makeup required more colour than the normal look. She used a brush to apply a touch of rouge, not below the cheekbones but just above them.

Her lips. First a deep-red lipliner. Then a deep-red and matt lipstick, a shade which contrasted with her scarlet hair. This lipstick was firmer than a glossy or a fatter type of lipstick. A pro knew how to choose lipsticks which didn't smear on glasses and napkins.

Her hair. A supermodel's hair was exposed to some form of wear every day. Meticulous haircare was essential. Next week's haircare would be at a more advanced level than in this weird and emotionally shattering week. Tonight, she wanted a hairstyle which was both simple and elegant. The earlier black dye was now all gone. She brushed her long, wavy hair backwards and adorned it with a dark and stylish headband.

She slipped into brand-new luxury underwear from La Perla. The chic bra had a list price of three hundred US dollars. The knickers, one hundred and twenty dollars. She chose a black set. *Roger loves black. Tonight, I'm going to ask Roger to relieve me of my underwear.*

Perfume? She sprayed her neck and arms with Elle, a favourite fragrance from Yves Saint Laurent. From the wardrobe she picked a short summer dress from Louis Vuitton. And matching stockings.

Shoes? Not the funeral shoes, not the black Prada. Tonight, she wanted something else on her feet. She snatched a pair of snow-white Christian Louboutins which carried a cool list price of seven hundred dollars. Shoes she had paid for with her own money.

She brushed her teeth and painted her nails.

Ready. She threw a flickering look at the destroyed full-length mirror. Mum was still unaware.

"I hope it can handle you, Cat."

"What do you mean, Jan?"

"I do hope the mirror can handle your beauty—without breaking."

"What did you say, Catriona?" Mum glowered and reduced the TV's volume. "Could you repeat what you just said?"

"I said you don't have to stay up late and wait for me."

"Aha? You have a date. You have met a new boy. Your fiftieth boyfriend. Who's the happy boy this time?"

"No date, Mum."

"Aha? You're going to party all night long. With whom?"

"I'm not going to party, Mum."

"Don't lie. You're wearing new makeup and you're dressed up for a party. Must you look like that?"

"I'm going out for dinner. I wanted to dress for the occasion. After all, it's Saturday evening. Can I go now?"

"With whom are you going to dine?"

"Dr. Stockmayer."

"Stockmayer? On a Saturday night?"

"We're going to discuss a new medicine. Both Stockmayer and I have extremely busy agendas. On Monday I'll be back at work. A scheduled meeting with my physician in a Saturday night-time slot simply became the most suitable solution. Also, Oberon Clinic has a new branch in the capital. We'll talk about that too. Stockmayer wants to transfer my case to the London branch, which would be more convenient, of course."

"But why dinner? At a restaurant? Why don't you see the man at the clinic?"

"Because now it's evening, Mum. It's dinner time. If you don't eat, you die. Stockmayer is a generous person. It would be impolite to reject his invitation."

"What kind of restaurant is it? Where is it?"

"A nice little restaurant next to Paradise Park."

"Stockmayer lives in Springlake. Doesn't he? That's my guess. It's possible to check. I'll check it. Trust me, Catriona."

Cat sighed. "I don't have time to argue. I must go now."

"Will you sleep in your mother's house?"

"Louise has said I can spend another night at her place, if I want to."

"Louise Drum again. All of a sudden, old schoolmates are more popular than your family. Louise is a rebel. A bad influence, Catriona. Bad influence."

Cat didn't comment. She left the house.

• SIXTY-FIVE •

HE LOOKED AT the gun in Baginski's hand. Then he gave the man renewed eye contact. "What you think is insignificant, Leo. You have no authority in Yolexus decision-making."

"Jarrow has modified the plan regarding Zimmer."

"In what way, Leo?"

"Zimmer will live, for the time being."

"Why?"

"Jarrow wants me to shadow Zimmer to the European Patent Office headquarters."

"Why?"

"Jarrow suspects Zimmer is in contact with triple agents in Central Europe. Triple agents with an unwanted attitude towards Yolexus Enterprise. I'll travel to Munich tonight."

"It's risky to let Zimmer live. He may find the time to enforce BioFutura Systematik's gene therapy concept."

"Jarrow says it's worth taking the risk with Zimmer a while longer. Jarrow weighs different risks against one another."

"You know I'm on the Yolexus board of directors. Why do I hear about a change of plan through you and not from Jarrow?"

Baginski smiled. He ignored the question.

Stockmayer glanced to the left, towards the space between two bird statues—the ostrich and the flamingo. He frowned. "Someone there?"

Baginski twisted his head in the same direction. Stockmayer pulled the spanner from his coat pocket and swung it with full force. The tool hit Baginski on the side of his head. The man dropped the pistol, stumbled backwards and fell.

Now intimidated by the gloom of the park, Stockmayer looked around. He saw no other shadowy figures but bird statues; heard no sounds but his own breathing and the whizzing wind in the treetops. He broke into a run.

• SIXTY-SIX •

"YOU LOOK AMAZING." It wasn't the first time tonight he had said it. Roger held her hand from across the table. He caressed her fingers. "Incredibly beautiful. As always."

She wanted to be held. She fantasised about being the new Mrs. Stockmayer.

Then he said, "Shall we take a look at the menu?"

Cat nodded, smiling. He released her fingers.

The Latin American restaurant had, just like Roger's living room, a splendid view of Paradise Park. All the colours of the rainbow dominated the interior, matching the shades of the exotic drinks. Simple yet elegant furniture. Dimmed lighting, soft instrumental background music. She was already enjoying herself at the little restaurant. Because of her fame, she had feared she would draw unwanted attention. It didn't happen. Tactfulness characterised the place, just as Roger had said. The majority of dinner guests were couples who wanted a level of privacy, just like her and Roger.

Roger seemed to be friends with the entire workforce. He was informal with the host, the head waiter, the cloakroom attendant, the waitstaff. Even the chef came out and exchanged a few words with Roger and took the opportunity to give Cat a delicate compliment.

She flipped the pages of the menu and said nothing for a while. She just wanted to feel the excitement of being here. A few seconds of silent drama too. A jittery moment to sort an array of feelings: her concern about the return of her dead father; the horrific images from Karl-Heinz Zimmer's study; her quarrelling with Mum; her conflicts with Sis; her anger with Roy; her longing for Ebba; erotic memories of last night with Roger; her expectations of the upcoming night with Roger; fantasies about the nice things she wanted to do for Roger tonight; visions of the pleasant things she wanted Roger to do for her tonight. The whirlwind of emotions made her dizzy.

They ordered cocktails. Cat had a non-alcoholic virgin Piña Colada without sugar. Roger had a Tequila Raspberry Smash.

His handsome gaze caught her eyes. "How are you doing tonight? You appear somewhat absent."

"I'm sorry. I feel a little strange."

"You've had a tumultuous week. Anyone who has had a week similar to yours would feel a little strange, to say the least."

"I've also been thinking about what you mentioned about a London clinic. And you said you're also the director of the London branch. Maybe we'll be able to make comfortable plans for ourselves. We'll be able to see each other often, won't we?"

"Perhaps we'll have time to see each other more often than we first dared hope. I've got some marvellous news for you."

"A surprise?" She sipped on her cocktail.

"I want the London branch to be my permanent base and the Blackfield clinic my temporary one. I'll keep my house here. My permanent residence will be in the capital."

"Wow." Her heart jolted. "You mean that?"

"Oh, yes."

"Kiss me, Roger."

From the starters section of the menu, Cat chose brie-and-mango empanadas with a mild salsa. For the main course, she had a vegetarian burrito with truffles. Roger ordered sliced and fried calamari with aioli for his starter. For his main course, he picked Xinxim—lime chicken in a crayfish-and-peanut sauce served with rice. As for drinks, Cat wanted a glass of freshly squeezed kiwifruit juice and Roger chose a glass of rosé.

"Roger?"

"Yes?"

"Do you know a firm called Yolexus Enterprise?"

"Why do you ask, sweetheart?"

"I read somewhere that Yolexus Enterprise makes medicines for the treatment of sleep disorders. Since I'm a patient with narcolepsy, I got curious about the company."

Roger took a sip from his glass. "I do know Yolexus. Not a gigantic corporation, but not an insignificant company either."

"Have I used any medicine that Yolexus has manufactured?"

"Never. There are several companies which produce drugs for the treatment of dyssomnias. As in any line of business, competition is important and, fortunately, patents have a limited lifetime."

"Okay. I was just curious."

He fired off his charismatic smile. "As I said before, it's healthy to be curious. I love your curiosity."

"Tonight I'll show you a thing or two which will awaken *your* curiosity," she whispered.

"I look forward to the surprise."

• • •

"Roger?"

"Yes?"

"Are we going soon?" She stepped out of a shoe, stretched her leg under the table and placed her stocking-clad foot in his lap. "When?"

"Are we finished here? You want us to go now?"

She felt his hand wandering up her stretched-out leg. "Yes," she said. "I think we're finished here. What do you say?"

Nobody in the restaurant noticed what they were doing. Fortunately, the tablecloth had a long drop length at two edges, one of which was facing the centre of the restaurant.

"Me too, Catriona." His eager fingers reached the inside of her thigh. He jerked at her stocking. "I think we're ready to go."

"Come on then, let's go."

"I'm just going to pay the bill."

She smiled at him. "Hurry up."

He let go of her leg. Then he signalled to the head waiter.

Sunday. Her final day in the City of Crows. At least, her final day this time. Tomorrow, her everyday life would restart.

Sunlight filled Roger's bedroom. On the bed, Cat sat naked between his legs. The quilt had slid down to the foot of the bed. He wrapped his arms around her waist. She rested the back of her head against his chest. Her rump pushed against his erect penis. She moved his hands upwards, placed them where she wanted them. His fingers started to caress her nipples.

"Roger?"

"Yes?"

"Do you have any children? Did you and Henrietta have kids?"

"No. I have no children."

"Didn't you and Henrietta want children?"

"We didn't rule out the idea of having kids at some point. It was just that we prioritised our careers."

• • •

"Catriona?"

"Yes?"

"When did you begin shaving your pubic area?"

"I think I was eighteen. Discovered it was convenient. When I shoot micro-bikini or raunchy-knicker adverts, I don't have to worry about pubic hairs showing."

"I love the little bright-pink area. It's sexy."

She giggled. "It showed a little in some daring shots I did for a prestigious magazine."

"Catriona?"

"Yes?"

He held her close to him. "How different you are. You and your twin sister."

"Eerie, isn't it?"

"What happened?"

She collected her thoughts and mobilised her strength. "Janice and I ... At the beginning, Mum's pregnancy proceeded well. She carried two dizygotic embryos. Janice and I would have become normal sororal twins. But then something went awfully wrong. Janice ... The foetus which would become Janice developed a severe malformation. I was the fortunate one. I was always seen as the fortunate one. Even after my diagnosis."

"Your twin sister's deformation is limited to her appearance. Her central nervous system is perfectly normal. She doesn't suffer from any brain damage."

Cat nodded. "I'm the sister with a neurological disease. A chronic sleep disorder. I guess everything has a price."

"Do you mean you think your narcolepsy was the price you paid for your unimaginable beauty?"

"Catriona?"

"Yes?"

"How much does your mother know?"

"She thinks I've spent the night at a female friend's place."

"We can't keep it a secret forever. It wouldn't be fair to anyone. Sooner or later we have to tell her."

"Later. Let's do it later."

"And when the time is right, I'll no longer be your official healthcare provider. Everything will be perfect."

"Except the age gap."

He shot her a curious look. "Serious?"

She laughed. "Only a joke."

"What amazing nights we've had together."

"Mmm." She paused. "I want you closer. Even closer, it's even nicer." She began to stroke his penis. "Even closer and even nicer means there's no room for a condom." With her free hand, she lifted her long wavy hair back and away from her face.

"Do you use pills?"

She shook her head.

"Then it'd be risky to ignore a condom."

"That second time the other night. Right after my horrible dream. I wanted to be comforted. You comforted me. We used no condom. But you pulled out just before you came."

"Something I won't try again."

"Risks are captivating." She continued to play with his penis. It was already rock-hard in her gliding hand.

"What if you became pregnant?"

"The probability varies with the menstrual cycle, my dear Dr. Stockmayer. Basic course in female anatomy?"

He panted. "You want to trust so-called safe periods?"

"Mmm." Her fingers continued working, up and down the shaft of his penis.

"Safe periods are not always safe," he said, his voice shaking.

"Would you like to have kids someday, Roger? With me?"

"I think so, Catriona. I want to spend the rest of my life with you." Roger panted again. He ejaculated in her hand.

• SIXTY-SEVEN •

WITH BOTH FISTS, Benke Bengtsson hammers on the inside of the maintenance hole cover. The emperor of the Karla School roars, swears and yawps. The utterances scare away deer, squirrels and sparrows. The bush-lined trail falls away from the idyll. The trail is transformed, distorted, into the Devil's open-air theatre.

The maintenance hole cover squeaks, clatters, slides, rattles, plummets and shatters. Movements pulsate in the blackness. Crawling shadows are glimpsed within the cylindrical abyss. The well trembles. The ground quavers. The subterranean shape advances. Benke's crushed head rises above the blackness of the sewer. Cherry-red blood, canary-yellow pus and oatmeal-grey brain flow out of the nail hole in his skull.

Storm winds fill the tomblike darkness. The crickets play funeral tunes. The ink-black sun sprays leaping shadows. The brook oozes like dragon's blood. Obnoxious amphibians swim through the fizzing water. The emperor laughs his cynical laugh. "Now we've got them. The four-eyes and the duckling."

Benke climbs out of the well. Sewage and putrefying body fluids drip from his rotting T-shirt and jeans. The boy grins, pointing at Ebba with his stiletto. "I want to start with the cocky duckling. Grab her, guys."

Benke's buddies appear. Berra and Sigge guffaw like pet monkeys. The emperor totters towards Ebba. She screams …

Ebba woke up with a jolt. Woke up—not in bed but rather *on* the bed. On top of the bedspread. Alone. With her clothes still on: last night's party outfit. She squinted. Bright light was crashing down on her from the ceiling lamp. The bedroom was at least her own. She was at home in Notting Hill. A clanging pain in her head. A desert-dry taste in her mouth. The walls rotated. The bedroom was spinning like a carousel. Fucking nightmare. Eleven years had passed since the horrors of that day. *Forget the past, Ebba. Focus on the future.*

She tried to think. She had no idea how she had got home, let alone when. She tried to remember the last thing which could be remembered, or rather the last thing worth remembering. The gap in her memory felt like a normal booze-induced blackout. Nothing strange. She lived up to the elite's expectations. After all, she was Ebba Sjödal, the unbeatable party princess. *The drop-dead gorgeous and filthy rich party princess, that's me.*

She let out a belly laugh. At once she became silent again. Her laugh had sounded like Benke Bengtsson's moronic guffaw. The same neigh-like laugh used to make the schoolmaster go apeshit. Mr. Stenlund. The howler monkey.

Damn Benke. Damn schoolmaster. Damn childhood.

She blinked, gasped, paddled with her arms, kicked out with her legs, shuffled off the bed and landed on the carpet with a soft thud. Lay still on the floor. Stared up at the ceiling lamp. Squinted in near-panic. The lampshade swirled like a flying saucer. For a crazy moment, she wondered if she had crawled on all fours all the way home from Cromwell Road. Impossible, of course. Also, her clothes were as clean and immaculate now as before. On the other hand, her body protested. Her aching body did suggest she had crept all the way home from the Kensington banquet.

Crept home like a turtle.

Ebba the turtle, that's me.

She guffawed again. Now she heard her own laughter (not Benke's) fly out between her lips. And now she remembered. The principal memory from last night's party bubbled in her brain. The brief meeting with the acclaimed Hollywood producer. He wanted to work with Ebba Sjödal.

Ebba, like many other fashion models, would take the step towards a Hollywood movie career.

She longed to tell Roy. Roy loved going to the cinema. Roy would be delighted to hear about her extra job as an actress in Hollywood's dream factory.

She rose from the floor, grimaced. Could her skull explode?

What luck, she thought. It happened to be her day off today. An ordinary Sunday. Certainly, as a supermodel, she had worked Sundays, worked any day, sometimes ten days a week, ho-ho, but today she was totally fucking off work. She had plenty of time to recover. She would be back on top form faster than anyone could say 'Holy crap, Tony Coca-Cola and the Roosters have a new album out and are touring again'.

Top form. Top form ...

A clear-cut alertness flared up in her mind. Today was no ordinary Sunday.

Jarrow. The meeting with Dirk Jarrow.

Tonight. The Golden Plaza Hotel, Paddington.

Ebba's bedroom was as large as a living room or a lounge. Here she had all sorts of amenities within a few seconds' walk from the bed. Bar cabinet, TV, a corner sofa, a coffee table. Even a fridge. An integrated room, one could say; which was more than one could say about Cat's bedroom. Cat's room was just a bedroom and nothing else. Cat didn't want a fridge or a TV or a sofa in her bedroom, let alone a bar cabinet.

People were different, Ebba thought. Differences between people were stimulating. Cat was captivating in her own way. It struck Ebba the contrast between the property's two owners was more important than ever. When you were tired of yourself, you were fortunate to have a best friend like Catriona. The best friends' differences became their rescue. As luck would have it, one's best friend wasn't a copy of oneself.

The mere thought of breakfast made her want to vomit. What time was it? She threw an eye towards the dressing-table clock. Ten forty-seven. She decided to skip breakfast. Better to aim for lunch. Sunday lunch around two p.m.? Lunch out? Champagne lunch out? Sundays existed for champagne lunches. If Roy had been available, she would have asked him to accompany her but Roy had a football match today. Instead, she would call a girlfriend. A girlfriend who loved champagne. Who? Martina Pieroni? Excellent idea. Talkative Martina could make Ebba forget Yolexus and Jarrow for a few hours.

She opened the fridge, plucked out an ice-cold beer, twisted off the cap and took three quick sips. Better than breakfast. She sat down on the corner sofa, put the beer bottle, her mobile and the sweet gift box with sparkling red cover on the coffee table, thinking she would make two phone calls only. To Martina and to Mum. Little did she know she would make four calls.

She dipped her index finger into the pretty little box and stirred the snow-white powder, moved her finger to her nose, snorted the cocaine and raised the beer bottle to her lips. Two sips.

Call number one. She called Martina's mobile.

"Hi, Hi, Ebba. What a fun surprise. Unbelievably fun. I was just thinking about you. Yesterday I shopped away three months' wages at Harrods, and you know what? I wondered what Ebba would say about the seven dresses I bought. And the scarves and the gloves and the eight pairs of shoes. On Thursday morning, the painters arrive. Pedro and I agreed on what colours we want on the walls downstairs. Can you imagine? What time-consuming distractions one has to deal with on a regular basis! And what an incredible heatwave. But the weather guy on TV says temperatures will soon drop. Maybe they have already begun to drop. What do you think, Ebba?"

"In my bedroom, it's January now." She shivered a bit but not because of the freezing cold beer. She guessed Martina's treacherous talkativeness was an invaluable asset to her. Martina had been born to be a real estate agent. The dashing Italian could sell any house for an exorbitant price.

"Your voice sounds a little odd, Ebba. You okay, darling?"

"Getting better. Could do with some encouragement."

"Hungover on a Sunday morning?" Martina laughed. "How unusual, Ebba."

"And how are *you*?"

"Hungover like a bitch."

"On a Sunday morning? How unusual, Martina. Shall we try to recover together?"

"Smashing idea. Pedro is on an out-of-town job and I don't like to dine alone. What do you suggest?"

"American Bar at The Savoy." One of the most famous bars in the world was good enough for Ebba Sjödal.

"That's super. What time?"

"Two-ish? I have to shower and change clothes. I woke up only a fucking moment ago, still dressed in last night's outfit."

"And the light's still on, right?" Martina laughed.

In new and clean clothes after the shower, holding a fresh beer in her hand, she started to feel a bit better. Soon time to head to the Strand. She lit a cig, jumped onto the bedroom's corner sofa and used the remote control to click on the TV.

The broadcaster: *"The news that super talent Roy Beckman has tested positive for cocaine detonated like a bomb in the world of football. Midfield genius Roy Beckman had a brilliant career in front of him, both in the Premier League and in the England national team. But not anymore. The devastating revelation this morning comprises more than one isolated positive doping test. A certain complementary test has detected long-term cocaine abuse. The FA is no longer interested in Roy Beckman. Top clubs in the Premier League as well as in overseas Europe are dropping their transfer queries regarding Roy Be—"*

Ebba turned off the TV. She swore and hurled the remote control across the room. The flying device collided with the stand-alone clothes rail and shattered.

Call number two. She called his home number.

No answer.

She dialled his mobile number.

Waited.

He replied. "What the hell do you want?"

"Roy? Why are you swearing at me? I'm calling because I'm worried. I saw the TV news."

"Don't call again. Don't call ever again."

Her heart jumped. "What do you mean?"

"I don't want to see you ever again, Ebba."

"Don't you love me anymore? Don't say you no longer love me. Whatever you say, do not say that. You mustn't hurt me."

"I don't love you anymore. I don't want to see you again."

"Don't say that, Roy."

"I'll say whatever I want. And I mean what I say."

"What about me? I still love you. Our future together?"

"I have no future anymore."

"Have you talked to Cat?"

He laughed, a hideous laugh without humour. A hoot of laughter which belonged to a horror movie. "I don't give a shit about Cat and I don't give a shit about you."

"Why are you taking your anger out on Cat and me?"

"Self-centred bitches like you bring nothing but bad luck."

She almost started to cry. She blinked hard several times to clear her vision. "Neither Cat nor I are self-centred. We donate vast sums of money to charities, and most people we meet at work or out of work think we're very social girls. We—"

Roy didn't comment. He hung up on her.

The day was still young. It was too early for Ebba to imagine that the already horrible day could become any worse.

• SIXTY-EIGHT •

THEY HAD A late breakfast in the kitchen. Or rather, a late brunch. Or an early dinner. The time was already three in the afternoon. Cat wasn't in a hurry to be contactable. Her phone had been turned off all day. Roger thought of his evening talk at Rainbow Tower. They sat together on the kitchen sofa.

"It's here, Catriona. The last day. You'll travel tonight."

She kissed him. "We won't be away from each other for long.

We'll soon be back together. In the meantime, our phone calls will keep us close."

He returned her kiss. "What time does your train leave?"

"Not until ten tonight."

"We'll still have some time together then, both before and after my talk." He rose and closed his briefcase.

"Sure." She nibbled at her toast. "We'll have time to do a lot of interesting things, Roger."

He smiled, looking at his wristwatch. "I'm just going to drive down to the clinic and get a few files."

"Do you want me to come with you?"

"You don't have to. I won't be long."

"I could play the decent patient. I promise to behave well. I promise not to come up with any rude suggestions within the walls of the clinic, especially not in the presence of other staff."

He chuckled. "I'll be back very soon, sweetheart. Make yourself at home. Have another cup of coffee. There's plenty left in the coffeemaker."

"Okay. I'll take the opportunity to make some phone calls."

"Good." He held her, kissed her, then left the house.

She refilled her coffee cup. The window next to the kitchen sink faced the driveway. Roger climbed into the Mercedes. He waved. She waved back.

She couldn't find her Alice band. Where was it? Not in the bathroom, not in the kitchen, not in the living room, not in the hall, not in the wardrobe where he had let her hang her clothes. She trotted about with her hairbrush in her hand, found the Alice band on the bedroom floor, partly hidden by a bedside table, picked it up and went over to the mirror on top of a chest of drawers at the end of the room.

The chair in front of the chest was reminiscent of a tall bar stool. She climbed onto the stool, placed her Alice band beside the mirror and started to brush her wavy waist-length hair. Next to the mirror sat a wooden lacquered box. Black with a pattern of red, blue and white flowers. The box was wide open. Earrings, necklaces, bracelets, brooches, nail polish, mascara, lipsticks and perfumes occupied the various departments of the box. She thought of Henrietta. Roger had said he had no photos of his late wife. Instead, he had obviously kept her storage box as a memory. He could never bring himself to get rid of it. The context was both fine and tragic. It hurt a little in Cat's heart. The box and its contents were well-kept and dust-free. He must have loved her without limit.

Sky-blue eyes, bright eyelashes. Mid-length, vanilla-blonde hair. She used makeup but never for a party-style appearance; only to emphasise her natural looks. She was a strong-willed woman. I observe the same willpower in you. I'm not saying you two are alike. I don't see you as a replacement for my deceased wife. I love you for the unique person you are.

Cat's intuition struck. Something just didn't add up.

Excuse me, Sherlock Holmes. Excuse me, Columbo. But now we're in my territory. Beauty products are a model's area of expertise, so I'm going to have to ask the distinguished gentlemen to step aside for a while. A blonde with sky-blue eyes and bright eyelashes who wants to cherish her natural looks does not choose black mascara. She chooses some shade of brown. The mascara in the box is black. Henrietta was probably brunette or black-haired—and dark-eyed. No guarantees, but likely. The key phrase is 'natural looks'.

Why would Roger lie about his deceased wife's appearance?

Was there anything else he had lied about?

Or concealed? What? Why?

Do you know a firm called Yolexus Enterprise?

Why do you ask, sweetheart?

She connected to the Internet on her phone and did a search on Yolexus Enterprise. A patternless search. She had no direct plans for what she wanted to do. The company proved to have a website. Cat opened it. It indicated a number of tabs containing information about YE's corporate structure and products. She clicked the tab entitled Corporate Management. A list of board members flared up on the display. Twelve names. The list had an international look. The top name was a certain Dirk Jarrow. What kind of a guy was he? The other eleven: Volodymyr Orlov, Ewa Potter, Ludwig Trexler, Sten Johansson, Marina Morientes, Walther Pearce, Lee Chang, Dagmar Bergkoff, Takashi Osugi, Melody Brown-Clarke, Pratap Anand.

She remembered a product name from the dead Zimmer's blood-splashed notebook. *Nargontanac.* Something like that. A strange name. That's why she remembered it. But she couldn't recall its spelling. *Patient subjects developed mental disorders.*

She clicked on the tab which listed YE's products. She didn't expect to find Nargontanac and she was right. No information about Nargontanac or something with a similar spelling. Such a scandal product must have been deleted. She shook her head. This didn't make her any the wiser. Browsing the Net without a proper plan was a waste of time. What was she looking for?

She couldn't help surfing for pictures of Roger. Were there any pictures of Roger online at all? Chances were good or great. Roger was a renowned scientist. And Cat was curious. Curious like a cat. She performed a search and did find photographs of her new love. Not many. Four. According to the captions, all four were taken in connection with international conferences and seminars. In two pictures, he was in the company of various delegates. The remaining two photos showed him with a young gorgeous blonde. Mr. and Mrs. Stockmayer, according to the captions. The woman's appearance matched Roger's description of his dead wife. The blonde was Henrietta. The images were seven years old. Henrietta Stockmayer had two years left to live. How snazzy she was, Cat thought. Beautiful indeed.

I'm sorry, Roger. I'm sorry for doubting you. I feel like a spy. I didn't mean to snoop into your private life. I'm ashamed. You spoke the truth about Henrietta.

She sighed and shut down the Internet and spent the next few minutes brushing her wavy hair.

• SIXTY-NINE •

CALL NUMBER THREE. To call her mother, under normal circumstances, was easier said than done. And now, with a lump in her throat and Roy's words on her mind, it was impossible to call Mum. Somehow, Ebba managed to defy the impossible.

The last time she had phoned her parental home was on Christmas Eve two years ago. No special reason, no other reason than to wish her family a Merry Christmas. No one had missed her. No one had longed for her. Furthermore, she had called at the wrong time. She had interrupted them in the middle of the traditional mulled-wine party. Dad and her bros got pissed off at her, of course.

Another swig of beer. She rang.

Someone answered. "Hello?" Mum.

"Happy birthday, Mum."

A painful silence enveloped the handset. Then, "Ebba?"

"Yes, Mum. It's me."

"Why are you calling?"

"Why do you think? It's your birthday, Mum. I'm calling to congratulate you. Which I just did. Didn't you hear?"

"Your congratulation sounds like an effort, Ebba. Like a necessary evil. Preferably, you want to forget about the family's anniversaries. Almost two years have passed since the last time you called."

She closed her eyes and sighed. "How are you doing, Mum?"

"Your voice sounds strange. Are you still doing drugs?"

She gritted her teeth, promised herself not to shout. "I asked how you're doing. You and the others. How you and Dad and my bros are doing."

"All your brothers are in prison."

"What?"

"Your brothers are dangerous bank robbers, Ebba."

She coughed. "I ... I didn't know."

"No wonder you didn't know. You never get in touch. You don't care what's going on in your old hometown."

"Not true, Mum."

"It is true."

"No. Not true." She wanted to cry again. Almost did. Changed her mind. Held back her tears. Drank more beer. "Must it be like this, Mum? Must it be like this?" She took some deep and shaky breaths. "My life is stormy as hell right now."

"Stormier than usual?" A mocking tone in Mum's voice.

"Yes." She wiped at her eyes. "But I want to say something. I want to say something, here and now."

"What?"

"I'm so tired of all the scandals, Mum. When the winds of this final hurricane have died, I want to become a better person. A few more scandal articles about me might end up in the papers, but I want to restart my life as a better person."

"Have you called Marja's family? When was the last time you phoned the Koskinens? Marja was your best childhood friend."

"Marja and I talked three years ago. We live stressful lives."

"Ebba?"

"Yes?"

"Call Artturi and Lisa."

"Why, Mum? Why now?"

"I can't say. Just do it."

"Why can't you tell me?"

Mum didn't answer. She said again, "Call Artturi and Lisa."

"Is it important I call right now?"

"If you think Marja is important, call now."

Phone call number four.

"Hi, Ebba." Artturi Koskinen didn't sound like himself. The usual cheerfulness was absent from his voice.

She concentrated her attention. "Er, I just talked to Mum, Artturi. She told me to call. How are you and Lisa? And Marja? It would be nice if Marja and I could coordinate our next visits to

Kungsör. It's been a long time since we had the opportunity to meet in our hometown. I think it would be great fun."

Artturi said nothing. Why didn't he say something?

She continued, "Three years have passed since I last spoke to Marja. Is she still at the same law firm in Stockholm?"

"Ebba?"

"Mm?"

"Marja is dead."

"Huh?"

"My daughter killed herself." He paused. "Six months ago. Overdose of sleeping pills."

Her nausea of today's awakening returned with a thunder. The soothing effects of the beer blew away. All of a sudden, she felt stone-cold sober. She raised the ashtray to her lips and spat out the burning cigarette.

"Your glass bear? You want to give me your glass bear?"

"Yes, that's what I want."

"I can't accept it, Marja."

"Ebba? Hello? Are you still there?"

"I'm here, Artturi. I don't know what to say. What you're saying feels completely unreal and so terrible." She shook a new cigarette from the pack. "I thought ... assumed Marja was happy. She had started a brilliant career as a lawyer at one of Stockholm's most prestigious law firms. I learnt she had her own family. A successful husband who loved her very much, and two beautiful children. A superb flat in the sought-after district of Gärdet. Marja mailed pictures. She—" Her voice broke.

"Marja left a suicide letter."

Ebba lit the new cigarette. Her fingers trembled. She waited. She didn't want to, *couldn't*, ask about the contents of Marja's letter. She suspected Artturi was about to tell her anyway.

"Marja wrote she could no longer cope with the burden of a horrid secret."

The phone line went quiet.

"Are you listening, Ebba?"

"I'm listening." She glanced towards the dressing table. At the moment, it sat on top of the dressing table. The glass bear in multicoloured mosaic. The memory of Marja. The symbol of old friendship and a rotten secret.

"Horrid secret," he repeated. "How would you interpret it?"

"I don't know," she heard herself say.

As if Artturi hadn't registered what she had just said, he continued, "What 'horrid secret' could have driven my daughter to her death? Any idea, Ebba?"

She had smoked the whole cigarette in less than a minute. The smoke stung like fire in her lungs. She coughed. Then she spat in the ashtray. "I have no idea." She almost vomited the beer. "What you're saying sounds incredible. Nasty and tragic." She gasped for air. "May I talk to Lisa?"

"Lisa can't talk about this anymore."

"Give my best to Lisa, Artturi. Imagine how many times we, Marja and I, sat in your kitchen as children, eating cinnamon rolls and drinking raspberry juice. We ... We ..." She couldn't finish what she was trying to say.

• SEVENTY •

BLACK MASCARA. A first intuition. Easy to have. Less easy to forget. *Think, Catriona. Think. You know people all over the world. Use the fact that you have acquired a global network of contacts through your profession. You know someone in the German Alps, or you know someone who knows a journalist in southern Germany. Right?*

Right. Hanna Schneider. Model colleague on the catwalk.

Hanna was from Ingolstadt in Bavaria. Although Cat and Hanna didn't hang out together in their spare time, they used to chat whenever they got the opportunity at the big shows in Paris, London, New York and Milan. They knew each other through their job. Cat made a decision. She would call Hanna. She had the German girl's mobile number.

"Yes? Hello?" Hanna sounded drowsy. "It's Hanna."

Hanna was one year younger than Cat. She had long bright wavy hair, clear-blue eyes, full lips and a unique radiance. She resembled a younger Doutzen Kroes.

"Hey, Hanna. It's Cat."

"Cat?" Hanna yawned. "If you knew what time it was here."

"I'm sorry, Hanna. I had no idea what time zone you were in. I could try to call at a better time instead?"

"Wait."

A rustling sound in the background. The swish of moving bedclothes and the click of a bedside lamp.

"It's okay, Cat. We can talk now. I wasn't asleep. The jet lag is bouncing around like an unquiet ghost in my head."

"Where are you, Hanna?"

"Hong Kong. Launch of a new perfume—stressful but fun."

"Sounds exciting."

"The hotel suite has a superb view of Victoria Harbour. The hotel has one of the best international restaurants in Kowloon. But the sauerkraut isn't as good as the Bavarian kind; not by a long shot."

Cat giggled. "Okay. I'll be brief. I'm trying to remember if you ever mentioned your dad was a journalist in Munich or Regensburg or something like that."

"Almost right. I have an uncle who is a reporter covering the whole of Bavaria and parts of Baden-Württemberg."

"Aha. I'm searching for information about a bus accident in the German Alps, about five years ago. It was a charter bus transporting orchestral musicians to a gig."

"Isn't there any info on the Internet?"

"There are a lot of articles, but I haven't found one which contains the special thing I'm looking for. I thought maybe someone would be able to give me some extra information. The less interesting details which didn't end up in the newspapers."

"You sound like a detective. What are you doing?"

"I'm just curious about the facts surrounding an outstanding female violinist. Henrietta Stockmayer. She was among the passengers who perished in this bus accident."

"Your talk makes *me* curious."

Cat considered her words. She didn't want to lie to Hanna. She wanted to win Hanna's trust. She had to give something in return. "Can you keep a secret, Hanna?"

"Totally." She yawned again. "I promise."

"This Henrietta Stockmayer is my neurologist's dead wife. My neurologist has told me a little about Henrietta, and I think some details seem a bit odd."

"Uh-huh. And why is all this so mighty important to you?"

"I've fallen in love with him. And he is in love with me."

Hanna tittered. "Congratulations."

"Remember what you promised. My new relationship is a secret for now. You're the only person who knows."

"I'm honoured." The German girl laughed again.

"Do you think your uncle might have reported something about that bus accident?"

"I don't have a clue. You want me to ask him, right?"

"I would be endlessly grateful."

"How urgent is this?"

"To be honest, it's very urgent."

"I can't be bothered to ask you why it's so urgent, Cat. But I'll contact my uncle for your sake. I'll do it now. I'll send him a message before I try to sleep."

"Kind of you, Hanna."

"You'll have to be kind in return."

"That's a deal. Make a note of it."

"I will."

"Dinner at La Tour d'Argent? Just you and me. Whenever we find the time. The bill will be on me. How does that sound?"

"Sounds great, Cat. Best restaurant in Paris. A reasonable compensation."

"During the next Paris week?"

"Let's try. The fish quenelles at La Tour d'Argent are the best in the world." Hanna yawned again. "Now I have to sleep."

"Good night, Hanna. And sleep tight. Bye."

As she waited for Roger to come back, she took the opportunity to make herself ready. She brushed her teeth, fixed her hair in a topknot, painted her lips, packed her handbag with toiletry kits and her phone, tablet and sunglasses, then returned to the ground floor. She was about to make a phone call to Sis (on Mum's home phone number) when her smartphone started to beep. She dug into her handbag and grabbed the phone. "Yes?"

"Miss Milton?" A man's voice. Unknown.

"This is Miss Milton speaking."

"My name is Wolfgang Schneider. You're supposed to be a friend of Hanna, my niece. I received a text message from her." The man's voice was dark and low-key. From a radio in the background bubbled instrumental music. It sounded like some Southern German folk music.

"Hanna and I know each other through our careers. Thank you for getting in touch so quickly, Mr. Schneider. I'm surprised. I just talked to Hanna on the phone. I couldn't have guessed you would contact me at once. In truth, I dared not hope to hear from you at all."

"Your request is strange, to say the least, Miss Milton."

"Mmm. I know."

"I usually don't engage in communications of this kind. I have neither the time for nor an interest in curious amateur detectives. However, I'm prepared to make an exception to my principles. You and your case are the very first exception. If you hadn't been Hanna's friend, I wouldn't have contacted you."

"I understand, Mr. Schneider. I do respect your principles."

The line went quiet.

Then, a tapping sound, as though the man was knocking on a computer keyboard. The dark voice came back, "I was one of the journalists who reported on that bus accident in the German Alps five years ago. Most authors overwrite their first drafts. The surplus disappears during the revision. However, I save old notes, all those insignificant details which only belong to a first draft. I can't throw anything away. Perhaps I'm superstitious. What would you like to know?"

"One of the passengers who died was named Henrietta Stockmayer. Mrs. Stockmayer. Violinist in the orchestra. Could you describe her? How did she look? Her hair and her eyes?"

"What a peculiar question."

"Yes, I know."

"Do you have more peculiar questions?"

"No more questions at all."

Quiet again, as though the man had had second thoughts about the whole thing. Then more clacking in the background, like sharp strikes on keyboard keys. "I have my old files here. On the passenger list, there was no Henrietta Stockmayer."

"Are you positive?"

"Are you certain about the surname? There is a Henrietta here. A Henrietta Trexler."

She was thinking. Roger had mentioned Henrietta, and Cat had taken for granted that her surname had been Stockmayer. Henrietta could have kept her maiden name, for some reason. Married women, career women, who kept their maiden names were not so uncommon. But who was the blonde in the pictures on the Internet, then? In the pictures with the captions, 'Mr. and Mrs. Stockmayer'? An error? Maybe. There were a lot of errors and poor-quality information in cyberspace.

"Miss Milton? Are you there?"

"I'm sorry. I was thinking. Now I'm not sure about the surname. It's possible, maybe, that the Henrietta I'm asking about is the one you mentioned."

"Henrietta Trexler was thirty years old. Shoulder-length, curly, ink-black hair. And dark eyes. Are you satisfied?"

Am I satisfied? Not at all. Anything but satisfied. "Don't you mean waist-length, straight, blonde hair? And blue eyes?"

"Are you insinuating I don't keep my notes organised?"

"No." She wrinkled her forehead. "No, of course not. Thank you for the information, Mr. Schneider. Thank you very much."

"How do you plan to use this information?"

"I won't use it for anything, Mr. Schneider. I'll keep it to myself. I needed to know what my neurologist was talking about the other day. You see, Henrietta was his wife."

"Aha. I have a digital photo here. Mrs. Henrietta Trexler in the company of her husband. A photo I took at a concert in Graz eight years ago. The woman must be around twenty-seven. The man seems to be in his late thirties but may be in his early forties. It's difficult to try to guess people's ages. Wait a minute ..." Pause. "Now I remember. The handsome man in the company of the female violinist is a scientist. Your doctor, uh? Some hotshot neuroscientist engaged in pioneering sleep-disorder research?"

Cat bit down on her lower lip. "Sounds like my doctor."

"Would you like the picture? I could send it to your mobile."

"Yes please, Mr. Schneider. Thank you very much."

"I'll send it as soon as we've finished. Are we done?"

"We're done. Thank you again for everything."

The photo arrived to her phone. A lovely couple. The scientist and the violinist. Henrietta had shoulder-length, curly, ink-black hair. And dark eyes. Just like Hanna's uncle had said. The man in the picture was a forty-four-year-old Roger. He was incredibly good-looking. As good-looking as today. The same charismatic radiance. The same magnetic gaze.

Roger had told an untruth about Henrietta. But things took a turn for the worse. The picture caption made Cat's world collapse. The caption read, 'Henrietta Trexler with her husband Ludwig Trexler'.

Ludwig Trexler? Her heart began to slam at high speed. She started to feel sick.

She fumbled with the phone. Her trembling fingers managed to open the Internet and navigate back to the website of the pharmaceutical company Yolexus Enterprise. Back to the list of

YE board members. Right. She remembered before she saw it. The fourth name on the list: Ludwig Trexler.

• SEVENTY-ONE •

A FEW HOURS later, and a bottle of champagne later, Ebba sat behind the wheel of the Porsche. The afternoon with Martina Pieroni had marked a refreshing break from her problematic life. Refreshing with a double meaning: Martina was hilarious and the champagne enticing.

Now, once again, darkness towered over the horizon.

The meeting with the Yolexus boss Dirk Jarrow.

She steered the Porsche westwards along Oxford Street and honked the horn twice at a lazy double-decker driver. The champagne almost made her forget you couldn't turn right at Marble Arch. You weren't allowed to drive straight ahead either. Left turn only. The Porsche stopped dead; it tore away. Stopped dead, tore away. Again and again. It was fun flooring the accelerator and scaring the shit out of people, then stamping on the brake pedal in the nick of time. She jerked at the wheel, swerved through the intersection, waved to the innumerable pigeons, changed lanes, steered right into Cumberland Gate, then right again, then changed lanes again and turned left, northwards along Edgware Road in the direction of Paddington and the Golden Plaza Hotel.

The thirteen-hundred-dollar Miu Miu handbag lay on the passenger seat. She let go of the wheel with one hand, peeked in the rear-view mirror, dug into the handbag, found the plastic can, peeled off the lid, dipped her index finger in the can and brought the snow-like powder to her nose.

She is daydreaming in the Porsche's driver's seat. Daydreaming a nightmare. She walks through a scorched landscape in the kingdom of death, an underground inferno of shaking rocks and fire-spouting volcanoes. The spasmodic ground coughs, spits, yawps and throws up whirls of fire and pools of shadow. There is some kind of heaven down here, but the sky of death is emptier and blacker than any other midnight she has ever seen. No stars. No wind. No birds. No smells. No sounds. The heaven, no real heaven, is nothing but an arch of sterile lightlessness.

She has just got out of bed. She wears only her nightdress. Her bare feet ache. The earth burns under her feet. Ebba wishes she had a pair of shoes or at least a pair of socks. She doesn't know why or where she strolls. She cannot turn back. She is unable to control her actions.

She has passed the point of no return.

The mountain ridge on the horizon trembles and squeaks. The rocks are melting, forming lava floods, which wriggle like killer snakes towards the valley. Ebba is the wrong girl in the wrong place at the wrong time. *I don't want to be here. I don't belong here. I'm a nice girl.* Without the least warning, it appears. The castle is mighty like a mountain. The entrance is as huge as the front facade of St. Paul's Cathedral in London. The windows are as wide and tall as the long sides of double-decker buses. The four spires, as tall as moon rockets, point at the dead anti-sky like disguised cruise missiles. The castle is darker than night, bleaker than death.

"I don't belong here", Ebba whimpers. Still, she can't control her footsteps. She passes through the giant portal. The interior consists of a single room, devoid of decoration. A naked space of incredible size. Vast like a dead, inner sky.

She screams when she sees the creature. The monster, as big as a three-storey house, sits on a kind of throne. The hammock-like throne is massive like Tower Bridge in London. The freak (the devil?) has olive-green fur. A bald, horned head. Eight eyes as wide as church windows. Four arms as thick as redwood trees. Teeth like elephant tusks. The beast gesticulates. Eight splayed fingers on one of the four fists wave at her.

She shrieks. "I don't belong here!"

"That's what you all say on arrival." The beast delivers a disgusting laugh. "You think there are people who belong here, Ebba? You assume I invited you here? Nobody belongs here. Like countless people before you, you're here not without reason." The voice of the demon shakes the night like thunder.

The tears which spill from her eyes feel real. Too real for a nightmare. "My mother used to talk about an eternal paradise."

"Your mother has not kept herself up to date with current events. That's a shame. It's important to stay on top of political developments. Paradise is a mere memory. A misguided idea of the afterlife. God lost the Cold War. We won. There's now only one superpower in the world, and that's us. Do you understand?"

"I don't understand anything."

"Mr. Jarrow freelances for us. You didn't know?"

"I want out of here. Whoever you are, let me go."

"There's nowhere to go. How many crossroads did you think a human being had in life or in death?"

"My mum—"

"I'm not interested in your mother. It's about you, Ebba."

"What do you want from me?"

"Tell me how and why you're involved."

"What does it matter?"

"I want to know."

She wipes the tears from her cheeks with the long sleeve of her nightdress. "It's this exclusive group of businessmen and businesswomen and scientists ... an international group of contacts and influences ... The four most important players are Dirk Jarrow, Chief Executive Officer of Yolexus Enterprise; Roger Stockmayer, neuroscientist and sleep-disorder expert at the Oberon Clinic, as well as member of the board at Yolexus Enterprise; Esmeralda Northcutt, top secretary and triple spy from NanoScoop Technology Group; and the late Umberto Antonetti, Professor Emeritus of Biochemistry at Liverpool University, and the insider at BioFutura Systematik."

"Continue."

Ebba blows her nose in the hem of her nightgown. "BFS is a biotechnology company founded by Victor Milton, the dad of my colleague and best friend Catriona. The conspirators want to either control or destroy some new discovery made at BFS. Their ideas and approaches are eccentric. They want to get to Milton through his daughter. And they want to get to Cat through me. The group has a hold over me, forcing me to cooperate. If I don't obey, Jarrow will sabotage my career."

"And?"

"Stockmayer said his patient Catriona's so-called automatic behaviour would be the key to my involvement in the plan. All I had to do was report what Cat said or did when she had a narcoleptic attack. Stockmayer said the everyday actions of a narcoleptic person in a state of automatic behaviour function automatically. For example, the person can talk or walk or drive a car while sleeping. When the person wakes up from this condition, he or she has no memory of what has happened during the time period in question.

"Stockmayer also said when Cat is in a state of automatic behaviour, she performs routine tasks and engages in communication with reduced awareness. Cat remembers no details from those episodes, something I utilised. Cat's own subconscious betrayed her. Dreams, hallucinations; her dad visited to tell her about BioFutura Systematik's revolutionary gene therapy concept. And when my best friend unconsciously talked about her dad's secret, I betrayed her."

The monster's jaws are working. The long fangs whoosh like guillotines. "Was it this Stockmayer who explained how it all would work out?"

"The scientific part, yes. The business part was orchestrated by Jarrow and, to some degree, Northcutt. Dame Esmeralda."

The monster knitted its eyebrows. "Dame?"

"*Dame* is a British title, derived from the English word *damehood*, an award the Queen assigns a female individual for a significant long-term contribution in an activity at national or international level. It is one of the highest honours an individual can receive. The masculine counterpart of the title and award are *Sir* and *knighthood*."

"So, who is this honourable Dame Esmeralda then?"

"A High Court judge who plays triple games on all fronts. She has offices in Montreal, Chicago, Buenos Aires, Sydney and London. Dame Esmeralda is the architect of several major political murders."

The beast fixes its eight eyes on Ebba and points at her with three of its four index fingers. "How profitable?"

"We're talking trillions of dollars. Stockmayer said a breakthrough in gene therapy which resulted in a cure for narcolepsy would pave the way for other cures and new insights across the entire field of the pathophysiology of neurological and neuropsychiatric diseases, including multiple sclerosis, cerebral palsy, Parkinson's disease, Tourette's syndrome, ADHD and autism. I want to add that the word 'pathophysiology' isn't mine. It's Stockmayer's word. I have no idea what it means.

"Moreover, Stockmayer said nano methods as gene therapy solutions are a topical research area. BioFutura's programme was the world's most successful one. The BFS nanotechnical concept would also have an impact beyond nerve diseases. The BFS method is a cure for several hitherto infectious and fatal diseases, including cancer.

"The explanation for the prominent versatility of the BioFutura method is that the nanotechnology involves free manipulation of individual atoms and molecules."

"You're a model, Ebba. You're sounding strange for a model."

"I know I'm sounding strange. I'm not talking like me. But this is a dream. A fucking nightmare. I want to wake up. I want a cigarette and a beer."

"Why did you do it, Ebba?"

"It wasn't my fault." She whimpers. "They made me do it."

"Nobody is ever innocent, Ebba. Everybody is guilty of

something. Human beings are corrupt and egoistic by nature. Individuals lie, cheat, and get elected."

She sobs. "Life is complicated and I'm only human. I want to get another chance to improve."

The devil's grin widens. "Why did you do it, Ebba?"

She hesitates, fearing saying the wrong words. "Roy ... Roy Beckman ... was mine. Roy was mine until he was evil to me and yelled at me and dumped me over the phone. Roy and I would have built our future together. Now that future is ruined."

"Was Roy your only motivation?" The phantom sweeps an eight-fingered hand, causing a current of air. The draft of wind makes Ebba's hair flutter. "Did you want Roy as a revenge on your best friend?"

"Roy wasn't my only motivation. There were also other reasons. Although Cat and I were ... are best friends, I wanted more influence. I was tired of being the permanent runner-up in prestige games against her. She made me jealous.

"Cat is the most beautiful girl in the world. She is more popular than I am. Even if I have an obscene salary myself, Cat earns more. I couldn't stand being overshadowed by my best friend in this way anymore. The more obscene the salary, the greater the prestige."

The beast shows a hideous grin. "Continue."

She blinked. "There's nothing more to tell."

"But there is. Have you managed to forget Herbert Krass?"

"What's this about? A kind of confession?" Tears trickle from her eyes. "The gossip journalist may have been double-dealing and his secret game may have turned sour. Will you allow me to return to the surface soon?"

"The surface?" The demon laughs. "Do you mean the surface of the earth or the decent portion of society?"

"The surface of the earth." She sobs. "I'm a decent girl."

"Are you?"

"I want to be. I want to change."

"You look scared, Ebba."

"I am scared."

"Why, if nightmares aren't real?"

"I don't like this place."

"No one has asked you to like it."

She takes a few shaky steps backwards. "I'm going now."

"You're not going anywhere, Ebba. We'll socialise, you and I." The beast scoops her up with ease, as if she were Fay Wray or Jessica Lange or Naomi Watts in King Kong's fist.

Ebba shrieked, woke up with a start and realised the Porsche was standing still and silent. In the car park. Outside the Golden Plaza Hotel in Paddington. The champagne and cocaine must have made her daydream. Then she must have fallen asleep at the wheel. When? Before or after parking? She didn't remember the drive from the Strand. Holy shit.

Knocks rattled on the driver's window. She turned her head and blinked. A geezer in a uniform peered into the Porsche.

A fucking parking attendant? She lowered the window.

"You all right, miss?"

She regained her photogenic smile. "Brilliant."

"You seem a little tired."

"I'm fine." She put a cigarette between her lips.

"Just wondered if you had fallen asleep, miss. This awesome roadster swung into the car park a quarter of an hour ago, but nobody got out to buy a ticket."

She preserved her smile, not without effort, hoping there was no smell of champagne on her breath. No traces of cocaine on the passenger seat. So far so good. "I was just resting for a while. Where's the ticket machine?"

The geezer pointed. Then he said, "You know, you look like that Swedish model Ella Sjödag or Elsa Sjödell or something like that." He scratched his head. "Know who I mean?"

"Yeah, I know who you mean." She sniggered. "That wild and scandalous girl? Do I look like her?"

The parking attendant scratched his head again and left.

She bought a parking ticket, checked her Gucci watch and put on a pair of dark glasses. The four-thousand-pound Moss Lipow sunglasses were framed in ostrich and alligator leather. She spat out the cigarette butt, left the car park and strolled into the lobby bar at the Golden Plaza Hotel. Half an hour early. Plenty of time to relax. It would be nice with a Bloody Mary.

• SEVENTY-TWO •

CAT COULDN'T BELIEVE what she had done. Through her discovery of a tube of black mascara she had come to the conclusion her doctor and lover Roger Stockmayer was living a double life as a Ludwig Trexler who was a board member of Yolexus Enterprise which had manufactured the scandalous product named Nargontanac which had caused brain damage and mental disorders in subjects associated with a clinical study.

Ludwig Trexler, M.D., Ph.D. Yolexus Director. Member of the Yolexus Science and Technology Committee and Lead Independent Director.

"*Have I used any medicine that Yolexus has manufactured?*"

"*Never. There are several companies which produce drugs for the treatment of dyssomnias.*"

Roger was involved. The man she had fallen in love with, the man to whom she had made love several times during two passion-filled nights and two passion-filled mornings was a man involved in the murder of Dad and Zimmer and probably also involved in the disappearance of the BFS Deputy Director of Research, Sandra Kallikrinos. Roger was involved in the plan to steal BioFutura's outstanding gene therapy concept, a theft which might have already been completed.

She couldn't care less what a prosecutor might say about the evidence. What mattered was what she thought and felt herself. The fact he had concealed his double identity and lied about

Henrietta's appearance was evidence enough for Cat. Proof he had things to hide. The sickness in her stomach worsened. Her foothold swayed. She rushed into the bathroom, vomited in the washbasin, spat, hyperventilated and cried out.

Filled with disgust, she felt dirty, both on the inside and the outside. If she had had more time, she would have showered again. All of a sudden, Roger's (Ludwig's?) kisses seemed as pleasant as the toxin from the most poisonous mushroom would have felt on her lips. Her memory of their erotic adventures changed from exciting to dreadful. The moments of his caressing hands on her waist, his playful tongue on her nipples and the feeling of his throbbing penis inside her, she now perceived as fragments of bygone horror visions.

A nasty sensation of Roger (Ludwig?) overwhelmed her. She must erase every aspect of this man. Eradicate every bodily and soulful detail associated with Roger (Ludwig?). Having another shower in this house would be a waste of time. The shower water in this house couldn't clean her. The water in this residence was as impure as the air she now had to breathe.

She scrambled her belongings together and was about to dash out of the house. She stopped in the hallway, trembling, swallowed her cry, considered her actions. A pain grew in the pit of her stomach. She had no plan. What would she do? What *could* she do? What did she *want* to do? Minutes ran away with a furious speed. He could be back anytime. He was only picking up some files at the clinic. Imagine if he turned into Paradise Park Street as she was leaving the front of the property. Or an even narrower margin: What if he turned into the driveway at the same instant as she walked out through the front door?

Panic started to chop like razor blades through her muscles. She fought it. She couldn't afford, had no time, to accept panic. She must regain her calm. The calm before the storm.

If he showed up before she had made it out of here, she would pretend nothing new had happened. To be alone with Roger when she revealed her discovery was unthinkable.

Make yourself at home, he had said. She discovered the house and the garage were connected via a glazed terrace facing the back garden. She judged no one could see from the street or from the front of the property if a person walked into the garage via the terrace in the direction of the back garden. She moved through the terrace, opened the garage door, slid in, closed the door, hit the light switch and surveyed the space. No windows. She guessed the light couldn't be detected from the outside. But who knew for certain?

She was in a two-car garage. Roger had driven off in his snow-white Mercedes. Here was an emerald-green Jaguar. (*Ebba would love a car like this*, Cat found the time to think.) The garage had three exits/entrances. In addition to the electric garage door and the door to the terrace, there was a side door. What did she want to do here? Search for evidence? Further proof which reinforced her suspicion about the conspiracy against Dad's company? Yes, she decided.

The garage resembled a well-stocked storeroom. And there was a lot of metal. The parking spaces for the Mercedes and the Jaguar were surrounded by a steel railing. In the space outside the three sides of the railing stood metal bookcases filled with metal file boxes, plus a rectangular metal-framed bench with a surface of some darker, probably spill-proof, material. The bench had two sinks and was reminiscent of a workbench in a chemistry, biology or physics laboratory. Although she had no scientific background, she knew what lab furniture looked like. She had seen pictures from Dad's company.

This was far from a regular garage. No garden tools or equipment, such as a lawnmower, brushes, rakes, trimmers, spades or digging tools, or a garden hose. The room was rather a combination of car park and scientific department. Incredible but true. And with superb ventilation. She couldn't sense the slightest smell of exhaust fumes.

If Roger came home while she was in the garage, the sound of the Mercedes' engine would alert her. She would have time to leave the room before he became suspicious. She walked over to the lab furniture. It appeared cleaner than clean, *clinically* clean, like an examination table in a hospital. The bench had ten drawers. She started to pull them out, one by one. In the first seven drawers there were all kinds of laboratory equipment, for example, test tubes, beakers, syringes, funnels, and loads of stuff she was unable to identify. The turn came for the eighth drawer. She pulled it out. The contents were staggering.

The items in the eighth drawer were packed in a plastic bag: a suit, a pair of latex gloves, a wig, a latex mask, three bloody scalpels and a notebook. The detailed mask showed a moon-pale face; lips as slim as shoelaces; a disturbing smile; a nose pointed like a bird beak. The wig was pinewood-blond, its style short. The outfit as a whole represented an imitation of the gunman from the tram. It was Roger whom Cat and Jan had seen at the Zimmer residence, not the corpse-pale gangster guy with the sick smile. Roger wasn't only behind the murder of Zimmer. He had carried out the bestial deed in person. What was going on? Where was the gun-crazy gangster with pinewood-blond hair and pointed nose?

A hand landed on Cat's shoulder. She cried out and whirled around. Her heart rushed. Roger stood right in front of her.

The side door, previously closed, was now ajar. Either she had not heard the Mercedes or had mistaken the sound of his car for the humming of other traffic on the street outside.

"What bad luck that you have to be so curious, Catriona."

• SEVENTY-THREE •

THROUGH A GLASS wall, she observed him at a table for two in the crowded Golden Plaza bar. Jarrow was reading a paper, sipping what looked like an Irish coffee. At the same moment as Ebba appeared in the lobby, he turned his head in her direction, as if he possessed panoramic vision and therefore knew she was there just then. He signalled to her.

"How nice that you wanted to keep me company, Miss Sjödal. Company is more pleasant than loneliness. Don't you agree?" Jarrow folded the newspaper. "Have a seat."

She sat down opposite the Yolexus boss. It was impossible to get used to his appearance. His face was a dust-grey shade similar to used dishwater. The chronically bloodshot right eye was surrounded by a birthmark which looked like a splash of brown sauce. His teeth were the same colour as resin, with the exception of a glimmering canine tooth in gold.

"What would you like to drink, Miss Sjödal?"

She didn't fancy a Bloody Mary any longer. She wanted no alcohol. It was high time she sobered up. In Jarrow's company, she wanted to be as crystal-clear and alert as possible. At once she thought of what Cat used to drink in bars. "Water, please."

"Carbonated?"

Carbonated? Doesn't matter to me. "Yes, please."

He snapped his fingers. A waiter appeared at the table.

"My wife would like carbonated mineral water," Jarrow said. "Your finest brand, of course."

"Certainly, sir."

Ebba couldn't help scowling. Fortunately, her angry gaze didn't show behind the dark glasses. She whispered across the table, "What do you mean by calling me your *wife*?"

"I've booked a hotel suite in the name of Mr. Acland. Since you're going to accompany me to the suite, it is advisable the staff think you are Mrs. Acland. Basic decency."

Ebba's heart froze. "Why would I follow you to the suite?"

"Because our topic is secret. We cannot discuss Yolexus secrets in a hotel bar."

"Why are we here at all, sir? Why didn't we meet elsewhere?"

"The Golden Plaza Hotel serves the best Irish coffee in London. I wanted one. And I enjoy it here. And I'm known here as Mr. Acland."

Ebba tried to calm down. She glanced around, with the greatest discretion. She wasn't the only woman wearing dark glasses. She noted three other girls wearing them. She guessed she didn't attract specific attention. "What if someone heard you call me by my real surname earlier?"

"Unlikely. The compact and continuous murmur in this atmosphere makes it impossible to overhear or to eavesdrop."

She listened. Jarrow was right. You couldn't even hear what the people at the nearest table were chatting about.

"By the way, I'm married," he said. "My love is Lisa-Marie. You don't have to worry about anything."

"I see."

"You and my beloved Lisa-Marie are much alike. Both you and my Lisa-Marie are very easy to converse with."

"I see." *Lisa-Marie must have a psyche of steel.*

The sparkling water arrived. She took the glass.

Jarrow produced a monstrous smile. He raised his drink. "Cheers, Mrs. Acland."

The Golden Plaza Hotel's top-floor suite offered a magnificent balcony view of Paddington Station, St. Mary's Hospital and Euston Road, including Euston Tower and University College Hospital. Jarrow wanted her to admire the view from the outer edge of the balcony. She obeyed.

"If you lean over the railing," he said, "you'll see better."

She stiffened. "I don't want to lean over any railing."

"It would be unfortunate if you made a mistake which resulted in a fall from a high place." He loomed over her. "It's important you consider your actions. A single mistake could lead to a fatal fall from a hotel balcony. Do we agree?"

She threw a glance at the balcony door. "What if you got to the point, sir? What were we supposed to discuss? Could we return to the suite? I don't want to talk here on the balcony."

"Are you scared?"

"The nice weather is over. And it's a little windy out here."

He grinned. The already disgusting Yolexus boss looked like

a zombie in the dimness of the balcony. "Let's return to the suite, Miss Sjödal. It'll be pleasant."

They sat opposite each other at the coffee table. Jarrow in an armchair, Ebba on the sofa. She shifted on her seat. "I thought Yolexus Enterprise no longer needed my services."

"I admire your optimism. However, life is a grey zone."

"What do you mean?"

"I mean your career would be crushed if certain colourful photos ended up in the wrong hands. And I mean your nice body would be crushed if it fell from a high place, such as a balcony. Do you understand? Or would you like a demonstration?"

She started. "No demonstration is necessary, sir."

"Fantastic. You're a reasonable woman. Like my wife, you do understand my thoughts. You and my wife have intellectual reasoning in common."

His creaking laughter made her shudder.

"It isn't blackmail," he continued. "Blackmail is immoral. Instead, it's *business*. Commerce, competition and prestige regulate our lives, Miss Sjödal."

"What happened to Mrs. Acland?"

"We're alone. When we're alone, you're always Miss Sjödal."

She was just dying for another cigarette. "I could lie to the CIA and Interpol about those saucy photos. I could argue the pictures are fakes. Montages. Or that the lady in the pictures isn't me but a porn actress who happens to look like me."

"You could come up with all sorts of lies. You're a talented and experienced liar. But dare you take the chance this time?"

The idea of lighting a cig in Jarrow's smoke-free suite was unthinkable. "What do you want?"

"I want to offer you a job, Miss Sjödal. A moonlighting job as a Yolexus agent. A job which pays forty million pounds, or fifty-five point two million dollars. Tax free, of course. About eight times your income of last year."

"Why pay me at all? Your company could force me to cooperate without compensation."

Jarrow's golden canine glinted. "I must be an overly nice person. Nonetheless, if I lost my good mood, the offer would disappear. If I lost my good mood, one Miss Sjödal would fall from a balcony and smash on the ground, two hundred and seventy feet below. That would be a shame, wouldn't it? Even if the company still uses you, it's important to remember you're not irreplaceable."

She had no interest in the Yolexus money. As a supermodel, she was already immensely rich. She had more money than she could ever spend. But Jarrow's hold over her forced her to listen.

"You travel to Gothenburg tomorrow," he said.

"Gothenburg? How would I have the time?"

"Your top mission has already been arranged. You'll fly from Heathrow to Gothenburg for an international conference in molecular medicine. You'll travel in the company of the Yolexus representative, the conference delegate and your husband, Dr. Boris Dolgorukov. According to your passport and your other identity documents, you are Mrs. Karin Dolgorukov. The conference banquet takes place on the night before the closing day. The venue is a hotel restaurant in Kungsportsavenyn.

"Apart from your delightful charm, you'll draw no specific attention to yourself. Spouses of conference delegates are invited. Nobody will suspect you're the famous model Ebba Sjödal. You're a specialist in changing your appearance from day to day. You'll choose your wig and makeup and dress for the banquet. Among the hundreds of delegates, there's one Professor Hirayama Koizumi. You'll let a tablet of P37 fall into Professor Koizumi's wine glass."

"What is P37?"

"A code name for a Yolexus-manufactured neurotoxin."

"Neurotoxin?!"

"A poison which will finish Professor Koizumi for good."

"That's murder."

"Professor Koizumi must die. The action is propelled by commercial interests, political morality and public prestige."

"Why me?"

"Two reasons. You're perfect for the role of Mrs. Karin Dolgorukov. And I like to work with you. You're a very social girl. As social as my wife."

"If I refuse, you'll kill me?"

"I would kill you without blinking. Your immediate future is determined here and now. In this hotel suite."

She hurled the flowerpot just as he dropped his eyes to open her handbag. The pot shattered in the violent collision with his head. Tulips flew. Water splashed.

"You damn bitch." Jarrow slurred, but he didn't faint. The flowerpot hadn't been strong enough. The man got to his feet, faltered. Blood trickled from his scalp. "Now I'm going to kill you, Miss Sjödal. Some other beauty will play the role of Mrs. Karin Dolgorukov."

She was already rushing in the direction of the door which faced the corridor. She slipped on a tulip, skidded, fell headlong, screamed. From the corner of her eye, she saw Jarrow coming for her. The monster grabbed her hair, jerked, pulled.

She shrieked, floundered, kicked out with her legs. One of her high-heeled shoes hit him. He growled and dropped his hold on her hair. She scrambled to her feet. Too late. He blocked the exit. She swore, threw herself into the bathroom, slammed the door shut and locked it.

She began to weep. He hammered his fists on the bathroom door. The door clattered and creaked.

He shouted, "You won't get out of here alive."

She couldn't call for help. Her phone was in her handbag. The handbag lay on the sofa in the lounge. She sobbed, sniffled. Jarrow continued to strike at the door with his fists.

How dare you defy me? Jarrow thought. The blood dripped from the cut on his head, down along one cheek and onto his shirt collar. He took the handkerchief from the breast pocket of his suit jacket and wiped at his scalp, cheek and neck. He threw the bloodied rag onto the hallway floor. Blood oozed between his lips. He hawked and spat a red gob onto the carpet. He raised the Heckler & Koch pistol. The silencer was already mounted. He aimed the weapon and fired multiple shots straight through the bathroom door.

• SEVENTY-FOUR •

"AS I SAID earlier, Catriona, it's healthy to be curious. But even healthy curiosity has its limits. I didn't need to get any files from the clinic. I already have everything I need for tonight's event. Instead, I wanted to leave you alone in my home for a while. It was an experiment." Roger pointed at the fluorescent lighting. "The garage is equipped with surveillance cameras. Images are sent to this tablet in my jacket pocket."

Cat froze, said nothing, couldn't say anything. Her tongue was stuck to the roof of her mouth. She waited, afraid to say the wrong words. Afraid to breathe.

Roger embraced her, kissed her. "It was a test, darling. You walked straight into the trap. A contact at the medico-legal centre informed me the day before yesterday that you had been asking uncomfortable questions about your father's death."

She stood still, allowed herself to be kissed. She remained neutral, forcing herself to be indifferent. She didn't answer his kiss with passionate body language. But she let herself be kissed.

"The latex mask is nothing short of an artistic masterpiece. It provides an excellent illusion of Leo Baginski."

"Uh-huh." She tried to look relaxed. Easier said than done. "As we both know, I've seen this Leo Baginski. The real guy. One of the gunmen from the tram. It couldn't have been you, Roger. I called you from bus 93 just after its departure from Hill Street and Denton Crescent. You couldn't have been in two places at the same time. By the way, your image doesn't fit the context.

You're a scientist, not a military-like action hero. Who is Baginski?"

"An assassin. The man you and your sister thought you saw from your hiding place in the wardrobe at Zimmer's house."

"You saw us? You knew we were hiding in there?"

Roger nodded. "And to reinforce your illusion of Baginski, I hung around longer than necessary in Zimmer's study. I wanted you and your sister to get a good look at me. Oh, and Janice sneezing like that wasn't very elegant. Bad timing." Then, like an afterthought, he added, "I didn't like what I did in Zimmer's house. Didn't like it at all. Believe me, it took a great effort to do something which only a mindless killer machine like Baginski would be able to do. My actions, and the style of my actions, had to fit the man I was impersonating. I'm not a cold-blooded murderer."

"How is it that you have a latex mask which gives the illusion of a professional killer, might I ask?"

"The mask, which you weren't supposed to find, is a leftover item from a previous Yolexus Enterprise mission. Some time ago, Baginski had to be in a certain place on a special occasion. Not the real Baginski, but an apparent version of the man. I want to add that this was a non-violent mission. I was the character who impersonated him back then, and I kept the latex mask. I thought it might come in handy again. Well, it did."

"Where is the real Baginski now?"

"I don't know."

"What about the other offender? On the tram? Bald, round cheeks, broad shoulders. Who was, or is, he?"

"You don't need to know."

"This other gunman shot at me."

Roger said nothing.

"This other gunman fired some kind of dart at me. I got the impression he didn't want to kill me. Did he use a tranquillizer gun? Did he want to sedate me and then kidnap me? Steal my body? How do you think this sounds?"

Roger said nothing.

"Then the two gunfighters ended up in a battle against one another. They fought over me. Without any police training, I've reasoned my way to a few, hmm, conclusions. Is there a secret linked to my disease?" She knew it was dangerous to talk but she wanted to gain time. Talking was better than silence.

Roger studied her. His attractive but insidious looks made her shiver. She steeled herself. "What are you going to do with me, Roger? Are you going to kill me?"

He laughed. The most terrifying part of his laugh was its genuine heartiness. He obviously found her question very funny. "I love you, Catriona. Earlier, I said I wanted to spend the rest of my life with you. Nothing has changed in that respect. Our love, our eroticism, will flourish. I want to marry you. I want to have a family with you. We'll have many children."

"How can that happen? After everything that's happened lately, how could we preserve our love life and make a family?" He's crazy, she thought. But how could a scientist be that crazy? Had his boundless love for her bent his mind out of shape? Had he succeeded in suppressing the absurdity of his talk of creating a family with a girl whose father was the victim of a murder plot in which he, Roger, was involved?

He hesitated. What was he thinking about? He certainly wanted to find out how much she knew. For example, the text message with an image attachment from Hanna's uncle was still in her inbox. What would happen when Roger realised she knew he was Ludwig Trexler?

"I need you, Catriona. You are the finest, the most beautiful, the cosiest and the sexiest thing in my life since Henrietta. At the moment, however, I don't have time to talk about our passion-laden future together. I'm on my way to Rainbow Tower. We'll talk and make love when I come home. When I come home we'll also talk about our forthcoming wedding. In the meantime, you'll wait here in the garage."

"Do you mean you're going to lock me up in here?"

"For your own good, sweetheart. But just until I get home."

"I have a train to catch tonight. I have to go to London."

"Because of the latest developments, because of your excessive curiosity, you have to postpone your journey."

"I have a return ticket for tonight. People in London are expecting me."

"We'll discuss the rebooking of your return ticket when I come home tonight. I'm happy to pay for your new ticket."

"Please don't lock me up in here, Roger."

"For your own good."

"I have to use the bathroom," she lied.

"There's a bathroom here." He pointed to a door which she had mistaken for a cupboard. "It's small, like a storage room, but functional. Give me your handbag, sweetheart."

Pointless to refuse, she thought. She handed it to him.

He inspected it. "Excellent. Both your phone and your tablet are in here. For your own good, I'll take care of the handbag with its contents until we see each other again."

She hoped he wouldn't inspect her phone.

"See you soon." He hugged her, kissed her, then walked towards the open side door.

"Wait, Roger."

"I'm on my way to Rainbow Tower." He left the garage.

Cat was alone. Locked up.

Nobody knew where she was. All the doors were closed and locked and impossible to open from the inside without a key. She inspected the control panel which operated the garage door. No instructions indicated. She pushed buttons at random. Nothing happened. Although she lacked an electrician's expert knowledge, she guessed Roger had done something special with its electronics. He must have predicted her idea of trying to walk straight out of here via the electrically operated door. She peered into the so-called bathroom and flicked the light switch. Indeed, the space wasn't any larger than a storage cupboard. But clean. A toilet and a basin. No window.

She was angry at herself for having walked into this trap. She had to get out of here. She had to get out now. She would need some kind of tool, some sort of battering ram, and then simply bash her way through a door. A battering ram? Her thought process stopped. The idea sparkled like fireworks in her head. *Do you mean it? Do you dare?* She stared at the sports car. She tried all the doors of the Jaguar. Locked. She returned to the laboratory bench, pulled out drawers, poked about in the plethora of gadgets, found a remote key. The Jaguar's remote key. She pressed a button. The car bleeped. She tried the door on the driver's side. Unlocked. She sat down behind the wheel and drew a deep breath. The first time in six years she had sat in the driver's seat of a car—and not just any car. The conspirator and murderer Roger Stockmayer's sports car.

After her diagnosis as a seventeen-year-old with a new driving licence, she had stopped driving altogether. Not because narcoleptics weren't allowed to drive. They were, provided they met the usual knowledge requirements and skills, and if they informed the driving-licence-issuing authority about their disease. The DVLA issued temporary driving licences for narcoleptics, with regular reassessments once a year or every second year or every third year. Cat, however, dared no longer drive. She had chosen to quit. But now she was here. Behind the wheel of a sports car. *Imagine if Ebba could see me now.*

She studied the dashboard. The gearbox. The pedals. Now or never. Her fingers touched the ignition key. She no longer had a driving licence but this was an emergency situation. She stepped on an arbitrary pedal and rotated the key at the same time. The engine started with a low-pitched rumbling.

All the doors in the garage are closed. Car exhaust fumes are toxic, lethal. What am I doing?

The Jaguar scampered backwards. The reverse must have—

The car slammed into the railing. There was a loud clank. She screamed and fumbled with the gear lever. *The exhaust fumes ... How good is the ventilation?*

A screech filled her ears. She grimaced. She had forgotten to step on the clutch. Which pedal was the clutch? She stepped on the middle one and pushed the gear lever. Nothing happened. Was that the brake pedal? She stepped on the pedal to the left and shoved the gear lever in some random direction.

The Jaguar rushed forward with the power and suddenness of a real and living jaguar. The car collided with the garage door.

Dead stop.

She was hurled forward, hit her forehead on the steering wheel, swore, using words she would normally never use, such as the four-letter f-word. (*Imagine if Ebba could hear me now.*) She groped for the seat belt, found it and fastened it.

The gear lever. The reverse gear. The clutch. The throttle. Her hands back on the wheel.

The Jaguar shot backwards. She had no time to brake. The car crashed into the railing again, even harder than before. A section of the railing gave way with a clang. The vehicle trembled and continued backwards and hit the workbench. One of the bookcases tipped over and banged against the car roof. *Illegal driving plus damage. See you in court, Roger.*

The correct pedal and the correct position of the gear lever. The Jaguar raged and flung forwards like a creature in a movie. A section of the still standing railing clashed with the right side of the car. Cat swerved. The vehicle collided with the garage door. Both the car and the door shrieked and groaned. Plaster crackled and popped, and chippings whirled from around the door frame.

The smell of exhaust fumes. However, not worse than in central London or Paris—so far. She snatched the gear lever, jerked it. Stamped on pedals, right and left. The car hastened backwards and lurched. The railing scraped the left side of the Jaguar. She stamped on the middle pedal. The vehicle stopped dead. Clutch, gear, steering, accelerator. Full on.

The car skidded across the concrete floor and rammed the garage door. The glass in one of the Jaguar's headlights exploded. She screamed. Metal groaned and squeaked. The garage door bowed and its hinges rattled. Chunks and splinters of plaster fell from the surrounding wall. The dead stop from the crazy speed propelled a pain through her and made her cry out. The seat belt hurt her shoulder and chafed a breast (*a breast which Roger has kissed and sucked*). She gasped, coughed, sputtered. The air tasted of petrol, dust and plaster. *Come on, Catriona. Come on. Come on. One more time. One more time.*

Her fingers found the gear lever. Her feet found the right pedals in the correct order, or so she guessed, or hoped. The vehicle rushed backwards. She caught a sight of herself in the rear-view mirror. She didn't recognise herself. Red-rimmed eyes stained with an insane intensity. Disordered hair with a straight-out-of-bed look. Teeth bared like a hyena. An uncool bead of moisture on her brow. She was one of the world's most coveted models but, given the reflection, she might as well have been a stranger from a dark and unwanted dream.

The mirror image had stolen all her attention. She forgot to step on the brake pedal. An ear-splitting thunder threw her back to reality. The car smashed into the workbench. The room trembled. Another bookcase tottered and fell onto the Jaguar, scratching the paint, and boomed against the concrete floor. The gearbox jangled. She coughed, croaked, panted, sobbed, pushed the gear lever, stepped on pedals and turned the wheel. The throttle pressed to the floor. The Jaguar rushed forwards.

• SEVENTY-FIVE •

THE FIRST ROUND shattered the bathroom cabinet mirror. Ebba shrieked and threw herself to one side of the room, away from the door. The hail of bullets clattered, slammed, rasped. Shards of tile and concrete sprayed from the opposite wall.

She crouched close to the wall in the corner by the bathtub. The window detonated in a cloud of dancing splinters. The washbasin cracked. Silence followed. As if it mattered, she put her hands over her mouth, trying to subdue the sound of her rapid breathing. Then she realised it did matter after all. Jarrow didn't know if she was dead or still alive. She looked up at the ruined window. A small window, not big enough to creep through. Not even a slim model could wriggle through it. Besides, the suite was on the Golden Plaza's top floor. The idea of escaping via the window was lousy from the start.

Jarrow listened. Not a peep from the bathroom. Was the rude girl dead? Was she alive?

Gun silencers were consumables. They functioned worse and worse, after only half a dozen shots. He couldn't fire any more bullets without attracting the attention of staff and guests. He had taken the opportunity to blow the bathroom lock to smithereens. If the stubborn lady was still breathing, he would break her pretty neck. It didn't matter if she was riddled with bullets and dying. If she breathed in the least, he would crack her cute neck.

He pushed open the door, entered. Debris from tiles, plaster, concrete, glass and white-gloss-finish ceramic everywhere. But where was Miss Sjödal? The space was empty. No dead or living or dying girl. The demolished window was too small to offer an escape route. No girl was in the thrashed shower cubicle. No girl could or would swim out of here through the toilet drain.

Wedged in the narrow space between the ceiling and the bathtub curtain rail track, Ebba swung the toilet brush with full force. At the same instant, Jarrow turned his eyes towards the ceiling. He reacted reflexively, managing to parry the strike with an arm. The hard blow made him grimace. "Damn girl. I'll get you for that. I'll break your cute neck."

"First you have to catch me, you dirty old man." She guffawed and sobbed at the same time. "You're bleeding from a wound on your head, fuckface. Did you collide with a flowerpot?"

Fresh anger flashed in his eyes. "I'll punish you for your rudeness. I'll torture you to death." He reached for her, missed.

She flipped him off with her middle finger, then swung the toilet brush again. He ducked. She swung it again. The toilet brush, with its shaft of steel, hit his extended fist. The man howled. He grabbed the bathtub curtain. Pulled, jerked, twisted. She yelled. The U-shaped curtain rail track rattled and squeaked. Then it swayed downwards. Hooks snapped. Runners burst. She screeched. The suspended chrome device lost several screws. Crumbs of plaster and paint rained from the ceiling. The rail track leaned, rocked, came loose. Ebba fell, screaming.

• SEVENTY-SIX •

JANICE WAS AT the kitchen table with Dixie on her lap. "Would you like a potato crisp, Dix?"

Dix looked up, purring, said nothing.

"Perhaps you're dieting, Dix. You should be dieting. I should also be dieting but I can't. I can't and I don't want to." She put both fists into the bag of cheese-and-onion-flavoured crisps. She scooped shedloads of crisps into her mouth, over and over again, chewing and smacking her lips.

"There, you see? All the crisps are gone. I'm a hopeless case."

Dix miaowed.

"Dix, you know what? Cat leaves tonight. Will you miss her, or do you think her leaving for London will be a relief?"

Dix shifted on Jan's lap. He said nothing.

"I understand why you're hesitating with your reply, Dix. I'm divided myself. Her visit to the City of Crows has been stressful, difficult, problematic and associated with all sorts of horrors. In a way, I think her leaving tonight will be a relief. I miss the peace and quiet. At the same time, she is my beloved sis, or at least the twisted shadow of the sis I want to love."

Dix miaowed.

"Dix? Do you suspect Cat has a new boyfriend? Sis always has boyfriends, one after another."

Dix purred.

"It's getting late, Dix. Where's Cat? Why doesn't she get in touch? Why doesn't she call Mum's phone? Shouldn't she start to pack her suitcase and spend some time with you and me and Mum before leaving town? You never know when you'll see Cat in Blackfield again. You don't even know if you'll ever see her here again. Sis doesn't like the City of Crows. I don't blame her. How could I blame her? I can't compare Blackfield to other cities since I've never been anywhere else. If I had Cat's appearance and if I were as radiant as she is, I would have looked at society from a different point of view." She paused. An afterthought surfaced. "Did you hear, Dix? What I just said? It seems as if I've begun to understand Sis and her perspective."

She lifted Mum's phone and dialled the number of Cat's mobile.

• SEVENTY-SEVEN •

STOCKMAYER DROVE HIS Mercedes-Benz towards the city. At the same time, he experienced a journey towards the future. His future with Catriona. There were lots of things to plan, accomplish and organise. Beautiful dreams and fantasies about Catriona would soon turn into earthly realities. They would move into a magnificent house in London. They would marry. He would take her on a honeymoon abroad. They would have children. He owned a castle in the Austrian countryside between Vienna and Graz, a castle he used to use as a holiday resort. A fairy-tale castle. Catriona would be his fairy-tale princess, or rather his fairy-tale queen. They would spend most of their leisure time between London and the fairy-tale castle.

He needed to maintain a healthy relationship with the rest of the Miltons. Rita and Janice Milton would always be welcome in the Roger Stockmayer-Catriona Milton family. The mother and the twin sister and their cat would be welcome both in the residence in London and in the castle outside Graz. He did hope Janice would contact his friend, Jakob Ratzinger.

The accelerating development of technology made corporate espionage and corporate theft easier and cheaper than ever. The plethora of readily accessible instruments and sophisticated innovations turned industrial espionage into a global problem which cost hundreds of billions of dollars a year. Cyberspace, phones, state-of-the-art video-chip technology, etcetera, offered alternative routes to obtaining company information. Industrial spies seldom used only one method but a collection of techniques which combined legal and illegal, traditional and forward-thinking methods.

The multifaceted nature of the activity made it impossible to quantify praxis. Yet it was possible to determine the damages. It was reported German companies lost fifty billion euros and thirty thousand jobs to industrial espionage every year. The British Government Communications Headquarters estimated Great Britain lost one billion pounds annually due to electronic fraud. The American Society for Industrial Security assessed the potential losses for the entire US industry due to domestic and foreign thefts of trade secrets could amount to two billion dollars a month.

Stockmayer braked at a red traffic signal. He checked the rear-view mirror, half expecting to spot Baginski in the backseat. No one there. He doubted the Yolexus hitman was dead or dying. The blow from the spanner had been hard, but not hard enough to kill a man.

When the traffic signal turned green, he turned right, along City North Road. It was high time to distance himself from Yolexus Enterprise. Jarrow had made a mistake. Stockmayer had seen through the Yolexus boss the moment Baginski had called.

Nobody knew Roxonodonol better than Stockmayer. He would build a new research team based on members of KNEPCOM, his international expert network.

Catriona's handbag lay on the passenger seat. He reached for it, took out the phone and the tablet. He noted his future wife had been in contact with a Wolfgang Schneider in Germany. The attached photo revealed Catriona now knew that he, Stockmayer, had lied about Henrietta's looks. Yet another detail they would have to talk about later tonight.

The web browser's history reinforced his perception of her curiosity. She had searched for pictures. The delicious blonde in the photos was Emma Auenbrugger, a secretary at Premium Star Pharmaceuticals, the Yolexus subsidiary and manufacturer of Rox-1 and the by now discontinued Nargontanac. Emma was the perfect secretary: affectionate, efficient, moderately curious. And she was great in bed. Emma Auenbrugger had acted as Mrs. Henrietta Stockmayer several times, assignments which had strengthened the credibility of Roger Stockmayer's identity. It had worked, as nothing could link Roger Stockmayer to Ludwig Trexler or to the clinical study in New Delhi.

He would arrange this Wolfgang Schneider's fatal accident through KNEPCOM. He had no time to contact KNEPCOM tonight. The task could wait until tomorrow. In the inbox of Catriona's mobile, there was an unknown phone number. He wondered who she had called. Many celebrities had secret phone numbers. She might have called a friend, not unlikely some model colleague. He knew staff within KNEPCOM who could crack unknown phone numbers. If the owner of this number was a link to Wolfgang Schneider, KNEPCOM would create *two* fatal accidents in due course.

He must explain to her why he sometimes found it convenient to be Ludwig Trexler. Or Enok Ripstein. Or Stefan Mahlau. So far, nothing indicated Catriona knew he was using four identities. His future wife didn't need to know everything. We live in a democracy. A democracy was a freedom-loving society. He had a legal right to his integrity and flexibility both inside and outside the framework of the forthcoming marriage.

He stopped at another set of traffic lights. He then turned left and drove southwards via Crowfield Way. At the western horizon of the cityscape loomed the modern masterpiece.

The rainbow-shaped Rainbow Tower accommodated radio stations, conference rooms, art exhibitions, shopping malls, cinemas, restaurants and cafes. The high-tech architecture style with exposed mechanical and electrical systems was inspired by the Centre Georges Pompidou in Paris. With its total height of three hundred and fifty feet, from ground level to the top (excluding the forty-nine-foot aerials on the roof), and comprising thirty floors, Rainbow Tower was the tallest building in Blackfield.

Finally there. He turned the Mercedes into the car park. Catriona's phone rang. He looked at the display. The caller's number belonged to Mrs. Rita Milton. It was either the mother or the twin sister who was calling. He let the phone ring. He tossed the handbag with its contents into the boot of the car.

Rainbow Tower, Hall 1A, thirtieth floor. A thousand attendees. Not a bad turnout. The size of the hall was just about big enough. The space comprised upper and lower stalls plus two balconies. In the foyer was a restaurant and a bar. Stockmayer sat in a chair next to the stage, waiting to be introduced by the hostess, Professor Paulina Venner. The title of tonight's talk was already projected onto a huge white screen:

IS ANYTHING UNREAL?
The human brain as a biological quantum computer requires new concept of reality

Roger Stockmayer
Oberon Clinic, Blackfield & London, UK

It was a talk for the public, and therefore he had to adjust his language. It was an evening in the spirit of pop science. Besides, he decided to abandon his original outline. Instead, he would improvise, engaging in a dialogue with his audience.

It pleased him the one thousand attendees represented a broad range of ages, from young kids to elderly pensioners. Boys and girls. Men and women. The gender distribution was fifty-fifty. Citizens from all walks of life. The broad appeal of tonight's talk warmed his heart.

The audience didn't need to know his speaking fee for tonight was fifty thousand pounds, or half a million euros. A fee funded by taxpayers. Nothing strange. As a taxpayer, you paid for invisible investments. With lucrative results, Roger Stockmayer's name was advertising Blackfield as a cultural city and intellectual centre. If local businesses were thriving, local taxpayers were winners. And anyway, half a million euros was a modest fee. There were out-of-date politicians who commanded better speaking fees. If Stockmayer received the Nobel Prize, he would double or triple his fee for cultural engagements—to start with.

• SEVENTY-EIGHT •

THE JAGUAR RAMMED the garage door with a thundersome noise, harder, faster, wilder, crazier and tougher than before—a boom and a screech and a clang and a squeal and a pang and a snap. Twisting, ripping, turning, squeezing.

Tortured metal, cracked concrete, splintered plaster. Fractures fanning across the car's side windows like spiderwebs. Another headlight exploded. The room's ceiling light flashed like a stroboscope. There was a crunching, crackling sound from the electrical control panel.

Cat shouted, swore, sobbed. Her body ached. The vibration from the collision had smashed straight though her. She experienced a taste of blood in her mouth. She grimaced, wiped her brow on her sleeve, clutched the steering wheel and continued to press the accelerator pedal. The garage door hinges protested. The already wrecked metallic door curved more and more. The car's engine rumbled like a bloodthirsty predator.

She assumed Roger hadn't studied any more surveillance-camera images since he'd left. Had he done so, he would have returned to stop her by now.

Hinges, screws and nuts groaned and burst in tandem with falling chunks and splinters of cement and wood. The door gave way. It swayed and wobbled like a battered sail. The Jaguar jerked forwards over an uneven bed of destroyed concrete, thrashed plaster and misshapen sheet metal.

A front tyre got stuck in the debris. The fear of a tyre puncture washed over her. She stamped on the throttle and turned the steering wheel in despair.

"Come on." She twisted the steering wheel, back and forth. The engine screamed. The chunk of rubbish, whatever it was, dislodged. The Jaguar forced its way forwards again.

Out. I'm out. Out, out, out.

For a second or two, she lost control of the car. She spun the steering wheel here and there. The Jaguar skidded, struck a flowerbed and crossed the lawn towards the edge of the property. When she spotted the fence and the drop to street level from the edge of the property, it was too late to brake. She kept her foot steady on the throttle. The car smashed through the fence. At the very impact, she closed her eyes. The Jaguar turned airborne, flew from a height of two or three feet and landed smack-bang on the asphalt, missing the rear bumper of a passing Toyota. The Jaguar shook like a dislodged roller coaster car in the violent contact with the street surface. The shock absorbers squealed and rattled. She was on Paradise Park Street.

Cat didn't see the lorry before it honked. She realised she was driving in the middle of the street. The head-on crash was only a few feet away. She spun the wheel with a frantic effort to the left, the Jaguar swerved and the rumbling lorry passed to her right, missing her by a hair's breadth. She panted, suppressing her tears. She heard a clatter, not distant. Something rattled on the undercarriage of the car. She could do with some luck, she thought. She said a silent prayer. The car mustn't break down. Not now. Not right now.

The Jaguar whizzed through the district of Springlake. She lowered the windows for fresh air. The smell of exhaust fumes could have been worse. The garage-laboratory, or whatever it was supposed to be called—she had never seen anything like it; departments like that didn't exist for the public, did they?—had superior ventilation. She felt sick. Sicker than ever. Not because of the fumes. The source of her horrible nausea was Roger. She could never forget. She had to learn to live with the memory.

She had no intention of driving to the nearest police station to report what she knew about Roger Stockmayer and Yolexus Enterprise and the conspiracy. She had already decided what she would do, without the least hesitation or fear. She steered the crash-damaged car towards the city centre, via City North Road and Crowfield Way. The fastest route to Rainbow Tower.

• SEVENTY-NINE •

PAULINA, THE HOSTESS, moved with precision to the centre of the stage, waving to the audience. She was a short lady with mustard-yellow hair, ebony-black eyes and pink-painted lips. In her daily life, she headed the Department of Molecular Biotechnology at Blackfield University of Technology. She wore a twilight-dark dress with a pattern of white butterflies. The hall was equipped with a large focusing screen. A camera team had arrived. An enlarged Paulina appeared on the screen.

She spoke into a microphone, "Ladies and gentlemen, welcome to Rainbow Tower and the informal special talk of the night." Her energetic voice sparkled in the speakers. Paulina had to have been an opera singer in another life.

"Scientists have basically two choices. Either they can choose to follow the conservative and typical route and mass-produce solid results, thereby guaranteeing themselves a comfortable life and a reasonable degree of success. Or they can break out of the ordinary and venture into uncharted and risky territories, where there are no guarantees, and where they must be prepared for failure. It is in this latter category, among the tenacious and fearless risktakers, where we find the most significant scientists, those we read about in the history books.

"In the science world, almost every new idea is wrong. If this were not the case, it would be too easy to push forwards the frontiers of knowledge. Frontier science always balances on the edge of absurdity and contradiction. Major scientists focus on these paradoxes because it is there where the answers to the revolutionary breakthroughs are hidden. It is a great pleasure, and a fantastic honour, to have one of the most spectacular and fearless scientists with us here tonight at Rainbow Tower, a world authority whom we will read about in the history books."

Paulina paused for effect. "Ladies and gentlemen, may I present no one less than the pioneering neuroscientist Dr. Roger Stockmayer."

A roar of applause and whistles filled the hall. Even toddlers clapped their hands, cheering. Toddlers imitating adults. The atmosphere in a crowded circus tent could not have been more exhilarating. Tonight was party night. Paulina left the stage and Stockmayer entered it. She touched his shoulder (her hand almost crossed the line between a clap and a caress), gave him her warmest smile and continued to her chair at the end of the front row in the lower stall.

The basic technology included a data/video projector, DVD/BD player, film screen, high-definition document camera, wireless microphones and a mixer station for audio, lighting and visuals. On a table which looked like a magician's prop table (the cloth was black and shiny and featured a pattern of golden stars and moon crescents) were bottled water and fancy plastic glasses. *Maybe Paulina sees me as a magician.* Stockmayer noted a close-up of himself on the big screen.

He picked up the microphone and surveyed his audience. A thousand pairs of eyes took him in. "In the science fiction movie *Hollow Man*, one of my favourite movies, the scientist Sebastian Caine, played by Kevin Bacon, says, '*You don't make history with rules. You make it by seizing the moment.*' Caine was right."

Scattered laughs blended with applause.

"Without rule-breaking scientists who seize the moment, humanity would be in a stagnant state. We wouldn't have our modern society. We would still live in a Stone-Age-like system." He paused, grateful that Jarrow wasn't in the audience. Out of the corner of his eye, he noted Paulina's mustard-yellow haircut. "What do all medications have in common?"

Silence. Then murmurs. The audience waited.

"I'm referring to something very basic and obvious, ladies and gentlemen, and therefore it isn't easy to guess what I'm driving at. My answer to this puzzling or even strange question is that pharmaceutical drugs affect the individual one way or another while the environment remains unchanged. But what if there were a substance which worked the other way around? A pill that altered objects and circumstances while the pill-taking person stayed unaltered."

• EIGHTY •

THE JAGUAR RAN red lights. Cat found no time to even think of the brake pedal. The traffic densified. The sports car coughed, turned onto Crowfield Way, managed to slide into the correct lane, passing restaurants, casinos, office buildings, banks and supermarkets. Now she spotted the city's tallest building.

"Your obstinate appearance is a growing problem, Cat," said Professor Antonetti.

Cat cried out. The reptile sat in the front passenger seat.

Antonetti wore his black raincoat and hat. His face seemed to belong to something from a theme park horror house. His jaw muscles were working like a cast-iron grinder and his eyes were blazing like candles on Judgement Day.

"What are you doing here? How can you be here?" She almost lost control of the car again. On her way through a right turn she rotated the steering wheel too late and too little. The Jaguar's left side bumped against a lamp post. The car careened. She tugged at the steering wheel clockwise. The vehicle wobbled back into the lane. "I killed you, Professor."

"Yes. You killed me." He coughed up and sputtered bright-green blood. The slime splashed across the dashboard and the windscreen. "You're a murderer, Cat. Therefore, you must be punished." A paw grabbed her knee.

"Don't touch me. Take your ugly paw off me."

"You commenced a passionate relationship with a traitor. How does it make you feel?"

"Don't touch me. Go away."

"You and I have unfinished business."

"Do you know what you're doing, Catriona?" Dad's voice.

The man in the front passenger seat was in his early forties. Clean-shaven. His long hair was gathered in a rubber band.

"You scared me, Dad. How and when did you get here? What do you want now?"

"I asked if you know what you're doing."

"Definitely not." *What is Dad talking about? My sex life? Does Dad know I've slept with my neurologist?* She repressed the presence of her dead father, tried instead to concentrate on her driving. Soon at Rainbow Tower. A few hundred yards to the RT car park. "Could you leave me alone for a while, Dad?"

"You have no driving licence. And this isn't your car."

"I'll explain later."

"Some green liquid has splattered on the dashboard and the windscreen. Green and sticky. Is it green blood?"

"Listen, Dad. Professor Antonetti, conspirator and spy, was here. Now I must concentrate on my *driving*. We can talk later. I have things to do in Rainbow Tower. Okay?"

"Miss Milton? Catriona Milton?" Zimmer's voice.

Cat whimpered. BioFutura's Deputy CEO sat in the front passenger seat. His right eye stared at her. The left was destroyed. A scalpel had been thrust into the man's brain through his left eyeglass lens and eye. The plastic eyeglass frame arms had been positioned not behind his ears but across his ears. Another two knives, driven through the eyeglass frame arms and buried into the ears, secured the glasses to the corpse's head.

"Dr. Zimmer ... What do you want?"

"The Milton sisters have sought me." Blood leaked from the man's mouth, ears and thrashed eye. "An urgent matter." The blood ran down the front of his shirt and trousers and dribbled onto the seat. "It concerns a letter from your father. You still have the letter, haven't you?"

"The letter is lost or stolen."

"You don't mean that, do you?"

"I'm sorry." She had nothing more to say. She had run out of things to say. Zimmer was already gone. Gone like a fading fog. Only the blood on the seat remained.

She believed the dead Zimmer's phantom-like appearance in the car and his subsequent disappearance into thin air marked the end of the freaky stuff. She couldn't have been more wrong.

An envelope flew out of the Jaguar's glove box and landed on the front passenger seat. A light-yellow envelope. It seemed familiar to her. She reached for it. The text on its front: 'To my twin daughters Catriona & Janice Milton'.

Her heart jumped. Dad's letter to Zimmer. Roger had stolen it. Given everything else which had happened today, she couldn't be surprised. She was beyond surprise. But why would Roger keep a stolen letter in the sports car?

She glared at the glove box and frowned. Something stirred inside its open door. Another envelope flew out. Same colour and same format as the first one. It landed on the passenger seat. The text on its front: 'To my twin daughters Catriona & Janice Milton'. Confusion and fear competed for new space in her head. Two envelopes. Two *identical* envelopes. There should, *could*, be only one. What was going on?

A third envelope flew out of the glove box and landed on the passenger seat. Light-yellow. Same format. She whimpered. The sports car swayed, drifting towards the wrong lane. Motorists honked their horns. She found the brake pedal and pulled the steering wheel, avoiding a head-on crash with a van. She thought of a rude swearword often used by Ebba but she stopped herself from saying it. She scrambled for the envelope. The text on its front: 'To my twin daughters Catriona & Janice Milton'.

She ripped open the envelopes with her teeth and fingers, while navigating the Jaguar through harsh city traffic. Her suspicions were confirmed. Here were not three copies of Dad's letter to Zimmer, or one original and two copies, but *three identical originals*.

The crease at the upper right corner was identical in all three and located at exactly the same place in all three. She had noted the crease the other day, at the tavern, and now she spotted something new: a millimetre-sized tear in the left edge, at precisely the same place in all three letters. Cat and Sis had read and studied *one* of these letters at the tavern the day before yesterday. What the heck was going on?

A fourth envelope flew out of the glove box.

A fifth.

Six. Seven. Eight.

Nine. Ten.

It was just the beginning. Envelopes started to spurt from the glove box at an explosive speed.

To my twin daughters Catriona & Janice Milton To my twin daughters Catriona & Janice Milton To my twin daughters Catriona & Janice Milton To my twin daughters Catriona & Janice Milton To my twin daughters Catriona & Janice Milton To my twin daughters Catriona & Janice Milton To my twin daughters Catriona & Janice Milton To my twin daughters Catriona & Janice Milton To my twi ...

Hundreds, no, thousands of envelopes were gushing from the glove box. Thousands of identical originals of Dad's letter to Zimmer. Cascading envelopes were piling into drifts on seats and on the floor. Shooting envelopes were spinning and pattering and clinging everywhere in the car, like frantic, light-yellow bats. Cat screamed, shielding her face with her hands.

• EIGHTY-ONE •

SCATTERED LAUGHTER IN the hall.

Stockmayer smiled. "Nice to see you're in a good mood tonight, ladies and gentlemen." Pause. "Is the idea of a substance which influences the environment—while the substance-taking individual remains constant—a crazy idea? Or, if we rephrase: Is the idea of a chemical, which realises the individual's dreams, fantasies and thoughts, a crazy idea?"

Scattered shouts from the audience: "Yes." ... "Crazy idea." ... "Completely crazy."

"And why is the idea crazy?" His voice reached the one-thousand-strong audience through multiple speakers in the upper and lower stalls and on the balconies.

Dispersed cries from spectators and listeners throughout the hall: "Impossible." ... "Illogical." ... "Irrational."

"Aha," he said. "But who decides what's impossible and possible? Who determines what's illogical and logical? Who stipulates what's irrational and rational? Who determines what's unreasonable and reasonable? Who is authorised to make such profound decisions? Who is to judge?"

The hall turned dead silent.

"Every scientific fact was once condemned by authorities, religions and the elite," Stockmayer said. "The resistance to innovation has often been aggressive. Researchers have risked imprisonment or the death penalty. Every invention was seen as idiotic. Every discovery was a shock to traditionalists. Every creative idea was a breach of law and solid proof of lack of judgement. The aeroplane was considered impossible, for the reason that machines are heavier than air. It was illogical and foolish to imagine flying machines. The atomic bomb was regarded as impossible. The rocket was considered impossible. The petrol-driven car was regarded as impossible. The television was considered impossible. It was decided it was impossible that the Earth was moving around the Sun. History is full of determined impossibilities which sooner or later turned out to be possibilities or downright truths.

"New thinkers have always struggled against headwinds in their fight against established knowledge. Dan Shechtman claimed he had found irregular crystals, or quasi-crystals. The statement was contrary to all logic and to all textbooks. He was ridiculed by his colleagues and was asked to leave his research team. But he persevered. Shechtman was awarded the Nobel Prize in Chemistry for the discovery of quasi-crystals.

"John Gurdon and Shinya Yamanaka showed something which many experts regarded as impossible: that the course of life doesn't have to be a one-way path. They found cell differentiation is reversible. Gurdon and Yamanaka shared a Nobel Prize in Medicine for the discovery that specialised cells can be reprogrammed to become cells capable of developing into all tissues of an organism's body.

"Ahmed Zewail did what many scientists thought impossible. He filmed chemical reactions as they occurred in real time, using ultra-short flashes fired by a laser which flashed at the timescale at which chemical reactions take place, that is, femtoseconds. A femtosecond is a millionth of a billionth of a second. Zewail was awarded the Nobel Prize in Chemistry for his studies of the transition states of chemical reactions using femtosecond spectroscopy.

"Enough examples. It would take all night to discuss curious people who have defied the impossible. Nothing is impossible. There are ways which lead to everything and, if we have sufficient willpower, we'll always have sufficient means."

The Jaguar rolled into the Rainbow Tower car park. All parking spaces were occupied. She managed to squeeze the battered car into the forbidden space between a Ford Ranger pickup and a bicycle stand rack.

She opened the driver's door and shuffled out. It looked like a few hundred envelopes fell out onto the ground before she could push the door shut.

Cat gathered as many envelopes as she could possibly carry, then moved in the direction of the RT main entrance.

She walked into the lobby and proceeded to the reception. "Dr. Stockmayer is giving a talk here tonight. Which room?"

One of the receptionists raised his eyebrows. He was busy eating a club sandwich and cheesy chips with brown sauce. "The event has already begun, and it's packed out."

"I asked: which room?"

"And I said it's packed out. Who are you?"

"Catriona Milton. I suffer from a chronic sleep disorder, and I happen to be Dr. Stockmayer's patient. I have to see him."

"Cat Milton? The supermodel of all supermodels? Not a chance. And not funny in the least. You don't look like her."

She puffed. "I've had a rough day."

The old man continued to eat his calorie bomb. "I can see you've had a rough day, miss. Your hair is untidy. Your eyes are red-rimmed. Your cheeks are moist. Your gaze is wild. And you have an attitude problem. Get lost before I call the police."

She noted four lifts opposite the reception. She walked towards the lifts and passed a tripod-mounted sign which indicated the venue of Roger's talk: Hall 1A, the thirtieth floor.

The receptionist, the grey-haired old man, shouted, "You're abusing the system, miss. You're forcing your way in despite not being welcome. You're abusing the system."

Now all the reception staff were alert.

She stopped in her tracks in the middle of the lobby. "I am Catriona Milton."

"No, you're not," called a female receptionist. "Cat Milton is one of the most famous models in the world. What would she be doing at Rainbow Tower tonight, huh? If she attended an event here, we would know, several months in advance."

"Things will happen tonight," she said. "I'll be on TV. Rainbow Tower will appear on TV. You'll see I'm right. I don't want to be on TV tonight but I won't have a choice."

A third receptionist called, "What are you talking about?"

"Never mind. I don't have time to chat with you."

A fourth receptionist shouted after her, "Stop right there. You're not allowed to use the lifts. You're barred from Rainbow Tower. We said you're abusing the system."

"Sue me, then, and see if I care." She had reached the nearest lift. "I'm going up to the thirtieth floor now. I must see my neurologist." She pressed the Up button.

Two security guards appeared from an adjacent corridor. They started to run towards her. "Stop right there, miss."

"In a renowned magazine," Stockmayer said, "I recently noted a few articles about reality. The articles came with headlines such as 'What is reality?' or 'Is matter real?' or 'Does consciousness create reality?'. Questions like those are frequently asked by philosophers and reductionists who want to highlight some kind of mysticism which isn't there. They aren't the right questions to ask. Matter is, of course, real, like the molecules of matter, like the atoms of molecules, like the particles of atoms, like the wave functions of particles. What we observe is a superposition of various reality levels. I would like to encourage questions such as 'Is anything unreal?' This question, as we've already observed, is the title of my talk tonight. I'm convinced there's no such thing as unreality."

A murmur rolled throughout the audience.

"I suggest the following reality concept," Stockmayer said. "To think about microscopic or macroscopic objects at fixed times at different positions in the room is not the right way of thinking, while a mental mapping of total particle pathways through the complete space–time universe is the right way of thinking. The bottom line is a superposition of many realities. Different realities may have different probabilities. However, no reality is less, or more, real than any other. It has nothing to do with actual measurements or consciousness. I'm talking about nature's pattern, an underlying structure whose existence is independent of human presence or human observations.

"I happen to have a substance which affects the nervous system in the strangest way. Instead of rejecting and eliminating the side effect, I wanted to manage it and refine it. I realised its potential. Brain activity requires energy. Energy can't be destroyed or created. Instead, energy is transformed from one form to another. In the present case, it's about some unknown mental energy which shows up among other, known energy forms. Let's give this unknown mental energy a name. For the time being, we could call it epsilon energy. Is that okay? Or would you prefer a different name?"

Dispersed laughter and chuckles.

"I take it nobody objects to the temporary name, epsilon energy." He paused, sipping water. "The cognitive revolution united the mental world and the physical world through the theory that we can explain minds and computers by applying specific common principles. The mind is connected to the physical universe by the sense organs, which transduce physical energy into brain-located structures of data. The mind, like the electronic computer or the quantum computer, is a processor. For this reason, the energy we call epsilon energy has both mental and physical properties. Furthermore, we can consider the brain as a biological quantum computer. Electrons and molecules shoot around the complex circuits of the nervous system. Those rapid blasts are charged with electrical energy, radiation energy, chemical energy and a certain amount of epsilon energy.

"A brain signal consists of a set of energy fluctuations. Epsilon energy may be an expression of a distorted quantum biology in the individual. Bizarreness arises in the balance, or rather in the imbalance, between different reality amplitudes. External reality is affected. The individual's thoughts, dreams, fantasies, turn concrete. I know it works. I have experimental evidence."

A new wave of murmurs and whispers propagated among the listeners. Stockmayer knew what he was doing. It was high time he informed the public about the dazzling side effects of the Roxonodonol products—both the prototype Rox-1 and tomorrow's Rox-2. A secret without commercial potential was a worthless secret. A captivating secret had to be converted into explosive news to be profitable. In order to win prestige, you had to publish reproducible results. He couldn't wait any longer.

Jarrow would be perplexed when he learnt Stockmayer had leaked the Rox project to the media and the public. Before the Yolexus boss reacted, KNEPCOM would convert the Rox project into a theft-proof programme with headquarters in an unknown location. Also, KNEPCOM would own the patent.

From the speakers: "Roger Stockmayer or Ludwig Trexler? What name do you prefer?"

His bloodstream froze. He raised his eyes. His gaze leapt across the audience, back and forth, and stopped. He couldn't believe it. Catriona. Catriona stood on the stairs of the upper stall. She had a microphone in her hand.

• EIGHTY-TWO •

"**LET GO OF** me, you damn thug. Let go of me." Ebba flopped around like a fish on the bathroom floor.

Jarrow yanked at her. "A flight from the balcony awaits you. It's safe to say your unruliness is worse than my wife's."

She kicked, yelled and snarled, and wondered if the suite was soundproof. Neither hotel guests nor staff had reacted to the noise. So far. People might not have heard any sounds they interpreted as mysterious or inappropriate. Or people had heard the noise but had chosen to ignore it. It was easier to ignore sounds than to examine sounds. With hundreds or thousands of people under the same roof, hotels were filled with strange sounds. Nothing strange about strange sounds in hotels.

Jarrow dragged her out of the bathroom and pulled her to her feet. His face was as white and moist as mozzarella cheese. He placed a disgusting kiss on her lips. She grimaced and spat in his face. He slapped her. She rammed her knee into his groin. He roared, groaned and lost his grip on her arm. She dashed to the main door of the suite and pressed down on the door handle.

Locked. She fumbled with the lock. Turned it. Tried the door again. Still locked. She felt a tug at the back of her hair.

She screamed and stumbled backwards. He grabbed her shoulders and swung her around. She squealed. He pressed the palm of his hand against her mouth. She bit him. Jarrow howled. Blood trickled between his thumb and index finger. His other hand grabbed one of her breasts. She hit him hard on the nose. He panted, lost his grip on her breast, pulled her towards him, seemed to consider the idea of kissing her again but then thought better of it. Instead, he hurled her along the hall, back into the suite, towards the lounge.

Ebba landed headlong, hit her head on the edge of the coffee table and shrieked. Adrenaline flowed through her. Fear and anger in a devilish mix. From the corner of her eye, and from a frog's perspective, she saw Jarrow approaching.

"Nobody will think your death is mysterious," he said. "If I'm right, you have both cocaine and alcohol in your beautiful body right now. Your death after toppling from the balcony will be interpreted as an expected end to your wild life on the edge. Oh, certainly no traces will lead to Yolexus Enterprise."

With enormous effort, she got to her feet. She sobbed and wiped her lips on the sleeve of her blouse, trying to wipe away the taste of Jarrow's obnoxious kiss. "Traces from gunshots don't fit any theory about accidental death, arseclown."

"It depends on what you mean by accidental death, you foulmouthed bitch. Both CIA and Interpol want men with whom you've been involved or with whom you're still involved. How would anyone know with certainty what happened here? The authorities will speculate as follows: You're a party princess and maybe you get a kick out of danger; Shootings in a hotel room will be associated with your challenging lifestyle, the consequence of something untidy and unfashionable from your controversial past."

"I hate you, fuckhead."

"I appreciate your sincerity, Miss Sjödal. You're very sexy when you hate. Your hatefulness is as erotic as my wife's self-control. But nothing lasts forever." He pointed the pistol at her.

The gun in Jarrow's hand boomed as the chair grew in his field of vision at tremendous speed. He heard the girl scream. The gun went off again and again and again.

She swung the chair at him and an ear-splitting noise filled the lounge. The first bullet twisted the chair out of her hands and sent it flying in the opposite direction, above her head. The next three shots smashed into a wall, thrashed a mirror and destroyed the glass pane of the balcony door.

• EIGHTY-THREE •

HE STARED UP at the stairs of the upper stall. Stared at her. How on earth had she managed to get out of the laboratory-garage? He tried to collect himself. Must save the evening. Must appear untroubled. Must trivialise the situation. Must reduce the new circumstance to an insignificant incident.

"Ladies and gentlemen," he said into the microphone, "it seems as though one of my patients has an urgent matter."

A thousand people turned their heads towards the girl on the stairs. A cheer rose from the audience.

"That's right," he said. "No one less than Catriona Milton, the model, born and raised here in Blackfield."

Catriona continued down the stairs via the lower-stall aisle, smiling (a strained smile) and waving to the audience. "Good evening, everybody. Fun to see so many nice and happy people. Fun to be back home in the City of Crows."

The crowd applauded, cheered, shouted.

She carried a stack of letters, he noted.

With a sweeping arm movement, she hurled the stack. A multitude of light-yellow envelopes sailed through the air like swallows. Most of them landed on the stage floor, scattering everywhere. "Dad's letter to Zimmer. There are many more of these, down in the car park. Have I mentioned I borrowed your Jaguar? I happened to crash it. Your lab-garage is also damaged, Ludwig. But I suppose you're insured."

He hurried to continue, "The fact that Miss Milton is my patient is not news. Miss Milton's neurological condition is not news. The fact that she's registered at the Oberon Clinic is not news. The private lives of celebrities are published in detail to the delight of the public. As we've all learnt by now, Miss Milton is on a temporary visit to her amazing hometown. Nonetheless, that she appears right here, at Rainbow Tower, and just now, is surprising even to me. I tend not to socialise with my patients at Rainbow Tower, if anyone wondered."

Was anyone listening? Listening to him? He threw a glance at the massive screen. He didn't see himself on the screen. Catriona was on it. The camera zoomed in on the famous catwalk lady. He, one of the most prominent neuroscientists in the world, was no longer in focus. Catriona had stolen the show.

"You didn't answer my question," she said. Her voice was devoid of love. "What name do you prefer? Ludwig Trexler or Roger Stockmayer? Or some other fake name you might be using every once in a while." She entered the stage.

"I'm in the middle of a talk, Miss Milton."

She turned to the audience. "Blackfield is the greatest of cities. Fun to be back home." She waved, smiling. "Hello, all you amazing Blackfielders. Extraordinary things are happening tonight."

The cheers, waving, happy whistles and shouts from the audience intensified. Catriona owned the stage. The presence of the catwalk queen made the venue explode into uncontrollable excitement.

Stockmayer coughed. "I have to ask you to leave the stage, Miss Milton."

She didn't listen to him. The audience didn't listen to him either. He was ignored, reduced to air.

The catwalk star raised a hand to the exhilarated crowd. The audience hushed, silenced. "I have something to say, dear Blackfielders," she said into the microphone. "I'll be brief. I don't need to be wordy because the whole story will be dealt with in the media. Also, the story will be investigated by professional investigators. I've been playing detective for a while but now I'm tired of it. Next week I have to be back at my real job." She had to fight to keep her tears at bay.

"Let me now talk about a truth. How I arrived at this truth, and how it is connected to Stockmayer's unimaginable truth about some substances called Rox and Nargontanac, will be all over the media before we know it. Right now, we only have time for the punchline. My neurologist is a conspirator and murderer. He and his collaborators were behind the murder of my dad and several other industry people. Their criminal organisation has stolen or destroyed corporate secrets."

Stockmayer broke in, "Nonsense, ladies and gentlemen. My patient's senses are not working to their full capacity. As her healthcare provider, I can assure you what she's saying is beyond the realm of truth. Let's return to the discussion about the phenomenal pharmaceutical which realises the individual's dreams, wishes, nightmares and or fantasies. We see at once that such a substance would cause boundless chaos unless its effects were controlled in some acceptable form. The prototype, which I call Rox-1, works beyond control, but the upcoming—"

"Stockmayer is a killer," she interrupted. "The man is associated with a shadowy corporation by the name of Yolexus Enterprise, which made a dangerous drug. He was involved in a criminal cover-up in New Delhi. And I think I'm a victim of this dangerous drug myself. Stockmayer and Yolexus—"

"I order you to leave the stage," Stockmayer hissed.

Catriona, into the microphone: "Any journalists or police officers in the audience?"

A few scattered hands in the air. A man shouted: "I'm a journalist, Cat. And I heard everything you said." A woman called out: "I'm also a journalist, Cat. I heard everything you said." Throughout the sea of people, dispersed screams: "We love you, Cat!" Another man in the crowd uttered in a distinct voice: "Police officers here. We three are from CID, even though we're not on duty tonight." A woman in the upper stall shouted in a shrill voice: "The clean-living businesswoman Catriona Milton is a role model! You couldn't imagine a better ambassador for the city of Blackfield!"

Resounding applause and happy whistles.

What would the hostess, his long-time academic colleague, think of tonight's outcome? He didn't dare look at Paulina. For his inner eye, he saw Paulina's altering facial expression, a transition he didn't like in the least.

His gaze jumped back and forth across the sea of people. Anxiety spread throughout the audience. People stirred in their seats, massaged their foreheads or wrung their hands. For the first time this evening, he was distressed. The police officers and the journalists worried him. Also, Rainbow Tower had its own security personnel. If the RT guards abided by the law, they were unarmed, but at any time anybody in the hall or anywhere in the building could alert external police via a phone call.

He had difficulty absorbing the consequences of what was about to happen. How *could* this happen? He was a Nobel Prize candidate, for Christ's sake. And he *would* get the prize. He would get the Chemistry prize or the Medicine prize. The Nobel Award Ceremonies and Banquet in Stockholm were a major international event which received worldwide media coverage. He would be there, for he was born a winner and a genius.

The hall entrance doors opened. Three men and two women marched in. The huge screen captured the advancing group. Two of the men and one of the women were blue-uniformed RT guards. The remaining man and woman were police officers dressed in summer-season uniforms. The policeman and the policewoman were armed. How many police officers were in the building right now? wondered Stockmayer.

The policeman spoke into a megaphone: "This is the police." As if nobody had understood they were the police. "A young woman has entered the building in a manner not conforming to the law. She's probably here in Hall 1A. A girl who claims she's Catriona Milton. That her? On the stage?" The policeman paused. "But, for hell's sake, it *is* Catriona Milton."

No one in the audience seemed to care about the newcomers to the hall. People reached for their mobiles, for it would be an evening to remember. On the front row of the lower stall, a man with bushy hair pressed a mobile-phone button in the same moment he gave Stockmayer an angry look.

"The use of mobile phones is prohibited in the RT halls," Stockmayer said. "Besides, it's poor manners." He hurled the microphone at the angry man, who dodged it by ducking.

Another voice over a microphone: "Good evening, Dr. Stockmayer."

The new voice chilled Stockmayer to the bone. He couldn't believe it was happening. His eyes darted to the far back of the hall. Leo Baginski pulled a firearm from his jacket pocket.

• EIGHTY-FOUR •

THE GUN IN Jarrow's hand failed to discharge. It must be out of ammunition, she thought. He swore and tossed the weapon onto the floor. Another chair came flying at him. She had let go of this one, so the chair was airborne. He swore again and parried the projectile with his arm. He snorted like a horse. "You damn girl. That hurt."

"You're a shithead, Jarrow," Ebba croaked.

"You're ill-bred," he continued.

She rolled her eyes. "Like I've never heard *that* before."

"Your gross language as well as your obscene finger gestures indicate a problematic childhood and a wasted youth."

"You're a fucking coward," she said. "A grown man who jumps a girl, huh?" She clutched a third lounge chair and was ready to throw it. This was the last chair within easy reach. Jarrow had knocked away the first two.

He spotted something. She understood what it was. He sidled to the sofa while keeping an eye on her. "Before I drop you from the balcony, we need to find out whether it's convenient that your handbag follows you down."

"Go fuck yourself, arsehole."

"You completely lack my Lisa-Marie's humility." He picked up her handbag and shook the contents out onto the coffee table.

A mishmash of makeup bottles and makeup jars tumbled and clattered against the tabletop. A variety of other items followed. A bright-pink purse with maybe a hundred UK and US banknotes of different values. A Porsche car key. A packet of Glamour Superslims cigarettes. The little jar with the illegal party powder. Two packets of Wrigley's peppermint chewing gum. A box of sweets from Harrods. A bag of salted peanuts. A hairbrush. Posh sunglasses in a posh case. A packet of birth-control pills. Even a packet of condoms (better safe than sorry, Ebba thought).

Jarrow grinned. "What's this ridiculous figure?" He held up the little glass bear in multicoloured mosaic.

Her heart skipped a beat.

"I want you to accept the bear, Ebba. I want you to do that."
"Why? You love that bear. You've always loved it."

"Please put down the glass bear, Mr. Jarrow. It's invaluable to me. A gift from my best childhood friend."

The man's grin deepened. "When I'm done with you, you won't care about this stupid toy. Dead girls don't care about anything." With violent force, he threw the glass bear at the wall. The bear shattered. Splinters of glass rattled against the floor.

She shouted. "No! No, let go of it! You can't!" Too late.

"I've made a decision. Your handbag with its contents, minus one glass bear, will follow you over the balcony."

Something burst inside her. Some kind of barrier. A rage she had never experienced infused her superheated brain.

He raked the items back into the handbag. A lipstick rolled off the edge of the table. He bent down to pick it up. As he moved his gaze away from her, only for a moment, Ebba flung the third and last chair in a frenzy.

The furniture struck his skull. The man dropped to the floor, yelling. She rushed forward and aimed a kick at his groin. He caught her high-heeled shoe, preventing her kick from finding its target. She screamed like a predator. He moaned.

• EIGHTY-FIVE •

GUNFIRE RIPPED THROUGH the night. The shot from Baginski's weapon hit the mobile-telephoning man on the back of his head. Blood and brains and skull fragments sprayed across the front of the stage. The distance from the far back of the hall to the front row of the lower stall was impressive to say the least. Baginski appeared to have fired without bothering to aim.

"Christ, can that man shoot," Stockmayer muttered.

Catriona yelled. People in the crowd roared. Children cried. Confusion arose about who had fired the thundering gunshot. Where had the shot come from? A balcony or one of the stalls? The police officers pulled their weapons and wheeled around, scanning the hall for the shooter.

Stockmayer squinted at the image of himself on the massive screen. Once again, he was in focus, but for the wrong reason. The screen annoyed him now. The already repellent atmosphere of the venue transformed into a blaring composite of swelling emotions. The idol, the cover girl, the celebrity Cat Milton's surprising presence, in combination with the surprising gun blast and the sudden death of a member of the audience, became too much for her youngest fans. Hysterical teenage girls shrieked and waved and wept. Gaping teenage boys were glued to their seats, their eyes huge and shiny like spheres of glass.

Neither the younger nor the older audience showed any further interest in new scientific achievements. Catriona, who couldn't tell the difference between an atom and a molecule, was all of a sudden more popular than he was, the Nobel Prize candidate. The public lacked any sense of proportion.

The many light-yellow, identical envelopes lay higgledy-piggledy on the stage floor. More proof that Roxonodonol worked. On the other hand, proof which contributed to the ruining of tonight's event. The letter had materialised, over and over, from Catriona's thoughts about the letter. Billions of neurons in the girl's brain lobes had fired epsilon energy. Uncontrolled epsilon energy, promoted by dancing subatomic particles. A risk he had counted on, yet a risk he'd hoped would first be diluted and then drowned out by the plethora of normal electrochemistry in the girl's head.

The police officers shouted something. He didn't listen. He didn't care what they were trying to communicate.

"And now I'm coming for *you*, Dr. Stockmayer," Baginski said into a microphone. "I have a score to settle."

At their earlier confrontation in Paradise Park, Stockmayer had had a special combination of luck and opportunity. 'Luck' was not something he had in abundance. He guessed Baginski could drop him with another long-distance gunshot if the hitman wanted to.

Stockmayer swung his gaze towards the lower-stall aisle—too slow, too late. Like a spirit who had surfed the pools of shadows, Baginski was already here. The left side of his face was swollen. A dark-brown fedora hat concealed to some degree the bandage which was wrapped around his scalp. The advancing contract killer squeezed off two shots as he slipped on one of the many envelopes, which now lay scattered everywhere, as though they'd moved into new and optimally dispersed positions. The first bullet whizzed past Stockmayer so close it singed his cheek. The round slammed into a wooden backdrop on the opposite side of the stage. With the tip of his forefinger, Stockmayer touched the site of the burning sensation. The fingertip came away with a narrow streak of blood. The second zinging bullet went very wide, taking out the big wall-mounted monitor and its electronics in a blaze of sparks and fizzing electrical discharge. Already falling following his slip on the envelope, Baginski was driven to the floor by the police officers' fire.

Stockmayer had no plans to hang around on the stage. He was already moving. Catriona passed right in front of him. She dashed across the stage. He took the opportunity and grabbed her shoulder. The girl's shoes skidded on the polished parquet. She lost her balance and started to go down. He caught her, embraced her, helped her to her feet. He handled her with care, as if she were a porcelain doll. One of the most sought-after models on the planet would be his ticket out of Rainbow Tower.

He would never hurt his love. The point was the police would think he was capable of hurting Cat Milton. The hostage situation was just for show. He calculated no one would call his bluff. No one would dare.

He would leave Rainbow Tower in a little while. He and his sweetheart would leave the building together. He would phone a KNEPCOM number. An unmarked KNEPCOM car would pick them up in Crowfield Way and drive them to an unknown place. KNEPCOM operated private flights. Later tonight, a KNEPCOM aeroplane would take him and his love out of Britain. The future was waiting for the two of them together.

She floundered in his arms and broke free. He blocked her way in the direction of the lower stall. The police officers shouted again, trying to be louder than the terrified crowd. Once again, he didn't listen to the police officers. He had other priorities, other things to think about. The police didn't dare shoot at him. Catriona was in the line of fire. But why would they shoot at him at all? he wondered. Police weren't supposed to gun down unarmed suspects.

Catriona left the stage in the opposite direction. She disappeared behind a set of backdrops. He had anticipated her move before anyone else. He picked up his pursuit of the girl. From behind, he heard the rapid footsteps of the police officers.

He found a door. Not an emergency exit but an unmarked door. The policeman and the policewoman rounded the stage backdrops and spotted him. He moved through the door and shut it behind him. Next to the wall beside the doorway was a toolbox and a stack of corrugated steel. He grasped one of the sheets of steel and propped it under the door handle. It wouldn't stop the police officers but it would slow them down.

Tripping footsteps echoed off the walls of the stairwell. *Catriona.* The staircase led only from the thirtieth floor to the roof. For technical maintenance staff, he guessed. There were several radio and television stations at Rainbow Tower and, on the roof, there were several aerials.

He hurried up short flights of stairs and noted movement from above. Catriona opened a door—in all likelihood the exit to the roof—stepped through it and pushed it shut. He followed her onto the roof. He shuddered. A cold, hard rain was slashing through the night from an overcast sky. The girl was twenty feet ahead of him. The distance growing. He increased his pace without running. He didn't want to frighten her. "Catriona."

She stopped, faced him, said nothing.

He glanced around. No maintenance staff in sight. They were alone, at least on this section of the roof. Alone for the moment. He approached her. "Catriona. We have to talk."

Her body language belonged to the coldest of ice princesses. Her lovely hair, matted by the downpour and stirred by the wind, was flowing over her shoulders.

"How did you know, Catriona?"

She looked at him. "Henrietta's mascara. Its colour puzzled me. One thing led to another."

"You're both smart and curious. That's not news to me. If I had closed the lid on Henrietta's box, we wouldn't have found ourselves in this stressful situation. Everything would have been just fine. Imagine if we could turn back time a few hours."

She didn't comment. She was too tired.

"We have to talk, Catriona."

She shook her head. "I've done enough talking, Roger. I've already said everything I wanted to say. Journalists and the law will take care of everything which follows from here."

"The nature of reality is complex," he said with a startling shift of subject. "By that I mean the nature of reality is simple. The world looks like it does, and behaves like it does, because the fundamental constituents of matter arrange and rearrange themselves in detailed patterns. These scenarios apply to both lifeless matter and living organisms. Biologists try to explain as much as possible about life in the language of chemistry. Theoretical chemistry is physics. And the theory behind chemistry is quantum electrodynamics."

She blinked at his discourse. "Leave me alone, Roger. It's over. It's all over."

"It isn't over, sweetheart. It's just the beginning. How we perceive, interpret and react to reality has consequences both for our intrapersonal and interpersonal circumstances. Differences between reality perceptions are the basis of hostile relationships, including political and religious conflicts. Reality is subjective as well as objective. Do you understand? An objective reality, such as a car, a tree, or the entire physical universe, isn't necessarily dependent on subjectivity for its existence. While subjective reality, such as the experience of a love affair, a nightmare or an impulse, isn't necessarily dependent on objectivity to be real. The subjective world is as real as the objective world." He closed the gap between them.

She recoiled. "I don't want to be up here on the roof. I'm afraid of heights. I'm afraid of you too. I want you to leave me alone. Could you please move out of my way? I want to return inside."

"I love you, Catriona."

"You must have lost your mind, Roger. Otherwise you would know I can't love you back. Your organisation was behind the murder of my dad. Yolexus Enterprise considered BioFutura an inconvenient competitor in the market of drugs for the treatment of neurological diseases. The breakthrough at my dad's company would have destroyed the potential future of Roxonodonol. Now there are no winners. We've all lost."

"I have the resources to charter a private plane out of Great Britain on the spur of the moment. You and I could fly out of the country together tonight. An international network called

KNEPCOM could arrange our private flight, with Austria its destination. Stealth-mode KNEPCOM aircrafts delay radar, infrared and acoustic detection. No one will be able to track us down in time. We'll disappear. We'll get married. We'll make love every night. We'll have children. We'll live in a fairy-tale castle in the countryside. We'll be happy for the rest of our lives. I'll resume my research in a brand-new direction. You'll start a new career. You no longer need to be a model. I already have new exciting plans for you. You'll be the new Mrs. Stockmayer. And the new Mrs. Trexler. And the new Mrs. Ripstein. And the new Mrs. Mahlau. All four wives in one, only on different occasions. I'll tell you more about that later."

She was dumbfounded. She just shook her head.

"To fall in love with you wasn't planned, Catriona. It just happened. Love is an uncontrollable energy. You can't deny it, or fight it, or suppress it, or destroy it. The power of love is as sharp and intractable as epsilon energy."

She took a few swift steps backwards and stopped cold. She had bumped into the roof's railing. She glanced over her shoulder. The view was hair-raising. Dizziness hit her. The evening traffic rumbled along Crowfield Way at the bottom of the abyss, three hundred and fifty feet below.

"I still admire you," he continued. "I can't help but desire you. Though you've sabotaged my talk and the rest of the evening, I'm prepared to forgive you. Because I need you. I can't live without you. I'm dreaming of a happy life with the most beautiful woman in the world."

"Your dream is over, Roger. No chemical substance can repair your fantasies, or my thoughts, or someone else's wishes. Your Rox project is no answer to eternal happiness."

He embraced her. "You're not listening."

She stiffened in his embrace but said nothing.

He looked into her eyes. "You won't just be my gorgeous wife. You'll also be my main research subject. Those flashing synapses in your brain will pave the way for innovative and motivated research on many other psychical effects, such as telepathy, EPS, clairvoyance or telekinesis."

What could she say? What could she do? He held her. She couldn't move. The railing pushed against her back. Where were the police? She listened for sirens or even the rocking noise of a police helicopter. She heard nothing but the distant city traffic.

She thought of Sandra Kallikrinos. "What happened to the BFS Deputy Director of Research? Did she drown in a bathtub? Or was she murdered? Did she investigate the circumstances surrounding the New Delhi affair?"

Something happened.

Cat whimpered. Roger groaned. They saw her on the roof. Sandra Kallikrinos moved towards them.

Lathering shampoo sat in her dark-brown hair, as though she had just stepped out of a bathtub. Her body was swollen, decaying, the skin discoloured. Her pubic hair looked like withering moss. The naked Sandra kept approaching.

"Stop, Catriona," Roger said. "Stop thinking about Sandra Kallikrinos. She's here because of your thoughts. Epsilon energy is quantum entangling across time and space. You're triggering the Rox effect. Stop it, Catriona. Stop it."

"Answer the young lady's questions, Stockmayer," Sandra said. Then, "Does the girl know who Jarrow is?"

Roger let go of Cat to focus all his attention on the former BioFutura employee. "Disappear, Kallikrinos. You're unwanted company."

Sandra laughed. An eerie cackle from the land of the dead. "You think you have the power to make me leave?"

"Well, to start with you're already dead."

"Dead but real," Sandra said. "Death is as real as life. It's about a superposition of realities. You already know that, don't you? After all, you're the expert."

A bead of sweat appeared on Roger's brow. His hands trembled. Cat took the opportunity to try to squeeze past him. Sandra seized Roger's arm as he discovered Cat was trying to escape. He gave Cat a gentle push towards the railing. Not at all a violent push. Still, the railing gave way.

She fell. As a paralysing horror engulfed her, Cat heard her own scream. She fell from the roof of the city's tallest building.

• EIGHTY-SIX •

EBBA WAILED AND tried to pry her foot from Jarrow's grip. A glowing fury pounded behind her forehead. She tried again, again, and got away from his clutch, tripped and fell. Her shoe remained in the panting man's fist. He fumbled for her leg. His nails scratched her nylon stockings. She crawled on the floor like a desperate turtle. A gurgling sound flew from her mouth. She propelled her arms and kicked out with her legs. His filthy nails slithered along her stockings. She imagined she was distancing herself from the coffee table, as though it mattered, but the Yolexus boss still clung to her like a parasite.

Despite the blurring veil of uncontrolled emotions, she believed her mind was clear enough to recollect the direction in which he had thrown the empty gun. Jarrow planted a hand on her rump. She glimpsed the pistol, stretched out an arm to grasp it, a fraction of an inch short of reaching it, whimpered, puffed, swore, reached for it again, a little bit further, her arm aching. The effort seemed eternal. Then, she did reach the gun, with the tip of her little finger.

He pinched her arse. His fingers searched the smooth valley between her buttocks. She managed to rake the pistol towards her. She snatched it by its barrel and swung it backwards. The handle of the pistol hit the dirty old man in the face. She heard a cracking sound. He squealed like a pig. Nasal blood spattered onto the floor. His eager fingers fell away from her bum.

"*You fucked with the wrong girl, arsehole.*" Her own voice frightened her. She didn't recognise her own voice. The voice which seeped out between her teeth belonged to some callous avenger she didn't know. "*You fucked with the wrong girl, arsehole. I told you not to touch the glass bear. You didn't listen. Why didn't you listen?*"

Her foot with the remaining high-heeled shoe kicked out. The stiletto heel rammed Jarrow's throat. The old man howled. She pulled her foot back. Kicked him again. Pulled back. Kicked out. Back and forth. The stiletto heel thrashed the old man's neck. Blood flew like deep-red-coloured water from a fountain.

• EIGHTY-SEVEN •

CAT WOULD BE crushed against the concrete ground far below. Something within her broke the paralysis at almost the same instant that her fall had started. Her paddling hands found the outermost edge of the rain-wet roof. The shock, the fear, the pain, the panic and the gravity-inflicted strain deadened her attempt to shout for help. Her lungs lacked the air needed for a resounding cry. Besides, who would help her? Roger?

She was alone. Alone with a killer, Roger, and alone with a living murder victim, Sandra.

She was tiring, faster by the second. Her hands hurt. All her remaining power and concentration was spent on clinging to the edge of the roof. She dangled like a marionette, as unstable as a voodoo doll on a string in Janice's room. Her arms trembled. She glanced over her shoulder, looked downwards. Her field of vision encased a terrifying image: city traffic at the bottom of a vast vertical space. She regained her voice. "Roger! Sandra! Help me! Help me! Help!"

She turned her head forward again and peered upwards. "Hello? Anybody there? Where are you? Hello?" She spotted them. "Help me. I'm falling. I can't hold on anymore. I'm falling." She could only glimpse them from this horrible perspective.

Roger and Sandra were fighting. The dead woman punched Roger in the face while Roger tried to strangle her.

Didn't they hear her calls for help?

Or were they ignoring her?

Untroubled by her nudity, the dead Sandra giggled. "You're going to tell me, Stockmayer. You're going to explain it all. Here and now. Talk about New Delhi. Both Miss Milton and I want to know. Yolexus Enterprise and NanoScoop bear the blame for my brother's suicide. Yolexus and Nano bear the blame for Miss Milton's damaged subconscious."

From beyond Cat's field of vision, a new voice shouted, "It's all over, Stockmayer. And you know it. Step away from the woman. A man of your intellect realises when it's over."

Police officers, Cat thought. The police officers were on the roof. She yelled for help again.

Sandra pushed Roger. Pushed him hard.

Roger fell from the roof, screaming. He paddled his arms. He fell straight at the dangling Cat. His shoulder brushed her hair. His hand found the hem of her skirt. She screamed. The skirt ripped and its elastic waist stretched before it snapped. She shrieked again. One of her hands skidded on the rain battered edge, lost its grip altogether, then recovered it. Her fingers ached. A dull pain throbbed behind her tear-filled eyes. She craned her neck, forcing herself to look down. She saw Roger's vanishing body being sucked deeper and deeper into the downward void towards the relentless end.

She sobbed, peering upwards, towards the roof. "Help me."

A head appeared. A malformed face. "Cat?"

"Janice? What on earth are you doing here? How did you get here? Help me up. I can't hold on any longer. I'm falling."

"Cat? What's going on here? Why didn't you answer your mobile? I read in a paper your neurologist was giving a talk here tonight and I thought you might be in the building. There are police and journalists everywhere, both inside and outside the building, and a tremendous uproar. And who was that nude woman, uh? She looked dead and rotten. She was here just now, and now she's gone—vanished into thin air. That's weird."

"Janice! Don't just stand there and prattle like an idiot! Help me up! I'm falling! I'm falling!"

Cat started to tumble. Her exhausted hands dropped away from the edge of the roof. At the same instant, she noticed her sister's outreaching arms in the rain-soaked twilight.

Three months later

November

London

CAT DROVE HER lemon-yellow Volvo south through the vast city. She'd started the trip from Notting Hill, crossed Holland Park Avenue and passed through Kensington, Earls Court and Parsons Green on her way to south Fulham. The morning was both sunny and rain-free, weather you had to be thankful for in London in November.

Her choice to start driving again after six years of avoiding it had nothing to do with the events in Blackfield. She told herself it was true, but suspected she was a bad liar. Her experience inside Roger Stockmayer's lab-garage had triggered something. A newly discovered longing for freedom. Driving a car was associated with a particular feeling of freedom.

She had re-registered and re-reported her disease at the DVLA. After an intensive ten-week course, she had met all the requirements and passed all the tests. She had received her temporary driving licence, which lasted for twelve months. Perhaps she wasn't the best of drivers. Hopefully not the worst either. She didn't need a top-of-the-range car. She enjoyed the everyday Volvo. It worked as expected. She regarded a car as a means of transport, nothing else.

The road sign appeared ahead:

SUNFLOWER – Rehabilitation Centre.

The main building was reminiscent of a cathedral, with tall windows and an exquisite dome on top. The surroundings consisted of lawns, trimmed hedges and autumn-coloured deciduous trees. Cat steered her Volvo into the visitors' car park.

She was welcomed by a silver-haired woman in a wool coat.

"How's my friend?" Cat said.

"Ebba is a strong girl." The old lady gave Cat a warming smile. "She's well."

"Is it true she'll be discharged tomorrow?"

"That's right, Miss Milton. Ebba isn't just drug-free, she has also lost her taste for cocaine. Here at Sunflower, we take care of our fellow human beings in the best possible way. We have very few relapses. Our statistics speak for themselves."

"I'm a bit early. Is she ready to see me?"

The old lady's smile could thaw a frozen heart. "More than ready. Ebba has been ready to see you ever since she woke up this morning. She can't wait to see you. I'll show you to her room."

The room was bright and cosy. Floral wallpaper. A pinewood table with an orange cloth. A motley bouquet in a clay vase. Two orange armchairs. A bed with a violet cover. Landscape wall art. Tall windows overlooking an autumn-coloured park.

They hadn't seen each other for several weeks. They had only talked on the phone twice since the end of the summer. Anita Scriver had also had a word with Ebba. Anita and the rest of the Supreme staff had given Ebba their full support. All the models were also supportive. People had understood she'd needed a break. She was welcome to return.

Her Hollywood contract was also saved. Ebba's tangled private life made her an interest to showbiz pros. After all, scandals and controversy sell the most in our times.

Ebba had just had a shower. The scent of shampoo—crisp grapefruit and green almond—lingered in the room. She lay on the bed wearing a blue bathrobe, flipping through a glossy magazine. She looked terrific.

"You look great," Cat said.

Ebba put down the magazine.

"Do you mean it?"

"Yes."

"Are you still mad at me, Cat? Do you hate me?"

"I've never hated you, Ebba. I've been furious at you. I was furious at you and Roy for what you did to me. But when I learnt he had been caught in a doping control, I wanted nothing to do with him. I have no interest in guys who use drugs."

"I know, Cat." Pause. "I've loathed myself."

"Don't talk like that, Ebba. Let's focus on the present."

Ebba swung her legs off the bed. "Your dad is dead, Cat. Murdered. I was, in some odd way, involved in related sinister plans at Yolexus Enterprise. How is it that you don't hate me?"

"I don't blame you for my dad's fate. How could I? You didn't know Jarrow planned to murder my dad."

"But I assisted Yolexus Enterprise. I betrayed you."

"I've been angry with you about that too. Again, it was a short-lived anger. You were a victim of blackmail. If you hadn't been available to the criminals, Yolexus Enterprise would have used some other method to harm BioFutura. I have the ability to forgive you. I'm glad I have that ability because it hurts to hate. It hurts in the body and the soul to hate."

Ebba moved away from the bedside. "Hug me, Cat."

The girls hugged. They stood in the middle of the room, clinging closely together.

Ebba sobbed. "Are we still best friends?"

"We're more than best friends. We're like sisters."

"Do you still want to share a house with me?"

"I love that house in Notting Hill. And I long for my best friend to come home. The house feels empty without her."

Ebba sniffled. "I'm coming home tomorrow."

"I'll pick you up. In my car."

"Oh, I almost forgot. You've bought a car. A Volvo."

"Yeah."

"How do you find driving again?"

"It's fun. Do you want a ride back home with me tomorrow, even though I don't drive a Porsche or a Ferrari or a Jaguar?"

"I sure do, Cat. I sure do."

"Even if I respect the speed limits and the road signs?"

"I do want to ride with you. It doesn't matter if you drive at a snail's pace."

They giggled a little.

"Cat?"

"Yes?"

"I have something fantastic to tell you."

"I'm listening."

"The other day I talked to Mum and Dad on the phone. They're planning a trip to London to see me." Ebba sobbed, wiping at her eyes. "Can you believe it? Mum and Dad say they want to travel to London just to see *me*."

"Your parents love you, Ebba."

The girls were still embracing.

Ebba sniffled. "Look how clumsy I am, Cat. Now tears are dropping on your coat. I'm so sorry."

"It doesn't matter, Ebba. It doesn't matter at all."

A Mr. Acland had been found dead in a suite at the Golden Plaza Hotel in Paddington. The cadaver, which lay in a pool of blood, had severe damage to its neck and throat. Mr. Acland turned out to be Mr. Jarrow, the CEO of collapsed company Yolexus Enterprise. Authorities didn't know who had killed Dirk Jarrow 'in such a bestial way', as they put it, and they didn't know why. Only two living people knew what had happened and why. Best friends were able to keep secrets.

Ten months later

September

Prague

PRAGUE FASHION WEEK (PFW) took place in the famous Pařížská Street, the most expensive street in the Czech capital. International companies such as Prada, Cartier, Hugo Boss, Louis Vuitton and Christian Dior had premises along it. There were also great restaurants, posh cafes, magnificent hotels and a fine selection of shops selling Czech porcelain and Bohemian crystal. The PFW was a project which supported domestic creativity and design, presenting forty-five shows, fifty-four designers, trademarks and art schools, twelve hundred and sixty outfits, and attracted seventy thousand visitors. The event collaborated with Czech and Slovak fashion designers and established them abroad.

Cat Milton, Ebba Sjödal and Hanna Schneider belonged to the group of international and exclusively invited guests. One night, their Czech model colleague Dorota Rybičková took them to the U Fleků restaurant and brewery in the New Town district.

The U Fleků venue was a complex which comprised eight lounges and a garden. Elegant furniture and decorations reinforced the atmosphere of the historic building. Visitors included both Czech and international celebrities, businessmen and businesswomen, sports profiles, artists and tourists. The September weather was pleasant. Still summer. The four girls sat at a table among the chestnut trees in the open-air beer garden.

"What would you like to drink, girls?" Dorota asked. She had turquoise eyes. Her hair was even blonder than Hanna's.

"Beer, of course," Hanna said. "The largest possible glasses."

The girls laughed.

"A cup of tea," Cat said.

"A small beer," Ebba said. "My only beer tonight." She lit a cigarette. "And this is my only cigarette tonight."

Dorota also lit a cigarette. "My first of fifteen cigs tonight."

More laughter.

Dorota, like Hanna, ordered a glass of the establishment's own beer. The drinks arrived. The waiter in white shirt, black tie and blue-green vest was Dorota's brother. His name was Pavel. He exchanged some Czech words with his sister.

"What would you like to eat?" Dorota asked.

"The Czech national dish, of course!" Hanna and Ebba shouted. "Roast pork, dumplings and pickled cabbage."

Cat pointed at the menu. "I would like the vegetarian option. Potato rösti, boiled vegetables, white cabbage."

Dorota's brother disappeared with their orders.

"I have an idea," Hanna said. The German looked secretive.

"What?" Ebba said.

"What kind of idea?" Dorota said.

"Can't wait to hear your idea, Hanna," Cat said.

"A business idea," Hanna said. "To start a cafe chain. Us four. What do you say?"

Cat, Ebba and Dorota snickered.

"I'm serious," Hanna said. "We could start on a small scale just for fun. A cafe in Cat's Britain. A cafe in Ebba's Sweden. A cafe in Dorota's Czech Republic. A cafe in my Germany."

"Would the four cafes be established in London, Prague, Berlin and Stockholm?" Ebba asked.

Hanna nodded. "If that initial phase became a success, we could expand with another four cafes at once."

"Why another four at once?" Dorota said.

"Where would the extra four open?" Ebba said.

"I think I know what Hanna means," Cat said. "The extra four would open in our respective hometowns. One in Dorota's Plzeň. One in Hanna's Ingolstadt. One in Ebba's Kungsör. One in my Blackfield. Was that what you thought?"

Hanna grinned. "Right."

"What would we name the cafe chain?" Ebba said.
"Yes, what name would we choose?" Dorota said.
"We could think about that for a week or two," Hanna said. The girls tittered.
"About your idea," Cat said, "could we be five girls?"
"Why not?" Hanna said. "Whom do you have in mind?"
It became Cat's turn to look secretive. "Before I reveal whom I'm thinking of, I want to have a word with her. I'm meeting her here in Prague tomorrow. She has experience in the restaurant industry. I think she would be an asset to us."

The girls looked at each other. Hanna and Dorota seemed to be deep in thought. Not Ebba. Although she hadn't yet been told, she appeared to have a good idea whom Cat had in mind.

Hanna shrugged. "Okay, Cat."
"I'm curious, Cat," Dorota said.

Pavel showed up with the dishes, plus a large plate of food they hadn't ordered, and which Pavel offered them free of charge. "Cold sausage with cucumber and butter," Dorota said. "A popular Czech starter."

"I'd like to try the cucumber," Cat said. "Not the sausage."
"We already knew," Hanna said. "Fortunately for the rest of us, you're a vegetarian."

The girls laughed.

The next evening. Grand Hotel Evropa in Wenceslas Square. The famous Art Nouveau-style hotel was one of the city's most important architectural landmarks. The address had also appeared in popular culture. Some Prague scenes in the action movie *Mission: Impossible* had been filmed here, Ebba said. The IMF agent Ethan Hunt (Tom Cruise) had met the villain Max (Vanessa Redgrave) at the hotel.

The Miltons and the Sjödals sat at a table in the beautiful restaurant. The Miltons: Mum, Cat and Janice (only Dixie was missing). The Sjödals: Ebba and her parents Pär and Ylva.

"How fun that we could meet in Prague," Pär Sjödal said.

"And how nice to meet Ebba's parents," Cat said.

They talked about all kinds of things, except for Victor Milton's death and Ebba's criminal brothers. They focused on pleasant topics. The most popular subject of discussion was Janice's transformation. Stockmayer had been right. The plastic surgeon Ratzinger had done wonders. Sis didn't look like a monster anymore. Sis was changed, no longer disgusting. She wasn't just changed. Sis had lost all her extra weight and was downright pretty.

Wenceslas Square was more than just a square. It was long and wide like a boulevard, with multilane traffic in both directions, crossed by the tram and the rapid transit systems, and lined with restaurants, hotels, nightclubs, cafes, banks and supermarkets. The neoclassical National Museum occupied the southeastern end, and there stood the statue of a horse-riding Václav, a duke of Bohemia in the tenth century, the first Czech saint and the patron saint of the Czech state. Cat, Jan and Ebba sat on a bench among flowerbeds in the middle of the avenue, chatting, joking, looking at people, enjoying the urban atmosphere.

"You're so pretty, Sis," Cat said. She must have said it a hundred times already.

"Thanks again, Sis," Jan said. "Dr. Ratzinger did do the impossible. He helped me."

"You look awesome, Janice," Ebba said.

"Thank you again, Ebba," Jan said.

"Cat?" Ebba said. "Those whatchamacallit effects in your head?"

"Yeah?"

"Do they still function? Do your thoughts and fantasies transform into reality sometimes?"

"It depends on how we define reality."

"Uh?"

"Never mind. Anyway, the weird effects in my head have disappeared altogether. I'm grateful for that. It turned out a continuous intake of those substances was required to maintain ... hmm ... epsilon energy. Now I'm a normal girl again. That is, a girl with her usual narcolepsy."

"How's your new neurologist?" Jan asked.

"Great," Cat said. "He's both nice and professional."

Ebba grabbed Cat's arm. "Warn me if you fall in love with your neurologist again, Cat. Warn me well in advance."

"Me too," Jan said. "Warn me well in advance."

Cat sniggered. "You don't need to worry, girls. I won't fall in love with my neurologist again. This man looks like a cross between a toad and a hippo."

Jan and Ebba laughed.

"Sis?" Cat said.

"Yes?"

"Are you still thinking of quitting your job at the pub one day to open your own establishment?"

Jan smiled. "It's just a fantasy. An impossible vision."

"Ebba and I were wondering if you would like to help realise a business idea suggested by a colleague of ours. If you join us, we'll be a team of five girls. Would you like to become our business partner?"

Jan raised her eyebrows. "What?"

Excerpt from

SCHIZOID

− 1 −

The knife flashes in the glow of a streetlamp and swishes through the darkness.

She screams. Terror burns her nerves. The wind whips her face. Tears dim her vision. The cloudburst splatters and she loses a high-heeled shoe. The handbag with crushed contents spins out of her fist, spilling cosmetics in a fragrant arc.

She glances over her shoulder, sees nothing but trees and shrubs and high-rise buildings. He's panting just behind her but he's invisible in a maze of swirling shadows.

The knife chases her again. It stings and bites.

Her skirt hem bursts at the back. She slips on the wet lawn, slides, falls, crawls to her feet, reaches the sidewalk, turns left, up the hill. The raven-black heaven descends over the cityscape, erasing the full moon.

The darkness sweeps and blocks. Cars, buses and trams are rushing through the curtains of rain, both up and down the road. Nobody takes note of her.

She tries to scream again. Only a beep dribbles out between her teeth. A coppery taste fills her mouth. In the terror-night-blackness, the flowing blood is as dark as the downpour.

The vicious words that resound in her head belong to her so-called boyfriend. The actual voice is the exception. The voice, the muffled whisper, is unknown.

The night begins to rotate like a carousel. Fast, faster.

The asphalt beneath her feet wriggles, vibrates and wiggles.

Excerpt from *Schizoid*

The minutes meander away with a serpent's deceiving suddenness. Memories diverge. Moments hybridise.

She shivers. Her teeth chatter.

The city spins and topples. The kerb strikes her cheek. Red saliva spurts from the corner of her mouth.

The claws of eternity snatch the girl from the world's edge. She closes her eyes and dives. And swims through the light towards the other side.

The next murder plan took shape. But a noise from somewhere in the house had begun to encroach on his psychological space. The clamour diluted his concentration, a little at a time, until the situation became unbearable.

What on earth was going on?

A switch in his head flicked. *The phone. At this hour?* A sparkle of hope flew through Kenneth Sorin's heart. He took the call. "Alison?"

"Wrong guess."

"So it's you."

"Alison wasn't your type, Ken. Forget the girl. After all, her parents didn't like you."

"I loved her, Uncle Ash. I still do. She's the only girl I've ever loved." He needed a moment to clear his throat. "Inspector Ash Sorin, of all people, what do you want? It's the middle of the night. I'm busy, working." He shot an eye at the wall clock. Seven minutes past midnight. Three manuscript pages in thirteen minutes. Thirteen was not the most excellent number but those three pages satisfied him. "Uncle Ash, let me guess. It's about the serial killer, isn't it? I've already told you the following. We all have priorities and, from now on, I want to focus on my writing career a hundred percent. Do you understand?"

"I thought you used to disconnect the phone cord and turn off the mobile before you kick-started the damn typewriter."

"Typewriters aren't kick-started."

"Whatever."

Although he used computers, like most modern fiction writers, he preferred to write his first drafts on the old electric machine.

"Listen, Ken. On my kitchen table is a stack of photos of slaughtered girls. I can tell you, boy, these pictures do my stomach ulcer no good."

"You have my sympathies."

"I want to chat about the details, Ken, but not on the phone. I'd appreciate seeing you in my house tomorrow morning."

The workroom door to the corridor was ajar. Kenneth heard a sound from downstairs. "This conversation must end now. I promised Linda the 'night's special'."

"Linda? And you say I interrupted your writing? Nice try. I dare not ask what the 'night's special' is."

"I was talking about my cat."

"Of course you were. Tomorrow at nine?"

"I think you mean today. It's past midnight."

"Not too early for a Thursday morning."

"Let me sleep on it. I'll call you back, I promise."

Uncle Ash chuckled. "Good night, sleep tight, don't let the bedbugs bite."

Kenneth went down to the kitchen, wondering what the miaowing Linda wanted for a speciality. A bowl of corn and salmon pâté satisfied her. "Enjoy your meal, Linda. Don't worry about the bill. Dinner's on the house."

He returned to the first floor, turned off the typewriter and swallowed two headache relief pills.

On the way to the bedroom at the end of the corridor, he discovered he was trudging on Linda's elongated shadow. The blue-black spot under his feet floated across the carpet like a puddle of swift-flowing oil. Linda often gave the impression of being in many probability-oriented places at the same instant, as if she were a cat at the quantum level, a cat with the ability to disappear and reappear somewhere else at the same time and at any time, like a subatomic particle. Her omnipresence and independence appealed to him. Without a doubt, Linda was the best housemate imaginable.

If someone, or something, was sneaking about in the street right now, potential footsteps would be inaudible in the screaming wind. Something which should not move at all at this pitch-dark hour could be down there right now.

Maybe in the house. No, he decided. A cat's senses were superior to those of humans. Since Linda was calm, there was nothing to worry about.

The hammering wind gusts against the house gave the window panes the voices of a hundred rattlesnakes. The roof was squeaking like a ship at sea. Against all odds he drifted towards unconsciousness. The last thing he registered before the night seized him was the voice of a female student who had been interviewed on the TV news:

"Nothing is worse than trying to sleep at night or being home alone in the dark. The mutilator and killer could be anywhere. He could be out there right now. Or here. Right here, inside, with us. He could be one of us here tonight."

Photo © Asioni Press

Dr. Johan Fundin is an author of thrillers and suspense novels populated by complex characters. His books cover the genres of psychological, occult, spiritual and medical thrillers, science fiction and paranormal horror. He has a Ph.D. in physical chemistry from Uppsala University in Sweden and a background as a scientist at several laboratories and high-tech research facilities across Europe. Also, he has extensive experience of clinical work at a major metropolitan hospital. Today he lives in Sheffield, U.K.

<u>Visit Johan Fundin online at</u>

JohanFundin.com

Lightning Source UK Ltd.
Milton Keynes UK
UKHW011002150522
403009UK00003B/488